Salt
&
Storm

Salt & Storm

KENDALL KULPER

Little, Brown and Company

New York Boston

Little, Brown and Company

Hachette Book Group
237 Park Avenue, New York, NY 10017
Visit our website at lb-teens.com

Little, Brown and Company is a division of Hachette Book Group, Inc.
The Little, Brown name and logo are trademarks of Hachette Book Group, Inc.

The publisher is not responsible for websites (or their content) that are not owned by the publisher.

First Edition: September 2014
First International Edition: September 2014

Library of Congress Cataloging-in-Publication Data

Kulper, Kendall.
  Salt & Storm / by Kendall Kulper. — First edition.
    pages cm
  Summary: "Sixteen-year-old Avery Roe wants to take her rightful place as the sea witch of Prince Island. When she foresees her own murder, a harpoon boy named Tane promises to help her change her fate and keep her island safe and prosperous, but salvation will require an unexpected sacrifice"— Provided by publisher.
  ISBN 978-0-316-40451-8 (hardcover) — ISBN 978-0-316-29727-1 (international) —
ISBN 978-0-316-40450-1 (ebook) — ISBN 978-0-316-40456-3 (library edition ebook)
  [1. Fate and fatalism—Fiction. 2. Magic—Fiction. 3. Witches—Fiction.
4. Mothers and daughters—Fiction. 5. Islands of the Atlantic—History—
19th century—Fiction.] I. Title. II. Title: Salt and Storm.
  PZ7.K9490164Sal 2014
  [Fic]—dc23

                                                                            2013041664

10 9 8 7 6 5 4 3 2 1

RRD-C

Printed in the United States of America

For Dave, of course

Part One

A Lesson in Killing Whales

One

DESPITE MY MOTHER'S BEST EFFORTS, I NEVER forgot the day my grandmother taught me how to tie the winds. That was ten years ago, when Prince Island was more than just a rock out in the Atlantic Ocean, when its docks choked with ships, when the factory furnaces spat out a constant stream of thick black smoke and the island's bars spat out a constant stream of laughing men, their faces round and shiny.

That was back, too, when the people on my island treasured my grandmother and her role in their fortunes. Every man, woman, and child on Prince Island knew the way to her cottage, had to know the way because their lives depended on it.

Even back in the good times, the pastor with the dried-apple face would spend his sermons lecturing the congregation against my grandmother's promises. A deal with her was a deal with the devil, he'd tell them, raising his fist and cracking it down on the podium. And the people on my island would nod with pinched lips, but they'd visit her all the same.

A man—although they were usually so young they could still be called boys—might ask for a fidelity charm. He'd be anxious, excited, more nervous about leaving his girl than about the years-long voyage he would soon endure. My grandmother would tell him: "Bring me a dozen strands of your sweetheart's hair and cut off a lock of your own." Once he returned with the items, her long fingers would weave and bind the hairs with sea grass, building a loose bracelet. "Put it on her wrist," she would say, "and your girl will remain true."

Often the boy would hold this flimsy thing in his hand, feeling its impossible lightness, and frown. "You're mad. This'll break in a moment and then what will my Sue get up to?"

"Never one of my charms," she'd say. "Never known one of them to break."

So he would stick it into his pocket, still frowning, and leave. Later he'd slide it over his darling's hand.

"Something to remember me by," he'd say, but the women of Prince Island had seen enough hair and sea grass to know the truth. Still, the bracelet never broke or faded or fell apart and the girl stayed faithful. My grandmother, of course, had no control over the boy.

Older men, the captains and ship owners, kept my grandmother in luxuries like pure white sugar wrapped in crisp paper, fruits so brightly colored they hurt my eyes, bolts of cloth as smooth and soft as skin.

"Caleb gifts," they called them, because once, many years ago when my grandmother was a young woman, a captain named Caleb Sweeny slighted her, refused to bring her any gift at all, even though he stayed on the island for months as our men restored his ship. Only days after the ship launched, word came back the whole thing had been smashed to bits, run into rocks and beaten into nothing but timbers and torn cloth.

The men of the island grumbled that their months of hard work had gone to waste and worried that their reputations as shipbuilders would suffer. But even today everyone on the East Coast knows there's nothing stronger than a nail hammered on Prince Island, and so, in the end, the builders kept their fine reputations while my grandmother gained a new one: storm-raiser, not to be crossed.

It wasn't only men who made the walk to my grandmother's cottage. Women visited, too, women who wanted to protect their men at sea or, every now and then, to curse them. Sometimes it would get tricky: A woman would arrive spitting mad, promising my grandmother anything if only the *Kingfisher* would fail on the sea and one of those colossal whales would take a mighty bite out of a certain Clarence Aldrich and drag his filthy body to the depths. And this would put my grandmother in a spot, because she had just sold Clarence Aldrich a talisman made from a bit of wren feather, a powerful magic against drowning. Now maybe my grandmother would try to calm the woman and convince her to spend her money on a love charm to find a man not quite so worthy of a bite from a whale. But more often she'd take the money and make the spell and tell herself that Clarence Aldrich would still be saved from drowning, even if the whale might get him first.

These were the simple tricks and common charms and minor spells, paid in trade or food, that kept my grandmother's life running smoothly. They cost almost nothing to make and barely any time to pull together. Trifles, she called them, the little charms that were, to her, as easy as breathing.

Tying the winds was a different thing altogether. Only the richest ship owners could afford it, and they'd send their captains to the cottage on the rocks with money and instructions. The money my grandmother took willingly, the instructions less so. The winds are tricky, shifty, and it was hard enough, she'd tell them, binding and tethering them without some fool going on about specifics. And these captains were proud men, more bird or fish with their knowledge of the winds and waves, so to say nothing against her insults must have been a hard thing. Still, I don't know of any man who visited her cottage with the money and intent to buy that charm whose tongue or pride betrayed him, no matter how much his blood might have boiled. That's small magic, as my grandmother would say, the small magic that keeps the world spinning.

When a man came to the cottage looking to own the winds, she would send him away until she was done. Once, a captain—an outsider, otherwise he wouldn't even have bothered to ask—wanted to stay, to witness her magic.

"I work better alone," she said, and the captain's gaze slid to me, her six-year-old granddaughter, watching narrow-eyed from the corner. But if he thought anything, he didn't say it aloud.

I didn't want him there, either. My grandmother's cottage was a world that belonged only to us, to her and me and maybe my mother, too, if she ever wanted it back. The Roe women made the magic that kept Prince Island running and had for generations, and that captain should be grateful instead of plain nosy. I scowled at him until he left.

My grandmother crossed to the back of her small cottage and reached inside a heavy black trunk tucked at the end of the bed. The trunk, as far as I knew, was as old as the witches themselves, a big, bulky thing that the first Roe brought with her when she came to Prince Island. It had been passed down since then, from mother to daughter, and it was where the Roe women kept their materials. The trunk should have gone to my mother years ago, but instead my grandmother kept it in the cottage, and although I had slept with this thing at my feet for my entire life, I'd never looked inside. I'd never been invited.

I could hear my grandmother's long fingers gently pushing aside things that rustled and clinked until she pulled out a white cord as thick as my pinkie and as long as my arm.

"Here, Avery," she said, sitting down in her chair, and I ran to her and climbed into her lap. She wrapped her arms around me, the fabric of her sleeves warm with the smell of wood-smoke and herbs. She held the white cord loosely between her hands and I laughed and reached for it like it was a toy.

"Not the cord, dear," she said, lifting it from me. I felt her lips press against my hair, her breath warm against my scalp. "Lay your hands on mine."

My chubby fingers twitched in my lap, and I lifted them up, where they hovered over my grandmother's hands. Her skin was almost sheer, the network of pale blue veins standing out like tree branches. I walked my fingertips up the backs of her hands from her wrists to her knuckles, pushing hard so that I left a trail of pale dots on her skin.

"Focus now." Her words tickled my cheek, and I slid my hands around hers.

The cord snapped tight between her fingers, every fiber fine and shimmering as though it were made out of spider silk. For all I knew, it was.

Faintly, my grandmother's lips moved, lifting my hair, but I only heard the rush of hot air, and I held my breath, my eyes wide.

Outside, the wind arched around the cottage, a low, deep moan that shook the windows. Something clattered against the door, so loud and sudden that I jerked, but my grandmother gently pressed her cheek against my head.

"Focus," she said again, her voice more air than noise. "Keep your eyes on the rope."

The rope... It vibrated, shivered, and even though my

grandmother's sun-browned, lined hands remained steady I could feel the fine shudders through her bones. The wind picked up, a howl of such high pitch that it sounded almost like pain, but I didn't dare pull my eyes away from the white cord, moving like the strummed string of a guitar.

"Granma?" I whispered, my heartbeat rising in little pricks. My palms began to sweat, my fingertips to shake and tremble, and I could feel something, something pulling at me, a force reaching through my fingers, through my skin, my bones, traveling deep inside of me, yanking, grabbing, clawing like a cat tearing apart a ball of string.

Tears rose to my eyes and I wanted to shrink away, but I couldn't. My bones had turned to stone, while my grandmother said nothing, while outside the wind blew even more fiercely, rattling the glass of the windows, struggling to get in, to get at us, at *me*.

The air escaped from my lungs, and when I tried to breathe in again, I found that there was no breath, no wind, no air, as though an invisible hand reached down to pinch my nose and mouth shut and I was drowning, suffocating.

"Granma!" I wheezed, jerking, the rope buzzing between her fingers, the wind slamming fists against windows, howling at the door like an animal, maddened and maddening.

Every window burst open and I squeezed my eyes tight as the wind clawed at me, scratching my cheeks and twisting my hair across my face. My grandmother's hands came together quickly, expertly, and my hands moved puppet-like on top of hers, working and tying the string, pulling tight. I screamed, a wail as high and pure-toned as the wind itself, and it was as though something precious to me was suddenly wrenched away, torn into the wind and gone forever.

"Shh...Quiet, love, it's over now."

My grandmother's hands pressed heavily on my shoulders, and I realized my own hands were free. I hiccoughed and held my breath, my eyes still shut, and in the silence I could hear that the wind had died down, the air now cool and still.

I opened my eyes, blinking wide. My hands pressed against my chest, the muscles of my body sore as though I'd just carried something heavy for a long time. But it was only the memory of pain; whatever feeling had pierced me was gone.

"I didn't like that," I said, looking back at my grandmother. "It *hurt*."

For a moment, it seemed as though she hadn't heard me. She breathed hard, her skin ashen, her eyelids fluttering, and I frowned. She often looked like this, after big spells.

"Granma?" I reached a hand to her face and she shuddered, snapping her chin up. She laughed, a papery sound, and pressed the palms of her hands against my chest. Under the weight of her touch I could feel my own bones, thin but strong.

"That's all right, dear," she said, whispering slowly into my ear, her voice quavering. "It should hurt. That's just how it should be."

The cord still hung limp from one of her hands, and I

reached for it. This time my grandmother gave no protest, letting me run it through my fingers and feel the three tight knots now twisted down its length.

"What did you do?" I asked, and I traced my fingers across each knot. If I pressed hard, I felt something deep within: a rumble, a barely-there thrum.

"What *we* did," my grandmother said, taking the string lightly from me. "Each knot means the winds. Untie the first for a light breeze. The second will bring a fair trade wind. The third—that's the strongest. The third untied means a hurricane, greater and more terrible than anything you can imagine."

"Why would someone want to call a hurricane?" I asked, tilting my head at her. She lifted her eyebrows.

"I don't ask, dear," she said. "Remember that. It's not our place to ask. Folks have their reasons."

"Will I be able to do that on my own now?" I asked, and my grandmother shook her head.

"Not for a long while yet," she said. "Someday, when you're older, I'll explain how the magic will come. But until then, you can help me." She smoothed my dark hair with her hand, and I felt a warm glow in my stomach to be a big girl, old enough finally for my grandmother to include me in her work.

She eased me gently to my feet and stood up before walking slowly across the cottage to the black chest. She limped, moving as though her bones had grown stiff in the few minutes it took to work the spell, and when she reached the chest she put a hand on the wall to steady herself and breathed hard.

I watched her carefully, just in case she fell or collapsed. Sometimes it happened after big spells like these; sometimes she would rise to her feet only to fall again, crying and clutching her body, and I'd know to get a pillow to put under her head and push away the table and chairs to give her some space and shove my fingers into my ears to drown out her keening (only I didn't tell her about that last bit). But she looked well now, and I thought it was probably because I had helped her, this time.

She lifted the lid of the chest and was about to drop the rope inside when she turned to me and paused.

"Come look," she said, smiling, and my stomach swooped.

I walked slowly, my breath held tight within my lungs. My grandmother reached out an arm to me, scooping me close against her legs, wrapping me tightly as my eyes widened.

String, feathers, stones, simple objects, but to me they were jewels, shimmering with the memory of my grandmother's magic. Beneath those little worked charms I could see neat stacks of papers, notes written in strange hands, diagrams and drawings I didn't understand but that called to me, called to me as surely as if they already were mine.

I stared into the chest at my feet, the box that kept the history of the Roe women and their short, wild lives. It seemed too small. How could they shape my island, my world, so much and yet leave so little behind? But they also didn't live long, the Roe women, lasting until their forties, just until their daughters were grown and capable of taking over for them—although my grandmother would soon prove to be the exception.

"That box holds generations of Roe history," my grandmother whispered. "Everything we've learned or created. It's been passed down from mother to daughter since the first Roe. My grandmother gave it to my mother, my mother gave it to me, and someday I will give it to you." I looked up at her in surprise, and she leaned forward to press her lips against my hair. "You're a part of them. A part of us."

Us. She meant the Roe women, yes, but also the witches, *the* witch of Prince Island, for there was always only one working at a time. (My mother, for example, had all the abilities but it was my grandmother who was the witch.)

"It will be up to you, Avery," my grandmother said, pulling me from my thoughts. "Do you understand?"

Yes. I knew just what she meant. It would be me, *me* and not my mother, who would take over for her and become the very next Roe witch.

I nodded, and my grandmother swept me up in her woodsmoke arms and held me close, and I thought about my mother, who had abandoned magic and me only a year after my birth, who had given up her place as the Roe witch and forced my grandmother to work long past her prime, making her weak and tired and worrying the islanders.

I was supposed to set it right, to become the witch and bring Prince Island back to the glory days, but before I could, before even my grandmother taught me how to unlock the magic that would have made me more than just her apprentice, my mother came back for me. Days after my twelfth birthday, she dragged me kicking and crying from the cottage on the rocks to New Bishop, the big town at the northern end of the island, and in no uncertain terms absolutely forbade me to become the witch.

Ever since then I knew it would only be a matter of time before I returned to the cottage, before I escaped. And when the days rolled into weeks, months, years, I didn't worry, I didn't panic. I did not care when my mother announced her engagement and then marriage to one of the island's wealthiest men and moved us to his home. (What was one prison in exchange for another?) And when she began dressing me in silks and satins, parading me around like a prize pony at church picnics and social teas, lacing her conversation with words that felt like mines—*gentleness, obedience, virtue, social grace*—I hardly even paid attention. Let her do what she wanted. Let her fantasize about the kind of woman she wanted to make me become. I did not care.

Because I was supposed to be the Roe witch, it was my destiny and duty, and how could anyone, even my mother, stop that?

Well.

I tried.

I hope the people of my island know that, at least.

I hope when they tell this story, the story of how they lost their witches and their luck and their fortunes, they don't judge me too harshly. I hope, also, that they remember none of it would have happened had my mother not turned her back on magic. Or had my mother left me alone in my grandmother's cottage. Or had my mother, drunk on the cult of domesticity and stuffed to the brim with 1860s morality, not been so determined to see me a proper lady. Or had she realized that when it came to magic, I would not make her mistakes.

So if the people of my island blame anyone, better her than me.

Two

I WAS SIXTEEN, STILL MY MOTHER'S PRISONER, the night I became the whale.

I am swimming and it is just sunrise, the sky so gray as to be almost invisible. I rise to the surface to breathe and that's when I see the dark shadow of a boat, gliding gently toward me in the water. Men ride in the boat, their faces grim and greedy and silent, and as I turn to watch them I feel a bite in my side, a piercing pain.

The word *harpoon* forms in my frantic mind when I see another man lift a long, heavy metal spear to his shoulder to strike again, but I dive, dropping down through layers of water. The ocean turns cold, dark, pressing around me, but the deeper I go the more the iron inside of me twists and pulls and

I know that I'm tethered to the boat, that even now the men pull the rope tighter and drag me back to the surface.

It does no good to swim, I know, but maddened with fear and pain, I press into the waves and the heavy boat tows behind me, casting up crests of waves in its wake. I swim and swim until the energy leaches from my burning muscles, energy that would have done better to be saved to fight, and now I can only pant into the water.

I lurch toward the boat, intending to attack, but they reach me first, a lance deep into my side. The rope connecting us tightens, pulls me ever closer, and the rising sun flashes against their bright knives. They aim not for my brain or heart but my lungs, and when the first knife hits, I gasp, breathing in blood and water and cold, cold air. Another knife hits and another, ribboning the pink tissue inside my body, and it's like trying to suck oxygen through a wet sack. My panic makes me lurch for air again and again, but when I breathe now, blood and water spray into the air, a column of red that clouds around me, and I can taste them mix, salty water and salty blood, and just as my eyes roll back into my head, I see the bright curve of a hook, a hook the size of a man's head, and I urge every last bit of strength I have into my scream.

It was then that I woke up, panting for air, my arms and neck glazed in sweat. I lay in the darkness, confused and blinking as the details of my bedroom solidified. Still heaving for breath, I sat up in bed, pressing my fingertips against my closed eyes until bright points of light shattered across my vision. My heart refused to slow, and I jumped from the bed and threw open the window, gulping in cold air.

I leaned my cheek against the edge of the window, the breeze cooling the damp hair stuck to my forehead. The world outside was drawn in grays and silvers, silent but for the soft nighttime sounds of birds, the rush of the black ocean only a two-minute walk from my bedroom. My chest ached, and I lifted a hand to press my fingertips against the cage of bones around my heart and imagined again the sailors' knives, the harpoons....

A nightmare. It was just a nightmare. A normal sixteen-year-old girl would laugh, shaking her head at her own foolish imagination before tucking herself back into bed. But I was not a normal girl, and this was not just a nightmare.

Every Roe woman receives a special ability, aside from water magic—a gift that appears in childhood and separates her from all the Roes before her. My grandmother could read high emotions, soothing and appeasing even the strongest passions. My mother—in a twist of irony that proved magic, at least, had a healthy sense of humor—had power over love, affection, and in her youth she would sell charms that promised love for the day, the year, the lifetime.

I could interpret dreams. I could see what they meant for the future, for the dreamer, and I knew what this dream meant for me.

For the first time in my life I thought I might not become

the witch. I might not ever have the chance. Because I could read dreams and I knew what it meant to dream I was a whale, to dream of men trapping me, hunting me, piercing me with harpoons and leaving me to drown in my own blood.

I will be killed. I will be murdered.

I've never been wrong before.

Three

PANIC REARED UP THROUGH ME, HOT AND blazing and blurry, and that was it. I had to escape to my grandmother's cottage, and I had to go *now*.

I spun and threw open the door of my looming black wardrobe before shoving aside the woolen winter clothing folded in the back. There was a false bottom to this wardrobe, and if I hooked my fingernail just right into the far left corner, I could lift it up, exposing a space about the size of a man's shoe. My fingers shook as I reached in, feeling in the darkness smooth stones, a handkerchief knotted around sand, a single delicate and empty bird egg: my version of my grandmother's black chest but without the magic.

I felt around in the hole until I found a short length of twisted, rusty wire, the kind usually wrapped around a fence post. Sailors say a bit of fence wire could protect a man against a curse, and so I carefully wrapped it around my wrist, staining my fingers with powdery orange-pink rust.

This will work, I told myself, although I knew I had not made a spell and remained just a girl with some wire puckering the skin of her wrist. Still, I rose to my feet, my mind already racing through my escape: down to the kitchens, out the back garden, loop around town, then down to the beach and straight south to the cottage and safety.

I didn't need a map, not when I knew almost from birth every inch of my island, floating forty miles east of Massachusetts's shore. Prince Island from above looked like a comma with a stretched-out tail, a pause before the open ocean, and I pictured myself standing at the northeastern tip of that comma, where my mother's house lay, and pointing my toes south, along the curving shoreline path all the way down, down, down to the very tip of the comma's tail, to the crumbling rocks where my grandmother's cottage sat. It would be a long walk, more than seven miles into the wind, but as soon as I left the town behind, it would be a nice walk, too, with nothing to my right but bowing fields of sea grass and nothing to my left but ocean. And then the sandy shoreline path would go brown and bare, sand turning to gravel turning to rock, and the land to my right would grow skinny and broken, and by the time the sun would rise, I would see the cottage before me, rosy with the dawn. The sky would be clear, colorless, mist blending together the air and the ocean, the waves whispering against the rocks. My grandmother would be inside, asleep, tired, maybe, from a long night of customers, and I told myself, *I will walk through the door, wake her, and say, "I am home."*

My breathing slowed as I held the moment in my mind, and then I turned and reached for the cloak hanging on the wardrobe door.

This will be the night I escape. The thought repeated in my mind like a refrain, over and over, and I believed it so hard that I whispered it aloud: "This will be the night I escape!"

I took a step, one step with the cloak still bunched in my fist, and my knees gave underneath me.

"No!" I whispered, catching myself just in time. I clutched the wire around my wrist and urged it to heat with magic, to protect me. Another step and this time I fell to the ground, the sharp points of my elbows and knees striking the carpet so that I gasped with pain. Bright stars peppered my vision, exploding into color and then into blackness, raining down over me, smothering me with sleep, but even as I could feel my arms and legs go tingly numb, hot anger sprang through my veins.

Stupid! Why did I possibly think I could escape that night? For four years, any moment I attempted to run back to the cottage, the invisible rope around my waist gave a tug, tethering me back to my mother's world. Cursed, I was cursed, and my mother said she'd given up magic for good, said it was a terrible thing, but she wasn't above using it to keep me at her side, and she's a hypocrite, a liar, a fraud and phony, and I hate her I hate her *I hate her!*

I stretched out on the carpet, eyes glazed over, my heart whirring with frustration and fear, and as my mother's curse slowly, firmly, pushed my eyelids closed, my body went still. But on the inside I was screaming.

I woke stiff and light-headed, my bones and joints aching. The wire still dug into my right wrist, and my hand tingled. It had been months since I last woke up on the floor like this, caught in an attempted escape, and my cheeks burned as I pushed myself to my feet and slowly, gently stretched.

I massaged my aching muscles and unwound the wire, blinking and fuzzy-headed, when it all rushed back to me: the dream, the knives, my shredded lungs full of blood instead of air, and what it all meant for my future. My knees trembled and I had to clutch the wardrobe for balance.

I am going to be murdered.

It wasn't any easier to face in the daytime.

Wincing, I leaned against the wardrobe, unused to the swooping, dizzying feeling of glimpsing my own future. I'd seen death in dreams before, of course: I discovered I could tell futures six years ago, about the same time more and more of our whale men signed up to fight in the War Between the States. My grandmother, ever the entrepreneur, set up a side business in future-telling that kept us both afloat during the war years (my grandmother had charms against whales, not bullets).

They made me famous, those dreams, and soon would-be soldiers began to visit the cottage not for the witch but for her little black-haired granddaughter. "Doesn't come up to your elbow," men would say, "but can tell you if you're gonna live or die."

I always suspected it was the dreams that attracted my mother's attention, because when she came to the cottage and pulled me away, she hissed at my grandmother, "You've turned her into a death-teller! My child!"

My grandmother said something in response, that magic was my birthright, that I belonged here, that I was doing what I was meant to do, and my mother's hands squeezed my arms so tight that they tingled.

"She's meant for more than *this*."

My mother forbade dream-telling, of course, but what she didn't know was that I still interpreted dreams, down at the docks for pocket money, even though her new husband had enough money to fill my pockets for decades. It was the only way I knew to relieve the tension that I constantly carried inside, the magic that coiled inside of me, begging to be put to use. Boys and men would sidle up to me, a dollar a dream, and I'd tell their futures.

Often the dreams meant silly, unremarkable things—a missed kerchief, a spoiled meal, a bad sunburn. Every now and then, though, I'd see something terrible. I'd see the boy standing before me blistered with fever. I'd see boats smashed into splinters, men slipping into black water. I'd see disease, danger, death.

When that happened, I held their money out and told them: "It isn't good. Do you still want to know?"

No doubt my business-minded grandmother wouldn't understand, but I think it's only fair. A bad death is a terrible thing but so also is to live your life under a shadow, asking with every moment or decision, is this it? Is this what will lead to my ruin?

Sometimes they still wanted to know, would rather have the knowledge, and sometimes they took their money back and said they'd rather just let what's fated happen. Sometimes afterward, after I told them all I knew of their terrible futures, they laughed and said it's all foolishness and they didn't believe me, which I didn't mind—after all, it wasn't my life.

Other times the sailors with the bad futures would ask me a question: "What can I do to stop it?" They'd ask me and I'd shrug. Can't do anything. It's the future. Can't change it. Then I'd leave, and quickly, before they demanded their money back.

But for the most part, telling dreams was fun for me, a lark, a way to try on the mantle of the Roe witch and prove to the people of the island that I was more than just my name and bloodlines. I liked doing it—or used to, I thought, and my fingers trembled as I buttoned up my dress.

"Calm down," I whispered, and the knot in my stomach twisted. "You'll gain nothing by panicking. The dream won't come true. It can't come true. You're not supposed to die, you're supposed to become—"

My words broke off as the answer came to me.

You cannot kill a Roe witch.

It's an old island saying, dating back to the very first Roe, Madelyn. More than a century ago, when Madelyn came to the island, a whipped-up mob plotted to throw her into the sea, but the wave that reared up from the rocks swept away not the witch but the would-be killers. Since then, grieving women and angry sailors, come to seek revenge on the witch, find their knives turned and their passions cooled. It's been proven true too many times to be mere superstition. You can't kill a Roe witch.

The thought filled me with relief. True, I was not the witch, not yet, and so not safe, but there was a solution. All I needed was to unlock the secrets of my magic and take over for my grandmother.

Laughter bubbled up through me, high-pitched and nervous, because I'd been trying to accomplish this for four years now and was no closer than the day my mother took me away.

What else could I do, then? I didn't know how to access my magic, how to transform into a real witch, but my mother knew. My grandmother knew. My mother, of course, would never tell me, but I was certain my grandmother would. If I could only send her a message...

I rubbed my temples, a headache growing at the very thought. My mother had forbidden messages between my grandmother and me. For four years now we heeded her because on the day she took me away, my mother had shouted the one thing none of us could have possibly expected: that if my grandmother ever tried to come for me, my mother would take me off the island.

What a thing to say, for what Roe, even my magic-hating mother, could have chosen to actually *leave* the island? Leave her home? Leave the only world she knew? It was as though she'd suddenly held a knife up to my neck. So strange, so reckless and violent, and while I doubted anyone—not my grandmother, maybe not even my mother—would have actually thought her any more capable of taking me off the island than slitting my throat, one does not test a madwoman with a knife.

Goose bumps prickled across my skin as I imagined her on that day, wild-eyed and wicked. Would she make good on her threat if she found out about a message? I'd been too scared to test her these past four years, and I knew a message would be dangerous, and it would be foolish.

But I was desperate.

Decided, I moved quickly out of my room, through the hall and down the stairs and out the front door, taking care to muffle my footsteps, although it was so early that I doubted anyone was awake—not my mother, not her husband, not his two rotten little children.

Your new family, my mother called them, and they were perhaps the worst of the many indecencies she'd forced me to suffer. I didn't believe my mother at first, two years ago when she came back to the oily, ramshackle little apartment where she had taken me and told me that she was going to marry William Sever, a pastor (pastor! Can you imagine my grandmother's heartbreak when she heard the news?) and wealthy widower with two small children: six-year-old Hazel and the terrible Walt, a boy whose primary interests seemed to be smashing insects and spying on his new stepmother in the bath.

Outside on the front lawn, I paused a moment to check that there weren't any little faces watching me from the windows of the pastor's big, glorious house, pinkish-white and perfect in the morning light. The house fit in with my mother's obsession with money and status, although when she first took me away, she seemed content enough with her modest life as a washerwoman. She claimed, often, over and over, that she married the pastor for me, to get me out of the cramped apartment, away from the refineries that kept me coughing, and into good clothes and a warm bed. But it was obvious that she enjoyed being the lady of a grand house, living in the nicest neighborhood on the island (a place the locals called, with airs most decidedly on, "up lighthouse"). And she was forever telling me how much better, how much safer our lives were now.

Safe, I thought, turning my back on the house, and the word sent a shiver down my back. Safety was important to her.

You can't kill a Roe witch, but you can beat her within an inch of her life, and that is what happened to my mother. Once, she'd been a beauty, impossibly lovely, with a face that made her more famous than her love charms and that set her apart from the other island girls, short, round-cheeked, gray-eyed, freckled, with wide mouths and noses that flattened out near the eyes and hair as wild and stiff and tangled as a mat of dried-out seaweed (this is what I look like, at least).

I don't know the particulars of the story, for my grandmother, whenever I asked, just pinched her mouth into a long, straight line and said nothing, but from what I pieced together from rumors and whispers, my mother had been young, teens, maybe, or early twenties, when a man beat her senseless and split open her lovely face from right eyebrow to the left corner of her lips (a small point: that man was my father). He left her with a baby and a scar and a devastating hatred for magic, which, in the end, had not prevented a half-drunk brute from taking away the only thing that had made her truly special.

She put her faith in money instead of magic now, but money wouldn't do a whit for me and my dreams, and I shoved open the beautiful wrought-iron front gate and stepped out onto Main Street. With the beach and water to my left and the homes of the island's elite to my right, I walked south, watching for any spying eyes: nosy society ladies who would love nothing more than to march over to Pastor Sever's home and tell my mother my doings (she had spies all over the island, and it was common knowledge that if a man saw the little Roe girl out of bed in the middle of the night, there'd be a fine reward for her return).

Gradually, the houses to my right grew smaller, humbler, and closer together, flapping sheets of laundry instead of manicured hedges decorating the front lawns. Unlike the richies in my mother's new neighborhood, these people were already out of their homes and at their work, and they knew me and nodded at me as I passed.

"Good morning, Miss Avery," one woman called, folding a sheet against her body. I waved back, recognizing her as the wife of a sailor still at sea. I had a delicate relationship with the people of my island. They loved and respected my grandmother and they feared and respected my mother, but I couldn't help them, not yet, and they watched me warily.

The houses thinned out as I reached the first of New Bishop's stores: dark and huddled dry goods, the musty-windowed milliner, the bright white apothecary where already a crowd of children stood outside, staring in at the jars and jars of dream-colored candies. My grandmother had once toyed with the idea of setting up her own little shop in New Bishop, to lure footsore sailors unwilling to trek out to her cottage. But of course, she hadn't come near New Bishop for four years.

Main Street narrowed as I continued to walk south into town, the buildings rising ever higher above me to crowd out the view of the sky and the ocean. The path underneath my feet turned to brick, the road to my side cobblestone, and when I inhaled, the sharp smell of coffee filled my nostrils, raising the hairs on the back of my neck. Low-ceilinged restaurants and food stalls erupted with the sounds of working men getting their breakfasts: sugared honey buns, fried sausages, wire baskets of clams that steamed and shivered water in the cool morning. I'd missed my own breakfast and couldn't help but pause and stare, my mouth watering, as a red-faced baker's wife laughed with a dock boy and wrapped up in a bit of news-paper a hot cake crumbling with heavy-scented cinnamon, her fingers leaving greasy smudges in the ink.

Beyond the breakfast market, the fruit and vegetable stalls crowded the already busy sidewalks with sweet rotting smells. Even this early, the women of Prince Island scoured the wares, shallow baskets swinging over their muscled arms, while a group of men sat huddled outside the green door of the tobacco store, the de facto meeting place for the island's whaling agents. Most of these men didn't share the island look of gray eyes and dark hair, and I could tell they were outsiders (the polite term is "off-islander," but behind their backs we call them "seagulls"). Still, they knew as much about the island's businesses as anyone, as they were responsible for manning whalers, negotiating sailors' contracts, running the business of whaling for the ship owners. Ringed in blue-gray smoke, they talked about the whaler schedules in loud voices that quieted as I drew nearer.

"Just one goin' out this week," a fellow with a thatch of red hair said to the group, and as I passed, his eyes narrowed and he called out softly, "Give my regards to your grandmother, Avery Roe."

I nodded at the men, their wolfish stares following me, and turned east onto Water Street, which led to the ocean and the docks, but had I continued walking south on Main Street, I would have run smack into the factory district, made up of boxy, sky-high buildings that belched black smoke morning to night—or used to, back when I was a child, when my grand-mother was younger, when there were more whales in the world.

The noise of the market and the stores faded behind me as I walked down Water Street through the shipyard, the blocks bordering the great wharf that stretched down New Bishop's shore. Men too old or too disinclined to sail often set up shop back on Prince Island to build and repair ships, and in the glory days the widened streets of the shipyards teemed with men and with the bits and pieces that made up the great whalers. Most shops would leave their doors open during the day, the better to bring in business, and a man could look left to right and see riggers busy twisting hemp into rope, coopers making careful planes down pure-white oak boards, blacksmiths grimacing as they lifted their hammers over sizzling red iron.

Today, though, mist rose over the empty shipyard streets. Half the stores were closed and had been for months, while in the other half, artisans meant for turning wood and metal into whalers instead swept their floors, cleaned their hearths, or sat on stools, hands clasped, talking in soft, absent voices.

A few watched silently as I hurried down the street, and Martin Child, a canvas maker, leaned out the door of his shop, lifted his chin, and called out, "Hey there, Avery Roe."

I turned to look at him and tendrils of fear snaked through me to see his hard expression, something almost like an accusation sitting in his familiar island features. He wasn't a sailor—none of the men in the shipyards were anymore—but they were islanders and still lived and died by the business of the whalers. A man on Prince Island was a whale man or he was a shipwright or he worked in the bank, financing excursions, or he worked for the ship owners as a whaling agent. Foreign sailors often visited and bought my family's charms, but the people of the island were the ones who truly relied on us. They were waiting for me, my islanders, waiting for me to take my grandmother's place and bring them back to glory. But I could feel their patience begin to wane as business trickled, could feel the lingering eyes of the shipwrights as I passed through the yard. I thought then of my dream, my nightmare, the cold, chilly faces of the sailors, and I shivered and picked up my pace.

Beyond the shipyard, Water Street ended at the docks, spread out a mile and a half down New Bishop's shore like brown and broken teeth. The exact middle of the docks, Main Dock, still catered exclusively to the big, square-rigged whalers, but the farther from Main Dock in either direction, the smaller the boats got, from whaleboats to fishing boats to sleek, rich sailboats, all the way down to rowboats, dinghies, and even a few flat-bottomed skiffs.

There was a time when so many ships crowded the docks, it was as though Prince Island's stubby, wind-stunted trees suddenly grew into a forest of masts and ropes and curled-up sails. *Skyscrapers*, the islanders call them, the straight black masts stretching three, four stories into the air to scrape the sky. But that was before whalers began hunting up north, before their ships got trapped in Arctic ice, before whales learned better to hide from hunters. That was before the War Between the States, when whaling grew so dismal that instead of sending their ships out on hunts, owners sold them south, to be filled with stones and sunk to the bottom of rivers, channels, harbors, all the better to keep the Confederacy closed off from the sea. All those lovely old ships, broken up and flooded, worth more as detritus and debris, and the owners shrugging away complaints, saying "What else am I to do? What else can I risk with the whales gone and the ice biting and the Roe witch unable to offer her protection?"

I headed straight for Main Dock, which in spite of everything still swarmed with men and boys, running, dragging ropes, or rolling barrels, their movements as chaotically in sync as a great school of fish. So much blood and waxy oil had seeped into the wood of the docks over the years that they were permanently stained, marbled dark rust and greasy gray. You had to shout to be heard down on the docks, shout over the noises of creaking ships, snapping sails, the constant hammerfalls and saws of the repairmen. And it always stank: of salt and brine and sweat, of rotting whale and sweet oil. In short, the docks were an affront to every kind of sense and, aside from the cottage on the rocks, my favorite place on the island.

I descended the rickety stairs to the docks without slowing, crossing the invisible line that separated the island's women and children from the world of the whalers. These men knew me, knew my grandmother, and they lifted their eyes from their work to greet me. They weren't just islanders, gray-eyed and dark-haired, but foreigners, too, of every continent and coloring, their g'mornings accented in French, Spanish, Portuguese, the lilting of the Southern states, the trill of the Pacific Islands.

"Hey there, Miss Avery," a red-faced man said, but when I nodded and meant to keep walking, he put out a hand. "Think you can make me a spell?" He held up a slim, six-inch-long metal spike attached around his wrist by a cord: his marlinspike. Good sailors had to know how to splice together ropes or quickly undo knots, and my grandmother had a tincture of whale oil and saltwater mud that made the marlinspike slide through even the tightest knots and kept its rope splices tight. But even if I hadn't been distracted by my nightmare, I couldn't make him the spell.

"Go see my grandmother," I said, and he scowled.

"I did. Made the walk last night, there and back, but she refused." He ran a thumb down the point of his marlinspike. A shiver worked through me and I frowned, because this was the second time this week I'd heard that my grandmother turned a sailor away. "What's she getting on about, sending me off? I had good money and my feet felt none the better for the walk."

"I'm sorry," I said. "Perhaps she was tired."

"She was tired, eh, but what's your excuse, then? Since when do the Roes think they can refuse us?"

"She would do it if she could," I said, and I frowned as a headache began to grow behind my eyes.

"And what about you? Can *you* do it, or d'you think your name alone gives you the right to act high and mighty down on the docks? You say you're a Roe, but all I see's a fancy little girl who likes to play at magic. This is my life! You'll play with that, will you?"

"I have to go," I said, and I pushed past him and rushed down the dock before he could say anything else.

"You're her? You're Avery Roe?"

Surprised, I spun quickly to see another man—no, a boy, only a few years older than me—standing behind me, his head cocked to one side. He had the coloring and look of one of the South Pacific islanders, whale hunters prized as harpooners and oarsmen, but he spoke nothing like those men I'd met in the past. Living on Prince Island had given me an ear for accents, and this boy's words rang with a mix of cultures: a bit of British, some French, even the casual slang of New England sailors.

"I am," I said, my heart still buzzing from the sailor and his marlinspike, "but there's somewhere else I have to be. Good day."

I made to move, but he held out a hand, smiling, his teeth white against his cinnamon-colored skin, and reached into his pocket, where I heard the jangle of coins. "I would be willing to pay you for your time," he said, and when he drew out his hand it shone bright with silver dollars. "I have a dream for you."

My eyes traveled from his outstretched hand up to his arm, where an intricate checkerboard pattern crisscrossed his skin, beginning below his elbow and disappearing under the roll of his sleeve.

"I can't," I said, looking over his shoulder into the crowd at the end of the docks. I needed to find someone. I needed to send a message to my grandmother. I needed to become a witch and stop my own dream before I worried about someone else's.

I realized the boy had said something.

"Excuse me?" I said, and although he smiled at me, patient, there was a hunger in his eyes.

"I said that I've heard stories about you. I came to the island just to see you." The light caught the coins in his palm, and when I glanced down I noticed that the long fingers of his outstretched hand trembled. "Will you tell my dream? I would like to know what it means."

He came to the island just for me. That's the way it used to be, when I was ten years old in my grandmother's cottage, holding court before a group of awestruck men as I described their futures in detail. I liked that feeling, being needed like that, but something pulled at me with this boy's words, an instinctual tug just below my rib cage, a warning.

I blinked, dazed, and he stared back at me, the smile on his face stretching with a look I'd seen before—desire, pure and all-consuming. This wasn't idle fortune-telling, and again the warning flashed.

"I can't, I—" The words froze on my lips as a sudden, sweeping wave of *need* crashed over me. The magic inside of me whipped up like a maddened dog, desperate to be put to use, to tell this boy's dream. I *needed* to tell dreams. It eased that terrible, constant pressure in my chest, if only for a little while, and even though I charged money for it (don't give them anything for free, my grandmother told me), it was as much a service for myself as my customers. And now, the magic inside of me screeched, a hungry baby howling for food, grating and constant and shrieking through my head *do it do it do it DO IT*, and I stuttered and stopped myself, overwhelmed. "No, I mean, all right. Tell me your dream. Quickly."

He pushed his handful of coins higher, eager despite his passive face, but I only plucked one from his palm. "I charge a dollar," I said, my voice tense, and he nodded and slipped the rest back into his pocket.

"You have to tell the truth," I continued, and I heard a soft laugh behind me. When I turned, I noticed that a small knot of young boys had paused their work to watch us, and my stomach twisted. The boys laughed because, lately, it had become sport to make up dreams for me to tell: wild, naughty, stupid dreams that made my head ache and my temper flare. "All in good fun!" they'd tease, because I wasn't my mother or my grandmother; I wasn't a proper witch and they didn't care about me. They didn't respect me.

The tattooed boy, to his credit, ignored them, and when I looked back at him, he began.

"I am alone," he said, his voice rumbling up through his lungs, through his throat. "It is night, and I am in the middle of the ocean. I float in a canoe, and I am flat on my back, staring up at the sky."

I felt it then: the sloping, slipping curve of his words, reaching out for me with spider-silk threads. He wasn't lying, not like the dock boys did; this dream was true, but I couldn't shake the feeling that something was wrong, the meaning of his dream slipping in and out of focus.

"The sky is full of stars," he continued, staring into my eyes. "I watch them grow bigger and brighter. Then, one by one, they wink out and disappear until the sky is black." He paused, and I bit the inside of my mouth, uncertain.

"I sit up and shout," he said, and his voice grew soft, but the kind of softness that means excitement. "But there is no answer. When I look around, the canoe is gone and I am in darkness." He lifted his hands into the air. "Then I wake up."

Those spider-silk threads wound around me, pulling out the meaning of the dream, and as it fell into place, my hands jerked into fists. I took a deep breath and pressed my fingertips against my temple, massaging away my headache. Not this, not after my own terrible dream.

Another breath, and I held out his money.

"It's not good," I said, because it wasn't. It wasn't anything I'd be happy to tell a person, and I felt a stab of pity for this strange boy. "If you don't want to hear, you can have your money back."

For a moment he watched me, his brown eyes deep wells, and I thought perhaps he would take back his money. I thought perhaps that no matter what he said, I'd give him the money and keep my mouth shut. But then he shook his head.

"I have to know what it means."

As he spoke, the full meaning of his dream slammed into place, and I understood suddenly why this felt so strange, why I shouldn't trust this boy. All the pity inside of me vanished as my cheeks grew hot with a mixture of anger and embarrassment.

"I told you not to *lie*," I said, and at my words, the boys watching us let out a swell of laughter. I turned on them, eyes narrowed. "Did you put him up to it? Told him it's great fun to lie to the witch?"

They only howled more loudly, slapping shoulders and knees and stomachs, and I pushed past them, shaking with so much rage that my vision blurred.

"Wait!" the boy said, his footsteps close behind me. "I didn't lie!" He ran to my side and threw an arm out to stop me. "That dream was the truth!"

"But you already know what it means, don't you?" I said, spitting out the words, because that was the strange thing I felt: certainty. Some other witch somewhere else in the world already told him this dream and so his hiring me was all a farce, just another joke like the dock boys, another chip at my family's moldering reputation. "Why ask *me* something you already knew?"

"You could tell?" He stared at me, stunned, and I squared my shoulders and moved to sidestep him. "Please," he said, moving to block my steps. "I'd heard rumors of your magic but I needed to know for certain if you could really do this. I wanted to test you to see—"

"*Test* me!"

"Good one, there!" a boy shouted. "Yes, give her a test! She says she's a witch but I think it's all stories!"

They exploded into laughter as my whole body shook red

hot, and I turned on the boy, fuming because he didn't believe in me, because he thought he could *expose* me as, as a cheat or a charlatan or a trickster! It made me sick.

I hated this boy. I hated him worse than any of the pranking dock boys, and I wished I were a man so I could punch him and it would hurt or a witch so I could curse him.

I was not a man. And I was not a real witch. But I could still hurt him.

"You want to hear your dream?" I asked, raising an eyebrow. "They're dead."

He flinched, and despite the flicker of pity I felt, my temper carried the words from my mouth.

"You had a mother and a father and three sisters but now they are all dead. All your cousins, your aunts and uncles, all your friends, every person you grew up with is dead, and they were murdered and their bodies thrown into the sea."

He stared at me, his dark eyes glassy with tears, but I just lifted my chin and rode out the waves of anger sweeping through me.

"Don't bother me with your dreams again," I said, and this time when I pushed past him, the boy didn't stop me.

Four

STILL TREMBLING, THE TATTOOED BOY'S silver dollar tight in my fist, I walked quickly down the docks and ignored the questions from the older sailors. Behind me, I heard one of the men shouting at the laughing boys, telling them they needed to show respect to the Roes or they'd answer to the cold waves. It made me feel a bit better, but my head swam with thoughts of the tattooed boy's lies, his terrible dream, my own dream and my murder, and still I was trapped, with no way to escape from my mother and no idea how to become the witch.

Air burned in my lungs as I tried to steady my frantic breathing, but finally I had to stop, resting a hand against a stack of barrels, blinking away the spots of light that peppered my vision. *Breathe, breathe*, I told myself, panic fluttering through my veins. *Focus.* The message. I had to send my grandmother a message so she could tell me what to do.

For that, I needed Tommy Thompson, and so I raised my head and set my jaw and scanned the faces on the docks, looking for one that was freckled and sunburned and gap-toothed. I found it at the very end of the docks, leaning up against the door of the counting house and chatting with a blond-haired boy.

Tommy Thompson grinned as I approached, and shouted, "Morning, Avery!" In return, I gave him a weak nod.

How would I describe Tommy? He was...my partner, I suppose, helping gather up dream-telling customers (for twenty cents' commission). But he was also the only person on the island I could properly call a friend. Since he turned twelve five years ago, he'd worked at the docks' counting house, the squat gray building where captains headed upon their arrival to log their wares and collect their payment. Tommy Thompson was perhaps the only boy on Prince Island who didn't dream of setting sail on the next whaler and leaving his home behind, a fact that endeared him to me as soon as I met him. He had a nice way about him and a pleasant smile, and I got the sense that he liked being friends with the witch girl—it gave him a bit of shine and specialness in a world where you weren't really a man until you walked a whaler. I also got the sense that he wanted more from me than just my friendship, but I kept our relationship businesslike. "The islanders must trust us," my grandmother would say. "You can't favor one more than another."

"Tommy, I—" But before I could say anything else he pushed forward the boy standing beside him.

"Jimmy Rickers has a dream for you," Tommy said, breaking into his grin. He nudged the boy again. "That's eighty cents to Miss Roe, lad, and another twenty to me."

I glanced at the boy, thirteen or so, smiling at me under a long fringe of blond bangs, and I felt a flash of annoyance.

"Not today," I said to Tommy, whose grin slid from his face.

"Really?" Ignoring the boy, he leaned in closer. "I need that twenty cents, Avery—I owe Joe King two dollars—and I told Jimmy you'd do it!"

My nerves frazzled, I shot Tommy a look. I didn't tell dreams on command, not even for him.

"Maybe later," I said, my eyes sliding from Tommy to the horizon. "Can we talk?"

There was a pause during which I hoped Tommy would not try to push the issue, and finally I heard him sigh. "All right. In the office."

He turned and I followed him inside the dock house, closing the door behind us. I frowned at the large windows that looked out over the docks. The counting house sat far out on the dock, easy for passing sailors to see, but also easy for people to spy what we were doing.

"What is it, then?" he asked, and my stomach churned.

"I . . . I need . . . I need to send my grandmother a message."

Tommy startled and stood up a little straighter. "A message, Avery? Een't that . . . dangerous?"

He would know. Years ago, not long after I met Tommy, he offered to pass a note to my grandmother, but my mother caught him almost instantly. Tommy swore backward and forward to my mother that it had been his idea entirely and that I hadn't even known about it. He came back to me, white as a ghost, shaking, and told me she said if she found him helping me again, she'd make him regret it. We both agreed it wasn't worth the risk.

"I wouldn't ask you if I didn't need it," I said, and although I tried to keep my voice steady, it shook as I spoke.

"But your mother said something bad'd happen to me. And your grandmother can't even come back to New Bishop or your mother'll take you away. And you can't—"

"I know," I said, cutting him off. I rubbed my temple, trying to think, but he was right. I'd lost my mind to chance something so risky. "Never mind." I sighed. "I'm sorry, Tommy. I'll... I'll try something else." I turned to leave, but Tommy put a hand out to stop me.

"No, Avery, it's all right." He rumpled his hair, face screwed up. "I'll do it."

I shook my head. "It's too dangerous. I shouldn't even have asked."

He just grinned. "I want to. I want to help."

I studied him for a moment before reaching into my pocket and pulling out the silver dollar, but Tommy waved it away. "Free of charge."

I didn't like that. "Do nothing that could harm our

reputation," my grandmother would say, and not paying for a service could harm our reputation.

"For Joe King," I said, laying the coin on the table, and I was relieved when Tommy didn't refuse it.

"What is it you need to tell your grandmother?" he asked. I opened my mouth, but my voice seized up in my throat. How could I tell sweet Tommy Thompson that I was scared I'd be murdered? And another, darker thought also hit me: Anyone could be my attacker, even sweet Tommy Thompson.

"I'll have to write it down, Tommy," I said, and his eyebrows knit together. Paper meant evidence if my mother found him out.

"Can't you trust me, then?"

No, I couldn't trust anyone with the truth, not even my only friend, not even if it put him in greater danger.

"You don't have to do it," I said. "If you're worried you'll get caught, we can forget about it." But he just sighed and handed me a scrap of paper and a gnawed-down pencil.

A rush of gratitude warmed my chest—dear Tommy, a better friend than I deserved—but as I suspended the pencil over the paper, I found I couldn't even write down the words. A chill swept over me, goose bumps rising on my arms and legs, and because Tommy still stared at me, waiting, I finally scrawled: "I had a dream. I need your help."

After folding up the note tight, I handed it over to Tommy, who shoved it into his pocket.

"Can you go tonight? You can leave her response with one

of the maids in the kitchens," I said, and when a note of panic crept into my voice, Tommy paused.

"Sure, then. I'll do it."

I nodded, my heart still beating fast, and I felt Tommy's hand on my shoulder.

"Whatever's wrong, it'll be all right, Avery," he said softly, and he sounded so sure and confident that for the first time since my dream, I smiled.

For the rest of the day, there was nothing left to do but wait for Tommy. Back in my mother's house, I paced the floor of my bedroom and counted down the hours until he would see me next. He had to work all day today and then he'd have a busy evening in the counting house, running over the accounts, putting everything in order for the next morning. Then back to the master's house for dinner, and perhaps he wouldn't get out to the shoreline path until ten or eleven in the evening. The walk, if he made good time, would take two or three hours. He might get back to New Bishop at three or four in the morning, but even if he went right to my mother's house then (although he wouldn't; he'd be tired; he'd want his bed), I wouldn't be able to sneak outside to wait for him.

Tomorrow, then. Another twenty-four hours to wait. And watch. And worry.

My stomach turned and I stopped my pacing to pick at the

scone I'd stolen from the kitchens before making my way back up to my room. Only twenty-four hours. I could wait twenty-four hours. After all, I'd waited four years to escape from my mother.

I could feel my lip curl as I thought about that day, four years ago, the day she took me from my grandmother and stood me in the kitchen of her tiny apartment, staring down at me like she hadn't had any thought of what she was going to do next.

"Well," she'd said. "I've just saved you. Aren't you going to say something?"

I blinked at her. I'd never seen anything like her with that scar that tripped and tangled across her face.

"You don't have to live in that hovel anymore," my mother said. "You don't have to see her anymore." Unmoving, she watched me, taking me in from head to toe. "I'll get you shoes. I saw some with little heels in town. Pretty. I'll get them for you."

I didn't know what to say. It felt as if I was breathing very fast.

"You'll need a new dress, too. You look so old-fashioned in this style. Did you even know that? When is the last time you played with other little girls?" She reached out to touch my sleeve, and I froze, eyes wide. "I made this dress when I was young. I had to beg for enough to get the pattern, and then the fabric.... I worked all winter, saving up, and then it took me another month to sew it just right, and my mother said it was a waste of money, but when I finally put it on, it was lovely." The fabric rasped between her fingers. "I'll make you something nicer. We can look over the patterns together. If you're good, I'll let you pick out the color."

"I don't want a new dress. When can I go home?"

Her hand dropped from my sleeve. "This is your home now," she said, spreading her arms wide, and the room was so small and cramped her fingers nearly brushed the walls.

"I want to go *home*."

She frowned. "You don't understand. I am your mother. I've brought you here to keep you safe." Her fingers twitched at her side and she brought them up to her waist, rubbing them together with quick, nervous motions.

"Becoming a witch is a brutal, terrible process," she said, something she would say often, omitting the details of that brutal, terrible process, believing that, far from scaring me off, it would only encourage me to try and unlock my magic (and on that point, she was probably correct).

"You must give up so much to be a witch. That cottage is no place for a little girl to grow up, strange men traipsing through all hours of the night," she said, and now she paced back and forth, punctuating her words with the sharp raps of her heels. "You need an education. There is so much you missed, trapped out there. You deserve better. You deserve the *best*. I should have taken you away from there *years* ago. You're going to go to school and stay with me and—"

Did she stop speaking? I don't really remember, because at that moment I'd begun to scream. *Scream*—as loud and as long and as violently as I could and I didn't stop for weeks. All the while my mother kept trying to calm me, telling me about the toys she'd bought for me, the hair ribbons, the charming girls' novels, hoping that, like the plucky-but-sweet protagonists, all

I needed was a few gentle reminders on proper morality and I would settle down.

"Stop! Stop it!" she shouted, but she hadn't realized what she had done. She'd thought she'd brought into her home her daughter: a miniature version of herself as a girl, a child who only dreamed of books and boots and baby dolls and would worship the woman who'd rescued her from the cottage. She tried to give me the things she had once wanted and then, bewildered when I rejected them, only tried harder, forcing me into frills, dragging me to concerts, spending her meager savings on carousel rides and sweets shops and puppet shows, where I only kept screaming, *kept screaming.*

"*Stop* it!" my mother said, her voice high and scared, and I remember she gripped my shoulders, shook them, rattled the breath out of my lungs, and in the silence said to me, "This is your home now, and you are staying with me! Listen! You're not going to see her again. She's not coming for you, ever, not if I can help it, and I am going to keep you safe. This is a good thing I'm doing for you! I'm never going to let magic touch you, *ever.*"

I squirmed in her grasp but she pulled me close, wrapped her arms around me in what she might have thought was an embrace but felt to me like a cage.

"My mother never protected me," she whispered, hot and fierce right in my ear, "but I am going to protect you."

That evening, almost a full day after my dream, I sat in the rocking chair in my room, in the house my mother said she found for me. I sat wearing the new dress she'd flown in from Paris, the boots from London, the silk ribbons from the mainland. For me, she'd said, all for me. Because if I was not to be a witch, I would be a lady. I would have beautiful clothes and paintings and music and a husband and the well-regard of society.

And just as she kept me in a net of her magic, she tried to entrap me with things—pretty things like dresses and bracelets and carriages and canopy beds. I could feel her tentacles reaching around me, slowly, soothingly, trying to convince me that I was warm and comfortable, that I belonged here, my every care addressed, my every want met, my days as shapeless and lovely as a never-ending dream.

"See what kind of life you could have?" she offered. "See what could be yours if you only gave up chasing magic?"

But anytime I imagined myself in my mother's world—shut up, shut in, a cosseted, treasured lady in a great, grand house—the force that flowed through my veins bucked and jittered. I was not a lady, no matter how my mother dressed me, no matter where I slept or what I ate or whom I socialized with. I was a witch, I was a whale, and I did not belong in an octopus's nest.

Five

I CAN NO LONGER COUNT EVERYTHING I'VE tried in an effort to unlock my magic.

I once cut off a curl of my hair and threw it into the ocean. For a whole year I swam in the sea—at sunrise, at sundown, at midnight, with the tide in and out, fully clothed and fully nude. I gave Tommy a dollar to rent me a little skiff and pushed off from the docks and rowed until I could barely see any land and called out to whales and water witches. My grandmother had a scarf that she wore around her neck every day and my mother favored scarves, too—scarves! that could mean something, couldn't it?—and so I spent a winter learning to knit, crafting a lumpy, gray, stringy blob of what could almost be seen as clothing, and I wore it around my neck and wished for my magic.

"It's supposed to hurt; that's just how it should be," my grandmother once told me, and so I pricked my fingers with pins until I bled, pinched myself until my arms and legs marbled with bruises. A week after my fourteenth birthday, a spooked horse knocked me down, breaking my arm, and despite the sharp fire of pain that forked through me, I felt a sudden flurry of hope: Surely *this* would be enough to do something. When I cried out a moment later, it was more from disappointment than from my splintered bone.

"Sacrifice," my mother often said. "You don't know what you must give up to become a witch." So I tried to stop myself from sleeping, slapping myself awake, my days turning hazy and dim. I went without food, until my mother noticed and forced open my jaws and poured soup and porridge down my throat. I had one last possession that tied me to my grandmother: the socks she'd knit for me and that I'd saved, like a holy relic, long after I'd outgrown them. They were the only things in the world that I loved, and right before we moved to the new house, I threw the pair into my mother's tiny pot-bellied stove. And I received in return a roomful of smoke and some unladylike swearing from my mother but not, unfortunately, my magic.

I would have tried anything. I would have cut off a finger except my mother and grandmother had all ten of theirs. I would have shaved my head or lived alone on a rowboat for a year or slit open my body to the sea. Nothing I tried ever seemed to work, although I knew, I *knew* that all my magic lay inside me, waiting, waiting until I figured out how to release it.

That night, I had the dream for the second time, and I woke up fighting, my hair plastered to my forehead and cheeks. I heaved for air, shocked to find my lungs whole and clear of blood and water, and as my senses returned I pushed away the terror to search for any clues, any new signs or details about my future.

Could I be wrong? What if I was wrong? I am not a perfect teller, and the meanings that float to the surface are sometimes not as exact as they first seem. Once I told a man, a ship owner, that Annie Perry would betray him and ruin his finances. Annie was his pretty young wife, a lady from the mainland prone to complaints of our shabby little island. He sent her away to relatives up in Maine, and it wasn't until his biggest ship faltered in Arctic ice that I learned its name was *Annie Perry* as well. The man lost his wife and ship and business in quick succession, and if I wasn't exactly wrong in telling his dream, I didn't have it entirely right, either.

There had to be more, I told myself. Sometimes when I tell dreams I can see so much—names, dates, faces, places— and perhaps I simply needed to concentrate harder. Perhaps I couldn't tell my own dream correctly; perhaps it didn't work like that. I jumped from bed and paced the floor, sifting through the images, turning them in my head because I *had* to have been wrong the first time, I couldn't be killed, and if there was some plot against me I must know who was behind it and why (and when and where and how).

A noise—a man's cough—made me turn suddenly, heart in my throat, eyes wide with fear, and I'm ashamed now to admit that I thought it was my murderer, there already to finish me off. But when the seconds of silence ticked into minutes, my breathing finally relaxed, and I realized it must have been the pastor, my mother's husband, rolling in his sleep.

I wonder if he *is my murderer?* I thought, and my lips pulled back in a tense smile. He disliked me enough (and why wouldn't he? Moody teenage girls who hate their mothers and hope to become witches must be hard enough for any man to stand), making my mother zero for two in regard to picking a father for me. Her first choice, remember, left her with her scar, and I knew even less about him than about the pastor, for, when pressed, my mother only told me that my father was a sailor and that he had soft hands. "He worked as hard as the others," she said once, "but his hands were as smooth as a child's. I used to wonder what he did to them." And then she sighed, as though it wasn't those soft hands that ruined her face.

Your mother had magic, a little voice whispered to me, and I shivered, *and still she couldn't stop a man from attacking her.* But I shook my head, fighting away the panic. You can't kill a Roe witch. No one can. Maybe my mother couldn't save herself, but magic would save me.

By the next morning I'd slumped over in a chair in the corner, the angles of the wood sharp enough to keep me from heavy sleep. When I opened my wardrobe to dress, my reflection caught my eye and I paused, staring at my sagging gray skin, the reddish clouds shot through my eyes. My grandmother had charms for sleeplessness, for staying awake through the night—popular with green-hand sailors, who usually got the unwelcome task of watching from the masthead all night—and I wished I had a few.

My stomach grumbled as I left my room and headed downstairs. My mother, her husband, and his children usually ate their breakfasts together in the dining room, but I took my meals down in the kitchen when I could, and no one complained because my mother's family avoided me almost as much as I them.

I got along better with the servants, anyhow. The senior staff—the butler, the housekeeper, my mother's maid—came from the mainland and cared little for the Roes, but most of the junior staff were islanders whose fathers, uncles, brothers, cousins whaled, and they enjoyed talking to me and would occasionally ask for a dream-telling. Magic under my mother's roof was risky but worth it, as in lieu of money the staff paid me in their discretion and assistance: saying nothing should I escape to the docks for a day or cleaning up the results of my magical experiments.

I especially liked the cook, Mrs. Plummer, who had a healthy respect for magic and my grandmother—she had a son, she said, whose life was saved by one of my grandmother's spells. If she wasn't distracted by cooking, she would tell me stories of my great-grandmother Almira, who'd lived at the turn of the century. "Now there was a woman with a lot of ocean in her," she'd say, as fine a compliment as islanders could fashion.

When I climbed down the stairs to the kitchen, Mrs. Plummer was in the middle of scolding Lucy, the scullery maid. Lucy shied away as I walked through the door, if not on account of Mrs. Plummer's reprimands, then on account of me. She'd never liked me much, ever since she got her Roes confused and asked if I could make her a love charm for, of all people, Tommy. (Poor thing. Of course I told her no and wished her well, although at twelve years old, scrawny as a wet dog and speckled as a hen's egg, she didn't have a chance.)

"Oh, Miss Avery!" Mrs. Plummer turned from Lucy and nodded at the back door, which led out into the garden. "Something left for you, outside." She leaned in, dropped her voice. "I didn't touch it. Just in case."

I glanced at her sharply, butterflies in my stomach. Mrs. Plummer understood magic, understood that charms meant for someone specific should only be handled by that person. And I could think of only one person in the world who would leave me charms.

I ran to the back door and threw it open. There, just by the frame and still wet from dew, sat a small package wrapped in brown paper. "For Avery" stood out in scrawled letters on the damp paper, and I bent down to pick it up. She was right, Mrs. Plummer—the little parcel vibrated with magic, fresh and tingling.

Granma! Tommy must have gotten my message to her and she must have figured out what I needed! My heart flew into my throat as I ripped the brown paper apart. I looked first for a note but, finding nothing, turned my attention to the charm.

"Strange…" I whispered. It wasn't what I expected: a dried-up something, spongy and light as air, like very soft, pale coral. A string wound over its surface, and tucked here and there into the string were fine knots, delicate, intricate, minia-ture versions of the knots that sailors make.

I stared at the little charm, confused, because I could be certain of only one thing: This didn't come from my grand-mother's hands. It didn't even feel like her magic, although the familiar tug told me it *was* still magic. A luck charm, in fact.

"Was I right, Miss Avery?" Mrs. Plummer called from the kitchen, smiling at me over a ball of warm, floury dough.

I turned as though in a daze. "Yes," I said, and because she really did do the right thing in not touching it, I smiled back. "Thank you."

The charm felt curious in my hand, pulling and push-ing, trying to wrap its threads around me, to worm its magic through me and change my luck to good. It tickled and vibrated so much that I walked quickly back into the kitchen and set it down on the counter. My fingers still burned, so I picked up the salt bowl and dipped my hand in, rubbing the rough grains against my skin.

"Something wrong?" Mrs. Plummer asked. She slowed her work and glanced over her shoulder at the open kitchen door before speaking again. "Not something... not something with your grandmother, is it?"

Is it? Could that be why this little charm felt so strange? Could I have forgotten my grandmother's magic already? But no, her magic is mine, too, and beyond the underlying feel, this one was entirely different. It felt a little like I'd bitten into a meal I'd never eaten before, knowing it was chicken, just covered with a strange and exotic sauce.

"No," I said finally. "No, I don't think so." I searched around the kitchen before grabbing a thick cotton towel. "May I borrow this?"

Mrs. Plummer waved a hand. "Of course," she said.

Wrapping the charm carefully in the towel, I picked it up. "I'll be back in a bit," I said.

"Where are you—" But I was already out the door, on my way to the docks, because this charm came from a sailor's hands, and I had to find him.

The Roe women don't usually use the charms they make, and they certainly don't use charms made of other magic. Once, a captain returned from the coasts of Africa with an ornate carving for my grandmother—his Caleb's gift, a gesture of goodwill for the weeks he'd spend in our port. Standing over five feet tall, the statue was inlaid with precious metal and carved with intricate patterns in the shapes of eyes. When the captain unveiled it with a dramatic flourish, I gasped, the wave of strange, strong magic hitting me as forcefully as a gale. Tears sprang into my eyes, and as the captain tried to explain—the statue represented knowledge and strength or something like that—my grandmother ran to the fireplace and snatched up a shovelful of burning embers.

"Out!" she shouted, holding up the steaming, sizzling shovel. "Get it out!"

The captain, startled, had enough sense to realize his beautiful Caleb's gift had been rejected and, instead of complaining, dragged the cursed thing out of the cottage without another word. My grandmother reached into her black chest, drawing out bundles of dried herbs and the delicate skeletons of birds, tossing them to the dirt where the statue had stood, muttering words rapidly under her breath. I watched from the corner, crying, gasping, and when my grandmother finally finished, she pulled me close into a hug. Her skin felt feverish, sweaty, her breath sweet and hot, but even her gentle hands couldn't drive the chill and shudder from my skin as I remembered again the force that knocked against me.

"Be careful," she had whispered to me, and I thought of her words again as I ran down the street, the charm burning my skin even through layers of cotton. "Be careful of strange magic."

I stumbled a moment and had to slow to catch my breath as

a terrible thought entered my mind—*could my murderer know magic?* But I dismissed it immediately. This little charm barely had enough power to numb my fingertips, let alone kill me.

My feet carried me down to the water, down to the docks, pulled by the foreign magic. I spared half a moment to glance around for Tommy—he certainly didn't make the charm, but perhaps he had an idea who did, and besides, he owed me my grandmother's response—and when my eyes swept over one sailor, he looked up with such expectancy that I knew I'd found the person who left me the little package.

The tattooed boy tossed aside the wet rope in his hands as I walked up to him and jerked the towel away, wincing at the fresh wave of magic.

"This is yours?" I asked, lifting the charm, and when he nodded, slowly, I added, "Why?"

"A gift," he said, his expression smooth. "With my apologies."

I narrowed my eyes at him. "Realized it's no good to make a witch angry? Scared I'll curse you to bits? Well, I don't use luck charms," I said, thrusting it out at him, and a corner of his mouth ticked into a surprised smile.

"You could tell it was a luck charm?" he asked, and when I said nothing, the charm still stretched out in front of me, he shook his head. "You should keep it. It won't do good to return it."

He was right. Just like Mrs. Plummer knew not to touch a charm intended for another person, this boy knew that to return an intended charm would ruin the magic, maybe even turn it around, good luck into bad. Although I didn't have qualms about giving this boy bad luck, I knew he wouldn't take it back now. I frowned and pushed the charm into my pocket, where it vibrated against my hip like a jar full of bees.

"Who told you how to treat charms?" I asked. "Was it the person who told your dream?"

"That was a shaman, not far from Tahiti."

"And he was the one who gave you this charm?" I asked, but the boy shook his head.

"I made it."

"Made it?" I pulled the little charm out again, feeling past its string and soft surface into the threads of magic within. It felt cruder, sloppier than my grandmother's refined and reliable charms, but it would still work (and that was more than I could say about anything *I* had tried to make).

"Where did you learn how?"

He lifted his eyebrows and smiled. "Where did you learn *your* magic, witch girl?"

I crossed my arms over my chest, studying him. "Well, where are you from? What are you doing here on Prince Island?"

His smile grew tense and stiff. "I came from an island, same as you. In the Pacific, not far from New Zealand." He glanced up at the brigantine floating in the slipway to my right. "I'm a harpooner with the *Modena*."

The big, blond ship stretched above our heads. Even in need of repairs, she was a beauty—square rigged on foremast, fore-and-aft rigged on the mainmast, and although I couldn't see the registration mark on her bow, I knew enough that she wasn't an island boat and, most likely, carried none of my grandmother's spells.

"Aren't you a bit young for that job?" I asked, and he studied me.

"I was born holding a harpoon. My name is Tane," he said, stretching out his hand, and I liked the way he said it, *Taah-neh*, his accent curling and breathing around the word.

"Avery Roe," I said, and I took his hand. As my skin touched his, a crackle of magic electrified the air and I jerked away.

"Yes. Avery Roe of Prince Island. Granddaughter of the sea witch. Dream-teller. You're famous."

"It's my grandmother who's the famous one," I said, ignoring the rush of pleasure at his words with a wave of my hand. "She does the real magic. I just tell dreams."

"That's not real magic?"

"It's not the same, no," I said, color rising to my cheeks. "But someday I'll leave New Bishop and take over for her, and then I'll know everything she does."

He said nothing for a moment, and I stared back, surprised at myself. There weren't many people on the island who knew that, for all my bloodlines and destiny, my magic was nothing compared to my grandmother's. This boy had too casual, too easy a way about him. He made me say things without thinking.

"And why don't you leave now?" Tane asked, speaking carefully.

"Perhaps you shouldn't meddle," I said. "I'm not so poor a witch that I couldn't make a nosy sailor boy sorry."

He shook his head. "That wasn't my intent." He glanced over his shoulder, his eyes lingering on the other men, and leaned in closer, dropping his voice. "I have a proposition for you, witch girl. I've heard the men here talk about your mother, that she's keeping you from your grandmother with a curse."

As he spoke, I struggled to keep my breaths calm, even as my blood sizzled through my veins. What chatty whale men! Silent as stones when you've a question for them, but slip some gossip into their ears and they're worse than fishwives with their tongue-flapping.

"Do you believe everything you hear?" I asked, my voice high-pitched and brittle, and he held up a hand.

"Wait," he said. "I might be able to help. I know how to ward off curses."

My eyes widened. That was tricky business and nothing familiar to me. My grandmother didn't want it known that magic could be fended off (or else what good would her threats do?), and when sailors came calling for protection against magic, she sent them away empty-handed.

"All right," I said, and I licked my lips. "Say you break my mother's spell. What then? You want something from me, don't you? I can't make charms for you. I can't do anything beyond dream-telling."

His mouth pulled into a long, thin line. "That's all I need, witch girl. Do you remember my dream, from yesterday?"

Fire, broken bodies, crying children, the rush-rush-rush of a surf turned red.

"Yes," I whispered.

"I told you a shaman in Tahiti interpreted it for me, six months ago," Tane said, and a muscle in his neck jumped and tensed. "He told me more, as well. He told me that the men who killed my people are American sailors. He told me to find another dream-teller, and he told me that she would help me." His words grew faster, softer, mixing with his hot breath, and I swallowed, my throat dry and sticky.

"I'm sorry for yesterday, but I had to test you. I had to be sure you were the girl he spoke of. Since the day I heard about what happened to my people, I've written down every one of my dreams. I want you to tell me what they mean and what they say about the men who killed my family."

My breath stopped in my chest as Tane stretched himself up to his full height, and the sun shining on his skin seemed to be sucked into the black marks across his arms.

"Find them, witch girl," he said, his voice as low as a rumble, "and I'll break your mother's curse."

I blinked at him and he stared back, his features so still and grim they seemed carved out of stone. How was this strange boy supposed to break my mother's spells? Because despite the crackle of magic around him, despite the charm buzzing in my pocket, I knew that in the end, he wasn't like me. He wasn't born into magic and it didn't spin out from him; somehow he knew how to tether it, shape it, maybe manufacture it. But even so, his magic was weak and my mother still a witch in her prime.

"How?" I asked. "How would you break her curse?"

"There are things I can try," he said, and my stomach sank. "*Try...*"

"I understand magic. My people have—" He choked on the word, paused, started again. "My people had ways of protecting themselves against magic. With enough time, I could teach you."

"How much time?" I asked, eyes narrowed. He thought for a moment, holding my gaze.

"I'm not sure. Perhaps however long it would take you to decipher my dreams."

That was the wrong answer. Six months of dreams, one hundred and eighty nights, with perhaps two or three separate dreams a night... Even if the dreams came to me easily, it still meant hours, days, weeks of work—time I did not have.

"And what if I told your dreams and learned nothing about your people?"

"You could see my future, couldn't you?" he asked, his words flushed with urgency. "You could tell me if I meet them and when. The shaman told me you could help me."

"No," I said, and the memory of my own dream sent a wave of nerves over me. "Not necessarily. Sometimes there are details and sometimes... not."

"I still want to know anything you could tell me. And in return, I could help you."

He stared at me, waiting, and I looked away from him with a sigh. Truthfully, I wasn't certain he *could* help me. The little charm purring in my pocket didn't inspire much awe for his talents. And besides, *be careful of strange magic.* Even should he prove powerful enough, I didn't relish reliving the pain and poison I'd felt when that captain brought his idol into my grandmother's cottage.

Tommy should have gotten a message to my grandmother last night, explaining that I needed her. Even if she couldn't help me escape New Bishop, she could tell me what to do to unlock my magic, and then I could break my mother's spell myself. Besides, I didn't have weeks to experiment with this boy's half-formed, foreign magic. I didn't have any time at all.

"No," I said, shaking my head. "I can't."

"Don't you need my help?" he asked, frowning, and I laughed.

"Unfortunately for you, I'm not nearly desperate enough to try your magic."

"But my dreams—"

"I can't," I said, and seeing his face fall, his mouth pulled down into a frown, I felt a funny jump in my chest. "I'm sorry. I am. I'm...I'm sorry about your family, too."

His shoulders jerked a little in surprise, and although I expected him to say something, to protest, he just nodded.

"I'll be here," he said, and when I opened my mouth to tell him I wouldn't be back, he moved, swift as a seal, to point at the buzzing, burning charm in my pocket. "And hold tight to that," he said softly, dark eyes glowing. "It looks as though you'll need it."

Six

WALKING BACK TO MY MOTHER'S HOME,
I rubbed over and over the spot on my hip where the charm
had sat, shivering and buzzing against my skin. Despite Tane's
words, I dropped the charm into the harbor as soon as I was out
of his sight, but I could still feel its itching, niggling residue.

I wished I knew where Tane got his magic. There are other
magic-workers out there in the world, other folk who make charms
and spells and bend the laws of nature. Every now and then sailors
will bring back stories of the strange things they've seen, of little
girls born with snake heads, of men who can transform into dogs,
of mind readers and animal charmers and fire manipulators.

Once, when I was very little, I saw one of these magic
people. Usually my grandmother didn't like to encourage outsiders coming to the island, but this one, this man, he was a

jester, an entertainer, no threat to her or her working spells. She took me to the docks to see him, whip-thin with dusky skin and a thatch of stiff black hair. He was bare-chested and wore only tight canvas britches and he stood in the center of the wharf with the whole town (even the pastors) around him in a circle, and then, as we all watched, he rose into the air. He went up and up and up, spinning and twisting like a feather caught on the wind, the ropy muscles of his back and arms tightening and flexing. He stayed up in the air for twenty minutes at least, long enough for even the most reticent islanders to fill his cap with money. He left not long after, and for weeks I pestered my grandmother, asking her if she knew any spells to fly. No flying, she finally said. Our women are made for water, not air.

But I didn't think Tane was one of them, one of us.

Sighing, I turned up the walkway to my mother's home. It was a Sunday, and the rest of the Severs would be at morning services by now (my mother had excused me from attending church, after one of the pastor's thinly veiled screeds against my grandmother caused me to actually leap up and call him a liar). The big house stood empty, but instead of climbing the front steps to bask in the peace and quiet, I sat down on the stoop.

Where was Tommy?

He wasn't at the docks—I had checked after my conversation with Tane. The counting house stood empty, while everyone I asked said some variation of "Haven't seen him all day."

I held my hands on my lap and waited, craning for any sight of him.

Ten minutes passed. An hour. Another hour. I stretched my muscles and frowned at the empty street.

Where was he?

The Severs would be home soon, and, sighing, I rose from my perch, took the stairs to my room, and sat at the big window, watching the stretch of Main Street below.

Maybe he wouldn't come to the house. Maybe he'd overslept; maybe he'd had to run down to the docks to work. But he *said* he'd come. And Tommy was, at the very least, reliable.

I leaned my head against the window frame, not moving, even when my neck cramped and my eyes burned and my head ached and my stomach churned as though I'd eaten a bucket of gravel. The lunch bell rang and I ignored it. The dinner bell rang and I remained in my room. A maid arrived with tea and toast and inquiries about my health, and I dismissed her and let the tea cool and watched the world outside grow dark. And still, he did not come.

Where was Tommy?

Every muscle in my body screamed with tension by the following morning. I'd fallen asleep with my face pressed against the glass, and although I didn't remember sleeping, I did remember my nightmare waking me, reminding me that Tommy was supposed to help me and instead he was missing.

Groaning, I pulled myself from the chair and blinked at

the morning sunshine. I would have stretched and resumed watching, but my stomach seemed to have grown claws overnight, roaring like a tiger for something to eat.

I paused just long enough to change my dress and curse under my breath at the sorry state of my face (slack, wan, with a perfect silver-dollar-sized imprint on my forehead from the window), and then I walked down to the kitchens.

As usual, the quiet of the rest of the house disappeared below stairs, and the closer I got to the kitchen, the more I could hear footsteps, clanging pots, the hiss of steam, and—crying. A girl's crying, in fact—Lucy, the little maid, upset again.

"What is it this time?" I asked, my voice strained from sleeplessness, and as I turned the corner into the kitchen Lucy peeked her red-eyed and ruined face up from behind her hands. She went rigid with shock and then her whole expression soured as though pinched by a giant, invisible hand.

"You—y-you!" she sputtered, shaking her head, before bursting into a fresh round of tears and scampering off to the maids' quarters.

"What was that?" I asked, and Mrs. Plummer clucked her tongue at Lucy's disappearing skirts.

"Oh, she's upset about that fellow she fancies," Mrs. Plummer said, throwing up her hands. "You know, the freckly one. The one who doesn't whale. He's gotten himself into a mess of trouble."

My stomach cramped. "Tommy?"

"That's the one." Mrs. Plummer shook her head and turned back to one of the six pots simmering on the stove. "I'm always telling her, you can't trust a boy who doesn't take to the water, he'll—"

"What *happened*?"

Mrs. Plummer raised an eyebrow as my shrill words cut her off. "Some men from the *Keene* found him wandering witless in the Great Gray Slough yesterday morning, three sheets to the wind and mumbling nonsense. Lucy heard it all from the milkman, and she's been making a fuss—"

I didn't even wait for Mrs. Plummer to finish before I turned and ran from the kitchen, back out through the garden and toward Main Street.

What could have possibly happened to Tommy? I knew that he did not drink and could think of no reason why he would go to the slough, the black marshy pond forever filled with icy, hip-deep water, even in the hottest summers. Half-mooned, it fits up against the island's northwestern shoreline, only a spit of sand and grass separating its fresh waters from the salty sea. It's desolate, even dreary, made up of nothing but quantities of pitch-black mud and long grasses barbed with fine stingers that slice open unsuspecting ankles and calves. There was nothing out there for him.

Tommy, wandering witless. Tommy, with a message for my grandmother. Tommy, who my mother said would regret ever helping me...

I'd just turned from Main Street to Water Street when I caught sight of a familiar figure walking by himself from the wharf—there he was, bleary-eyed and haggard.

"Tommy!" I turned and ran toward him, and he lifted his face, looking as though his whole world had just turned upside down. Breathless, I stopped before him. "I've just heard—what happened?"

Glancing around the crowded street, he nodded toward a side alley. "Down there."

As we walked, I watched him carefully, red-rimmed eyes on the ground, his hair greasy and falling across his face.

"Did she find you?" I asked, whispering, but Tommy shook his head.

"I don't know what happened," he said, his voice creaky. "I had your note in my pocket, and as soon as I left town, everything went all black. I found myself sitting up against Jack McDuffy's house—you know the one, right on the edge of town—and I thought maybe I'd ate somethin' funny, so I dusted myself off and walked back out to the shoreline path, and the next thing I know, I'm on my knees in the slough and the boys of the *Keene* are pullin' me up by my shoulders." He looked up, his face hollow with fear. "She said I'd regret it, Avery, helpin' you."

I twisted my fingers, uncertain. It sounded like he'd been cursed, but how?

"I didn't even get to deliver your note." He reached into his pocket and pulled it out, grubby and water-stained. Gingerly, I took it and held it between my fingers.

"It's all right," I said. "I'll send another message. I'll find someone else. Someone she won't suspect."

Tommy nodded. "You should be on your way, then, and I

should get back to the counting house. I wasn't in any fit state to work yesterday, and the master says if I step out of line again—"

"Tommy Thompson! All righ' then? How're you doing today, lad?" A man appeared from around the corner and slapped an arm around Tommy's shoulders, grinning. I recognized him as Mitchell Grays, one of the oarsmen for the *Keene*.

"Oh—fine. I'm fine," Tommy said, keeping his eyes on the ground.

"I thought you were done for yesterday!" Mitchell Grays laughed. "I've seen plenty o' drunks in my day, but I've never seen a boy walk into the water without a look on his face. If we hadn't been on our way to do some fishing, you'd have drowned yourself in knee-high water!" He let out another laugh and slapped Tommy on the back. "That's what you get for not going to sea! Drowning in the slough—hoh! My little Nan can paddle around in the slough and she's not six yet!"

The blood drained from my face as I tried to catch Tommy's eye. *That* was what had happened? My mother's spell had sent Tommy to the slough to...to *kill* himself?

Mitchell Grays let go of Tommy and winked at me. "Unless you weren't drunk at all, eh? We know how you are with the witch girl! Got yourself into a lovers' spat? Maybe you got cursed!"

Mitchell Grays threw his head back in laughter, and my heart raced. The islanders couldn't know that Tommy had been cursed—they couldn't even suspect it. Their opinion of the Roes had already fallen over the years. What would they do if they thought we'd started *cursing* islanders?

Tommy pushed Mitchell Grays's hand off his shoulder, so fast and hard it looked like a shove.

"Avery had nothing to do with it," he said, and the smile slid off Mitchell Grays's face.

"Well, that was just a joke, then, lad, I didn't—"

"You didn't think, that was what happened!"

"I didn't...well, hold on there, boy, where do you think you can get off talking to me like—"

"I already told you," Tommy said, pink-faced, breathing hard, "I was drunk, and Avery had nothing to do with this. And you should know better than to talk about the Roes like that!"

"Tommy—" I said, reaching out a hand, and Mitchell Grays's eyes narrowed, his expression dark.

"A fine way to thank a man," he said, and he moved to leave but kept his eyes on Tommy. "You would have died if not for me, you know that! You're an odd one, Thompson, and no good will come of you—you mark my words!"

Tommy started to go after him, but I grabbed his arm, my heart pounding. I'd never seen him like that, riled up, spoiling for a fight. I'd never seen him lie before, either, and he did it for me, he did it even though Mitchell Grays was sure to go right to the docks and tell every soul he met that Tommy had well-nigh lost his mind.

"Tommy, that—you could get in trouble for that!" I said, although I couldn't help the rush of relief I felt. The men at the docks might soon think Tommy had gone mad, but at least they wouldn't think he'd been cursed.

Tommy watched Mitchell Grays's retreating figure for a moment, every muscle in his body tensed, and then he glanced at me and his shoulders fell. "I don't want them thinkin' you had any part of it." He shook his head and looked in the direction of the docks. "Eh, I'd better get down to the counting house before Mitchell Grays tells everyone what's happened." He let out a sigh. "And you need to find another boy to carry a message. You'd better get looking soon, before your mother curses this whole island."

I frowned and nodded my head. Slowly, I reached for one of Tommy's hands and squeezed it.

"It'll be all right," he said again, only this time he didn't look like he quite believed it.

He turned back toward the docks, and I picked up my skirts and hurried to my mother's house. As I ran, I thought about my conversation with Tommy. One thing didn't make sense: I could not figure out how she found out about the note quickly enough to curse him. How could she have known? Did someone tell her? And when did she—

I stopped running, my blood cold.

...before your mother curses the whole island...

Tommy said...he only felt the curse when he left town. Not when he decided to go to my grandmother's cottage, as my mother's curse worked for me. I pressed a hand to my face, feeling hot tears form under my fingers.

How could I be so stupid?

There were spells tied to specific places meant for specific people, but I'd forgotten about them. My grandmother would use them all the time; just outside the cottage, for example, she'd buried an iron stake wrapped in canvas, a cursing charm meant to turn away anyone who came to the cottage with the intent of robbing it.

My mother *hadn't* cursed Tommy—not intentionally, anyway. And why would she, when it would be so much simpler, so much easier to bury a charm somewhere out on the shoreline path, a magical net to entrap anyone trying to leave New Bishop with a message from me to my grandmother.

Anyone.

That meant no more messages.

No more help.

I was well and truly trapped.

For a moment I felt the ground tip underneath my feet and I reached out a hand to the brick wall by my side. My knees threatened to buckle, hot panic washing over me as the thoughts tumbled through my head—*I will never reach my grandmother, I will never escape, I will never stop my future!*

Dropping to the ground, I covered my face with my arms, pressed my mouth against the sleeves of my dress, and screamed, screamed, *screamed.*

I screamed until my throat burned and rasped, until all the air inside of me had been squeezed out, and when I had finished screaming, I rose to my feet and kicked the brick wall so hard that I let out a yelp of pain. Panting for air, I leaned against the wall, pressed my forehead against the cool brick, and felt the frustration and fear and anger seethe inside of me.

This was my mother's fault, all of it. She kept me here in this town, she prevented my escape, she hurt my friend and nearly killed him—killed him!—and I had to make her pay.

Sometimes, when I am very angry at my mother, I like to imagine her big and bloodless and all alone at the bottom of the ocean, like a giant squid. I imagine her in the darkness, in the cold, all her sticky tentacles wrapped tightly around her. The squid live far down in the ocean, farther down than any man could ever dive. Only whales can go from the surface to the depths, where they chomp-chomp on squid and come up for air with skin slashed by sharp beaks and puckered with sucker marks. Once, a whale ship caught one of these squid—kraken, they called it—and hauled it to the docks and hung it up. Its skin was translucent and pale and fragile, the color of something that hates light, and its body looked saggy and swollen, full of all kinds of decaying gas.

That is how I imagine my mother, a monster deep in the ocean, reaching out with her tentacles to catch stray fish and stray sailors and pull them apart like a bloated, underwater spider.

And that day, as my feet drummed across the cobblestones back to my mother's house, I imagined my body cutting through the air like a whale's slick skin through water. I imagined that each step through town was another foot deeper into the cold ocean, deeper into my mother's territory. But I was a whale, strong and muscular, long-jawed and sharp-toothed, and I was going to find my terrible squid of a mother and chomp-chomp her so she'd learn to keep her blasted tentacles to herself.

Seven

BEFORE I CLIMBED THE FRONT STEPS OF the big house, I stopped, took out my handkerchief, pressed it to my face. I spat on my hands and smoothed back the wispy strands of hair that had come undone from my plait. I waited until my breaths evened again, and then I turned the doorknob and stepped inside.

Calm. Stay calm.

A noise from upstairs made me turn my head: fast, small footsteps followed by the door to the nursery slamming shut. The Severs had finished their breakfast and now gone their separate ways: children to the nursery, pastor to his study, my mother to her fussy little drawing room.

Carefully, I closed the door behind me and turned to make my way up the stairs when I heard my mother's voice, calling for me, reaching out a delicate tentacle to draw me closer.

Nothing is wrong. Don't let her think you're scared. You're not scared.

She sat in her parlor, dressed, as usual, like she was meant for this fancy new world, in a trim, green-and-cream-striped dress of summer satin. Sitting just at her side, ready should she choose to leave the house, was a white straw hat decorated with a bunch of real flowers and a thin line under the band to show where she'd snipped out the veil that would have hung there. She did that to all her hats, even when veils became fashionable, choosing instead to show off the scar on her face as though it were a particularly radical accessory she could never remove. Despite—or perhaps due to—her scar, she had a kind of terrible beauty, and between the parlor, the dress, the sunlight bringing out some pink in her cheeks, she looked every bit a hand-tinted fashion plate out of *Godey's Lady's Book*.

"Did I hear you on the stairs earlier?" she asked, and her voice flowed like honey, so sweet, so gentle. "Where were you this morning?"

"Just out for a walk," I said. Calm. Calm. *Stay calm.*

Something bright in my mother's hand caught my eye: the nib of her pen, long and sharp and delicate. She had a sketchbook open in her lap—blank. Art was one of the many things she'd tried to impress upon me, claiming that it would ennoble my spirit and reveal the world's true beauty, not realizing, I suppose, that if she wanted true beauty, all she had to do was walk out to the cottage on the rocks and watch the sunrise over the water.

"I heard there was quite a fuss in the kitchens today," she said, scratching the pen across the paper in bold, sweeping lines. "One of the maids reacted terribly to word that Tommy Thompson tried to drown himself in the slough." Her eyes flickered up to my face, her expression serene, but I knew she was watching me, waiting for me to respond.

"Is that what they thought at first?" I said, and *oh yes*! My voice was smooth, just as though my heart wasn't strangling itself in my chest. I kept my eyes on my mother's face as I spoke, daring her to see any fear or hesitation. "I heard that in the end, Tommy was drunk on rum. I bet he thought he was at home, drawing himself a warm bath."

"Well," she said, a tight little smile at her lips. "With all the stories flying about, who knows the truth?" Her shoulders lifted into a sweet shrug, and she turned back to her drawing. "The rumors in the kitchen are that some people think Tommy's bewitched. Did anyone mention that to you?"

I hate her. I hate her. I wanted to scream at her, at her lies, her duplicity, pretending to be nothing more than a gentle-woman, sweet and caring and good. I wanted to leap across the room and rip the paper from her hands and shout at her that Tommy almost died, *died* because of her! But I knew what would happen then. She would stare at me, cool as a pitcher of water, letting me get excited, letting me get scared, letting me admit that I tried to defy her. And then she would have every excuse to pack me up and send me off to the mainland—to keep me away from magic, to keep me *safe*. If I wanted to beat my mother, I would have to play her game. I didn't blink.

"Yes, someone did mention that to me," I said, studying the mask that was my mother's face. "But I told them that would be impossible. Because there are only three Roes on Prince Island. Granma would never harm a dock boy, out of fear for her business. I *can't* make a spell like that." I paused, staring at her. "And we all know that you have given up magic for good." Beat. "Unless, of course, you've changed your mind, which I suppose would be something the good Pastor Sever would care to know, for doesn't he always say that proof of your witchcraft would be grounds for divorce?"

She didn't move. Neither did I.

And then: a silver flash from her pen. A flinch. She flinched. And I allowed myself the teeniest, tiniest smile.

"How good of you to straighten that up," she said, and she cleared her throat. "And I'm so glad to hear that Tommy is all right. Poor boy. I hope his experience serves as an example to others of the dangers of... *liquor*. These island boys think it's all fun until they see a friend ruin his life with it."

Concern laced her voice, but her gaze was steady, steely. I'd never risk asking another boy to send a message for me, I'd never jeopardize my relationship with the people of Prince Island like that, and she knew it and she knew that I knew it. She thought she had won.

But then, perhaps there was someone else who could help.

So I let my smile grow, and as I walked out of her little parlor, I said—so easily, so indifferently, "Oh, *Mother*. You know there are plenty of men on this island capable of handling a few drinks."

It took me five minutes to make it down to the docks, and I arrived breathless, shrugging off questions of Tommy from the sailors and dock boys. My heart pounded so fast my vision blurred and my hands and feet tingled, but I couldn't stop to think this through, any of it, because I was trapped and Tommy couldn't help me and neither could any of the sailors, but perhaps I had one last chance.

One last chance that made me swimmy with nerves and my stomach turn, but what choice did I have? I had to do it, I had to stop my dream, I had to beat my mother and get to my grandmother and escape to the cottage and become, once and for all, the witch of Prince Island.

One last chance, and I found him, pausing to drink water, sweat beading along his checkered arms, and when he saw me, he didn't ask any questions or look surprised, and I didn't even mind that he knew I would be back.

"Can you really do it?" I asked, breathing hard. "Don't lie to me, tell me honest: Can you break my mother's curse?"

Tane tilted his head, studying me, and nodded. "I can."

"She's a strong witch," I said, panic fluttering in my

stomach. "You'd need to make something better than that little charm you gave me. If that's the best you can do, it's nowhere good enough."

He stood up a little straighter. "I can do it."

"And I need you to work fast. Start immediately. Tomorrow, and every day after that."

"All right," he said, his voice careful. "You'll tell my dreams in exchange."

It wasn't a question, but I nodded anyway, my head bobbing up and down in a nervous tic. Tane stood still, water dripping from the dipper in his hand, and frowned, uncertain.

"I thought you said you weren't desperate enough to take up with my magic," he said. "What happened?"

I let out a high-pitched laugh. "What do you think? I got desperate enough. So you'd better be telling the truth, because you're my last hope."

Eight

THE FOLLOWING DAY, FOUR DAYS NOW since my dream first woke me in the middle of the night, I stood with my forehead pressed against the glass window of Luewellen's General Store, staring at the neat, velvet-encased bottles of Wm. F. Nye's N.Y. Oil—*for Lubricating, Polishing, Cleaning, Preventing Rust, Product of New Bishop, Mass., U.S.A.*

I read those words over and over, forcing myself to stay calm and distracting myself from what I really wanted to do: pace the sidewalk like a madwoman, muttering and thumping strangers who got in my way.

Tane was late.

Yesterday, we'd agreed to meet at two in the afternoon outside of the general store, as it was the only time I could get away. But it was ten minutes past at least, and I had to be back at the house no later than three thirty.

I sighed and stared through the plate-glass window, counting all the wares on display. They nearly all had a bit of whale in them, in some form or another, and not just because this was a whaling island. Any general store in the country would look like this, shelves filled with stuff that came from animals that the men of this island hunted and killed.

Every rich lady in the country has a jar of whale on her vanity. She dabs whale on her wrists, at her neck. She uses whale to pull in her waist and lifts up whale to keep the rain and sun off her lovely face. She reads by whale and washes with whale and has whale to brush her hair and pin it in place. Her husband takes some whale to polish his shoes, to keep his buggy wheels clean and squeak-free. The factories that chug black smoke up and down the East Coast must have whale to grease their millions of working parts and whale to light their workrooms, and even a garden benefits from a bit of whale sprayed daily. You could glue things together with whale, strip off rust with whale, whip your horse with whale, and at night stroll the streets warm in the glow of whale.

What would all those people in this country do without their whales? What would they think if they knew, as the islanders did, that there were fewer whales in the world now, thanks to the wanting of corset boning, of umbrellas, of grease and soap and lamp oil and buggy whips? Fewer whales and more wanting and a weak witch who couldn't keep the whalers safe like she used to, like she should. To catch the whales, the sailors needed more than just skill and luck. They needed magic. They needed me.

"Avery!"

I jumped at the sound of footsteps running toward me, and the relief I felt upon recognizing Tane vanished in a rush of annoyance as I realized just how late he was.

"I'm sorry," he said as I opened my mouth. "I didn't know it would take so long for me to get this." He reached around for a bag on his shoulder and pulled out a large green-glass bottle.

"Not yet," I said, the words snapping out of me. "Come on, then, I haven't all day!"

I pushed open a red door next to the plate-glass window— not the door to the general store but instead one that led to a narrow staircase and the second floor.

"Would you tell me what we're doing here?" Tane asked, following me up the stairs.

"Maybe if you'd gotten here early enough," I hissed, "you could have heard some explanations."

"I said I was—"

"Shh!" We reached the second-floor landing, bare except for a green door with the words M. DUBIARD, MUSIC AND LANGUAGE INSTRUCTOR written in curly gold script. I leaned against the door, listening, and when I heard nothing, opened it.

In a warm patch of sunshine, a large, red-faced man with exceptionally tiny feet sat snoozing, the ends of his very long, very blond mustache trembling with each breath. I crossed the room and, frowning, rapped lightly on his arm.

"Monsieur?" I said, raising my voice a bit. "Monsieur!"

He startled and blinked once, twice, before focusing on me.

"*Excusez-moi!*" he said, jumping to his feet. "*Allons, allons, commençons.*" He rushed to a sleek black piano in the corner of the room and lifted the key lid, but I pulled his arm.

"No, no, Monsieur! We spoke yesterday, do you remember?"

"Ah!" he said. "Mademoiselle Roe! *Oui, oui.* Ah...*Avez-vous pensé au vin?*"

I glanced back at Tane, who, after a moment, pulled the bottle from his bag. Monsieur Dubiard's eyes lit up, and he rose from the piano bench with arms outstretched.

"We'll have the room for the hour, then?" I asked, and he nodded.

"*Je vous laisse maintenant. Au revoir!*" Taking the bottle, he waved and disappeared through a back door.

"What was all that?" Tane asked as I found a place to sit on the floor.

"An arrangement," I said. "You said we needed to find a place to do this. Monday through Friday I have to take piano and French lessons with Monsieur, and yesterday I made him a deal: He'll let us use his room during the times when I'd normally have my lessons so long as we bring him a bottle a week of red wine."

"Won't your mother get suspicious when your piano and

French don't improve?" Tane asked as he sat on the floor across from me.

"Considering as she hasn't got a piano and can't speak a word of French, I believe she never will suspect a thing." I glanced over at the hated piano, smiling slightly. "My great-grandmother Almira had the gift for languages. Our cook told me that back in her day, she would come to the docks and translate for all the sailors and shipmasters."

"For a price, I imagine," Tane said, lifting an eyebrow.

"Of course!" I said, and when he laughed, I found, to my surprise, that I quite liked the sound. Out of the sun, indoors, I could see him a bit better, see how his eyes weren't the dark black-brown that I thought but a deeper amber color that blended bluish just around his pupils, making him look more thoughtful, smarter than I'd given him credit for.

Still smiling, he turned and reached into his bag, and I leaned forward to watch him.

"What did you bring for my mother's spell?"

He pulled out a small, squarish book. "That will take some time yet. I thought we could start with my dreams."

"Did you now?" I asked, and the warmth I'd felt seconds before vanished.

"I can't do much of anything today," he said, lifting his shoulders into a shrug. "You'll need to bring me something belonging to your mother."

"Why didn't you tell me that yesterday?"

"I didn't know for certain. We can take care of it tomorrow."

"But you agreed we'd begin today!" I tried, but didn't quite succeed, to keep the hysteria from creeping into my voice. I planted my fists against the floor and moved to stand when Tane reached out a hand to stop me.

"Avery," he said, and my name came out like a growl, but soft. "You'll have to have patience with me. I will help you as well as I can, but you must know better than anyone what can happen with rushed spells performed badly. I need to get to know you. I need to get a feel for your family's magic. Tell my dreams today, and when we meet tomorrow, I'll be prepared."

He spoke so gently, his voice the quiet of a man talking down a skittish horse, and although I'd been ready to fight, to argue with him, I realized he was right. The extra time *would* help him get a better sense for Roe magic. I didn't know what impressed me more—that he understood that, or that he could talk me out of a temper. As far as I could remember, only one other person could cool me down when I was spoiling to fight, but I always suspected my grandmother used her gift of emotion-work.

"All right, then, get on with it," I said, and although I sounded as sullen as a child (or perhaps *because* I sounded as sullen as a child), Tane laughed again, sending another strange ripple through my stomach.

"Here." He opened up the leather journal on his lap and smoothed down the pages, dog-eared and swollen from moisture. "We'll start from the beginning, then? This one I wrote down the day after I visited the shaman." He cleared his throat. "I am running along a straight, bare path."

As he spoke, I closed my eyes, letting his words sink into me, feeling the weave and warp of the dream's meaning.

"The road slants into the sky, straight up, and I run along the road and into the clouds."

But I opened my eyes and shook my head. "No," I said.

"It's true!"

I shook my head again. "That's not the problem."

His face fell, eyes narrowed. "Is it not working?"

Again, I shook my head, impatient now. "We don't need to hear this one. It isn't important. Go on to the next one."

"But Avery, how do you know? Any little detail could mean something."

I blew air out of my nose, my lips pressed together tight. "*This* dream doesn't matter. We don't have time to waste on meaningless dreams. Go on."

He sat up, staring at me, and closed the journal. "Tell me," he said, and I glared back a moment before sighing sharply.

"It means that you will find a ship to take you to the United States and the name of the ship is the *Modena.*"

Tane's eyebrows lifted. "Oh."

"Can we move on, then?" I asked, drumming my fingers against the floor. Tane opened his journal again, flipping to the next page, and looked up at me.

"At least we know these dreams will tell the future," he said.

"Of course they do."

Tane paused, the journal loose in his hands. "But what if I went to the shaman the day after this dream and he told me I'd find the *Modena*, but then I decided to take another ship? Then the dream wouldn't have come true."

I crossed my arms tightly over my chest. "It doesn't work like that," I said. "You would have gone on the *Modena*."

"But what if I decided to change my future?" he asked, his eyes bright. "If you tell me what my future is supposed to hold, I'm given a choice, aren't I? I could change it."

"They all think that, but no one has ever managed it. No future I've told has failed to come true."

"But—"

"You don't understand. These dreams do not mean the future *unless you do this one thing differently*. Not what might happen. It's fate. It will happen."

"I still think—" Tane cut himself off, thought for a moment. "Let's say you told a man—"

"Two years ago I told a whale man he would die by a harpoon to his throat," I said, breathing hard. "He wouldn't go anywhere near the docks after that, gave up whaling for good. He picked up and moved to a little clay desert town named Santa Fe, a place where they've never even heard of whales. One day, his sweetheart comes to visit for his birthday with a big present, and she sneaks up behind him where he's napping on his back porch and shouts "happy birthday" at him, and he gets so scared he falls right out of his chair, topples onto her, and, to her surprise, starts choking and bleeding and is dead ten seconds later. And what do you think they found in his neck?"

Silence, and then Tane cleared his throat. "I suppose I can guess."

"The girl found out he whaled once and had the blacksmith make it up special, just for him."

Tane shook his head. "But if you hadn't told him, he never would have moved, he wouldn't have—"

"You don't understand," I said, pressing my lips together. "It would have happened, if not there, then on a ship or in a bar or at the bottom of the ocean—it would have happened. I didn't tell that man that he would meet his end in some dusty little town after his silly sweetheart got a romantic notion about seafaring and chose the wrong moment to wake a napping man. I didn't see any of that in his dream, no details, no time or place. I told him that someday a harpoon would pierce his throat and he would die. He tried to change his future, don't you see? And he couldn't escape it, no matter how far he ran! They all try, all of them with their bad futures and all of them, all of them fail!" Flames crept into my cheeks, and I closed my hands into such tight fists that my nails pressed deep into my palms. I suddenly felt stupid, so stupid, as tears formed in my eyes and clouded my vision.

"Avery?"

Tane had one hand stretched out to me, and I looked away, rubbing my eyes.

"I don't think that's true," he said softly. "We must be able to change our fates, somehow. Don't you think so?"

"No," I said. "Yes. I don't know. Does it matter what I think?"

He didn't say anything, and when I looked back at him, he was staring at the dusty floor.

"Is there something..." He paused. "Did you have a—"

"Let's keep going," I said quickly. "We don't have time to waste."

For a moment, he said nothing, and then he lifted the journal back onto his lap.

"All right," he said, and he paused again before speaking quietly, his gaze on the journal. "I would still like you to tell me every dream. Even the ones that have already come true." He raised his eyes to my face. "Please."

"Fine," I said, and I bit my lip. It came out harsher than I intended, and even though I hate apologizing, I swallowed and added, "I'm sorry. Just...keep reading."

It took a moment to shake off the hot flutter of nerves, but the more Tane spoke, the more I relaxed against the quiet calm of his voice. And the dreams, of course. It felt good to put my magic to use in the only way I knew how, even as none of his dreams revealed anything.

Most dreams mean nothing; they're simply dreams, and it just happens that the ones people are willing to pay a dollar to learn more about are the ones with deeper meanings. Tane had hundreds of dreams collected over the months, each one written in detail, but few meant anything and those that did were simple, insignificant—"You'll trade with another whaler for a sow and two piglets"; "At some point in the next week, you'll hit a bad storm"; "There is a man on your ship who will steal your pocketknife." Still, Tane wrote down their meanings just the same, pausing occasionally to ask me questions.

"Why are some more specific than others?" he asked, and I shrugged, picking at a loose splinter in the floor with my fingernail. "But sometimes you know the exact moment when something will happen. Why not all the time? How does your dream-telling work?"

I rolled my shoulders forward, eyes on the floor, and said, "I do not know. I see what I see."

"But you must—"

"Must what?" I asked, lifting my face to frown at him. "Do you think when I was born I received a manual of instruction on dream-telling? Do you think there are rules? If there are, I haven't learned them yet. I see what I see. If you don't like how I do it, find another witch."

I wondered what he would say, but he was silent and, after a moment, returned to his notebook as though nothing had happened.

At ten minutes to three I jumped to my feet, telling Tane I had an errand to run before I had to get home.

"Already?" he asked, gripping the edges of his journal. "But we haven't found anything yet." He closed the journal and threw it back into his bag.

"We'll get back to it in two days," I said, waving a hand,

and when Tane looked as if he might protest, I asked quickly, "What do you need of my mother's? For tomorrow."

He said nothing for a moment, blinking down at his hands. "Something she values. Something she uses a lot and loves."

I frowned. I couldn't think of anything that my mother loved, but I didn't have the time to debate, so I simply nodded. "Until tomorrow, then."

He let out a sigh. "Yes. Tomorrow."

My footsteps echoed slightly as I left the room, and I glanced back at Tane, his face dark with disappointment. Poor boy. For all his experience with spells, he still didn't understand what I have always known so well: Magic seldom works the way you want.

Bells rang as I reached the docks, an eight-note chime, repeated over and over, that announced a home ship leaving port. The wharves crowded with women, children, old men, families of the whale men on board and leaving. In other ports, this might have been a sad occasion—the men wouldn't return for years, if they returned at all—but on Prince Island, these boys carried a king's ransom in charms and spells, good-luck magic to keep them safe and alive. The *Eagle Wing*, the Prince Island ship leaving today, near floated on spells, my grandmother's magic woven through every inch of that ship like invisible rigging.

But I wasn't there to see off the *Eagle Wing*. I was there for—

"Tommy!"

I squeezed through the crowd, edging past tight knots of people until I reached the very end of the wharf and the stairs down to Main Dock. Tommy stood at the bottom of the stairs, looking out onto the ocean, his body swaying slightly.

"Tommy," I said again, running down, and he startled and turned, his surprise fading away into a look of pain.

"What . . . what is it?" I asked, slowing to a stop.

"They sacked me, Avery," he said, his voice creaky. "The counting house."

"What? Why?"

"Mitchell Grays. He went right to the master and told him I was raving, lost my wits and unfit to handle the *Keene*'s accounts. As soon as I got back to the counting house, they dismissed me." He let out a shaky sigh. "Five years of apprenticeship." His boot picked at a loose nail in the dock. "All over."

I bit my lip. "What will you do now?"

He laughed, a hollow sound closer to a cry, and raised his face. But I knew the answer already. What else could a boy on this island do?

"When?" I asked, my voice soft, and Tommy glanced over at the *Eagle Wing*, her sails already snapping in the wind.

"Captain found me a spot this morning," he said, his voice flat. "Two-year contract. I get a 120th lay."

"Oh!" I said, and a smile limped to my face. "That's... that's fine, Tommy." In fact, it was. It meant that at the end of the voyage, Tommy would receive 1/120th of the ship's total take, and on a successful trip, that could mean as much as two hundred dollars. Most green hands started off with a smaller take, as small as 1/200th or even 1/300th. I suspected Tommy's years of generosity in the counting house had paid off.

Tommy just nodded, staring between the whalers at the blue line of the horizon. He shook his head, his fists tight at his side. "I didn't want that life, Avery. I wanted roots. I wanted to stay here. Have my own little house. Marry a respectable girl." He glanced at me, his cheeks coloring, and he shrugged again.

The dock bell rang, cheerful, calling the men of the *Eagle Wing* to board, and slowly they began to drift down the steps, waving good-bye to friends and family. Tommy watched them for a moment before letting out a sigh, and the twisting in my chest grew tight and painful.

"It... it's my fault you're going," I said, and Tommy turned to look at me. "I'm so—"

"I don't blame you, Avery," he said, his voice suddenly steady and sure. "I knew some bad thing might happen to me, but when you asked me to deliver your message, you looked so... scared." He frowned, the lines etching deep into his face. "It een't right for your mother to keep you trapped here. You don't belong here in New Bishop and anyone who thinks otherwise is a fool." The toe of his boot chipped away a softened splinter of wood. "I wanted to help you. I still do. If I could, I'd do it again."

He looked away, embarrassed, and I wished I knew what to say in return. I wanted to tell him that I'd never met a finer boy in my whole life. I wanted to tell him that he was the greatest friend I could ask for and that I would always remember what he did for me and that I'd miss him more than I could imagine. I wanted to tell him I was sorry, so sorry for what my mother had done to him, what I had done to him, and I would give up anything if he could just stay. But you can't say these things to a dock boy on Prince Island, not even a brave and brilliant one. So instead I just nudged him gently with an elbow.

"You should get going, then. You don't want the boat to leave without you," I said, smiling. "You're such a terrible swimmer, you'd never catch up."

I watched for his grin, but he only nodded, his expression dark and blank. And that was what finally did it for me: That sweet Tommy Thompson couldn't laugh at a well-meaning bad joke meant he'd lost hope, he'd changed. He was leaving the place he loved for the first time in his life and he was scared and angry but mostly just resigned to it. What do you give to a boy who feels he's lost everything and has nothing to be happy for, nothing to hold on to? I gave Tommy Thompson a kiss.

"For luck," I said, smiling. And Tommy stared at me and touched his fingertips to his salty-sweet lips, feeling for my ghost.

"I thought you couldn't make spells," he said.

"I can't," I said. "That was just me." He blinked, blinked, blinked back until finally the clouds broke and the sun shone and he smiled, just a little. And my grandmother's words about small magic, the kind inside everyone, came back to me: "Just because it's common doesn't make it less powerful."

Nine

Hot, hot, the witch's pot,
Full of bones an' stones an' rot!
Hot, hot, the witch's pot,
Run away or you'll get caught!

THE WORDS RANG OUT AT ME AS I OPENED
the gate to my mother's home. My stepsiblings, Hazel and her
bratty big brother, Walt, and a knot of bumping, jumping children swarmed the grass in front of the house, shrieking at each
other. In the middle of the lawn, a girl with long blond pigtails
ran, hands outstretched, chasing the children. Whenever she'd
touch one, the child would fall to the ground, lying still as a
stick, arms crossed over his chest—dead, until another child
jumped over him, and then he'd leap up and rejoin the game.

I recognized it. "Witch's Pot," the children call it, and it only ends once the witch has touched all the children and reduced them to giggling, wiggling corpses stretched on the grass. It comes from the stupid and terribly misguided notion that witches eat children, and while I've wished to skewer half the children on the island from time to time, I've never desired to eat them.

I watched them play for a moment, hesitating at the gate, because after the disappointment with Tane and having to say good-bye to Tommy, I didn't want to deal with these children. It used to be that children caught playing this game risked a telling-off from any adult on the island. Disrespectful, they'd say, a disgrace to the good, strong magic that keeps our fathers and brothers safe. So Witch's Pot had a bit of forbidden thrill to it, and children, if they played it, kept out of town and out of sight. Not on the front lawn of one of the grandest houses on the island.

"Witch! Witch!" Walt the terrible whirled around, pointing at me, his squashed-in face ugly with cruelty. "Run away!"

The others let loose a stream of squeals and laughs, the pig-tailed girl completely forgotten now that there was an actual, real-life almost-witch in their midst.

I ignored them and headed up the front path to the porch, the children swirling around me like gnats. A freckle-faced, dark-haired boy stumbled in front of me, bumping his shoulder against my arm, and he leaped into the air, his face a comic mask of exaggerated agony, before dropping to the grass like an anchor into sand.

"She cursed me!" he cried, his voice a high-pitched squeak.

"Send for the doctor! Send for the gravedigger! I'm dead an' cursed!"

Waves of giggles washed around me, and I scowled at the boy, now rolling around on the grass.

"Have a little more res—"

"Don't let her speak!" Walt shouted, and he picked up a stick and tossed it in my direction. "She'll put a curse on us!"

One of the girls shrieked, and a boy—bigger than most— ran at me, head bent low. I sidestepped him, but not quickly enough, and he clipped my shoulder so hard that I fell to the sharp flagstone path. The heels of my hands burned and my bones jarred inside of me, and when I lifted my head to stand, a small stone whistled past my face, thrown by a tiny little girl with a pushed-up nose.

I stumbled to my feet and ran to the house, moving so fast that I nearly tripped over my skirts on the stairs and tumbled again. I slammed the door behind me with a boom and leaned against it, panting, my heartbeat a whirling thrum.

Outside the house, the children had picked up their game again, calling and screeching at each other with high, grating voices, and I pressed my fingers into my ears.

"Stupid children," I whispered, my eyes shut tight. "No respect. They have *no* respect."

They'd never have done that to my mother, to my grand-mother. Even the children of the wealthy families knew that the Roes played a part in providing their fine clothes and hot food. But I wasn't the witch and my grandmother faded bit by bit every day, and underneath the children's cruel game, I could feel something deeper, more malicious.

"We walk on a razor's edge, Avery," my grandmother had often said.

They needed to remember how much they owed the Roes, how important we were to them. I couldn't let them forget, and they would see as soon as I got back to my grandmother, as soon as I became the witch. As soon as I helped Tane break my mother's spell.

What did he say he needed? Something my mother used and loved. I knew how those spells worked. Personal spells, my grandmother called them, magic intended for one person. Love spells were often personal spells, and so were curses, and I knew they worked best when they had a little bit of that person in them, their hair or a photograph or a favorite glove.

But my mother wasn't a sentimental person. She adored her dresses, her hats, her cunning little boots, but money had made her careless when it came to items, and it was not long before the tissue-wrapped dresses imported from France or the delicate, much-cooed-over baubles wound up boxed and forgotten in the attic.

I sneaked carefully through the house, pausing with each step to ensure my mother wasn't around, and stopped just outside her bedroom door. I had a notion to steal a few strands of her long black hair—since marrying, she seemed to care a great deal for her crowning glory, brushing it nightly and dressing it every morning to the pastor's demanding specifics (his morning assessment of her hairstyle certainly factored in my decision to breakfast in the downstairs kitchen).

I eased into her bedroom and headed for her trim little vanity, the silver-backed brush sitting neatly on a tray. I lifted it up and checked and yes! One fine strand of hair coiled through the bristles.

The weight of the brush felt good in my hand, heavy like a weapon, and I held it loosely, digging with my other hand into the thick bristles, when a noise from outside made me lift my head: the children, shouting and singing again. My heartbeat drummed a faster rhythm, and I felt my stomach twist at their laughter. I'd dealt with childish cruelty most of my life, as, other than Tommy, I'd never made friends with any of the island children; but it had been easier to let their taunts roll off my back when I'd lived in the cottage, knowing that in a few years, they'd be coming to *me* with their requests and wishes.

I frowned and caught my expression in my mother's vanity mirror, thinking about the children, about the stings of sadness running through me, when my grandmother's words suddenly came to me.

"It's supposed to hurt," she'd said, and so I'd pricked my fingers and broken bones, but I had to admit that was quite a narrow definition of pain. Gently, I set the brush down on the table and leaned forward, almost touching noses with the pale, gray-eyed girl in the mirror.

Pain. Becoming a witch has something to do with pain.

I thought for a moment while the girl in the mirror blinked at me.

"You're . . . ugly," I said, whispering the words. "You're . . . you're . . . *short*." I contorted my face into a stern, disapproving grimace that only made me and the mirror-girl laugh. "This won't do. What was it Anna Granger used to say to me when we were little?" The girl's nose scrunched up. "Freakish-odd. No, no. Freaky-odd. Freaky-odd little witch girl. You're smelly. You're poor. Oh, no. I suppose I'm not poor anymore, am I?"

Another frown from the mirror-girl. This was harder than I had expected. Because when sausage-curled Anna Granger called me *smelly*, she really meant I smelled like the sea, and when she called me *poor*, she meant the cottage on the rocks, and as for *freaky-odd witch girl*, that was a high compliment, in my opinion.

I took a breath, thinking.

"The dock boys think you're a joke. The children of this island treat you as a sideshow." Hot, uncomfortable tingles swept across my skin. "You'll never figure this out," I whispered. "You'll be stuck in New Bishop forever. Everyone will hate you."

The mirror-girl winced.

"You're too stupid to figure out your own magic. You're always going to fail."

The air in the room felt suddenly close and dry, and I heaved a breath and kept going.

"Your dream will come true," I said, and the mirror-girl's

face darkened, her features growing small and tense. "You won't be able to stop your own murder because you're too stupid to be a witch. You won't ever make it back to the cottage. Your mother will keep you here!" The words came out faster, louder, before I even knew what I was saying. "You'll fail, and everyone will blame you!" Was it working? Was it? "Everything the Roes built for generations will disappear and it will be all your fault! The Roes will be hated forever and all because you are too *stupid*, too *weak*, you can't do *anything* right, *you're a failure*, a *disgrace*, and *you will never*—"

"Avery?"

I swirled around, bumping the vanity so that the tray of silver-backed implements rattled. My mother stood in the doorway, one hand gripping the frame.

"Avery, what were you shouting?"

Shouting?

"I—nothing."

"I heard you shouting," she said, eyes narrowed. "What were you doing?"

She sounded beyond curious. She sounded horrified and confused.

"Nothing," I repeated, and I turned and grabbed her hairbrush. "I had a knot and—I came in to borrow—mine keeps shedding bristles." Head down, I moved quickly, trying to pass my mother before she asked any more questions, but as I neared her, she reached out and drew the brush from my hand.

"Let me," she said softly, still studying me, and she walked back up to her vanity and stood, waiting. Every muscle in my body tensed, my mind screaming to escape, but I still needed something of hers for Tane. I couldn't leave. My nerves lit up with fear as I walked to her, taking my place facing the mirror. I didn't like to have my back to my mother, to be vulnerable like that, but when I turned my head to keep watching her, I felt her fingers in my hair, pressing my gaze forward and down.

"Who were you shouting at?"

Her fingers flitted like birds around my head, pulling down the pins I had hastily inserted that morning, and my hair fell in dark waves down my back.

"No one. I wasn't shouting."

The stiff bristles dug into my scalp before my mother pulled the brush down and through my hair, sending a wave of tingles across my skin.

"If you're going to lie," my mother said lightly, "you should at least try to be a bit better at it."

Her hands felt cool and soft as they grazed against my flushed neck, expertly weaving my hair into elaborate loops.

"Is this the fishing hook all over again?" she asked, and I bit the inside of my mouth so hard that I tasted blood. The *hook*, the tiny hook she'd found two years ago sewn into my sock, so that every step brought me a little shiver of pain. Another experiment in unlocking my magic. Another failure.

"No."

"Because I thought we agreed how silly and dangerous that

was. Didn't we agree that someone who wanted to hurt herself like that was sick?"

The muscles in my jaw flexed and clenched.

"Avery?"

"Yes." I breathed carefully through my nose. "Someone who wants to hurt herself is sick."

"Besides which," she said, and paused, reaching for a handful of pins, "I don't know what anyone could possibly achieve from it."

I couldn't help it: My head jerked up and I stared at my mother's reflection. She watched me carefully, and I could see in her face she knew what I was trying to do. So did she warn me off because my attempts were wrong? Or because they were correct?

Gently but firmly, my mother turned my head back down.

"I've wanted to fix your hair like this for so long," she said, and I tensed. "You can wear it like this the next time there's a party, and you'll look so lovely. You'll see. You'll charm every fellow there."

"I don't care about that."

She laughed. "What girl doesn't want to be the belle of a party?"

"Me," I said, and this time she didn't laugh but paused, reached for a hairpin, swept a strand of hair back from my forehead.

"It's more than just attention. You know that, don't you? An attractive girl can make herself a good match with a good boy, someone to take her sailing and to museums and the theater and to show her all the marvelous things in the world."

I breathed hard through my nose. "I don't care about *that*, either."

"You should," she said. "You can't have any kind of life on your own, Avery, not as a woman, not in this world."

"Granma manages just fine."

"No, she survives. And she goes barefoot in the winter and skins seagulls for supper and has never read a proper book or seen a painting or heard a waltz in her entire life. What kind of a life is that, without wonder or discovery, filled with drudgery and danger?" She paused, her fingertips raising goose bumps on my neck. "You can have so much more, Avery, but to truly succeed, a woman needs money. Money and status and security. If you're lucky, the right man can provide all three. With the right man, with enough money, you could sail to Egypt and see the pyramids. You could attend the opera in Paris or the ballet in Russia or the theater in London. You could climb a mountain. You could see an elephant. You can have a beautiful life, Avery, the best kind of life a Roe can expect. There's power in these things," she said, and her voice dropped to a whisper as she slid another pin into my hair. "Don't deny it. All these dresses and dances, these graces I try to teach you—they are powerful."

"No!" The word slipped out of me like a gasp, and I jerked my head forward, away from her. Something like a shudder rolled through me as I turned and faced her, her outstretched hand still between us, my heart beating very fast. "I don't want that! Anything they can get me—I don't want it!"

Her hand lowered and I leaned in and said through my teeth, "That isn't me, that isn't my life, and *why can't you ever understand that?*"

"No," she said, and the smile on her face faded. "You don't want it. You'd rather stare into the mirror, hurling insults until you hate yourself." She shook her head, studying me. "What would you give up? What would you give up to be a real witch?"

To be a real witch...and return to my grandmother and she would teach me how to take over for her and the ships would return and everyone would love me. And I wouldn't be murdered; I would stop it, somehow, because you can't kill a Roe witch. And no one on the docks would fear being friendly to me, and my mother could never control me, ever, and what would I give up? What would I give up for all this?

"Anything," I breathed. "Everything."

My mother's mouth twitched, twisting down along the line of her scar so that it looked like her face had split in two. She leaned in closer, close enough that I could hear her quick, shallow breaths, and my heartbeat sped up.

Is she going to tell me?

Will she actually tell me what it takes to become a witch?

"That's too much, Avery," she whispered.

She held my gaze for a moment; then my mother looked past me to the mirror and clasped her hands to her chest.

"Look at you," she said softly, her blue eyes lighting up,

and I turned back to my reflection. She'd dressed my hair like a fine young lady's, perfect and delicate and charming. For the first time in my life, I looked as though I actually belonged in this world she had created.

"What a lovely face," she said, and she had to mean my face because her own had not been lovely for a long, long time. "What a smart, lovely, beautiful girl. You know that, don't you? You are talented and intelligent and capable of so much in this world. And you deserve the best, nothing but the best." Her lips curved into a smile, her fingers pressed gently against my shoulder, and before I could say anything else she turned and left, her lavender-scented perfume lingering in the air, on my skin.

I watched her go, my eyes narrowed on the empty doorframe, my hands shaking. It took me a moment to remember why I had even come to my mother's room in the first place, and I turned quickly, reaching for the hairbrush.

"No," I whispered, because its bristles were thick with my own black hair, impossible to separate from my mother's. Useless.

I threw the brush down on the ground, the heavy thud a small measure of satisfaction, and pressed my fingertips against the vanity, leaning forward to study myself in the mirror.

What had she done to me?

Because even though I had never seen my mother's face whole and well, and even though her eyes are a vivid blue while mine are a clear, cloudless gray, standing here in her room with my hair dressed by her hands, I finally realized what she had done. She hadn't turned me into a lady. She'd turned me into the girl she once was.

It hurt, pulling out the combs and braids and yanking my hair free, but I didn't stop until pins littered her floor and I scratched out and killed that pretty girl in the mirror.

The next day, I paced across Monsieur Dubiard's apartment, studying Tane.

"Well?" I asked, and he glanced up at me.

"This is the best thing you could find?" He held up a green scarf, delicate and embroidered and the closest thing I could find to something my mother might actually care for.

"What's the matter with it?" I crossed my arms over my chest. I hadn't slept again last night, the fifth night in a row that my nightmare jarred me from sleep (five nights already—how much more of this was I supposed to endure?), and I could feel the sleeplessness stretching my nerves ever tighter, reminding me of my ticking future. "It's my mother's."

"It doesn't feel like it belongs to anyone." Tane spread the cloth out on the floor, and the fabric glowed in the sunlight. "I don't know if my spell will work."

"You're still going to try, though."

He sighed, a long, slow sigh. "Yes, I'll try. But sit down. You make me nervous stalking around the room."

He gathered up the scarf in his fist as I sat before him,

tucking my skirts under my ankles. His bag was open at his side, and he reached in and pulled out some fine string—the same kind of string from the luck charm he'd given me. His lips moved, and although I couldn't hear what he said, I felt a stir in the air around him, the quiet, tense anticipation that came with making spells.

And I was back in my grandmother's cottage, sitting in my trundle bed and watching her work. My hands would mimic her movements, cupping a shell, dusting it with sand, swirling the sand with my pinkie finger, slowly, slowly. I used to help her, after she showed me how to tie the winds—not with making charms but with preparing her materials, scraping shells clean or plucking birds for their feathers—and although I didn't know how to use my magic, just being around her while she worked would stir the force inside of me, awakening, itching. It felt good and right, and I would smile, thinking of the day I would become a proper witch.

But now, as I watched Tane work, the beast that lived inside my chest roared with desire. I wanted to snatch the charm from Tane's hands and work it myself, even though I didn't know how. I simply could not tether the power inside of me, although I could feel it pulse through my veins. I felt like a starving, mouthless person sitting in front of a banquet; I felt as though my hands were bound together and my skin was mad with itches that I couldn't scratch. I just wanted *it*—magic! Gasped for it, burned for it, and finally I couldn't sit anymore; I had to jump to my feet and keep pacing, never mind what Tane said.

I ran to the window and shoved it open, breathing in deep the New Bishop smell of smoke and salt.

"Are you all right?" Tane asked, and I nodded my head quickly. I waited, hanging out of the window, breathing hard and trying to ignore the swell of magic behind me. Soon, soon, I reminded myself. Soon enough I would be at my grandmother's house and soon I would know how to master my magic. And then, once I was the witch, the dreams would stop; my future would be secure and so, too, the future of the entire island. Soon. I heaved a breath. Soon.

"Done yet?" I asked, my voice tight and tense.

"I'm not sure. Maybe."

I turned around. The scarf had been balled up tight, the string wrapped around it and secured with a series of tiny, delicate sailor's knots. I could already feel the magic, Tane's magic, nestled within the scarf. As with the luck charm, the magic sucked and pulled at me, strange and cloying. Here, though, there was no clear pattern to the charm, nothing recognizable.

"Your people did this?" I asked, lifting an eyebrow.

"Just try it."

He held it out to me and I hesitated. *Be careful of strange magic*, and this clumsy spell certainly was strange, reaching out sloppy tendrils that wrapped around my wrist. It felt oily, slow-moving, like some half-dead, reaching thing, but still I took the scarf from Tane's hands and held it between my own.

"Well?" Tane asked. I glanced at him and squeezed the scarf tightly, wincing as the spell sank into my skin.

"I need to imagine leaving for my grandmother's house," I said. Carefully, I walked forward, but nothing happened—no exhaustion, no blackout.

"Did it work?" Tane's voice rose with excitement.

"Hold on." I closed my eyes, ignored the jumbled magic in my hand, ignored Tane's quick breathing behind me. The cottage. My grandmother. I pictured myself leaving this room, leaving New Bishop, running down the coastline and into my grandmother's arms. I pictured telling her about my dream, my murder, and hearing her say it would be all right, she would teach me to become the witch and that would secure my future.

Hope swooped through me, huge and sudden, and I ran forward, squeezing the scarf tightly in my hand. For just a moment, I could feel it, Tane's spell closing around me, cocooning me, and I nearly made it to the door, my fingers reaching for the brass doorknob, when my mother's curse cut through and darkness slammed down on me.

I woke with Tane leaning over me, his dark skin bloodless and shiny with sweat.

"Avery!" he said, breathing my name. I sat up and felt my head explode with pain, throbbing waves radiating from the back of my skull.

"You collapsed," Tane said, speaking quickly. "And you hit your head."

He stared at me, so concerned that I shrank back a little, surprised and embarrassed by the attention.

"Are you all right?" he asked, and he reached a hand out to touch my temple, but I pulled away.

"Yes," I said, my voice tight. "Yes, I'm fine."

Relief washed over his face, so fast and sudden that I stared at him, confused. I couldn't remember anyone—not my mother, not even my grandmother—taking such care over my bumps and bruises.

"Good," he said, and I gaped at him and his relief. Warmth rose through my cheeks, but then I realized that he shouldn't look so happy, because his charm had utterly failed; his charm failed and my mother's curse wasn't broken and I was still stuck here in New Bishop, alone and vulnerable with my own murder before me and he was *smiling*—actually smiling!

"You failed," I said, throwing the bundled scarf across the floor. Ignoring the pounding in my head, I pushed myself to my feet and crossed to the wall, where a row of mirror-bright daguerreotypes hung. My reflection stared back at me, and I lifted my hair gently to get a better look at the side of my head. Already, a blue-purple bruise had risen on my skin, not quite hidden by my hair. I bit back a swear. What would my mother think if she saw it? That I'd tried to knock myself out?

"That charm wasn't powerful enough," Tane said, and I glanced back at him.

"Obviously."

He stood and watched me. "It was the scarf. I couldn't do anything with something like that."

"My grandmother could have done it," I snapped. "You're not trying hard enough."

He was quiet for a long moment and then said, carefully, "I did the best that I could."

"No, you failed on purpose." The words seemed to march out from my lips before I even knew what I was saying. "You're fooling with me until I interpret all your dreams."

A muscle in Tane's jaw tightened. "That's not true."

"I bet you don't even know how to make this spell," I said, breathing hard. "You think that as soon as my mother's spell is broken, I'll leave New Bishop and then you'll never get your dreams told and so you're delaying things on purpose!"

I narrowed my eyes at him, waiting for his reaction. He made me hope, and I hated him for that. He made me believe that four years of powerful magic could be undone by a tattooed boy, believe that my future could be changed and my own death avoided, believe that I would succeed my grandmother before she died. I felt furious, at him, at myself, and I wanted to fight, to *scream*, to hear him explode back at me.

"Would you really leave me as soon as I broke the spell?" he asked, calm and quiet.

"Yes," I said. He opened his mouth quickly and I tensed, waiting for him to shout, but instead he smiled, a crooked half-smile that sent another wrenching twist through my stomach.

"I don't think so," he said softly. "You look like a girl who keeps her promises." He crossed the room and bent down to pick up the bundled scarf before returning it to my hands. Already, I could feel the fragile, untidy threads of magic slipping away, smashed completely by my mother's curse. I dug my fingernails into the folds of the scarf, as though I meant to rip apart what little shreds of magic remained.

"Are you sure you can do it?" I asked, looking down at the scarf. "This was a disaster. Can you really help me?"

"Yes. Do you believe me?"

I lifted my eyes to Tane's face, wanting to tell him no. But there was magic there, undeniably—better and stronger than what he'd tied to the scarf, magic that maybe was powerful enough to beat what my mother had created. I sighed.

"Yes. We'll try again tomorrow."

He nodded and hoisted his bag to his shoulder. "Tomorrow."

I waited until his footsteps had disappeared down the stairs before I followed after him. I had much to think about before our meeting tomorrow, beginning with what belonging of my mother's could possibly be better suited to spell work, but after a few minutes I found, to my utter confusion, that all thought of work or magic or curses always seemed to end in the exact same place: Tane's soft, sincere smile of relief.

Ten

AT NIGHT, I FELT THE DREAM TAKE ON A
life of its own, as though I was nothing but a spirit to fill the
whale's body, something to watch and feel as it died.

And trapped in the dream, I remembered something I'd
forgotten in my rush to become the Roe witch: I don't like killing whales.

Actually, I rather like whales, especially the sleek, strong,
gray-bodied whales that very occasionally swim past my grandmother's cottage and nowhere else along the island. Sailors
sometimes call whales big and dumb ("Cow fish!" they laugh.
"And just as easy to kill!"), but they're wrong. The whales I've
met, the whales I've seen, are smart, fast, fierce.

If I had any say, the men of Prince Island would make their
fortunes hunting something the world could use less of, like

seagulls that swoop down at you if you have a bit of food in your hand, or those horrible biting blackflies that rise from the surface of the Great Gray Slough like a menacing cloud.

When I think of whales, I'd rather not think of them hunted and scared, penned in by a dozen strong men carrying six-foot-long spears. I'd rather not think of them harpooned, steel points dug into their bodies, their lungs, the frantic death flurries that make them swim in a panic, towing behind them the whaleboat that cuts through the water so fast and so manic the whale men call it a "Prince Island sleigh ride."

When they are close enough to pitch their harpoons, the whale men aim for a spot just between the whale's great lungs: a vulnerable, fragile spot that the sailors have named, seemingly without irony, "the life." Aim for the life, they say. And bury the iron to the hitches.

I've never seen a whale die, outside of my dream, but I know well enough what it's like, the water spouting through its blowhole suddenly turning so red. "The red flag is flying!" the men shout, or "Chimney's afire!"

They drag the whale onto their ship, hoisted by its tail, and then they truly get to work, from top to bottom, peeling the skin off the whale like a child peels an orange on Christmas Day. There's a great furnace right on deck, the tryworks, in which the blubber is melted into rich oil, ready for barreling, and every whaler hopes to fill at least forty-five barrels, a good take, an honest take, enough to make killing the whale feel worth it.

It's a dirty and messy business, although most of the men

I know on the island understand how it needs to be done, and they see the whales as more than just floating barges to be transfigured into money and liquor and shoes for their children.

But still.

After nights of my dream, I could not deny that as much as I hoped to become the witch someday, I wished my magic didn't go toward killing things.

Back in Monsieur Dubiard's apartment the next day, I drummed my fingers on the floor, trying to pay attention while Tane spoke. It was his day to tell dreams, and although I enjoyed the work, I felt anxious and snappish. I missed Tommy and his smiles and his jokes. I missed the comfort of my grandmother's soft, smoky arms. Even dream-telling couldn't cool the nervous fever burning through me.

"Well?"

I snapped out of my thoughts to see Tane looking at me over the edge of his journal, his dark eyebrows arched in a question.

"Well what?" I asked, and his face settled back into a calm mask as he laid the journal in front of him.

"I was asking what my dream meant. I didn't realize you weren't listening." He said it too coolly, the thinnest note of accusation in his voice, and my brittle nerves crackled inside of me.

"It's too hot in here," I said, fanning myself with my hand. "I can't concentrate."

Without another word, Tane rose lightly to his feet, crossed the room, and wrenched open the window. When he returned to his seat on the floor, he watched me for a moment and then lifted the journal again.

"Ready?"

In response, I waved my hand like a flyswatter.

Tane's words rolled out of him in that steady, solid voice of his, the sound nice and strong, like the feeling of knocking your knuckles against the hull of a well-built ship. I rested against it and felt the dream grow clearer in my mind, but this one was short and not important—"You'll lose your lantern," was what I told him—and in the seconds of silence as Tane scratched a note in his journal, I felt as jangly and unsettled as when we'd begun.

"What's that?" I asked, leaning forward. Below the entry for his dream, I'd caught sight of something large and dark stretched across the page. Tane raised an eyebrow.

"It's my journal," he said, and I frowned and reached out for it.

"Silly. I know. I mean, what's on that page?"

For a moment, he lifted the journal up closer to his chest, almost as though protecting it, and I wondered if I had reached the end of his good nature and if he would tell me no, to keep my nose out of his doings. But then he shrugged, or seemed to shrug, anyway, holding out the journal in one long, rolling gesture of reluctant assent.

"I didn't know you could draw," I said, because that's what they were—drawings, beautiful little drawings, perfect and angular and vibrant.

"Why would you know?" he asked, but when I looked up at him, he stared out the window.

I flipped through the journal, quickly at first, just anxious to give my hands something to do and my eyes something to look at: the spirals of seashells, the curved wing of a gull, the scratch marks of a knife on scrimshaw. But after a few pages, my hands stilled. My heart stilled, and I simply looked.

I'd seen naturalists' books and the decorated scrimshaw that sailors brought back from their trips, but this was something else entirely, a different way of looking at the world. I flipped a page to a drawing of a man, and it was a man like I'd never seen before: the lines cleaner, more exaggerated, the shapes closer to a suggestion than reality. In the picture, the man bent over a plate of some food, his eyes half closed with exhaustion or hunger or relief. His hands, his impossibly long fingers, took up the center of the drawing, larger than they'd be in life, almost another animal altogether. He looked a little like a monster, all those sharp angles crowded together, bones stretched and elongated, but there was something alive to this drawing, something that made every other sketch or painting or etching I'd ever seen in my entire life feel flat and empty.

"You're...very good." I couldn't take my eyes off the pages.

I flipped back to see a picture of a man sitting watch, perched on the edge of a wooden locker. At his feet, practically leaning against him, another, younger sailor lay, facedown, with his ankles crossed and eyes squeezed tightly. The men—boys—looked so at ease, close and familiar with each other in the way puppies and kittens will roll into a ball for warmth and comfort.

Another page, a seagull, flying into sunset, cradled in clouds. Another page, a whale dripping blood and water and oil onto the deck as it's hung over the ship. I turned the pages and saw hands, whales, bits of the ship, bones and hooks and faces, squinting, staring, laughing. I'd thought I'd known what it looked and felt like to sail a whaler, but Tane's drawings turned those ideas upside down. It looked lonelier than I thought. It looked sweeter than I thought. It looked violent and beautiful and thrilling and sad. And he had captured it all, scratched into soft pages with a hand and eye I could not even imagine.

I wanted to hold this little book, this life and this world, in my lap, explore it all slowly, carefully, but I could feel Tane's impatience, the itch of something precious in someone else's possession. Gently, I closed the journal and handed it back to him.

"How did you do this? Who taught you?" I asked.

"I just did it," he said. "I taught myself."

I had so many questions for him—how did he make his drawings so naked, so raw? Did he draw them from life? From memory? Did he have more?—but he didn't look eager to talk, his eyes down and focused on the journal, the muscles of his hands tense around the cover.

"I've never seen anything like that," I said, and he drummed his fingers against the cover.

"Something to pass the time."

"Well." I bit my lip. "I like them. I like them a lot. They're... they're very well done. My mother always goes on about art and how only the purest, most refined minds are suited to be artists. I wouldn't have thought someone like you could draw like that."

He raised an eyebrow. "Someone like me?" he asked, the words careful, and I shook my head, frowning.

"No, no, that's not what I meant. I mean, someone who didn't go to school for this. Someone without the means."

He just stared at me, and I let out a tense breath, because the words were coming out wrong and I wasn't sure how to tell him what I really felt.

"I don't... My mother drags me to look at paintings all the time, and she always says that it's... it's about beauty or grace or... Those artists, the ones my mother makes me look at, their pictures... They paint flowers. Horses. Everyone looks pretty and happy and all the drawings look the same. Your drawings—they... they're so unsophisticated."

"Oh," he said, the word coming out forced, tight.

"No, that's not—I mean, your drawings are better than that. They show life like it is, not dressed up or overpolished." I sighed and rubbed a hand against my temple. "They're all the same, those paintings my mother shows me, and they're pretty, they're nice to look at, but they want something that doesn't exist. She keeps telling me that art should reflect life, and I always thought it to mean that she wanted her life to be as pretty as a painting, but I never thought of it...the other way around. I mean, that...that a drawing could capture what it is like to be...alive."

I let out another breath, quick and uncertain. Tane didn't move.

"I always thought I knew what it was like for...for you, for all the men who come to Prince Island, but I...You make it real. Does that make sense? I don't think I ever really thought about your lives, out there, but your drawings..." I closed my eyes and thought of another drawing, a boy with his head down, face cupped in one hand as though crying, his other arm stretched out to hold tightly to the rigging, so fragile, so strong all in one moment.

"Your drawings made me see them. You. Your drawings made me see." I shook my head again, still not certain I said it properly, but Tane was staring at me now with a hunger, an urgency that surprised me. I held out my hands, helpless. "Just...thank you. For showing me."

I felt the seconds tick in silence, Tane not moving, his grip still tight on the journal. I felt suddenly stupid for demanding to see his drawings, like I barged into his boardinghouse bedroom and saw him in his underclothes, and I wondered if I should apologize, if he would get angry with me, when he set the journal carefully on the floor and opened it to the last page we'd worked on.

And then: a smile like a flame licking across a blade of grass.

"You're welcome," he said, and he picked up his pencil and held it over the page before glancing up at me, his eyes glowing and eager. "Ready?"

Away from Monsieur Dubiard's apartment, I felt each passing second like a leaden weight in my stomach, and I itched to run back to Tane and our work. Despite the effort Tane put into breaking my mother's curse, it wasn't going well. A week after our first attempt, Tane's spells hadn't proven any more effective, although he was at least a bit better at catching me before I crashed to the floor. Every time I woke from the curse to see Tane frowning over me, his words apologetic, encouraging, a screw of frustration tightened within my chest. He meant well, I knew, and I liked him—as a person. But his magic was as effective as a handkerchief against a hurricane, and his excuses began to wear thin.

His dreams, if anything, went worse; we scoured the whole first month and discovered nothing more exciting about his future than that he would try out a new barber on the island.

"You're supposed to find those men," he'd said after our last meeting, determined and confused and hopeful and nervous, and to myself I replied, *I'm supposed to be the witch.*

I would have filled my spare time with more experiments, more meetings with Tane, but ever since our conversation at the mirror, my mother had taken renewed interest in my time, filling up my daily schedule with all manner of high-class events.

"Oh, what a sweet smell!" my mother said, pulling me through a garden so perfectly manicured it seemed the flowers had been beaten into submission. "Isn't that lovely, Avery?"

The next day at a parlor concert, overstuffed with ladies in tent-sized dresses that rustled almost as loudly as the pianist: "Listen to that music, Avery!"

Everywhere she took me it was "Taste this wine" or "Feel this velvet" or "Can you believe that?" as though this would be the time I'd look at her and smile and agree, as though I hadn't told her, over and over, endlessly, that I did not care about any of it, none of it, not a whit.

I'd seen her do this kind of selective hearing before, anytime the pastor spoke to her about anything other than the weather or what she was wearing. It was a remarkable trick; whatever she didn't want to hear seemed to slip right past her, leaving her serene smile intact.

"Look at this!" She'd taken me to a private exhibition of paintings and pulled me before a portrait of a girl in white.

Elizabeth Greengrass read the little placard by the painting, and I stared at it, amazed that this girl could actually exist in real life. She sat as carefully as a doll, hands in lap, feet tucked under skirts, buttoned up and still and fragile and soft.

And I wondered: What did she look like with her hair down? What did she look like when something made her laugh? What did she look like running down a hallway or eating something delicious or washing her hair?

There were a million different ways that Elizabeth Greengrass could have been painted and any of them would have been better than a portrait of her looking straight ahead with her hands in her lap and her mouth shut.

"She's beautiful, isn't she?" my mother asked, a hand on my arm.

"Yes," I said, because she was. But she was the only kind of beautiful my mother could appreciate: neatly tucked away in a frame and all surface.

Back in the house, at night, my whale-body slipped into cold water, the sailors' dark faces regarded me, they pushed their knives into my chest and left me gasping and choking on my own blood, and I would hold myself in that nightmare for just a few moments longer, scouring the dream for a deeper meaning. But when the images cleared through my mind, I was left with the same: I will be murdered, and underneath that message I began to feel an urgency, an alarm bell, no exact date or time but a warning that my future was not many years or even many weeks away but soon and creeping closer.

I began putting off sleep, instead throwing myself into my experiments with renewed fervor. Alone in my room, I reached into my wardrobe and pulled out my collection of trinkets and trash, experimenting with the secrets of my magic. I rubbed across my skin sickly-sweet ambergris, the waxy substance taken from whales and worth its weight in gold for its perfume. I anointed myself with whale oil and freed the long, flexible strands of baleen from my corset to wrap around my arms and ankles. I pricked and prodded and pried, and I remained the same: a normal girl with a tempest of magic inside of her.

In the half-world between sleep and wakefulness that I lived in every night, I thought about the Roes, their legacy, their lives unfolding around me like the bedtime stories my grandmother would tell me, every night, without fail.

"Tell me about Great-grandma," I would say to my grandmother, tucked into my little trundle with the covers pulled up to my chin.

"Almira? Or did you mean Frances?"

"Almira. The one who could speak all the languages."

And my grandmother would smile, because Almira was her mother and she loved her and missed her and she had been a good witch, smart and strong, the witch who decided that the Roes should know how to speak the common sailor languages, French and Portuguese and Spanish, and wrote a little book for us to learn. As part of my training and apprenticeship, my grandmother made me study that book, so that if a man came in asking, *"No quisiera ahogarme. ¿Tiene usted un amuleto para eso?"* we could say, *"Por supuesto, señor. Tome asiento por favor."*

But it was also a book full of other kinds of languages, the languages of birds and cats and grasshoppers. Anything that spoke, she could understand, and my grandmother would weave her histories with fairy stories and island folklore, and if I didn't know what was true and what was made up, I knew it was all wonderful.

"And everyone in town thought that little dog had gone mad, but she knew right away the poor fellow just had a hurt paw, and that was why he had growled when anyone tried to approach!" my grandmother would say, and I'd laugh.

There was Almira, with the languages and the book. There was Frances, who could pick up any plant or stone and know instantly what it could be used for, what was best for fevers and what could cure sadness. She made a book, too, a beautiful book filled with drawings so lifelike and perfect it looked as though someone had dropped a handful of wild-flowers across the pages. We used the book when people came to us with little ailments—less common now that the apothe-cary set up shop in New Bishop—but I often liked to look at the pictures, tinted and delicate, and Frances's spiderlike handwriting, instructing, "Boil in salt water for a quarter of an hour, wrap in a cloth, and wring out to dry." Each drawing had a initial, H.K., in the corner, and when I asked my grand-mother about it, she frowned and said she thought that was Frances's beau. I didn't even bother to ask about him, my great-great-grandfather, I suppose because I already knew he didn't matter. Roe women didn't marry, didn't pass on their men's names, and only bore girls. They were the ones I wanted to hear about, and my grandmother told me all she knew.

Frances's mother, Martha, could read minds and know what everyone was thinking, which was different from Lenora, the first Roe woman born on the island, who could change or erase memories but only with the memory-keeper's permission. She was popular among widows but not quite as popular as Abigail, her daughter, who could actually communicate with the dead. Abigail's daughter, Ida, also developed a following among the women of the island, but in her case it was because she could see anything that anyone in the world was doing right at that moment, so long as she held something that belonged to that person. To this day, naughty children or carousing sailors are admonished with "Careful now, the Roe witch is watching you!"

And then there was Madelyn, the first Roe, the one who came to the island already round with Lenora inside of her, who was among the very first people ever to set foot on the island and who could control animals. It is island lore that Madelyn began as a simple girl who knew no magic. Born in another country (some say Britain, some say France), she sneaked aboard a ship sailing for the New World already pregnant with her daughter. Somewhere in their journey, a huge storm broke the ship to pieces, throwing Madelyn into the sea, and she thought she would die until a whale rose up from the water and carried her miles and miles to the safety of Prince Island.

Those were the Roe women, strong and strange and powerful, who made the things that made our island safe and rich.

They grew up knowing their purpose in life and dedicated themselves to carrying on the Roe tradition. And they left things for the future: books or clothing or a shell particularly good for scrying or a new method for gathering fish or scars on the islanders' impressions of us. I couldn't let them down.

"Tell me more," I'd say to my grandmother. "Tell me all about them." And she would.

Eleven

"WHAT'S THIS ONE?" I'D STOPPED ON A PAGE of Tane's sketchbook showing a kind of bird, delicate, colorful, with a curved, intelligent beak.

Tane looked up from his notes. This was our agreement now: On days we worked on my mother's curse, Tane brought his sketchbooks for me to study. It kept me from hovering over him, distracting him with questions and worries, and the drawings calmed me in a way I'd never felt before. The drawings made me forget—at least for a few minutes—about my dream, about my mother and my grandmother and even my family's magic. He had a dozen sketchbooks, some beautiful and leather-bound, others not more than a handful of papers held between two pieces of flimsy cardboard.

But I loved them, their energy and expression. They almost

didn't make sense—I'd seen so many of these people, so many of these things, in my life before, but I didn't see them the way *he* saw them, and it made me feel strange and young, like Tane was retraining me in how to study the world. It made me feel differently toward Tane, too. He didn't make me laugh, like Tommy; he didn't make me feel like less of an outsider, like my grandmother; but just being around him, in this space, with his voice in my ears and his drawings in my lap and his magic curling around me...it quieted me. And I wasn't often quiet.

I showed Tane the picture of the bird—most of the drawings were confident, energetic, but this one had been scratched out, erased, and redrawn many times over—and a funny expression came over him, as though I'd just kicked him in the stomach.

"It's a kind of...parrot," he said, and I raised an eyebrow.

"Was it flying around a lot when you tried to draw it? It looks like you didn't quite get it right."

"No. I tried to draw it from memory after not seeing it for a long time. It's...it's dead now."

"You killed it?" That wasn't uncommon, sailors landing on remote islands and discovering exotic new creatures only to put those creatures on their dinner plates. Once I met a group of sailors who swore giant turtle was as sweet and tender as turkey, and besides which, the shells made handy bowls. But Tane shook his head.

He put out a hand and took back the journal. "I haven't thought about it in a long time," he said. "It was my sister's pet."

His face grew drawn, quiet, and my cheeks flushed. I'd forgotten. Of course, he'd had sisters.

"Tane," I said, and I reached out a hand but stopped just short of him.

He closed the book suddenly and looked up at me, smiling. "It's a terrible drawing. I should throw it away."

I must have made some face, because, laughing, he added, "It's all right, Avery. It doesn't matter."

But I knew already that his drawings did matter. They were bits and pieces of himself, his thoughts and dreams and jokes and fears. Why did I not realize he never drew his family, his home?

Handing me the journal, he turned back to his work as though I hadn't said anything at all, and I knew it would be easy to do the same, flipping through pages as though I'd never noticed the bird, but something trembling inside my chest made me set the journal on the floor.

"How much do you remember? About... about your home, I mean." I frowned, because I wanted him to know he didn't have to answer me. I didn't want to sound demanding.

He lifted an eyebrow. "As much as anyone remembers of the first nine years of their own life."

"But not enough?" When he didn't say anything, I tapped on the cover of the journal, my fingers jerky and nervous. "Maybe... Did you ever try... Perhaps you should try drawing something, something you remember. Something else. Or... or someone?" I didn't know why I said it except it had been a thought I'd had lately, a wish that I could draw as well as Tane because I would have liked to record my own memories: the cottage, the shape of the windows, my grandmother's hands.

"I couldn't," he said, and he said it almost like an apology. He gave me a grim smile. "I forget their faces. When I left it didn't even occur to me to try to fix them—anything—in my mind."

"Why not?"

As soon as I said it, I knew I had pushed too far. Tane snapped his gaze back down to his notes, riffling the papers between his fingers.

"It's getting late, and I know you'll want to try this before you have to leave." He rose to his feet, a tangle of string in his hands, and after a moment I followed him. He asked me to hold out my right hand, and when I did, he looped the string around my wrist, knotting it from time to time. His hands flew, sure and steady, but he seemed too careful to not touch me, his fingers just skating above my skin so that I could feel warmth, air, a stir around me, but not him.

He paused, eyebrows knit in concentration, hands cupped around my own as though around a flame. My mouth opened and I was about to ask him if he had finished and if I should try to leave for the cottage when I realized that he wasn't breathing.

My hand was still held out, upturned and facing him, and he studied it, a frown on his face, and then, softly, touched the tip of his fingers to the curve of my palm. I had to suck in a breath to feel the shock of heat, the electricity of his magic and—and *him*. Gently, he traced his fingers up my palm, over the string that webbed my wrist, tickling, teasing, trailing across the inside of my arm, raising hairs and goose bumps and moving so slowly that all I could do was stand there in shock, not sure of what he would do next.

A shiver began in my chest, a flutter like panic or like hunger, I couldn't decide which, and I wanted to pull away and I wanted to laugh, nervous, and I wanted to ask him what he was doing but instead I did nothing and just waited.

"Avery..." He whispered my name as quiet as a song, and something leaped up from inside of me, something that had to do with the drumbeat of my heart and the heat of his touch. For the first time since I left the cottage on the rocks, I felt the way I did when my grandmother would hold me in her lap and work her magic through me, as though my body was nothing but a conduit for something more powerful than I could understand, something I couldn't control or stop. But this wasn't magic, this was something else, and that nervous heat shuddered through me again, a rattle through my body that made me, of all things, *angry*.

My arm jerked away, leaving Tane's hands stretched out over nothing but air.

"Is the spell ready for me to try?" I asked, my voice higher and faster than usual. I didn't like this, this electricity and adrenaline that made me feel the way I did waking from my dream, my heart leaping from my chest and my head swimmy with fear.

"You should..." He trailed off, blinked, shook his head. "You should concentrate on—"

But I didn't even wait for him to finish before I began moving, and I didn't even get a dozen paces before the curse crashed over me like a black wave.

Seconds, minutes, maybe hours later, I blinked awake on the floor of Monsieur Dubiard's apartment, my head cradled in a pillow Tane had brought just for this purpose. He was watching me, concern and something like guilt on his face, and I jumped to my feet and kicked the pillow across the room.

"What was that?" I asked, and I wasn't sure if I meant Tane's spells or something else. "Your magic is too weak. You can't even see me safely to the street!"

"I'm working as well as I can," he said, running a hand through his dark hair. The movement made my stomach catch, a flip-flop of nerves that I didn't like. "Maybe in a few weeks—"

"*Weeks?*" Just the very thought squeezed my heart. Never mind weeks of sleeplessness, of my nightmare jolting me awake, but if I didn't escape from New Bishop soon, I wasn't even sure if I'd live that long. "I don't have that time to waste! Why didn't you tell me it would take so long!"

Tane didn't open his mouth, and I didn't even care that I was being unfair. I was so angry—angry that he wasn't as good at breaking curses as I'd thought, angry that my mother had gotten me into this whole situation, angry that I wasn't a witch and that I would be murdered and that I'd believed this boy when he said he could help me.

"Never mind," I said, letting out a breath in a sharp sigh. "We are getting nowhere with this. I can't—if it's going to take so long, it's no use for me. Don't bother coming tomorrow." I turned to leave, but as my hand touched the door I felt Tane's fingers on my wrist and—again! That current of magic within him flowed into my skin, so much stronger than the spells he'd made for me, as strong as even my grandmother's magic, but if he had so much power, why did it fade away the moment he tried to make a charm? Why couldn't he do it to save my life?

"Stop it!" I said, jerking my arm away.

"Stop what?" he asked, blinking at me. "What is it?"

"I can't do it anymore." I shook my head. "If it's not going to work, then my time is better spent elsewhere."

His eyes narrowed. "Why is time so important?" He paused, his expression hard. "What did you dream?"

My stomach dropped and I stared at him. "How—"

"You got upset our first day together, explaining how dreams work, how no one has ever changed their future." He lifted a hand, his fingers just inches from my face. "And you're not sleeping. You look like a seasick cabin boy on his first run."

He reached for me, leaning closer, but I pulled away, my jaw clenched tight.

"Fine," Tane said. "You don't have to say anything."

"Then it's settled. Our arrangement is over."

But Tane didn't speak, didn't move, and I watched him for several seconds, hearing the tick-tick-tick of my heartbeat, before turning to go.

"Wait. Avery, wait."

I shook my head, hard and fast as though I wanted to shake his words from my ears, but he spoke again. "Wait. I . . . I might know one more thing that could work."

Hope—that stupid, silly creature that lived within me, no matter how often I tried to beat it to death—lifted its nose and sniffed at the air.

"What, then?"

He wasn't looking at me, the faint line just under his left eyebrow deepening, like it always did when he had something important on his mind.

"I told you my people knew spells," he said, speaking low. "And they do." He shook his head. "Did. But they didn't use charms. Actually, I haven't tried any of my people's magic, not yet."

I breathed hard through my nose. "Why not?"

"I didn't think you'd be desperate enough to try it," he said. "And it's forbidden to share with outsiders. But there's no one left alive to object to my teaching you." His mouth curled suddenly, a wince as though he'd been slapped, and then he steadied himself. "So if you'd like to, I'm willing to try."

I could feel the word—*yes! yes! yes!*—on the tip of my tongue, but Tane's expression gave me pause.

"What's the magic?" I asked slowly, ready to smother my foolish, tenacious hope once more. Tane opened his mouth, closed it, opened it again, closed it. Finally, his fingers moved deftly over his chest, unbuttoning the long-sleeved blue shirt he wore. Underneath, he had an undershirt that, many washes ago, had been white, and he then shrugged off his blue shirt, pulled his undershirt over his head, and I gasped to see the intricate crisscrossed designs blackened into his skin, a maze of angles, of sharp lines that glowed, *burned* with magic.

And I knew it, without even his saying it, and maybe I had known all along, where he got his strength from, why the magic he carried seemed not to come from him but instead floated around his body. His tattoos.

"Someone my age should have more," he said softly. "But I left before I could earn them."

I couldn't speak as my eyes hungered to take in the full effect. I had spent enough time down at the docks to become used to the sight of men in short sleeves, unlike the cotton-headed young ladies who occasionally perched at the edge of Main Dock to ogle, twittering like birds and hiding their giggles behind tiny hands. Still, this was the closest I'd ever been to a man's bare chest, and I found myself looking past the dense mass of tattoos to study the lean curve of his muscles and his ladder-like ribs; and the structure of his body, of him, seemed to me more beautiful than even the artwork he wore.

It wasn't proper, I knew, to be here alone with him undressed, and even our bottle of wine wouldn't stop Monsieur

Dubiard from reporting us to my mother if he walked in now, but I couldn't bear to have Tane cover the tattoos again. Trembling, I reached out a hand and touched a finger to a single, swirling design just above his heart. A tendril of magic jolted through me, reminding me of that terrible idol that my grandmother had to banish from her house, but this time I kept my hand to his chest, riding the rush of magic like a wave, and I could tell that this was a tattoo for health against illness.

"There were many more, with many meanings and powers," he said, his voice shaking a little. "They've been lost now, forever. But these"—he spread out his hands—"I know what these can do." He tilted his body slightly, showing me a curious little design on the side of his arm where it met his shoulder: a grid of twelve triangles about two inches wide and arranged into a star, a little like the compass rose that adorns nautical maps.

"That's the one," he said. "It means protection against magic meant to do you harm. We give it to people who are precious and who need protecting. Young women wear this tattoo when they become pregnant, and hunters receive it before long hunts. It has even healed our sick."

"And why do you wear it?" I asked, and without meaning to, my words came out in a whisper. Tane said nothing for a few long moments, his eyes tracing the design.

"My sisters gave it to me when I left my island." He lifted his gaze to my face. "It's powerful. If you wore it, your mother couldn't hurt you, not with magic." He turned away suddenly and picked up his undershirt, and I could see he wore even more tattoos across his shoulder blades and down his spine, tattoos that whispered to me *strength, power, luck, skill.* He was a walking universe of spells.

"Why didn't you tell me this on the first day?" I asked, and he turned, surprised, as though he'd expected me to be angry and couldn't understand that I was, truly, curious.

"It's our magic," he said softly. "No outsider has ever worn our tattoos, although I saw many sailors ask when their whale ships came to our island. They like the designs. They like returning to their ships and showing off their skin, but our tattoos are not for adorning. Our tattoos have meaning, and they should be earned." He studied me, his brown eyes catching the light so they glowed blue-amber against his skin. "Something is going to happen to you, witch girl, something you won't even speak of. You've earned the right to wear a tattoo."

Twelve

OUR LIGHTHOUSE IS SOMETHING OF A JOKE and a curiosity, as it no longer works and even if it did, we would rarely need it. Sailors call New Bishop's harbor "the little pond" because of how gentle and even its waters flow (not by accident, of course—Lenora Roe set the harbor right nearly two hundred years ago). The sand, smoother than talc, caresses any ships that run aground, although for a captain to miss New Bishop's mile-long docks, he would have to be drunk and blind (and even then would need an inordinate amount of bad luck).

If the people who govern my island had any sense, they'd plop the lighthouse somewhere it might do some good, like down in Prince Island's little fishing village, Weld Haven, which sits on the southwestern shore of the island, just a bit below the Great Gray Slough and a bit before the long tail that reaches out to the Roe cottage. "Haven" is a touch of island humor, because unlike New Bishop's bathtub waters, the sea at Weld Haven's shore bites at ships and swimmers alike with rows of jagged, rocky teeth. Only tiny, flat-bottomed fishing skiffs can navigate safely out to sea, and if there hasn't been a wreck in those waters, it's only because there's no captain fool enough to try them.

In the end, though, the people on my island decided that a lighthouse in Weld Haven would be a waste, because the only folks to see it would be a dozen crumbly-teeth fishermen and their brown-faced, bowlegged wives, and besides, a fine town like New Bishop needed the mark of honor a lovely, large lighthouse would bestow. And so, to commemorate the hundred-year anniversary of the island's English settlement, the people of Prince Island erected the harbor lighthouse: white, sixty feet tall, with black trim around its windows and a little black cap.

Now, as we neared the island's two hundredth birthday, the lighthouse was little more than an eyesore; the island's children had long ago smashed its windows, and faded rust leached through the white paint so that it seemed as if the poor thing was bleeding. Every now and then a ladies' committee would sponsor a "Save the Lighthouse" drive, but the beautification of useless lighthouses was not the way the men of Prince Island chose to spend their hard-earned money.

All this meant that the lighthouse was the perfect place for Tane to carve a magical tattoo into my skin. We would be far enough out of town that I could scream my head off if needed and not a soul would hear. The lighthouse would be empty, especially as we planned to go in the middle of the night, and we could stay there undisturbed for as long as we wanted, or at least until dawn. My only worries concerned the lighthouse's dubious structural integrity and, ironically, the poor light.

The night of our meeting, I stretched out in bed, my ears straining for any noise that might mean disaster. I'd retired early, too nervous to trust myself to sit in the parlor under my mother's ever-suspicious eye, but that had proven a mistake. It would be hours yet before I'd have to meet Tane, and I was forced to spend the time clenching my fists and urging my whirring heart to calm. I thought I would die of nerves before the town clock struck one, but when I finally heard what I'd waited for, that one solemn *BO-ONG* echoing through the streets, I found I was frozen to my bed.

A curse! Ice seized through me that she knew, my mother *knew* I planned to escape! And I was ready to break down, crying and screaming, when I suddenly moved. I could move and stand up and walk around my room, and my cheeks flushed as I realized it wasn't magic that held me to my bed but plain old fear.

I dressed quickly, throwing an old black cloak around my shoulders. Sneaking downstairs to the kitchens proved easier than I would have guessed, my path smooth and silent, the air unbroken but for the quiet, steady breathing of my mother, her husband, and his children. I found Lucy the kitchen maid's boots, and they pinched my feet but still felt steadier than any of my delicate little slippers. Out the back door next, pausing only to grab a lantern and a handful of matches from the garden shed.

My mother's house, like all the big, grand houses, had a view of the shoreline unobstructed by trees or other buildings, and as the lighthouse sat far out on the beach just a little south of the house, that meant I didn't have to go through town to reach it. Instead, I went straight down to the beach, and it thrilled me, to run like a shadow from my mother's house as I had imagined so many times.

The lighthouse marked the north end of the docks, but these were the public docks, the boats tiny and half-full of dirty rainwater, and, unlike busy Main Dock, they were completely silent at night and deserted. As I reached the lighthouse, heaving for breath, I realized that Tane and I would be really, truly alone for the first time.

My fingers scrabbled in the dark for the crumbling, rusty door before I managed to wrench it open.

"He-hello?" I called, stepping inside.

"Up here!"

Tane's voice echoed down from the lamp room, and I squinted in the darkness. Fumbling with the matches, I struck one and carefully lit my lamp. The inside of the lighthouse was a mess of broken brick and twisted, rusted metal parts, and the staircase—rotted wood that had once been painted gray— looked barely able to support itself, let alone me.

"I thought we'd stay on the ground," I said, and I could hear Tane's soft laugh from above.

"You're about to spend the next few hours getting your skin pricked open," he called down, "and you're concerned about heights?"

I frowned and tested my weight against the bottommost step. In truth, I hadn't given much thought to the actual process of getting a tattoo. I knew from hearing sailors talk that only the boldest men would get tattoos, that it meant pain and that it required determination to get through. Every now and then a story would reach the docks of a tattooing gone wrong, of bleeding, of infection, of marks that refused to heal and instead turned streaky red and festered.

As I climbed the rickety stairs, I pushed those images from my mind and reminded myself that I didn't have the luxury of being scared. Fear was for a normal girl, the kind of girl who wouldn't even speak to someone with a tattoo, let alone get one herself, a proper girl like my mother wanted me to be, a girl who would grow into a lady, not a witch. I had my own murder to stop, and in that light, a bit of pain didn't seem so bad.

Tane waited for me at the top of the stairs, his lantern shining the way. The lamp room would have a spectacular view of New Bishop and the ocean in the daytime, but at night, the world outside was reduced to endless darkness so that it felt as if we were not at the top of a lighthouse at the edge of town but up the mainmast of a whale ship, surrounded by miles of black ocean.

Tane had set up already, a coarse white blanket laid across the floor (a gesture that surprised me with its thoughtfulness). A small bowl of black ashes pinned one corner of the blanket to the ground, and next to it sat a delicate paintbrush and two thin sticks: one a plain wooden dowel, the other a foot long with a curved tip of jagged teeth, a bit like a narrow, miniature rake.

"Is that it?" I asked, and my stupid voice quivered. I coughed quickly, clearing my throat. "That stick thing makes the tattoos?" I said, and this time my voice did not shake.

"Yes," Tane said. "I made it myself. Take a seat."

He gestured to the blanket, and as I tucked my skirts and eased to the ground, I realized how, in any other life, this would be a silly and romantic adventure. A midnight meeting in an abandoned lighthouse! The stepdaughter of the pastor out with a tattooed harpoon boy! Practically a penny dreadful.

For a moment, Tane stared at me while I stared back, ignoring the anxiety creeping over me.

"What?" I finally snapped, and he ducked his head.

"Ah," he said, and the light might have been low and his skin might have been dark, but I swear he blushed. "Well. Where should I..."

"What do you mean, where should—oh!" And this time my cheeks flushed. I hadn't even thought of that. Where was Tane going to tattoo me?

"Does...does it have to be in a certain place?" I asked, not meeting his eyes.

"Usually we tattoo the shoulder," he said, speaking quickly, and I frowned, thinking of those stupid low-cut dresses my mother made me wear to her endless society picnics and parties.

"But it shouldn't matter," Tane continued. "It will work no matter where it is."

And then he really did blush, and so did I, because where was a place on my body that my mother wouldn't see but that I also wouldn't be too embarrassed to show this boy? I had a fleeting thought then of the two of us hemming and hawing until daybreak, too hindered by our own self-consciousness to do anything.

"Hang it," I said, and before my nerves could fail me I kicked off my left boot. "Good gracious, Tane, turn around!"

Blinking fast, he covered his eyes and turned his head and, heart pounding, I yanked off my lace-trimmed cotton knickers and threw them in a corner. Keeping my left leg bare, I gathered my skirts underneath me and around my right leg. It was as much propriety as I could manage, given the circumstances.

"All right," I said, and as Tane turned back around I stared hard at his face, trying to read his expression, his eyes that seemed unable to settle on one part of me. I'd never been alone with a boy like this, never even in my imagination, and I'd never shown so much of my body, unclothed. My skin glowed in the darkness, unearthly and pale, the fine hairs catching the lantern light like tiny filaments.

"Here," I said, pointing at the front of my hip. "No one will see it."

"It will hurt more," Tane said. "Against the bone."

But I didn't want to think of that and I didn't want to think of another spot on my body, so I just clenched my jaw and said, "That's fine."

Tane nodded and said nothing, but I could hear his quickened breath and I ordered my own lungs to calm down.

"Lie back," Tane said, and I did it without thinking, my knuckles white as I clutched at my skirt. No doubt a proper girl, if she ever found herself in such a situation, would have shut her eyes tight at this moment, but I forced myself to focus. This would likely be the only time in my life that I ever saw someone get a tattoo. I didn't want to miss it.

"You did this as a child?" I asked, and Tane nodded.

"But on my island, women and children drank a tea first that put them to sleep," he said. "Only the strongest men received a tattoo with their eyes open."

A little flurry of panic stirred in my chest, and I managed a smile that felt like a grimace. "Haven't got any of that tea on you, by any chance?"

Tane laughed, quick and nervous, and opened up his bag to draw out a bottle of clear liquor.

"I brought it for disinfecting," he said, pouring a little of the liquid first on the jagged end of the tattoo stick and then (I sucked in a breath here) on the exposed skin of my hip.

Well, it wasn't tea. But it was something.

"Can I have a bit?" I asked, holding a hand out for the bottle, because I was alone with a boy, half-naked, about to get a tattoo, and since it was an evening for first experiences, hang it all, I might as well be a bit drunk, too.

"Easy," Tane said as I swallowed and coughed up some of the liquid. It burned as it flowed down my throat, but I took another, smaller sip and this time felt the fire slide to my stomach and explode in fireworks of warmth.

"All right," I said, lying back down. "I'm ready."

Tane moved the lantern closer to my body, his shadow looming large on the lamp room wall, and softly began to chant in a low whisper of words and breaths. The force inside my chest stirred, all the hairs on my arms stood up, and I felt the threads of Tane's magic reach out for me.

First, Tane dipped the paintbrush into the bowl of ashy ink. It tickled as he drew across my skin, his movements careful and small. As he drew the entire design, the compact rose of triangles, he kept up the chant, a strange, dreamy mix of words and noises and melodies that sank into me, calming me. I wondered if that was the point of the chant, to soothe the nerves of whoever would receive a tattoo, but Tane looked so focused on his work that I didn't dare interrupt with a question.

"Ready?" he finally asked. I glanced up at him, and for a moment I wanted to tell him no, forget it all, I couldn't bear whatever pain this would mean.

"Avery," he said, breathing out my name. "You can do this."

He smiled, and it was like I'd taken another sip of alcohol, the warmth rising from my stomach to my chest. I smiled back, and it began.

When I was seven years old, I would climb the natural jetty of rocks that stretched out into the ocean beyond my grandmother's cottage. She had warned me, many times, how dangerous it could be, that the waves made the rocks slick and sharp, that she was too old to come out and rescue me if I ever fell. But I never paid her mind. I was going to be the witch of Prince Island, lady queen of water and wave, and no harm could ever come to me in the ocean. I climbed and clambered over the wet rocks, my bare feet confident and sure, and when I reached the end, I laughed that anyone, especially my grandmother, could be frightened of a bunch of rocks.

It was on the return trip that one of my confident feet took a wrong step, and before I knew what had happened, my foot and ankle and knee and whole leg, all the way up to my hip, crashed down into the jagged space between two rocks, slicing open my skin and pinning me to the jetty. For a moment, the shock of my fall stunned me dumb, my breath knocked from my lungs, but I soon recovered my wits and planted my hands firmly against the wet rock to hoist myself back up.

But I couldn't. The rocks had trapped my ankle, squeezing it with a sandpaper grasp, and every movement I made only opened more cuts on my skin, only made tears rise to my eyes.

"Granma!" I called, lifting my face to the beach. "Granma, I'm stuck!"

I saw her face at her cottage window, watching me for several long minutes before she opened her door. The beach was far away, but I could still hear her clearly as she shouted back, "Get yourself out, then."

Her words chilled me even more than the waves now lapping at my toes, for the tide would soon come in and these wet black rocks would be swallowed by the sea. I cried out for her then, but she only watched me from the shore, her face set and serious, waiting for me to return.

I knew the jetty would be underwater in a matter of minutes, but the more I struggled, the more I only tore apart my skin. Still, I pushed myself up, my muscles quivering with strain, and with every wave I had to gasp against the stinging pain of my cuts, the icy fingers of the sea. The waves crashed up over the rocks, foaming and fizzing, and still I pulled, still I struggled. Tears squeezed from my eyes and I had to suck in breaths as the waves crested ever higher, and panic, true, desperate panic, clawed up through me, for I was not going to be the witch of Prince Island. I was going to drown out in the jetty, my leg trapped between two jagged rocks.

With the water swirling, sucking around me, my heart throwing itself against my chest, I let out a final scream of pain, of fear, of anguish, and wrenched my body up up up and free. I could feel my skin peel away, shredded and sliced off by the rocks, the churning water pink with my blood, but I was free of the rock and, gasping, I bobbed like a dog for the shore, not stopping until I had hauled my aching, slit-open, exhausted body to the sand and crawled to my grandmother's feet.

Up until the moment my tattooing began, I would have said that was the worst pain I had ever experienced in my entire life, and yet that day paled in comparison as Tane, again and again, beat the jagged point of the tattoo stick into my flesh. The first strike took my breath away, but there were hundreds more, and each brought me to a new dimension of pain. I tried not to cry out, squeezing my teeth together, but after a few minutes of agony I couldn't prevent a whimper from escaping my throat and soon I was screaming, my whole body on fire, my whole skeleton jarred and jolted and shivering.

Tane paused only to slip off his leather belt and hold it out for me to bite down. My tongue pressed against the salty leather, my screams muffled only slightly as tears slid down my cheeks. And through it all, I could still feel Tane's magic, slipping inside of me, knotting at my hip and expanding through me, a stunning pain of its own magnitude. I wanted to stop. I wanted to die. I had to fight against the blinding nausea rising within me, the dizziness that exploded through my skull. But still Tane continued, his movements sharp and methodical and never ceasing: place the jagged point against my skin, lift the second stick and use it to drive the tattoo stick down where its teeth bite into me, leaving behind a mess of blood and ink.

Every now and then he would pause to wipe my skin clean, and each time he would glance at me, just once, and he would speak to me in calm, soothing tones: "You're doing well, Avery; just hold on."

And then he wiped my skin and sat back on his heels.

"All right," he said. "This is going to hurt."

I wanted to laugh because if I wasn't already hurting, then whatever he had in mind would surely kill me. He lifted the bottle of alcohol and I spat out the belt, shaking my head.

"No, no!" I said, trying to draw away from him, but he pinned one strong hand against my waist and bit down on the bottle's cork, pulling it out.

"Tane, no!"

"I have to," he said, his jaw clenched.

"No! No, n—" My words cut off as the alcohol hit the fresh marks in my skin, and I was burning, my skin peeling away, boiling off me, and all I could do was shake and sweat and sob, over and over again.

"That's it! There, it's over! You did it, Avery!"

Through the haze of pain I felt Tane wrap his arms around me, pressing me close to him. Skin to skin, his magic blinded me, but I was too weak to fight it and instead I let it slip around me, wrap me up in a strange, fiery cocoon, my wrecked body stripped and ruined until all that was left was the coil of my own magic inside of me, reaching out for him, enveloping him. I felt the pulse of his heartbeat ricochet through my body as I sobbed into his shoulder and his hands curled and tangled into my hair, his breath whispered hot against my cheek, and he lifted my face to his and pressed his lips against mine.

The pain fell away. The burning fell away. And in their place rose up a hunger that I had never felt before, rearing up through me and expanding out to the tips of my fingers, to the ends of my toes. I kissed his lips and it wasn't enough; I had to press my hands to his cheeks and feel the jolt through my skin. I had to reach inside his collar, feel the ridge of bones at the base of his neck, and it still wasn't enough.

Why had no one told me about this? Where had this hidden world been all my life? I felt fresh tears rise to my eyes and Tane broke the silence, pulling away, asking if I was in too much pain, but I told him *no, no* and I whispered his name and he kissed the wet trails on my cheeks.

"You did it," he breathed, relief and pride and amazement mingled in his voice, and I laughed and kissed him again.

"Wait," he said finally, his voice a rumble against my throat. "I have to know. Did it work?"

We broke away and I glanced down at the swollen, bloody, jagged mess on my hip. It looked nothing like Tane's neat triangles, but I could feel its magic swell within me, spreading over and around me. Gently, I rolled to my knees, and Tane leaped to his feet, steadying me as I rose and smoothed my skirts over my new tattoo.

Think, I told myself. *The cottage, the escape.* I closed my eyes and tried to block out the pain, the feeling of Tane's skin, and I took a step. Then another. Another. *Refocus! The cottage! The escape!* But I did not black out. I did not stumble or fade away, but instead my fresh tattoo throbbed, sweet pain that whispered to me that I was, at last, *free.*

Part Two

Dreams and Designs

Thirteen

IF NOT FOR TANE, I WOULD HAVE RUN from the lighthouse, ignoring the fire in my leg that consumed my whole body. I would have likely passed out from the pain still en route to my grandmother's cottage, and I would have ridden out my feverish sleep alone.

But the moment I made for the lighthouse stairs, Tane stopped me, holding tightly on my wrist, telling me what I didn't want to hear. My leg wouldn't make the seven miles down to the cottage. *But I was free.* It would soon be daylight. *But I was free.* My mother, discovering me gone from my bed, would go out looking for me. *But I was free.* She would find me on the shoreline path and bring me back to New Bishop and this time she wouldn't use magic to keep me in her house but locks and chains and windowless walls.

Trembling, sweating, I stared hard at Tane before letting out a long sigh. I nodded.

"Get better," he said, placing his hands on my shoulders. "Get strong. We'll go together."

"Together?" In all my imaginings, I made the trip back to my grandmother on my own. What would she say if she saw me with this tattooed boy? Besides, my mother's other curse, the one that had sent Tommy stumbling into the slough, remained in effect, and Tane knew nothing about it.

"But you—"

Tane shook his head, cutting me off. "I've the same protection as you, remember?" He tilted his shoulder toward me. "Your mother's magic can't hurt me, either."

I blinked in surprise. Of course he was right. I wanted to ask him about it, but a sudden wave of dizziness overtook me and I bent over, clutching my stomach.

Be careful of strange magic. That was what my grandmother told me, and I could feel Tane's magic, foreign and strange and fighting against the force inside of me. But this was an infection I wanted, and as Tane pushed his body under my shoulder, urging me down the lighthouse stairs and back across the beach, I gritted my teeth and rode out the sickening waves.

"It hurts," I said, my hand searching not my torn and bloody hip but my chest, where a terrible tension burned.

"You'll be all right," Tane whispered back. "You did well." There was that note of surprise and pride again, and even through my feverish haze, a smile limped to my lips. I impressed him.

"We're here," he said, and I squinted through my half-closed eyelids to see we had reached my mother's house.

"Around the back," I gasped. "Through the garden."

Tane half-dragged, half-carried me down the side path and into the garden. The moon sat low in the sky and it would be at least another hour or two before the dawn, but it wasn't safe for us to stay out here, where anyone looking out the window would see. Still, I leaned against Tane's chest, his strength, not ready to say good night.

"Leave me a note in the garden when you're ready," Tane said, his voice raspy. I had my head tucked into the soft curve of his neck, his pulse beating gently against my forehead.

"Don't go," I whispered, and I knew it was madness to ask, an impossible thing, but I was sick and aching and wanted him to hold me. I felt his hand reach under my chin and tip my face up to his.

"I'll come back. Be strong. Get better."

One cool press of his lips and then he pulled away, and it was as though all the warmth and heat of my body went with him. I watched him place my lantern beside the garden shed and disappear back into the dark streets, and an ache of longing opened up inside of me. When he had gone, I turned and glanced up at the big house, shivering and scared, for all I wanted to do at that moment was collapse to the cool dirt of the garden, but I still had to cross to the kitchen, climb two flights of stairs, and make it to my room unseen and unheard.

I took a tentative step and winced, sucking in a breath of

air through my teeth. It wasn't the pain of the tattoo so much as Tane's powerful magic, disorienting enough to throw me off balance. I could barely see, my vision swimming in and out of focus, chills and burns alternately racking my body. I stumbled and tripped my way inside, holding tightly to walls and counters, reeling like a drunk. Bile clawed up my throat but I couldn't vomit, not in the kitchens and not on the stairs.

Make it to your room, I told myself, sweating and sick. *Anywhere else will give you away. Get to your room first.*

And that was the thought that kept me going, that all I had to do was cross the kitchens and climb the stairs and walk down the hallway and then I could throw up.

When I finally reached my room, I didn't even bother aiming for the basin in the corner, my dim thoughts casting out pity for whatever housemaid would have to clean up after me. My vision grew fuzzy and dark, but I knew I had more to do to keep up appearances, and through a fog of pain and misery I shucked off my dress, wrapped my swollen, bleeding hip with a scarf, kicked off and hid Lucy's too-small boots. Satisfied at last, I fell to my bed and let the fever take me.

Witches don't get sick. At least, none of the witches in my family. We seem to be immune to sniffles and common colds and illnesses of any kind, and no Roe ever died from sickness. As far as I knew, Roes only died in their forties, after handing over their title to their daughters, although with my grand-mother now in her sixties, and my dream, I didn't know what to think anymore.

I understood that the fever that confined me to bed was supernatural. Still, it came as a shock to feel the strength sap from me, to lie sweating and shivering and icy cold. At least my silly dream, with its promise of murder, assured me that I wouldn't be done in by a fever but would come through it alive, and I did, waking to the most startling sight I could imagine: my own mother, watching me with hawkish, suspicious eyes.

"You're awake," she said, and I blinked at her. She looked a mess, her hair disheveled and loose on her shoulders, her dress old and dirty. Even back in the stinking apartment, she had been immaculate, not a thread out of place. Appearance mattered to her, and it was unnerving to see her so sloppy, careless.

"Three days you've been out." She said it almost like an accusation. "How do you feel?"

Dizzy. Confused. Anxious. But I whispered the safest thing I could imagine: "Hungry."

"What happened to you?" She leaned forward in the chair at the side of my bed. "You seem...different."

My chest tightened and I felt the raw bundle of magic at my hip twitch. "Just hungry," I wheezed, my voice raw from disuse, and this time my mother seemed to hear me.

"All right. I'll be back with something for you to eat."

She rose slowly from the chair, still staring at me, while I struggled to keep my face blank and passive. The moment she left the room I threw back my sheets and yanked my night-gown up to examine my hip, ignoring the waves of dizziness that rolled through me. I winced as I peeled back the sweat-stained fabric and touched a finger to my puffy, swollen skin. But I hardly cared that it still looked unhealed; I was simply grateful it looked undiscovered. Ethel, one of the housemaids, likely changed my sheets during my illness, and if she saw my bandage, she kept her mouth shut—which she should have, given that only a week ago I'd told one of her dreams.

Carefully, I rewrapped my hip before pulling the sheets back up. I could feel the force of the tattoo working around me, sliding over me like armor while the core of magic that sat inside my chest remained untouched. It was bizarre, like carrying around someone else's ghost, but at least it no longer poisoned me.

My mother's footsteps echoed down the hall and quickly I smoothed my sheets and settled my hands in my lap.

She carried a tray before her and set it down on the night-stand, just enough out of my reach that instead of eating, I could only watch the curls of steam rising from the bowl of broth while my mother sat back in the chair.

"We had the doctor come in," she said, her voice tired. "He couldn't think of what was wrong with you. I didn't even think you *could* get sick. What happened?"

My eyes slid from the bowl of broth to her face. "Nothing."

She shook her head. "No, there's something.... You haven't... Tommy Thompson left, didn't he?"

"Yes." I swallowed, my mouth sticky and dry, and frowned. "Two weeks ago. What does he have to do with—"

"And you haven't been down to the docks lately?"

"No." It was the truth. My experiments and Tane's dreams more than occupied me; I didn't need to find customers. And besides, the docks had lost much of their charm after Tommy left. They reminded me too much of him and made me miss him and worry about him. I avoided them now.

"It's not... There's not anyone...?" My mother studied me, and I felt limp as a bit of rope, gray and tired.

"I just woke up," I said, not hiding the exhaustion in my voice. "Perhaps you could save your questions for another time?"

Instead of answering, she rose to her feet and paced the floor, one hand rubbing over and over the end of her scar.

"I was worried about you," she said, although if she was relieved to see me up and awake, she didn't sound it. "You're always down at the docks. I thought perhaps... perhaps someone had hurt you."

She sounded so frail, scared, but I just frowned.

"You think I'm one of those delicate ladies? I'm a Roe. No one is going to hurt me."

"No." My mother stopped her pacing to stare at me. "It's because you *are* a Roe that I worry." She took a few steps closer. "We're not normal, Avery, and everyone on this island knows it. They know we're more powerful than they are and they hate us for it."

My stomach growled and I glared at the bowl of soup.

"That isn't true."

"Why? Because your grandmother says so? They fear us...." Her fingers searched the side of her face, running across the jagged scar.

"I thought...I thought something had happened to you," she said, her voice weak. "I thought someone had hurt..." Her words trailed off in a mumble, but she stroked her scar and I knew what she meant to say.

"I'm not you," I said quietly, and she blinked as if coming out of a trance. "I'm not going to make your mistakes."

"And you're certain about that, are you?" she snapped. "You think it's possible for someone like us to get close to one of *them*? Even if it was, it would only lead to their ruin."

Tane's face rose before my eyes, and I snorted in disbelief. "Your ruin, maybe."

Her eyes narrowed. "And Tommy's."

Prickles of heat ran across my cheeks while the rest of my body turned very cold.

"I've been too careless with you," she whispered. "I've let you run around, go where you please...."

"You *have*?" I asked, letting out a laugh, and her eyes flashed.

"Why do you act like this? What have I done to you?"

I sat up in bed, my heart pounding. "What have you—you took me away! You keep me here!"

"Yes," my mother said, letting out a short laugh. "This is such a prison, Avery. A prison where you can have anything you want at any time you want."

"There is nothing here I want."

"Then tell me! What is it?"

I stared at her, my sheets gripped tight between my fists, and wished I was strong enough to leap out of bed and run away, now, go, now, prove to her that she could not keep me anymore. Why was I still fighting with her? Why didn't I just say what she wanted to hear so she would go away? It didn't matter anymore. In only a few hours I would be gone from here forever and on my way to becoming the witch. I would never have to see her again if I did not want, and none of this mattered anymore except—*four years*. Four years she lived by my side, and still I was a stranger to her.

"I know what you're trying to do," I said, and I had to fight to keep my voice steady. "I know you want me to think that this—all these *things*—are worth giving up what I am."

"It's more than that, Avery, and it's not about giving up; it's—"

"You need to *understand*." My breaths came fast now. "There is nothing you could do or say or show me that could ever make me forget: I am a Roe, I had a life and a duty and you ripped me away from both."

"You want to be a witch, then," she said, and her voice had gone very quiet and very hard. "Fine. Imagine your life in ten years. Twenty. When you are alone. When you are starving. When your roof caves in. Imagine your child, friendless, ignorant, exposed to violence and misery and fear every time someone knocks on the door. Do you think that living our legacy means happiness? Do you even understand how much you have to give up to be a witch? There will be a day, Avery, that you will look at the life I offered you and *long* to get it back."

"Stop it," I said, and I squeezed my eyes tight because I could no longer look at her, white-faced, still, towering over me like a judge.

"I'm tired of begging you to see what is right in front of you," she said. "And what's worse, I know you don't believe me. You wouldn't believe anything I told you about how hard it is to be a witch."

"What would you know?" I asked, raising my hands from my face. "What did you ever give up?"

For the first time, she startled, the calm mask slipping, just a bit, and she reached up, like I knew she would, reached up and touched, very lightly, the line of her scar.

"Too much."

A scuffle, a slosh, and she slid the tray from the table onto my lap. She turned and headed for the door, but before she walked out she paused, held my gaze. She was so still I wasn't even sure she breathed. "And what is worse, I gave it up before I even knew I had it."

Then she was gone, and the tray warmed my lap, and I listened to her words again in my head.

She didn't understand me. She didn't know. She didn't even realize that all her plans and plots were about to come to nothing, because I was leaving, forever. I'd always imagined that moment—the moment when I looked her in the eyes and *knew* she no longer had power over me—would be a triumph, something to savor. But instead, I felt very cold. My stomach knotted. What had she done to me?

Sighing, I shook my head.

"Stop this," I whispered. I couldn't worry about my mother anymore. My leg had healed. It was time to fetch Tane and make my escape.

I packed nothing. I planned never to return to my mother's house. When I heard the town clock chime one in the morning, I retrieved Lucy's boots—hidden in the back of my wardrobe—and slipped down the stairs, through the kitchen, and out the garden door. I paused just long enough to glance up at the big house, milky in the moonlight, before I turned and walked through town.

The night air cooled my cheeks, feverish with thoughts of my escape, with thoughts of Tane and what my mother had told me.

I knew she had not had the best record when it came to love, and my father and the pastor were, at least, two men incapable of loving a woman as strange and powerful as the Roe witch. And it was true that the cottage on the rocks belonged only to the Roes and that no man, no outsider, had ever been invited to stay.

That didn't mean Roe women lacked for suitors—real suitors, not men hoping to take advantage of a lone woman on the rocks (and I doubt I'll shock anyone when I say that a man meaning to attack a witch met quite unpleasant consequences). Rough-edged mariners visited my grandmother with their hair slicked down and a fistful of daisies, and gentlemen called, too, with offers for sailing excursions or trips to the mainland, but they were sent away all the same. ("The idiot," my grandmother said once, closing the door on a bucket-faced fop from Boston. "What would I ever want to do *there*?")

My grandmother rarely spoke of the man who fathered my mother, but I admit I never much asked her. If she burned a candle for this man, she kept the light well hidden from me, saying only that she didn't know him very well and that the story of their courtship (quite short, I imagine) wasn't fit for a little girl's ears.

"He was just like a ghost," she said once, and I remembered this because she had spoken unbidden, lifting her eyes from her work to stare out the window at the ocean. "He passed through my life like a ghost and when he was gone, I had your mother."

But Tane was not a ghost like my grandfather or a monster like my father but real, warm, kind. And I wanted him. I wanted him as surely as I wanted to breathe, as I wanted to return to the cottage and become the witch. And if Roe witches never shared their home with their men, then perhaps I would have to be the first.

The town was dark and silent as I picked my way carefully down side streets, taking special attention to avoid the busier spots: the pub near the docks, the row of boardinghouses on the other side of town. I kept closer to the center of town, near the businesses, closed now although not abandoned, as most shop owners slept above their stores with their families.

I knew I had to be careful, keep my hood up and my chin down and stay to the shadows, for there was still a price on my head for any man who happened upon me, and so when I turned a corner and near ran into Billy Macy, island-born rope-maker, I jumped a mile and put out my small fists.

"Don't touch me, Billy Macy," I said, backing away, although he was well over six feet and nearing three hundred pounds and could have swatted me as easily as a fly. "Or I'll—I'll—"

"Whoa, wait, there," Billy said, raising his hands up, his gray eyes wide with alarm. "What's all this, then? It's late for you. What're you doing out of bed?"

"Nothing," I said, fists still out in front of me.

"Running off to your grandmother?" Billy leaned in close and I flinched, ready to spring, when his broad face split into a grin and he laughed. "'Bout time, if you want my opinion!"

Seeing the look on my face, he laughed again. "Did you think I'd run off to your mama with you squealing like a pig over my shoulder? I'm not going to say a word, you can believe it. Whatever your mama'd do to me for keeping mum can't be worse than sitting here starving, waiting for you to grow up and take over the witch's work."

I eyed him, still uncertain. "You're not afraid of my mother?"

"Afraid! Of course I'm afraid! I know she could turn my insides out, even if she's got the upper class thinkin' she's given up on magic. But the way I see it, some things're just meant to be, and all of us on the wharf and the docks know you don't belong in town. And I've done nothing wrong, true? I'm not helping you escape. I'm just keeping my mouth shut for a bit. The pastor's wife's a tough woman to find, all those grand houses lookin' the same, and I've a hard time navigating up lighthouse," he said, and he winked and leaned in close. "Keep running, Miss Avery, and don't look back."

With a bit of a smile on his face, he turned and very deliberately stepped around me, heading off toward the dockside pub and humming off-tune as he went. I could only watch him at first, not entirely sure what had just happened.

They were waiting for me. They were hoping for me. They knew I was their only chance.

Warmth seeped from my stomach all the way through my body to my fingers and toes, and I ran off once more.

Tane stood waiting for me at the town border, an unlit lantern looped over one wrist, the collar of his jacket turned up. He smiled when he saw me, and when I ran to him and touched him, I was amazed to discover that I didn't get a jarring jolt through my skin. Instead, the magic in my tattoo stretched out and met his, recognized it and welcomed it like something familiar, like coming home.

I clasped my arms around his neck, breathing in his smell, his hands soft and warm in my hair, and my heart pounded happily inside my chest. Color rose to my cheeks as he tilted my chin up to kiss me, and, oh, he was so soft, feathery and gentle and strong, his mouth pressed against mine and my eyes closed and my veins full of fizzy happiness.

"I missed you," he said, and he squeezed me gently to his chest. He kissed my eyes, my forehead, his breath stirring my hair, and every place his lips touched, I felt a spark on my skin that made me shiver.

"Ready?" he whispered. I could hear his smile. "One more step and you've left New Bishop."

My breath felt tight in my throat, like too much excitement had made my lungs fail to work properly. Tane reached down for my hand and twined my fingers between his. Leaving. It was time to go.

With the lights of New Bishop behind us, we walked into the darkness.

Fourteen

WHEN WE WERE FAR SOUTH OF TOWN, Tane lit the lamp, and the grassy path slowly veered toward the beach. We walked close enough to the waves that the salt spray turned the ends of my straight black hair thick and curly and cooled my flushed cheeks. Hardly anyone ever came to the beach this far south, and so the sand stretched smooth and even, packed hard by wind and rain. Our feet left clear prints, but I knew that, come morning, the rising tide would wash them away.

"You can stop worrying," Tane said, reaching for my hand. "No one is following us."

My eyes swept across the horizon behind us. I could see the shadows of town loosely silhouetted against the paler sky, and I knew Tane was right, we'd made it, I'd escaped, but I couldn't shake the jangly, shivery feeling that my mother would suddenly swoop down and whisk me away.

"Distract me," I said, and I gritted my teeth together to keep them from chattering.

"And how should I do that?" Tane asked, dropping my hand to wriggle his fingers against my ribs. I shied away and caught his hand between mine.

"No, I don't know," I said, because Tane's laughter, his assurance, only made me more nervous. "Talk. Tell me something. Tell me a story. I like hearing people talk."

"You do? You can hardly sit still more than five minutes when I try to tell you a dream."

"Dream-telling's different," I said, pushing a damp piece of hair off my forehead. "When I was little, at my grandmother's house, I used to sit and listen when customers came. They'd tell my grandmother...everything. They'd talk about themselves. About things that scared them or things they'd done." My voice faded as I remembered: Stiff married women, so dried up as to be more sand than flesh, told with trembling hands and watery eyes their secret fantasies about the broad-shouldered dock boys. Well-respected captains talked fondly and sadly of their brown-skinned, blue-eyed bastard children, cradled in the arms of their tropical mothers. The memories of dead sailors were routinely resurrected on my grandmother's table, their bloated, swollen bodies described in detail by seamen barely out of short pants.

"They'd sit down at the table and spill their souls, and

afterward my grandmother would say that there was magic in talking aloud, like drawing out poison. Small magic." I glanced at him and realized he was staring at me. My cheeks warm, I looked away.

"Why don't you start, then, witch girl," Tane said quietly. "I want to hear a story about the Roes."

"The Roes..." I knew so many, hundreds maybe, the stories of the Roe women and their doings as familiar to me as the lines across my own palms, but it was hard to pick just one.

"My grandmother always said I reminded her of Abigail Roe. She was the youngest witch. She took over for her mother, Lenora, when she was seventeen, just a year older than I am now."

"And what could she do?" Tane asked, smiling. "Breathe fire? Curse anyone she didn't like with freckles?" He reached up to tweak my nose, and I laughed softly.

"No," I said, the smile fading. "She could speak to the dead."

Tane seemed to stumble for a moment, his eyes wide with surprise, before he collected himself again. "That is...some gift," he said, and he frowned and looked away from me, and I wished suddenly that I'd picked another Roe, even though Abigail really *was* my favorite, so young, so unafraid, and she was the witch for a long time, thirty years almost, second only to my grandmother.

I was about to change the subject when Tane slowly reached his hand for mine and squeezed my fingers. He felt cold, colder than he should on a warm summer night.

"Tell me about her," he said softly, and I cleared my throat.

"She used to walk up to New Bishop every Saturday afternoon, when the widows and their families would visit the graveyard, and she'd wait at the gates and tell them she could help them talk with their husbands and fathers and sons."

"For a price," Tane said, the corners of his mouth lifted into a wry, mirthless smile.

"Actually, no. She never charged for that."

"I thought the Roes didn't give away their magic for free."

"Well." I tilted my head, thinking. "She'd lost people. Her mother. Her grandmother. Perhaps she thought it wouldn't be right, asking money. But she had rules. A person could only speak to their dead three times. Three times and that was it. People used to offer her all kinds of things to change her mind—a ship, a mansion, all the money she could ever want and more—but as far as I know, she stood firm. According to my grandmother, she used to say that a person could waste away, thinking of the people they'd lost. So she settled on three times: the first to say 'I love you,' the second to say 'I miss you,' the third to say 'Good-bye.'" My voice faded and I looked quickly at Tane, who stared straight ahead, his gaze unmoving on the dark horizon.

"What would the dead say?"

"I don't know. She said everyone was different, and she wouldn't say any more. The dead deserved their privacy, she said, and their messages were only for certain ears. But usually..." I paused, feeling Tane's hand shake within mine. "The dead wanted the same as the living. A chance to say I love you, I miss you, and good-bye."

"She must have been quite a woman, Abigail Roe," Tane said, and I smiled, my cheeks glowing with pleasure and the small magic of talking. I liked this, walking in the dark with Tane's hand in mine and the memory of the Roes to lead us forward. I could feel them all around me, listening, watching, urging me on. I would be one of them soon. I'd have a daughter and then a granddaughter, and maybe someday she'd walk along this beach at night and say out loud, "And the Roe who saved the whole line after her mother made such a mess of things, the one who made sure it kept going—that was Avery, the dream-teller."

"Tell me about yourself now," I said, tugging a little at Tane's hand, and when he said nothing for several seconds, I added, "Tell me about your island."

"My island." Tane sounded surprised. He dropped my hand to adjust the wick of the lantern but then didn't reach for me again. "It is very hot."

"Is that all? What is it called?" I glanced at Tane, and he shrugged. "You don't know?"

"We never gave it a name," he said, pushing his free hand into his pocket. "We lived alone and untouched on the island for generations. We never left and no one ever visited us, so we had no reason to name the island. If we needed to, we called it *toka*."

"What does that mean?"

"Rock. When the English came, they gave it their own name. Hovell Island."

I nodded. "They did the same here. Ages ago, Prince Island had a different name. The name's been forgotten, but not the meaning: Island at the End."

"The end of what?"

"No one knows. I don't think anyone ever lived here before the English came. You can't farm this island, you can't raise anything here. The only thing it's got in abundance is distance from the mainland, and that's only valuable if you're launching ships into the ocean. But as for the name, after the English landed here in 1685, someone hoping to get in the royal family's good graces decided to name the island in honor of the infant Prince George." I shrugged. "I doubt the future king of England ever knew he had a scrubby little namesake out in the Atlantic, or surely he would have had the name changed."

Tane laughed, swinging the lantern so that the beam of light swept across our feet and the dark, smooth sand.

"When did they first come to your island?" I asked, and his smile faltered.

"Years before I was born. Before even my father was born. They first came with maps and notebooks and we thought we would be left alone after that. When I was a boy—old enough to walk and talk and run around on my own, but still young—then the whalers came."

"Was it a surprise to see foreigners?"

"For some." Tane lifted his shoulders into a slow shrug. "Our legends told us that we came from another island, *Aotearoa*, New Zealand, where the Maori live. But we have been alone for centuries. We have our own culture, our own traditions. And once we had another legend, one that said that the world had flooded and that our little island was the only land left. Even after the explorers came, there were many who believed that, but I never did."

"Why not?"

Tane raised his face, the lantern light striking him under the chin and casting deep shadows over his eyes.

"My father was a hunter," he said. "But if he had not taken a wife, if he had not had my older sisters or me, he would have packed a canoe and sailed off across the ocean. When I was very young, he took me out in his canoe and paddled until we could no longer see our island. 'Don't be afraid,' he told me, and I wasn't. He told me that the waters ended on the shores of lands we could only imagine. He told me that our island was so small and the world so vast and there's so much to see. He told me about cities, animals, factories. I don't know how he knew about all that. But he did.

"When the whalers came, he wanted to go with them and see the world, but he couldn't. So I told him I would take his place."

I glanced at Tane, studying his strange, cold expression. "You weren't scared to leave?"

He shook his head, slowly. "I knew every rock and leaf on my island. I knew the face of every person. I knew the girl I would marry and the house I would live in. Even as a child, I already understood everything my life would become, and I hated it. I felt like I couldn't breathe.

"Then the sailors came, and they brought their stories. It drove me mad, to know how much of the world lay beyond our shores. I begged them to take me. My mother did not like it and my sisters did not like it, but my father understood. He told me to go, and I left without looking back. I would have been about nine, then."

Something strange happened to Tane's soft voice. It grew hard, clear, his words cutting through the hiss of the waves and the moan of the wind. I watched his eyes turn to polished glass, shining in the darkness. He didn't seem angry. And he didn't seem sad. But I had seen that kind of expression before, on the faces of young men—new husbands or new fathers—as they left in their ships for a many-years-long journey. Sailors can't cry. But they can square their shoulders and set their eyes and turn hollow long enough to leave port and lose themselves in their work. That was how Tane looked.

"I hated my island," he said, and his clear voice seemed to speak more to the waves and the wind than to me. "When I left, I promised I would never return. But I should have stayed."

I stopped walking then, and Tane slowed, too.

"You would be dead now," I said softly. "If you had stayed."

"I would have been a fighter like my father. I would have killed before I died, and I would have died with honor, protecting my land and my people."

I stared at him for a long time. "But you still would have died."

He laughed, a hollow noise. "I *did* die," he said, and the end of his mouth curled into a smile. "I died the moment the shaman told me that everyone I ever loved and everything I ever cared for had been destroyed. They died, but I died, too, and it was my punishment that although I was dead there was still breath in my lungs and I still could walk and talk and think. All I wanted was to slit my throat with my harpoon, and the only thing that stopped me was vengeance."

He looked out on the dark waves.

"Every morning I woke up thinking of my parents, my sisters. Every night I fell asleep imagining how I would find and kill their murderers. I hunted whales. I ate my meals. And I breathed in and out, but it was only because I needed breath in my lungs to take my revenge." He paused, and a smile like a grimace pulled at his lips. "Ghosts haunt, don't they? Then I was just a ghost, bent on haunting."

A tremble worked through his body, a shudder so strong that it seemed he would fly apart, and I reached for him, pressed my arms around him until he stilled.

We stood like that for a long time, and it was several minutes before I realized he had spoken in the past tense. I lifted my face to his. His eyes were closed, and bright, wet paths shivered down his cheeks.

"Are you still a ghost?" I asked softly. His heartbeat, slow and steady, burned against me. He opened his eyes, ignoring the tears pooling at his long, dark lashes.

"I think..." He took a slow, rattling breath and brushed the knuckles of his fingers, gently, against my cheek. "I think...I am coming back to life."

Fifteen

THE PEOPLE ON MY ISLAND FORGOT THAT
my grandmother was a real person. They thought she arrived
on this island fully formed, with no other intent than to make
them charms. They forgot that, aside from her magic, she was
just like them. She made herself dinner and slapped at biting
flies and did her laundry. Although she looked older than her
years, she was still not quite so old as they thought. And she
had been young once. She had a name (Jennie. Jennie is her
name, still).

But no one called her Jennie anymore. Since the day she
took over from her mother, she had always only been the witch.
Or the Roe witch. Or Mother Roe. And the sailors who, a
week earlier, had called out sweetly, "Hey there, Jennie Roe,"
promptly ignored her old name and her old life.

It was like its own kind of magic trick, this easy forgetting. In the islanders' minds, the witch never changed. One day the door would open and the woman inside would be young. She would perform the same spells and act the same, and it was as though she had picked up someone else's conversation without missing a word.

For many years, there was even a rumor that the woman who lived out on the rocks was the *same* woman, that she'd managed to cheat death and make herself young again, over and over. When I was a child, my grandmother got visits from wrinkle-faced, fat old ladies who knocked on her door, all dainty and desperate, and asked if she might have something to give them back their youth. My grandmother always would explain that she didn't work that kind of magic, but if they really pestered her, sometimes she'd be persuaded to sell, for an astronomical sum, a tiny pot of mud mixed with fish scales and bird droppings. It did nothing for the skin, she'd tell me, but for those kinds of women—and they were always the rich ones, because the poor ones had more worries than wrinkles— just the act of paying out a fortune was a kind of relief.

"What happens when she doesn't get pretty?" I asked once. "Won't she get mad?"

"Never, dear," she said. "Because then she'd have to admit she's a fool paying to smear mud on her face. She'll convince herself it's working, you'll see, and she'll be back by the end of the month for more."

My grandmother was right, of course, as always. But even

when they'd come back, she'd turn them away. She didn't like trading in foolishness, no matter how much those dainty old cows offered, and the threat of being found out, of getting labeled a charlatan, outweighed the satisfaction of revenge against the islanders' erased memories of Jennie Roe.

Tane held my sweaty, cold hand as we walked the last bit in silence, my body jumpy and jangly with nerves.

And then, there it was. The cottage. A small beacon against the silvery-gray rocks, against the deepness of the ocean. Had it always been so tiny? I remember it looming and large, but that had to be my baby memory, magnifying over the years. Even in the dim gray of early morning, I could see that it still had the ramshackle, fall-down quality that I loved—crooked shutters, messy woodpile. Sun and wind and water had bleached the whole thing as white as whalebone, had freckled and stained its wooden walls so that the cottage seemed a natural part of the landscape, a giant speckled egg within a nest of rocks. My home.

The windows were dark and yet I didn't pause as the path wound to the front door. Even if my grandmother was asleep, she was well used to late-night knockings, and I didn't fear waking her.

"Wait," Tane whispered, but my feet tripped into a run, a dash to the cottage, joy and relief rising up from the pit of my stomach through my chest and bursting onto my cheeks as tears.

I knocked once, quickly, a rap that seemed to shake the whole cottage with the force of its intent, but I didn't pause for an answer. This was my cottage as much as my grandmother's, and I didn't have to wait on the doorstep. I threw the door open, my whole body trembling as the smells hit me: woodsmoke, salt water, sweet dried herbs.

"Granma," I said, my voice twisted and choked in my throat.

She slept, curled on her bed, and I saw with a wrench that my own little trundle bed was tucked away underneath, its sheets made up and ready for me. I crossed the room slowly, making my way to my grandmother's side.

"Granma."

The squeak of her bed, a mumble, and then a sharp breath.

"A-Avery?"

It was too dark to see her face, but I reached out my fingertips and touched her, touched her skin and her hair, blinking away tears. I bent my face down closer to her, burrowing through her blankets to press my cheek to her chest, the thud of her heart loud to my ears.

"I'm back, Granma," I whispered, and although tears ran from my eyes, I was happy, happier than I'd been in four long years. "I'm *home*."

Her fingers crept through my hair, slowly, delicately, almost as though she didn't believe I was real. She said my name again.

"It's me," I said, laughing, raising my face. I felt her hands cup my cheeks, the bones under her skin trembling, trembling.

"Oh," she said. *"Oh, oh, oh."*

A noise made me turn to the door: Tane, with his lantern. I looked back at my grandmother and my heart jumped. In the light, I could see now just how she'd aged. Four years, only four years, and when I left my grandmother she was stooped and slowed, but the woman in bed before me looked like a skeleton, skin stretched tight over her bones, her hair loose and stringy across her face. She couldn't have been much more than sixty and yet she could have passed for a hundred, old like she'd been stretched past her time—which, in a way, she had, for no Roe had lived as long as she. Her eyes, though, looked exactly the same as I remembered, clear and quick, and they moved from my face to Tane's.

"Who...?"

I smiled at her and motioned for Tane to come in.

"He's my friend, Granma. He helped me get—"

"Go away!" she shrieked, and I jolted. Tane froze where he stood, just inside the door, the lantern stretched out in his hand, and my grandmother, moving with the speed of a younger woman, sprang from her bed, rushing at him.

"Get out! Out!"

"What—what—"

Breathing hard, I spun and put myself between my grandmother and Tane. "It's your tattoos!" I said, speaking quickly over my grandmother's shrieks. "Your magic, it's too much for her!"

Without another word, Tane set the lantern on the table and left the cottage, his expression hard and unreadable. I closed the door behind him as my grandmother moved quickly around the room, snatching at dried grass, tiny leather pouches, and muttering to herself.

"He's gone," I said, leaning against the door. "I'm sorry; I should have known."

"It's still here," she said, shaking her head so furiously I didn't know how she could see. She tossed the bits and pieces she carried onto the table and sorted them. Her nails, long and yellow, tapped delicately with each tiny movement. "I can still feel it."

For a moment, I could say nothing, only stare at her as I tried to swallow the lump in my throat. She looked mad. Sick.

"Oh," I said finally. "That's . . . that's me, I think."

She turned her eyes to me, narrowing her vision to slits. "You."

"Tane, my friend, he knows magic. He had to make a spell for me, so I could come down here," I said, talking quickly. "My mother put a curse on me; did you know, Granma?"

No response.

"Th-that was why I couldn't come down to see you, but Tane, he figured it out. He—he gave me a tattoo, Granma, and the tattoo had a spell in it and that's how—"

At my words, my grandmother sprang for me, grabbing my shoulders and shaking me hard.

"A tattoo!" she said, so close to me that I could smell the sickly sweetness of her breath. "Poisoned with foreign magic!"

"No, no," I said, my voice weak and whiny. "I had to do it, Granma, I had to come back to you. I came back to be the witch!"

Her fingernails dug into me, pressing hard, her eyes searching. After a moment, she softened and the fear left her face. She sighed, a rattling, trembling sigh. I had never imagined she could look so old and fragile.

"Good," she whispered, nodding. "You're back. Good..." She blinked at me and reached up a hand to pat my cheek.

"I missed you," I said, and my grandmother smiled.

"Let's get to work."

Relief swept through me, so strong that my knees nearly buckled. My grandmother turned and walked toward the black chest, and already I could feel the magic calling for me, shining at me in the darkness. Just as the day we tied the winds together, my grandmother stopped at the chest, looked up at me, crooked a finger.

"Come," she said. "Open it."

A smile spread across my face, and my fingers tingled as I crossed to the chest. All the work of the Roes, and it would belong to me. I would know, I would learn. The magic inside of me roared with triumph, and I bent down, I touched a hand to the lid, I took a breath and held it and felt as though the whole world had disappeared or shrunken down or blacked out, leaving just me, my grandmother, the secrets of the Roes.

There. Just as I had remembered after all these years: the papers, the notes, the charms and neatly bound spells. Quickly, my grandmother reached inside, picking through the objects, and, like a magnet, I felt my own hands drawn forward, shaking.

"There's much to do, still," my grandmother said as she continued to pick through the chest. "We don't have much time left."

Time.

A needle of fear slid through me, and I put a hand on my grandmother's arm.

"There's something else I need to tell you," I whispered. "I came back because I had a dream and I need your help."

She cocked her head toward me, blinking in the dim light. "You still tell dreams?"

I nodded. "Two weeks ago I had a dream that told my future." I took a breath. I'd never said it out loud, not to anyone, and it scared me, as though by speaking it, it would really happen. "The dream showed me that I'm going to be murdered, Granma, and I have to stop it."

Her body went rigid and it took several long seconds before I heard the breath rattling through her lungs again. She closed her eyes then and she looked so frail and uncertain that I reached for her, still bent over the chest, but the moment I touched her thin shoulder, she rose to her feet and jerked away, eyes bright with anger and fear and—my heartbeat quickened—tears.

"Tell me what I need to do," I whispered, standing.

"How do I become the witch? I need to stop my dream from happening."

"Stop it?"

Ice slipped through my stomach. "Wh-what?"

"You cannot change dreams," she said, shrinking away from me. "And the Roe witch cannot be murdered."

"But—" I choked on the word, a tremble working through my body. "I *know*. That's why I came back to you now; that's why I need to know how to use my magic."

"No, no..." She squinted at me as though in pain, her hands reaching up to claw at her chest. "No one can kill the Roe witch," she whispered.

"Yes, Granma, yes, I know, I know!"

But she shook her head and closed her eyes. I saw a tear slide from beneath her short lashes, but when she opened her eyes to look at me again, her expression was blank, cold.

"No, you do not understand," she said, and her words were like stones, thudding from her mouth. "Dreams don't change. The future doesn't change. The witch cannot be killed. Teaching you how to unlock your magic will not save you. You are destined to die, not become the witch."

Falling. I was falling, and I had to step back and grab the wall to keep steady.

"But I returned to you," I whispered.

"It is too late."

"I'm here now. Help me stop it."

"It cannot be stopped."

"I was born for this. I can tell dreams. I have magic inside of me."

"Not enough. You do not know how to make spells and I cannot teach you if you're going to die. You will never be the witch."

My mind reeled. I couldn't speak. I couldn't breathe. I couldn't stand and I dropped to the ground and crawled, crawled like a dog, to my grandmother's feet.

"How could you do this to me?" I asked, choking on the words. She turned, looking at me down her nose as though I were a worm—an ugly, worthless thing and not her own flesh and blood.

"Me? What did I do?" she growled. "What did I do but wait for my granddaughter to return to me? If you had come sooner, before this *dream*—" She made a choking sound of disgust.

I was crying now, silent tears rolling down my face, catching at my lips. "You never came for me! You let her take me!"

"I put my faith in a girl who was supposed to be the witch!" Her face twisted, revulsion and rage sitting in her wrinkles. "How many nights did I lie awake, waiting for you? How many times did I have to assure myself that you would come? That you would use your skills and your gifts to break your mother's spell?"

I shook my head. "But you never told me how."

"And I shouldn't need to tell you how! Even without knowing spells, a real witch would have been back here in a fortnight, not crawling back four years too late, poisoned with a stranger's magic and marked for murder!"

My body curled in around itself, and I wept.

"Stop that," my grandmother said, sounding embarrassed. "Stop your crying."

I peered up at her through my fingers. "How can you be so cruel?"

"Cruel?" Her voice scaled with anger. *"Cruel?"*

She spread her hands out, showing off the sagging skin below her elbows, the joints swollen with arthritis.

"Look at me," she said. "Look at what I have become. And that is only the surface. On the inside, I am *rotting*." She bent low, bones snapping, and I had to turn away from the hot reek of her breath.

"Why do you think we only live short lives?" she whispered. "Look at what this life does to us!"

I turned away, unable to bear her anymore, but she grabbed my face tight between her ruined hands and forced my gaze up into her eyes, her eyes that seemed to look as young as my own, healthy and hale and inside a wasted shell.

"Pain," she hissed. "That is all I live with anymore, but I bore this pain for you. I bore it assured that when I went to my rest, the line would continue." She let go of me and stretched back up to her full height. "Cruel?" she asked, arching an eyebrow. "You cannot *know* my disappointment."

I had to press my hands to the ground to steady myself.

"Then stop my murder. Help me. What if I told my dream wrong, what if I couldn't understand...?"

"Do you think you were wrong?" she asked, and I said nothing. Her lip curled back and she jerked away, eyes on the table of herbs and dried grass. "No one can help you now."

She spoke her words with such careful lightness and yet they struck me like hammers. I wanted to scream and rage at her and beg her for help, but when I opened my mouth, I did none of that. Instead, I said the one thing that I had not allowed myself to think, not even once since I had my dream:

"I do not want to die."

A shiver vibrated through my grandmother's body, so strong and sudden I wondered if she would fall, but then she steadied herself and said nothing. I dropped my head and sat back on my heels. That was it. She couldn't help me, and there was nothing left for me to do.

"If I could," my grandmother said, her voice quavering, "I would feed you something that would give you an easy death."

But we both knew that she could do nothing of the sort.

"I would have trained you if you hadn't had that dream," she continued. "You would have been my successor."

"Please stop speaking," I said, my voice a little clearer than it had been. And underneath the mountain of grief and pain and confusion that threatened to crush me, I felt something: a cold, cruel realization that if there was nothing to be done, then nothing mattered anymore. It was freeing, but in the way that madness is freeing.

"Will you die soon?" I asked her, because to think of myself at that moment would have destroyed me. She jolted slightly, a spasm of pain crossing her face for just a moment.

"Yes," she whispered, and the word ached with longing. Her eyes lifted to the dark window in the far wall of the cottage, the window that, in the daytime, would show a view of the waves, and she tilted her head, just a bit, the way someone would when listening to particularly beautiful music. "Yes. I will go soon and it will all be over."

Over. All over. No more Roe witches.

I let them down.

I failed.

I rose to my feet, my legs so wobbly I wasn't sure they would hold my weight. My grandmother turned to watch me. She looked angry. She looked uncertain. She reached out a hand—to steady me, I think—but after a moment pulled away. I repulsed her now, with my tattooed body, my strange magic, my destiny. And I wondered what had happened to the warm, soft woman who had raised me, if she had ever even existed.

"Be careful," my grandmother said, and I laughed. Who tells a girl about to be murdered that she must be careful? I turned to leave without another word, but she stopped me, placing one gnarled hand on my arm, her mouth twisting into a frown of displeasure.

"Be careful of that boy," she said, searching my face with hard eyes. "He might hurt you."

I jerked away from her as anger rose through the layers of

numbness within me. "How dare you?" My words hissed out of me, sputtering like steam. "How dare you accuse anyone of *hurting* me? He cares for me. More than you would ever know."

My grandmother drew her hands up close to her chest, clutching the fabric just over her heart. She seemed to grow smaller, weaker before my eyes—her skin losing its color, her gray hair turning lank and wispy—and her expression took on such sadness, such ache, that I wondered if, finally, she felt some remorse for what had happened to me.

But she just closed her eyes and said softly, almost to herself, "Yes. That is what I am worried about."

I stared at her for a long time, so long that it looked like her body no longer lived or breathed but had dried into an empty husk. And when I thought she might have gone, right then and there, she turned away, eyes closed, the air in the cottage dusty and still.

She had rejected me. I would never be the witch. And she wouldn't even watch me go.

I swallowed the choke inside of me and opened the cottage door to the pale dawn.

Sixteen

ONE FOOT IN FRONT OF THE OTHER, I LEFT the cottage, my muscles cold and stiff as though my body had already turned corpselike. Tane leaned against a wall of the cottage, just outside one of the windows, and as my eyes found his, I knew he had heard everything.

I will be murdered.

My grandmother cannot help me.

I will never be a witch.

I didn't know whether to be angry or relieved. I didn't know whether to cry or collapse. And Tane didn't move, didn't speak, waiting for me to break the silence. Finally, I opened my mouth and said the first thing that came to mind:

"I forgot your lantern."

It was as though I'd released a dam, and I felt my whole

body crumple, a sob racking, tearing through me, but Tane rushed at me, rushed at me and wrapped one of his large, callused hands over my mouth and said, "Shh, shh, not here. Not where she can hear you."

He gathered me up in his arms and pressed my face to his chest, carrying me down the path, away from the cottage and toward the beach. Each held-in sob stabbed at me, clawing to get out, but Tane was right: I wouldn't cry and let my grandmother listen.

When we hit the water, I gasped, the icy shock stinging and reviving. And then I was under the water, under the waves, and I could finally scream in peace, the sound muffled and softened but still real in my ears. My body tingled with the cold water, the cold air, but I dived deeper, opening my mouth to taste the bitter ocean. I drank it in, as much as my stomach could hold, and it didn't choke me, it didn't make me sick.

I don't know how long I stayed under the water, letting myself float, letting the waves sway my body back and forth as if I were nothing but a caught piece of sea grass. A long time, I suppose. From far away, I heard something—a shout—and then Tane's hand was on my skin and I was coughing, sputtering up the sea, which suddenly seemed to burn me from the inside out. He was saying something to me but I couldn't understand him, and finally he placed his warm hands on my shoulders and pulled me, so gently, from the waves.

"Time to go," he said softly, and I let him lead me away, let him strip off my sopping-wet clothes and wring them out and brush them free of sand. I felt hopeless, helpless; so it was a good thing, his babying me.

As the sun rose, turning the sky pale white, Tane dressed me, and I didn't even feel embarrassed to let him see me, shaking and shivering in my thin chemise. Lucy's boots were ruined, and he carefully pried them from my feet before knotting the laces together and swinging them over his shoulder.

"Where are we going?" I asked, my voice not more than a mew. Tane wove his fingers through mine and led me back up the beach, back to the rocky path.

"New Bishop," he said. I closed my eyes.

"I said I would never return."

He squeezed my hand. "And now you must."

We walked slowly, picking our way up the rocks as the rising sun stretched our shadows across our path. Without my boots I stumbled, and if not for Tane's solid weight beside me, I would have fallen more than once. It would take a long time to return to New Bishop and I knew, dimly, that it would be well into morning before we made it back. I could not slip back into my mother's house without her noticing. She would know I had run away.

I didn't care. If I could never be the witch and if I could never escape my fate, then I didn't care what happened. She had finally gotten what she always wanted: an end to the Roe witches. What more could she take from me? What else was there left in the world that I cared about?

But of course, there was something left to care about, and there he was at the end of my hand. I looked at him now, and with the sun throwing his features into relief, I could make out the expression on his face.

Determination.

"You can't do anything to stop my murder. You heard what my grandmother said."

"I heard everything she said." He spoke softly but carefully, as though he were making a threat. "That doesn't mean I believe it."

"You can't change my future."

"My people had spells that would keep you from murder. I'll give you another tattoo."

I stopped suddenly and our hands broke apart before he stopped and faced me.

"It won't do anything."

He lifted his chin and the light struck the high arches of his cheekbones, illuminating his entire face with a golden glow. "You don't know for certain unless you try."

"I *did* try," I said, and a sudden heat swept through me. "Why do you think I needed to see her so badly?"

"And she did nothing. Let me help. Let me at least—"

"No!" My voice echoed across the rocks as the ocean within me pitched and roiled. "Why can't you understand?

Why can't you see that there is nothing to do? Why do you still care to help me?"

I took a step forward, my hands tight in fists, but he didn't move. I wanted him to leave, I wanted him to get away, because my life was like a powder keg, rigged to explode, and I didn't want him near me anymore.

"What is it?" I asked. "What is it about me that you want to save? Do you think it will make you feel better? Do you think it will make up for leaving your people to be slaughtered?" I shook my head, heat radiating from my skin. "You think if you save me you will be released from your guilt—is that it? But I am not one of your people and you can no more save me than you can raise your sisters' bodies from the surf!"

My words seemed to fly from my mouth of their own accord, without first taking leave of my head or my heart, and I was too far gone now, an ocean of fury, and Tane was a rock, passive and solid and so, so still.

"Say something!" I shouted, and when he refused to move, I ran to him and beat my fists on his chest, wanting him to hurt, wanting him to shout back at me and turn away and forget about me. But if there are waves strong enough to crack rock, I have not seen them, and it was not long before my tide went out and I spun away from him, my shoulders rolled forward, my head down. "Go away," I whispered. "Please, please go away."

I stood there, shivering in my damp, salt-stiffened dress, and heard nothing, not Tane's breaths nor his footsteps.

Then, a light touch on my shoulder: his fingertips. Slowly, carefully, his fingers and then his hands and then his arms wrapped around me, pulled me until my back rested against his chest and his body formed around mine like a warm, sturdy cloak.

"I am not going to leave you," he whispered.

I shook my head, but I wasn't strong enough to pull away. "You can't stop it."

He drew in a ragged breath. "Maybe not. But I'm not ready to say good-bye to you yet."

We walked in silence after that. The sun climbed higher, drying my clothes salt-stiff, and still we said nothing, Tane's hand firmly around mine, our eyes set ahead for the first signs of New Bishop. There was so much to think about, and yet my mind failed to focus on anything beyond the feel of Tane's hand and the soft sand under my feet.

When the town came into view, he told me he would have to leave me, that it would draw too much attention for us to be seen together but that he would find me, he would figure something out to keep me safe.

"I'll keep you safe." That's what he said. I wanted to believe it was true, so I nodded.

"You wondered why I care for you," he said, holding my face between his palms. "It's because you're strong, stronger than anyone I've ever met. Be strong."

He kissed me, a kiss so sweet that it warmed all the parts of me that had grown cold on our long walk, and I closed my eyes and kissed him back, lacing my fingers behind his neck and holding on, and with my eyes closed and my mouth full of the taste of him and his hands pressing hard against me, I never wanted it to stop, I never wanted it to end. Shut the door and lock me away in that moment forever.

But it did end; he pulled away and handed me my boots and left me to walk through the streets of New Bishop alone.

I took the back ways; still, I drew more attention than I would have liked. I could feel that my hair had dried into a rat's nest of salt and sand, my clothing wrinkled and stained, my feet bloody and my eyes bloodshot. I passed the row of boardinghouses and met a group of sailors coming to bed after a night of carousing, and I heard one of them lean in to his friend and say, "Didn't Billy Macy say she'd escaped? What is she doing back here?"

Exhausted, I reached my mother's house and paused at the front gate. How little time had passed since I left it, vowing never to return, and yet how much had changed. The gate squeaked long and mournful as I pushed it, and I didn't even make it to the front door before it sprang open and my mother raced down the front steps.

"Avery!" she said, grabbing tightly on my arm. "Where have you been? Where did you go?"

With every word she shook me, scrambling my already frazzled wits, but when I tried to pull away she turned and yanked me back up the stairs and into the house. The floors shuddered as she slammed the door closed.

"I came in at sunrise to find your bed empty!" my mother said, her blue eyes vivid. Anger made her pale cheeks pink and her scar stand out, gruesome and savage. She had her hair up, dainty as a lady's, and wore one of Pastor Sever's favorite dresses: lavender with pale pink stripes. "Where were you?"

But I was too tired to yell back, too tired even to speak. "Nowhere," I mumbled, looking at her with half-closed eyes.

"What did you do?"

"Nothing." I tried to push past her but, fast as a whip, she grabbed my arm and dragged me back to her.

"Answer me!" She squeezed, her hand hot, nails digging into my skin like the teeth of a trap.

"Just let me go to sleep," I said. "Just let me go!"

I wrenched free and stumbled up the stairs, moving as fast as my feet would carry me. I heard my mother behind me, racing to catch me, shouting at me to stop, but the last bit of energy I'd managed to save forced me just ahead of her, pushing me on until I reached my room and slammed the door behind me.

"No!" my mother said, shoving inside. Her whole body heaved as she breathed great, gasping breaths, her finely dressed hair now wispy and lopsided. I ignored her and tossed the ruined boots into a corner before collapsing on the bed, but I had barely hit the mattress when she was upon me, dragging me back to my feet.

"Get off me!" I shrieked. "Get away!" Frantic, I tried to

wriggle from her grasp, but she did not let go until I stood before her.

"Answer me! Where were you? Who were you with?"

"Who do you think?" I spat back, and she blinked, her mouth dropping open.

"Why—how—" She blinked again, uncertain. "I told you never to see her! I told you it was forbidden!"

I turned away from her, not wanting her to see my tears.

"What happened?"

"Nothing," I whispered.

"What did she do to you?"

"Nothing!" I turned and screamed at her. "She did nothing! Nothing!"

My mother's face drew up tight and tense, studying me. "She rejected you," she said softly.

Her words sent waves of hurt over me, and I was tired, so tired, and although all I wanted to do was shut my mother out and fall asleep, my exhausted body seemed to spring back, fueled by anger and frustration and pure, steaming rage.

"Because of you!" I shouted, and I was a wild, raving, whirling thing. "Because of your curse! It took me too long to get back to her and now it's too late! I'll never be the witch!" I threw myself down on the bed, my temples throbbing, sobs racking me like a dry heave.

"Good."

I squinted up at my mother, all my bitterness curdling into hatred, but she just stared at me.

"I never understood why you want so badly to be the witch."

"You *wouldn't* understand."

My mother's mouth curled with anger. "Then explain it to me. You dislike half the people on this island, and yet it is your dream to devote your entire life to giving them spells and charms."

"Not giving," I said. "Selling."

"For pennies," my mother said, shaking her head.

"I was born for this. It's our tradition."

"As the person who gave birth to you, I can assure you, I did not bring you into the world to lock you up in a cottage at the end of nowhere." She breathed slowly and carefully through her nose, her eyes unblinking and unmoving. "As for tradition, I had already broken it."

"I have magic inside of me," I said, and this time my words lost their hard edge and I spoke with desperate pleading. "I can feel it all the time, begging to be used."

"And do you think it gets better once you tap into your power? You do." Her voice had grown very cold. "But it's a trade, don't you realize? The Roe witch has to lose something in order to gain her magic."

"What?" I whispered, trembling, because even if I was never going to be the witch, I wanted to *know*. "What do we have to give up? What do we have to sacrifice?"

She took a breath, her eyes hard with pain. "Love, Avery. Magic should protect the things we love, shouldn't it? But instead it takes them away."

I groaned, reaching my arms around my head as though I could block out her words. It was more of her nonsense, her cautionary tales and irrational worries.

"Enough!" I shouted, the word muffled against my pillow.

"You have to know!" my mother said, and she lifted her voice over my growl of frustration. "It's what we are, Avery, we're—"

"Stop it!"

"Sacrifice, Avery! I lost what was most important to me, and I'm trying to make sure you—"

"Stop it, stop it! I don't want to hear it anymore!"

"A curse—listen to me! We're cursed, and you can never be—"

"No!" I howled, leaping to my feet. "The only thing I can never be anymore is the witch, and it's your fault! It's all your fault!" Tears bubbled up through me, shook me, and although I did not want to cry like this in front of my mother, the wail of frustration and fear building inside finally burst out. I covered my face with my hands, my body shaking as I tried to choke back my crying, and when I looked up at my mother, I saw she was watching me, her features calm and still. And then—she smiled.

"*What?*"

"Do you see now?" she asked, and how did she compose herself so quickly? How did she tamp down and smooth over every little feeling in her body? "She's sent you away. She won't train you. I'm offering you something else, Avery," she said, and she leaned in. "Will you accept it now?"

My hands dropped from my face and I stared at her.

"Look." She reached into her pockets and pulled out half a dozen folded pieces of paper: letters. "Look at this. Oklahoma. Oregon. Texas. Churches all across the country, all offering positions to Pastor Sever. I've prepared for months, Avery. We can go at any time. All I must do is make him accept a position, and then we can leave."

I couldn't speak. I couldn't even breathe.

"We'll get away from this island," she whispered. "Forever. For good. We'll build a new life somewhere else, a better life. There's nothing here for you anymore, don't you see? But we can go away...."

Her voice lifted up, floated like a dream, but with every word, my nerves strained until my whole body stretched tight as a piano string. I didn't care what idyll my mother spun. Leave Prince Island? Leave the water? I could feel my heart wrench in two at the very thought. Maybe I would never be the witch, maybe I would soon be dead, but if I had to die, I wanted it to be here, in my home. I wanted my body to be a part of the ocean. Until I breathed no more, I wanted my lungs to fill with salt-scented air. I couldn't leave the island.

"No," I whispered, and I shook my head, said it louder. *"No."*

My mother's smile only grew, and she fanned the letters between her hands, held them out to me. "Take one. Take one and we can go."

Revulsion turned in my stomach, clawed up my throat, and when I didn't move, the papers in my mother's hands fluttered.

"Just—take one," she said, and still she smiled, but her expression had gone tight, the scar stretched painfully across her face, her eyes desperate. I looked down at the letters, shaking now, and my mother said softly, "This one? You want this one?"

Slowly, the letters dropped through her fingers, gliding to the floor until she held a single long envelope. She opened it, trembling, her smile waxen. "The mountains of Pennsylvania. We'll leave next week. Won't that be nice?"

Again, she held out the letter, and when I didn't move she reached forward, pressed the paper against the palm of my hand.

I wanted to shred the letter between my fingers, turn it to confetti and throw it back in her face, but all I could do was look down, stare at it, dumb. Words, lines jumped out at me, jumbled together: *cottage, river, your daughter, my son Joshua, amenable to the match, arrange the wedding, we are we can we look forward to meetingherreadythedayafteryouarriveahouseforthenewlyweds.*

My head swam. Exploding streaks of color floated before my eyes. I could no longer feel my legs, and a very small, very remote part of me wondered if I was going to collapse.

"You found me a husband," I said, and the words thudded from my mouth.

"You're going to be safe, Avery. You're going to be happy."

"You can't make me," I said, shaking my head. "You can't force me to leave and you can't force me to marry some stranger."

My mother suddenly looked very sad. "But I could force

you. If I wished." She took a breath, almost a gasp. "There is nothing for you here anymore. I am going to keep you safe."

For a moment, I could only stare at her, her plans, her dreams for my future, and then: A riot stirred inside of me, a mad explosion, and I was *laughing*. I laughed, my whole body shaking, my lungs stripped of air, I laughed until tears filled my eyes and my stomach cramped and my mother leaned over me, asking what was wrong, what was I *doing*, because it was so funny, so ridiculous—her thinking she could keep me safe when she did not know that soon I would be murdered!

"Avery! Avery!"

Oh, I wanted to tell her, bark it out at her that I was going to die, that there was nothing anywhere in the world she could do to stop it. I wanted to shatter all her careful certainty, reach into the bubble she had built around her hard as diamond, and tell her something she *would have to hear*.

I opened my mouth, but just as soon as it had started, the laughter died on my lips. What would she do if I told her? Maybe she wouldn't believe me; maybe she would think I was trying to fool her. Or maybe she would get scared and frightened and never mind one more week but run from the island *now*. And then I would never see Tane or hear his voice or touch him and I would go to my grave with only his memory to sustain me.

Close your mouth, Avery.
Say nothing of your dream.
Just get away.

"All right," I said. I could still feel hysterical tears on my cheeks. "This is what you want, isn't it? All right."

"Really?" She didn't move. "You'll do it?"

"Until we leave, my time is my own. You won't forbid me to leave the house anymore. You'll let me go anywhere on the island at any time I wish."

She held my gaze for a moment and then nodded, just once, and let out a breath I didn't realize she had held.

"This is for the best, Avery," she said. "It's just the beginning. A beautiful beginning."

One graceful white hand reached out to touch my cheek and I tensed, fighting the urge to bite her. And because I was going to die and because my skin and scalp burned with salt and because I just wanted her to leave me alone so I could blot out her words with sleep, I let her touch me and I said nothing.

Seventeen

WHEN MY DREAM WOKE ME AGAIN THAT
night, I didn't get scared; I didn't panic. I sat up and leaned my
forehead against my knees, eyes closed, breathing hard.

"I know," I whispered. "I know."

I pushed my hot, sweaty hair from my shoulders, cooling
my neck, and stretched out on the bed, staring up at the dark
ceiling. For the first time I thought, really thought, about what
it meant to be murdered.

All I had was questions. How would it be done? Would it
be quick? Would it hurt? And the biggest question of them all:
Who who who?

Was it someone I knew now? Faces ran through my mind:
sailors with lingering eyes, pinch-faced widows, boys from the
docks, the servants in the house, Pastor Sever, the step-beasts,

my mother, my grandmother. And...? I squeezed my eyes tight. And Tane.

My heart knocked against my chest, quick and quiet, as I remembered my grandmother's bony hand on my arm, the urgency in her warning, my mother's warnings. But Tane would never hurt me.

I pushed my fingertips into my temples, my eyes shut tight. I wished I could talk with someone about this, someone who wouldn't try to solve my problems or dismiss them but who knew just what to say to make me feel better. Someone like Tommy, who by now must be floating out on the *Eagle Wing* in the ocean, wondering if I'd forgotten about him.

I've told twenty-eight men that they were going to die. Twenty-eight. Sixteen died in the War Between the States, from bullets or infection or starvation. Seven died on the ocean (drowning is the most common way to go). Three met their ends from incurable maladies: burst heart, chewed-up lungs, swollen limbs. One went for a walk after having too much to drink, climbed the church bell tower, and thought he could fly. One took a harpoon through his throat.

For the first time, I wondered what they actually thought and did, hearing about their own deaths. Not just the foolish things, like picking up and moving out to the desert, but if they could feel their own hearts beating, like I do, ticking fast and loud like a watch about to wind down. Did they spend all their money? Did they hug their children? I had never really wondered, and now I wished I had tried to find out.

I did not know how much time I had remaining to me, but I knew it could not be very long. If I could not stop it, at least I could prepare for it. I could make sure that whenever and however I left this world, I didn't leave any loose ends behind.

"You look like a girl who keeps her promises," Tane had said, and hadn't I made a promise to him? I told Tane I would help him. I told him I would tell his dreams, and I clung to that promise like a drowning man holds fast to a bit of wreckage.

The lighthouse looked different in the daytime, its haunted, mysterious aura fading into the forlorn quality of an abandoned wreck, with paint peeling and curling from its skin like the scales of a lizard.

I pressed a hand against the door, squinting up its length and into the bright, clear sky. I'd been all over New Bishop looking for Tane, but he hadn't been at the docks or in the boardinghouse where he slept. The thought had even entered my mind that perhaps he'd left the island—and me—and now I stood outside the door of the lighthouse, the last place he could possibly be, and wondered if I wanted him to be inside or gone, gone away to live his life without the thought of my death looming over him.

The door squeaked and groaned as I opened it, and my heart squeezed tight to hear something from the lamp room: a hurried rustle. Carefully, I climbed to the top of the stairs, one hand trained on the side of the lighthouse, and I emerged in the lamp room to a dazzling view: the blue, blue, blue of the sky, the harbor, the flashing white sand, and Tane, red-eyed, tousle-haired, huddled over a stack of papers.

"Oh," he said, the tension leaving his face. "Avery."

His skin shone with sweat, his dark hair limp. It wasn't past morning and yet I could tell he'd been up in the lamp room for hours, probably since last night. Papers littered the floor, some balled up, others a mess of hurried notes and slashed lines. Slowly, I knelt down before him.

"When have you eaten?" I asked. "When did you last sleep?"

"I slept a bit, last night."

"Here? What have you been doing?"

He relaxed his body, lowering the papers he held back to the ground, and I could see they were crisscrossed with sharp, angular shapes that reminded me not of his drawings but of his tattoos. But unlike the tattoos, which fairly reeked with magic, these were just pictures, flat and blank.

I picked one up and traced my fingertips across the lines. He'd pressed hard with his pencil, the designs almost carved into the paper. Something faint rose up from the drawing to my skin, but it was so wispy, so weak.

"There are ways to beat this," he said. "There are spells, and I just need to remember them."

"You've been drawing all night?" I asked, and Tane took the paper from my hands. He pointed at one design, a pattern of tiny octagons arranged into a grid.

"That one prevents stabbing," he said. His eyes clouded over for a moment. "At least, I think it should."

"No," I said softly. "I don't think it means anything."

His face flashed with anger, flames flickering behind his eyes, and, with a cry of frustration, he crumpled the paper between his fists.

"This magic existed once!" he whispered. "If my father were here, he would know how to save you!" One of his hands beat against the floor, so hard that I jumped. "I can't make myself remember!"

"You were a little boy when you left," I said, struggling to keep my voice clear and calm. "You can't expect to carry all your people's knowledge."

He lifted his head and stared at me. "But that's it, isn't it? If not me, then who?"

Shaking his head, he gathered up his papers and slowly shuffled them. I could catch snippets of magic, frail as spider silk, broken, meaningless, and my stomach sank. Tattoos couldn't save me.

I knelt down next to him and put a hand through his dark, shaggy hair. "You need to rest," I said. "You have to take care of yourself."

He blinked as though dazed, and I could see how exhausted he truly was.

"I made you a promise," he mumbled.

"And I made *you* a promise," I said. I reached around him for his bag and pulled out his slim journal, the dream journal.

A thin piece of rope marked the page where we'd last stopped, and I could see we were only about halfway done. Months more of dreams to tell, hours more of work.

I fitted Tane's hands around the journal and looked into his eyes, those brown eyes that I would never tire of.

"There's still work to be done."

First, I made him sleep. He wouldn't tell me the last time he'd gotten a real rest, but I knew it had to have been some time before we made the trek to my grandmother's cottage, and he would go mad if he didn't get some good sleep. And food, too. While he rested, I slipped down the stairs and headed for town. I didn't have money, but the good thing about living on an island where everyone knows you and knows where to find you: The grocers are kind with credit.

Back in the lighthouse, I studied Tane's journal. Underneath the dreams I'd interpreted, Tane had added small notes, explaining what each dream meant. The vast majority had a single phrase: *no significance.*

Based on the dreams I'd told so far, it seemed as though his future was one big blank spot, as though nothing important would ever happen to him. That wasn't anything to worry about, not necessarily. Not everyone lives an exciting life, and I'd never heard of a person having more than one big, prophetic dream. Tane had already had that dream, and so there was a chance that he'd never have another one like it again, that for all his meticulous note-keeping, he'd never learn anything more exciting about his life than what he'd have for breakfast the next day or if he'd get a blister out walking.

Still, Tane meant to find the men who had slaughtered his people. He meant to hunt them down and kill them, one by one. And if that was in his future, it should be something I could see.

Closing the book, I let out a sigh and reached for another of Tane's journals, one of the sketchbooks. At first I thought I was wrong—the pages all seemed to be blank—when I caught a glimpse of something and opened the book to reveal a drawing of a girl.

Me.

He'd drawn a picture of me, only this was a me that I almost didn't recognize, my features exaggerated and distorted and transformed into something extraordinary, like all his sketches. In the picture, I was sitting in the shallows of the ocean, the waves eddying all around me, my hair like string hanging across my shoulders. Spray fanned out from my body, and water dripped from my hair, my cheeks, my mouth, which had fallen open in surprise or shock or just stillness. He'd drawn me looking away, a faraway stare that made me look like a little child, but my body was stiff in the water, tensed as though ready to spring, and the girl in the picture didn't look lost or broken or scared or—no, she looked all those things, but she also looked strong. It was the breath before the fight, the moment when a soldier, waiting for battle, lets his mind flit away to his family and friends and his own fragile life, but it's only a moment—and then he's ready to fight again.

I stared at the picture a long time and then, in one quick, quiet movement, tore the drawing from the book and put it in my pocket.

After glancing up to make sure Tane was still asleep, I continued paging through the journal until I stopped at a drawing of another girl. She had a fine, delicate nose, small with a bump near the end that made her look regal and beautiful. High, round cheekbones set off her eyes, and her mouth was curved into a smile. Next to her was written a single word in Tane's hand: *Tuahine*.

I frowned, not sure who this girl was, but as I tilted the book up toward the light, I realized I had seen her before. I had seen her bleeding, her mouth open, hair swimming around her as she lay motionless in the ocean. Tane's sister.

I turned the page and saw a man emerging from the water, rivulets streaming down his finely muscled, dark back, hair pulled up into a neat knot at the top of his skull, his body twisted and striding forward, fighting against the push of the waves. *Matua*, the note said, and opposite that page, next to a drawing of a woman bending low over a fire, her hair braided over a shoulder, *Whaea*.

I turned the pages, knowing what I would see: two more sisters, one laughing, reaching forward, the other lifting a large bird into the air. I saw mountains, trees stretching into a canopy overhead, a detailed image of a spearhead. And I pressed my hand to the page, my fingers feeling for the marks curving into the paper as though just by touching the drawings I could touch the people, the places they showed.

"I remembered more than I thought."

I glanced up to see Tane watching.

"You should be asleep," I said, because he couldn't have gotten more than four hours, but he just eased himself into a sitting position and shrugged.

"I'm all right," he said, and he held a hand out for the journal. When I gave it to him, he looked through the pages slowly, letting his eyes wander over them. "It's coming back to me, bit by bit."

"Good."

"Is it?" He looked up from the book. "Remembering them just makes me remember how much I've forgotten."

His hand traced the lines across the page, and I realized he had closed his eyes.

"My sisters used to sing songs to me, but I can't remember the music." His voice was quiet, thoughtful. "On special days, my mother would make a stew, something with fish and spices, and I know it was my favorite thing to eat, but I could not tell you what it tasted like. My people had songs, stories, jokes that I have forgotten. They had a language, their own language different from any other in the world, but other than a handful of common words, I can't speak it anymore. My father always told me: 'We keep the dead alive by keeping their memory alive.' But the only memory of them that exists, anywhere, is in this book." Gently, he placed a hand on the page before closing the journal.

"It is my fault that they were forgotten," he said, and he set down the book of drawings and leaned forward for the book of dreams. "But it is not my fault that they were taken away from me. I want to find the men responsible," he said, opening the book to the last dream. "I want to kill them."

"Tane, maybe this isn't..." But my words trailed off as I saw the determination in his eyes. And I had promised him.

"All right," I sighed. "All right."

Without another word, he began. His voice fell into a rhythm as he read, pausing only to eat a little of the food I had brought, and he showed no emotion even when we went pages without a dream meaning anything. An hour and a month of dreams later, we finally reached one that had some actual significance.

"Well?" he said when he finished, and I blushed.

"It means you're going to kiss the granddaughter of the witch of Prince Island," I said, and I couldn't help smiling. For just a moment, Tane looked disappointed that the dream wasn't helpful, and then the meaning sank in and he laughed and leaned forward to press his lips against mine.

"At least we know that one is true," he whispered, and he dropped the journal to the floor, one hand warm on my leg. Heat rose up within me as he pulled me closer, reaching his free hand up to brush my cheek, my ear, my neck, so exquisitely gentle that I had to bite back a moan. The hand on my leg arched up, pressing against my skin and sliding toward my hip, and his weight leaned into me, pushed me down to the gritty lamp room floor. I could feel my heart pulse through every inch of my body, and as we sank back I put out a hand to catch my balance.

"Oh!" I said, jerking my hand away. A half-inch bit of glass dug into the heel of my palm, and already blood welled up around the cut. I yanked out the shard and winced, pain rocketing up my arm.

"Are you all right?" Tane asked, reaching for my hand, but the moment his fingers touched my palm I shuddered and turned away.

"Fine, fine," I said, my heart racing. I looked at my cut, at the blood spilling from under my skin, and my head spun. Tane moved in like he was about to kiss me again, but as I closed my eyes an image sprang up behind my eyelids: Tane, leaning over to kiss a bloodied, broken corpse.

"No!" I spat out the word, and when Tane blinked at me, confused, I plastered a smile to my lips. "I mean, we aren't— we're not done yet. Keep reading."

I looked away and breathed slowly through my nose, urging my heart to slow, trying and failing to shake the image of my dead body from my mind. That was all I was now, just a walking corpse, not a girl to be kissed. Shudders rolled through me and I pressed my hand to my lips, rubbing hard to erase the feeling there.

"Please," I said, my voice tight. "Go on."

Tane stared at me for a moment, so long that I wondered if he would ask me what was wrong and what I would say in return. But finally, he picked up his journal and continued.

For the next several hours, we worked through the dreams, taking short breaks now and then so that Tane could drink some water or I could stand and stretch, my hands pushed against the small of my back. From our perch in the lamp room, we watched the sun cross the sky before turning the clouds orangey-pink. I knew we would have to stop soon, at least to quiet the grumbling hunger in my stomach, but we were so close to being finished. Already, we'd reached the entries Tane had written after he'd arrived on Prince Island. And still, nothing, nothing that hinted at his future.

"Last one," he said, his fingers hovering over the page. "I wrote this three days ago, the last time I dreamed." He glanced up at me and swallowed. I nodded.

"I'm swimming in the waters of New Bishop," he said, "and it's very hot."

I closed my eyes, my heart beating faster. I waited for him to finish, just to be sure, and when it was quiet again, so quiet I could hear the waves of the ocean, I opened my eyes. He was waiting, almost leaning forward, his face honest and open. I shook my head.

"Nothing?" he asked, his voice tight.

"You will go for a swim at night," I said. "That's what it means."

He let out a long, hitching breath. "I don't have any other dreams."

"I know."

"But then..." His knuckles turned white as he gripped the journal. "Why? Why didn't my dreams tell me anything?"

I shook my head. "I'm not sure, Tane."

His arm jerked out, throwing the journal hard against the window, which shuddered but didn't break.

"What does it mean?" he asked, both hands clenched into fists.

"I don't know. Perhaps it means nothing."

He stood up, staring out the window at the harbor, now purplish in the dying light. I could see he was thinking, his face still, his eyes far away.

"The shaman *told* me you would help. There's no chance..." He let his words linger, and I tried to ignore the sting.

"I didn't make any mistakes, Tane," I said. He glanced back at me before turning to the window.

"And if you saw something, anything about my future," he said, his voice quiet and careful, "you would have told me, right?"

"Of course."

His shoulders slumped and he turned around. His face looked like a deflated ball, stretched out and worn.

"I'm sorry," he said, shaking his head. "I didn't mean to accuse... I swore to find them, Avery. I swore to kill them."

"I know," I said, but he only shook his head more vigorously.

"No, you don't understand. I *need* to know. I need to. I need something worth doing with my life if you're going to—" He looked away suddenly, clamping his mouth shut.

"If I'm going to die?" I asked, my stomach flipping within me.

"I still believe I can help you." He took a deep, shaky breath. "But I lost it all once, Avery. And the only thing that kept me alive was knowing there were men out there who needed to pay for what they did."

"Revenge? Revenge is what you'd live for?"

He closed his eyes and took a breath. "I did once," he said, and when he opened his eyes again they were steady and clear. "And I will again, if that is all that remains for me."

I stood up slowly and ran a hand through his hair. "Maybe you aren't supposed to find them. Maybe revenge is not something worth living for."

"What, then?" he asked. But a girl about to die is not terribly well suited to answer a question like that.

"I promised myself that I would avenge their deaths," he said, letting out a sigh, and I thought of my own promise. We'd gone through all his dreams, true, but I still had a name. I still had a reputation. Half the men on this island owed my grandmother their lives and fortunes, even if the other half might hate her for lately withholding her magic. That had to be worth something.

"I'll find them," I whispered. "You said I'm supposed to help you and I promise you, I will."

He lifted his face and it settled so perfectly into the curve of my hand, but as his lips pressed against the cut in my palm, a blaze of pain arced through me, pain that had nothing to do with the throbbing under my skin, and I pulled away and left without another word, before he could even wonder if he should kiss me good-bye.

Eighteen

NEW BISHOP IS A SMALL TOWN TO HAVE
three bars, and although they are not as full or as happy as they
were back in the lush times, all three have survived. Actually,
they've more than survived—they rode out the dip in fortunes
better than half the businesses on Prince Island. The biggest
towns of our two sister islands, Martha's Vineyard and Nantucket, don't allow the sale of liquor, and sailors looking for a
drink anywhere on the islands find it easier to hop a ferry to
New Bishop for the evening than to try to make it to the mainland. And because sailors will sacrifice rent, clothing, and dinner for a good pint, the three bars continued their brisk trade.

This means two things. First: The Prince Island Ladies'
Temperance Union, which occasionally writes columns for the
Island Gazette about the ills of liquor, has had very little success

indeed. Second: If you want news on the dealings of any man or any boat that sails the open waters, there are no better places to start than the New Bishop bars.

Each has its own character and its own regulars. The Jug o' Molasses (named for its signature drink: molasses mixed with rum and boiling water) sits half a block north of the eastern end of Water Street, not far from the docks themselves. It is the busiest of the three, the one with the longest lines on payday and the one most favored by the dockhands. Boys getting their first pint head for the Jug o' Molasses, which has a tradition of letting the boy in question drink as much as he likes for free, so long as he manages to keep it all down. Because of this, mostly young, unmarried men favor the bar, moving in singing, dancing packs that spill out into the streets in the wee hours of the night.

If the Jug o' Molasses proves too busy or too loud for your business, the Mansion House Inn and Tavern might do the trick. The name isn't to be taken seriously: It is neither a mansion nor a house, and the only people who might call it an inn are the drunks who fall asleep on their barstools. It is, however, a tavern, set into the basement of a beautiful brick building in the quieter northwest part of New Bishop. Its ceiling has the low-down, smoke-stained character of a ship's berth, and perhaps for that reason it is the special favorite of captains and ship owners, men with a bit more money who don't need quite so much singing or dancing, just a dry, warm place to sit with a glass and tell fish tales.

The last bar, and certainly the least, is the Codfish. The Codfish is way to the west of New Bishop, almost out on the grasslands that separate the town from the Great Gray Slough. "As good as a 'Fish regular" is a common saying on the island, and it means, in short, not very good at all. The Codfish is a place for shady dealings, a place where you're as likely to get stabbed as to get drunk. But you'll never see Prince Island clear it out because it also has the only whorehouse anywhere on the cape.

Dozens of men crossed in and out of New Bishop's bars every day, and I knew if I had the time and the patience, I'd find the answers I looked for. I had patience, but I did not have the time, and so I needed to get moving.

I visited the Jug and Mansion House first, weaving through sailors' songs and conversations, slipping questions whenever I got a sympathetic eye. I had to be careful, because some of these boys knew Tane and I didn't want to let on that I was doing this for him, but it didn't matter how well I phrased my questions: Either no one knew about the massacre at Hovell Island or no one wanted to tell me.

But I did learn one thing that I was grateful to know: The captain of the *Modena* had just decided to ship out at the end of the week.

Tane would have to go with the crew. He'd signed a contract, the standard two years, and still had another year and a half owed. For a moment, I wondered if he would stay on the island, forget about his contract, but I dismissed the thought immediately. Green hands jumped ship all the time—whaling was not quite as romantic as mainlanders thought—but for career whale men, desertion was, simply, out of the question. Contract breakers, especially if they held important positions, especially if they were not white, earned a place on the whaling blacklists: long columns of names printed in the back pages of every whaling newspaper. "Tane—harpooner for the *Modena*," it would say. "Oath-breaker and savage. DO NOT HIRE." Those lists ruined men, and while some might be able to find employment elsewhere, there are few places indeed that would open their doors to a tattooed islander like him. If he ever wanted to work on a ship again, he would have to keep his contract.

Outside the Mansion House, I leaned against a fence and let the news sink into me.

My whole life, I'd thought I would grow up, become the witch, live in the cottage, and someday meet a man to give me a baby who would become the next Roe witch. The man didn't matter—that was what I'd always believed; men were simply a part of our job, meant for buying charms and procuring supplies and giving gifts, but not anything to take seriously. And they didn't own the cottage. They didn't own us.

"Why would I want a husband, my darling?" my grandmother would say, cupping her hands below my chin. "Why would I want a man to cook for and to darn socks for? What man in the world could ever hold a Roe witch? We belong to the water, my love, not any person."

But she was wrong. Because a part of me did belong to Tane. And a part of him belonged to me. I couldn't ever be the Roe witch or stop my own murder. I'd failed to take over for my grandmother and to continue the line, but part of me had thought that I would perhaps get to keep the boy.

Maybe he would break his contract, for me, and never mind the consequences. Maybe he wouldn't ever need to work again, because somehow I'd manage to stop my dream and prevent my death and unlock my magic, and the earnings of a witch were more than enough to keep two people fed and warm. Or maybe I wouldn't live very long or maybe my mother would take me away, but Tane would stay with me, until the end.

I didn't know what to think anymore. I wanted to collapse. I wanted to sleep. I wanted to lean against this fence for the rest of my life (however short). But instead, I reminded myself there was still one bar to check and still my promise to keep.

From the outside, the Codfish looked like a lovely two-story house that had gone to seed. Scraggly, unkempt grass choked the front lawn, and thin, ten-foot-high bushes strategically blocked the windows and made a narrow entry to the front door. The bushes stopped just short of the upper story, and someone had taken some thick black cloth and covered every window so that only a thin mix of rose-colored light and women's laughter could seep out.

It had to be close to midnight by the time I walked through the Codfish's door, yet it still felt as though it were darker inside the house than out on the street. A dim fire, more coals than flames, glowed in one corner, and the only other light in the room came from a handful of stubby candles stuck to windowsills and tabletops and from a greasy lantern above the bar.

I walked through the room, glancing at the unfamiliar men. Most sat silent, watching me, although a few bent over their drinks to talk in low, quick voices.

"Don't serve girls." The bartender—a thin, yellowy-pale man I didn't know—narrowed his eyes at me, not pausing as he wiped a cracked glass clean.

"I'm not here for...that," I said, and in this dark space, with so many unfriendly eyes, my voice came out squeaky and tense. I had just realized that for a girl who knows she's about to be murdered, a visit to the Codfish was terribly stupid.

The bartender paused in his cleaning and glanced up at the ceiling, the upstairs rooms. "Madame LaGrange een't in, and she don't do interviews at night. Come back in the morning."

Despite my fear, anger flared up inside of me. I'd never had a particularly high opinion of whores, mostly because some men (erroneously) believed that Roe women, in addition to selling their spells and magic, also sold their bodies.

"I'm here for information," I said, and, figuring my name was the only real bargaining chip I had here, I added, "I'm Avery Roe."

"Avery...*Roe?*" the bartender asked, leaning in closer. "Your grandmother's the witch?"

I nodded and my heartbeat quickened as the bartender's eyes widened and the men sitting behind me hushed.

"You know, I went to her two years ago, askin' for a luck charm," the bartender said, his chin tilted up so that he stared down at me, appraising. "She turned me away. Weren't two months later I got my hand caught in a winch." Slowly, he drew his arm from the glass and shook off the rag. His wrist ended in nothing but a stump, the skin shiny and stretched red.

"Quite liked my hand," the bartender said, his voice low and gruff. "Dead useful for shippin'. Necessary, really, 'cause I een't had a job on a whale ship since the day I lost it."

His good hand snapped out and grabbed my arm, and I gasped, pulling away, but it was as though his fingers had turned to unyielding steel.

"I always said I'd make that witch pay," he said, yanking me so close I could smell the sour odor on his skin. "But she's got spells against that, don' she? Got any spells on you?"

His fingernails clawed into my arm, almost lifting me from the ground, when a voice said, "Let her go, Leewin."

The bartender's eyes focused behind me, and I heard a noise, a series of crisp, mechanical clicks: the hammer of a gun slowly being cocked. The steel fingers released and I backed away, rubbing my sore arm. A man stood behind me, straight and slim as a blade, a silver-bright pistol hanging loosely from his right hand and his eyes on the bartender. He glanced at me and sat down at an empty table.

"Why don't you join me," he said, waving his gun at a spare chair. "I've got no grudge against witches."

I could feel my eyes widen, every nerve on high alert. I wanted to turn tail and run out the door and forget the Codfish ever existed, and I certainly did not want to sit down with some shadow-faced stranger who carried a gun and seemed raring to use it.

This is for Tane, I reminded myself. *Do it for him.*

And after a few anxious seconds, I pulled the chair out and sat down.

In the flickering light of the table's candle, I studied the man across from me. He had shagging black hair, green eyes like lit coals, fine cheekbones darkened by a few days without a razor, and when he lifted his hands to light himself a cigarette, I noticed that his knuckles were red and raw, torn open as though he'd just done some fighting.

"I'm Avery Roe," I said, and I licked my lips, nervous. "Who are you?"

The man smiled.

"No names, girl," he said, wagging a finger at me, and from some other table I heard a quiet, scoffing chuckle. "I'm nothing but a humble businessman."

A smuggler, no doubt. During the war, many of our sailors discovered that their knowledge of boats and sailing could be put to use smuggling goods through the naval blockades, and even though the war stopped, the smuggling didn't. Few returned to do trade on the island, as the risk of being recognized was too high, and at first I thought this man was an outsider, a seagull. He looked the part, at least, with his bright eyes and fine features, but he spoke with a lilt as familiar to me as the sound of waves.

"You're from Prince Island," I said, and it wasn't a question. The man gave me another sly, slow smile.

"I lived here when I was young," he said. "I knew your mother, before her...accident. She was the prettiest girl in New England." He took a long drag on his cigarette, studying me, and his face had the soft, wistful look of a much younger man. I wondered if he was one of the many who had fallen in love with her. "You know," he said, tilting his head at me, "you don't look much like her."

When I frowned, he laughed. "What is it you're looking for?"

"Information," I said, leaning forward. "Less than a year ago, a boat of sailors landed on a little island in the South Pacific. Hovell Island. They killed the tribe that lived there. I want to find out more about them."

"The tribe?"

"The sailors."

"What for?"

"What do you mean, what for? They killed innocent people."

The man pushed back in his chair, rolling his eyes.

"Savages. What do you care for them? You're not one of those girls always going on about social reform, are you? What'll you do? Organize a ladies' march? A protest in the town square?"

I took a deep breath through my nose. "Those savages, as you call them, were slaughtered. All of them—the old and women and babies. They were murdered and their bodies thrown into the sea."

"A tragedy, sure, but what of the boys who did it?" the man asked, shrugging. "You're going to bring them to justice?"

I paused, considering. "Something like that."

The man studied me, the lit end of his cigarette glowing red in the darkness. "You've never been on a whale ship before."

"No. Of course not."

"You don't know what it's like." He rubbed his chapped and scabbed knuckles. "The time when a man could feed his family on greasy earnings is coming to an end. Sure, they say look up north, up in the Arctic, and maybe there'll be whales there, and then you get ships trapped in ice. There are whalers now that make it back to port as clean as the day they sailed. Ever wonder what happens to a man who spends three years hunting something that doesn't exist? He goes a little mad out on the ocean. He gets a little desperate. Maybe he gets a little drunk, too. I'm not excusing what they did, and a whale hunter'd rather kill whales, but if he's pressed hard enough, he might use his harpoon any way he can."

A note of accusation hung from his words and I leaned back in my chair.

"That is not my fault," I said evenly, and the smuggler shrugged.

"Never said it was."

I glanced around at the other men in the bar, many of whom had stopped their conversations to listen to ours, their faces hard with deep-seated anger.

"You would be in the minority, then," I said, dropping my voice low.

The man followed my gaze to the stone-faced listeners, but when his eyes settled on them, they turned away, focusing again on their drinks.

"Well, I'm not a whale man, then, am I?" the man said. "They think your grandmother's to blame for their bad luck, but she's simply an excuse." He leaned in and looked over at the bartender, pouring a drink with his head down.

"Look at Leewin, there," he said softly. "Fool lost his hand in a winch and blames your grandmother. But where was his head when the mate explained how to use the winch?" He lifted his shoulders into a slow shrug. "Your grandmother's charms made folks comfy and lazy, and even if it's a rude awakening now, they can't stay asleep forever. And besides, you want to know the real reasons why you can't make money in whaling anymore?" He pointed a long, scabbed finger in my face. "Too few ships and too few whales. Unless your grandmother can make a spell to call the whales out of hiding, her magic een't good for nothing. And anyway, even if she could, whale oil won't matter much, not in a few more years."

"Why not?"

He glanced around at the other men again and reached into his coat, retrieving a small vial filled with a clear, runny liquid.

"Know what this is, girl?"

I wrinkled my nose and said the first thing to enter my mind: "It looks like . . . liquor."

The man laughed. "Not quite," he said, caressing the vial. "It's kerosene. And it's going to kill off whaling."

My eyes narrowed. I'd heard of kerosene. You could use it to heat a home. You could use it to cook with. It burned brighter and cleaner than whale oil, and that meant it was something that most of the people on Prince Island hated.

"You sell it," I said, and again, it wasn't a question. The man tucked the vial back into his coat pocket.

"And with a lot of success, too. Kerosene's forty cents a gallon. Know how much whale oil costs?"

I didn't.

"Fifty-one cents. And while kerosene only gets cheaper to make, whales only get harder to find. Mark my words: In a decade, you'll be able to buy five times as much kerosene as whale oil for the same price. In two decades, no one will care anything for whale oil. The folks of this island had better understand that."

I stared at him for a long time as he lifted his cigarette to his lips again. "They will still blame my grandmother," I said.

The man tilted back, balancing on two legs of his chair.

"What you need to watch is who they'll blame when your grandmother een't around."

He dropped forward, the front legs of his chair landing with a thud on the floor.

"I can't help you with your murdering sailors," the man said. "But maybe you'd best let it go. Folks don't like their business getting poked around in, and I'll bet more men than you'd care to imagine have gone a little crazy out on the sea."

He couldn't help me. I wished he'd just said that from the beginning. I pushed myself to my feet and headed for the door, prepared to leave, when I felt his hand around my wrist.

"I always liked your mother," he said, narrowing his eyes at me. "So on her account, let me give you some advice. This island will see hard times soon, and it's no place for a smart girl like you."

"It's my home," I said, glaring at him, and for a moment, the fingers at my wrist tightened, hard, before releasing.

"You'll find other homes," he said, "where you can walk the street and half the people don't know all your business. Home's just a place to make a future." His eyes lingered over my face. "And there's no future here for a witch."

Nineteen

THE NEXT DAY, I WALKED DOWN TO THE
docks in the early evening, my nerves jangly and electric. All
through dinner I'd had to sit and listen to the pastor discuss
his new church and the work he'd do out in the mountains.
Every now and then he'd turn to me, his high voice imperious,
as though just by addressing me at the table he had done me a
favor. My mother had assured him that, away from the water, I
would be quiet, obedient, a sweet and humble little wife to the
dull Joshua, and Pastor Sever could not help but explain just
how lucky I was.

When he'd asked me if I looked forward to my wedding
and change of address, I told him, with more honesty than
he could have guessed, that I sincerely hoped to be murdered
before either of those two happy events.

The pastor blinked at me in shock before slamming down his glass so hard that it shattered, little pieces flying like shrapnel. Tiny Hazel burst into tears, and even the terrible Walt moaned a bit. My mother, like the good wife I hoped I'd never become, calmly called one of the maids to collect the jagged glass while her husband barked that he'd had enough, and didn't my mother realize that I was a menace, impossible, and "a mess, always a mess with this girl, causing trouble and ruining my name and I am sick of your excuses for her behavior!"

And that was it. I rose from the table without a word and left the house, followed by the pastor's shouts but (thankfully) not the pastor himself.

Now I paced Main Dock, shaking off the memory of my mother's husband, looking for the golden prow of the *Modena* among the bottle-brown schooners and rusted fishing boats. I found her at the end of one of the piers, the ship farthest out in the water, her deck littered with empty barrels and busy workers.

There could be no doubt that the *Modena* readied for a long journey, for she was scrubbed clean, hull to deck, and even her tattered sails had been replaced with pure, fresh canvas. Half a dozen men climbed her rigging, stringing the ropes that made up the veins of the ship, and it was there, at the very top of the mainmast, that Tane sat, legs swinging over the spar as though he were on a kitchen stool and not three stories up in the air.

I paused, watching him work. He held a length of rope in his hands and gently eased it through a pulley before dropping it down to a sailor waiting on the main deck. It made me dizzy, staring up at him so high above the ship's deck that a fall would have killed him in an instant. (Indeed, green hands so often feared a tumble from the rigging that my grandmother created a special charm against it.)

But I knew he would never fall. He moved with the ease and the grace that came from years aboard a ship, and even from my spot far below on the docks, I could see his muscles relax against the whaler's gentle swaying like a baby in a cradle. After a moment, he paused from his work, looking up past the mast and out onto the horizon. Light from the setting sun struck his back, casting his face into shadow, but I could just make out his eyes, open and steady, and the calmness and peace that came from sitting at the top of the world with nothing but sky above and before you.

He belonged there. The thought made me shiver. He belonged on a ship as surely as I belonged on my island. I felt the same way I did the first time my grandmother took me out on a boat deep into the ocean and I stretched my hand down and touched the rubbery-soft skin of a dolphin, thrilled and terrified and humbled all at once to see a creature so perfectly in its element.

Was that it?

Was that the moment when I fell in love with him?

I think it must have been. I stood, dizzy and dazed, at the edge of the docks and stared up at a boy staring out at the world and felt my heart thump inside of me, happy and sad and grateful and angry, all of it, all at once.

Oh, I was such a sorry fool.

How could I ever think, even without his contract, even without consequences, that he could stay on this island with me? No matter if I became the witch or defied my mother and my dream—Tane might have belonged to me but he was meant for water, and I could no more keep him here than I could willingly leave my home.

I closed my eyes and saw him there on the inside of my eyelids, suspended and perfect, and I had to let him go. If this thing that sparked inside of me really was love, I had to let him go.

The church bells rang seven o'clock, and Tane turned, his face and body crimson from the sunset, and dropped through the rigging like a spider in her web. One of his mates said something to him and he smiled and laughed before noticing me, and I felt a tug of guilt to see how quickly the smile slipped from his face. He walked over to me, and I appreciated that he didn't say anything, that he didn't ask if anything was wrong (because, of course, everything, everything was wrong).

"Tane," I said, and I glanced toward the beach that stretched north. "Care for a walk?"

He didn't answer except to keep to my side when I turned and walked back down the pier, across the dock, up the stairs, and out to the beach.

I could feel the heat of the sand through my flimsy slippers, and I stumbled, my balance uncertain, but when Tane reached out an arm to steady me, I instead pulled away, pulled myself up to my full height, my hands balled into fists at my side, my heart vibrating in my chest.

"Avery," he said, and I shook my head, walking more quickly now down to the hard-packed wet sand.

"You want to help me," I said, my eyes on the water, which had turned deep turquoise in the setting sun. "Will you do something for me?"

"Of course."

I glanced at him. "Do you promise?"

He stared back, and I could tell he was careful to keep his face blank. "No. I won't promise a thing that I don't know."

"The *Modena* sets sail in less than a week." I stopped walking to turn and look at him. "I would like you to go with her. I would like you to do that for me."

But he already shook his head, almost angry. "I won't go. I won't leave you."

"You signed a contract. You know what will happen if you break it."

"I don't care what they say about me," he said softly, and a little firecracker of anger exploded inside of me.

"That's your *reputation*, Tane. Your *name*. It's what gives you a job and keeps you fed and clothed and you can't ruin it! Who would ever employ you if not as a harpooner? You would give up your life and your future and for what?"

His hand slipped around mine. "I'm not going to leave you until we stop your dream," he said, but I pulled away, my heart beating fast.

"And even if I'm not murdered, what then?" I choked on my words, my whole body shaking while he stood with his feet planted, his body still. "This isn't your home, Tane; you'd hate it just as you hated your own island once."

My vision blurred and I turned away from him. Already the sun had slipped below the roofs of New Bishop, and the sand at my feet and the air in my lungs had chilled. I felt like an icy, unreal thing at the edge of the water, and when Tane reached his hands and then his arms around my body, the warmth of his skin was so sweet that I couldn't even fight him.

"Come with me, then," he whispered. "Leave with me."

I closed my eyes and leaned back against him, his words slipping inside of me to settle within my chest. *Come with me.* Those words meant safety and warmth and all I had to do was say yes. All I had to do was abandon my life and my home and leave.

But no Roe woman had ever left Prince Island since the first one had made it her home, not even my mother. The island sang to us Roe women the low, intoxicating music of waves and wind, and even as I thought about leaving and about Tane's strong arms, a deep, forceful wrench within my bones had already decided for me. This was my home. I would not leave, not even for him.

"I can't," I said, and I stepped forward, loosening Tane's hands from around my chest. I turned around to face him. "I can't leave the island."

He shook his head, his face dark. "There's a world out there, Avery. You can't even imagine how much you're missing.

When will you realize an island is nothing but a walled-up room?"

"What kind of a home doesn't have walls?" I asked, and he turned and walked down to the water, not stopping until the waves lapped at the top of his boots.

"I've heard rumors," he said, looking out at the dark horizon. "Men around the docks say Pastor Sever has accepted a new job, out in the mountains of Pennsylvania. They say he means to take his whole family with him." He glanced back at me. "Does that include you, witch girl?"

"He's not my family. But my mother intends for me to go."

"And you won't go with me, but you'll go with her?"

"Not willingly."

"Still. If you must leave, come with me."

I took a breath and wished I could tell him yes. I wished it was that easy, but I could see it, see myself standing at the docks, ready to board a whaler but forever unable to take that last step.

"I can't," I breathed, a panicked ache rising in my chest. "I can't ever decide to leave the island. If you want me to come with you, you would have to be like my mother and use magic or chains to take me. And I would hate you for it."

He stared at me, unblinking. In another moment the tide would swallow up his boots, but he didn't move, his body still as stone.

"So you would have me leave," he said. "You refuse to

come with me and will not have me stay, and even if I did, your mother will take you away from me."

"Yes."

"And all the while, your death grows closer and there is nothing I can do to stop it."

"Yes."

"Whether by the *Modena*'s departure or your mother's doings or your own death, we will have to part," he said, his voice so soft that I had to lean in to hear him above the rush of the waves.

I took a breath. "Yes."

His footsteps splashed in the water as he took two quick steps closer to me. "Then for as long as I can, I won't leave you."

"No. We can't, we...Tane, we should say good-bye now, on our own terms, before we're made to. That's what I wanted to tell you."

"Good-bye?" he asked, raising an eyebrow. "Why? What are you scared of? That I'll forget you?"

I could feel my mouth pinch into a miserable frown. "No. That you'll remember me."

He blinked, surprised.

"Someday you'll find out that I'm dead," I said, and I swallowed hard. "News will reach you, wherever you are, that the Roe girl on Prince Island was killed, and then what will you do? Will you stop everything and hunt down my murderer?"

"Is that what you want me to do?"

"No! No, of course not!" I shook my head. "I don't want you to think of me like that. I'm your friend, just your friend, Tane, and when friends die it's sad, but you don't...it isn't...When you think of me, I don't want you to think of revenge. I won't be responsible for turning you back into a ghost. I won't have you regret me."

He lifted a hand to my face, and this time I squeezed my eyes tight but didn't move.

"Avery. Open your eyes."

But I didn't want to look at him. I didn't want him to be real to me, not anymore, not now that I could never have him. Still. I opened my eyes and found him watching me, felt his palms against my cheeks, his breath against my lips, and it was as though I'd been swimming for miles, fighting a current and kicking for the shore, and had suddenly found an island where I could rest, just for a moment.

"I do not regret my sisters or my father or my mother," he said. "If I could erase the pain I felt at their deaths by erasing the memories I have of them, I would not do it. These days with you have meant more to me than anything else in my life. For the first time in a very long time, I can breathe again. Food tastes good. I go to sleep thinking about you, and I wake up with your name on my lips. It's like a gift, Avery. I do not regret meeting you, not even knowing that I'll lose you, not even if it is certain to bring me more pain. No matter what happens, I will always remember you. Do you understand what I'm saying?" He spoke so softly. "I love you. I do not regret that."

"And what happens when I die?" I whispered, my voice shaky, and the lines in his face grew deep as he swallowed hard.

"What is it you want me to do?"

"Say good-bye now. Before we're forced to." The words had barely left my lips before he shook his head. "Then at least, when I die...when I die...when you hear why and how and who...Let it go, Tane."

"Let it go?"

"You think you're doing something good with your revenge, making up for something, making up for injustice. But you wouldn't honor me. And you wouldn't save me. Give yourself a good life. That's what you could do for me," I said, and his breathing grew short and he looked away, but I grabbed his hands and pulled him back to me. "*Listen.* Please. See the world and sail and find new things to be happy about. Find another girl. Fall in love again and have babies. If you can promise me anything, promise me that.

"And...and give up chasing those men. Your sisters, your parents...I don't think they would have wanted you to carry their deaths with them, either."

But he was already pulling away from me. "No, I—I *have* to. They were murdered, Avery, don't you understand? I can't just let those men, I can't—"

"Tane, please!" I said, and I squeezed his hands so hard I could feel my nails dig into his skin like claws, and when he let out breath that sounded like a gasp, I didn't know what had hurt him more: my nails or my words.

"*Please*," I said, and the word was softer now even though I could feel my heart pounding and my head spinning because I had to save him, I had to do this for him, and if I couldn't live, then he would have to do it for both of us.

When he tilted his chin back down to my face, I wasn't sure what he would say or do. I knew he carried guilt and pain and fear within him, carried it on his skin as surely and as permanently as his tattoos, and now I had asked him to throw it all away, forget about it, find something new to sustain himself. His fingers searched my face, light as a breeze, running over my eyebrows, my cheeks, my lips.

"All right," he whispered. "All right."

"You promise?"

He lifted his hands, his long, strong fingers fanned out to show me they weren't crossed. "Promise. But you have to promise me something, too."

My heart thudded in my chest. "What?"

"Don't leave me tonight."

And here was the tricky part. Because I knew then that Tane would survive my death, no matter what happened tonight. He would be shaken, maybe, and sad, but he was strong, he was made to weather rough storms and emerge with slit sails and frayed ropes but a hull sturdy and intact. But I was not so certain of my own seaworthiness.

I thought then of my mother. I thought of my grandmother. I thought of all the Roe women who had never married, who had found a man to give them babies, and I wondered if they ever thought of their men again. I wondered if they loved their men, if they had the strength to fall in love and then forget them. Did they know, I wondered, did they know what I knew now? That to love someone, no matter what happened, meant carrying them with you forever?

"Avery."

He called me back to him, steady and sure, but there was a question in his voice. I could turn away from him then, and he wouldn't follow me. I could tell him good-bye now and be done with it and remove the temptation to never let him go. I could do it. I could.

But I didn't.

I reached for him—hands and heart and body and soul— and he kissed me. He kissed me, kissed me, kissed the breath from my lungs so that I had to pull away, gasping for air and for him.

"I love you," I whispered, and I said it again, whispered it against the hollow of his throat, "I love you, I love you, I love you. . . ."

He pulled me, so gently, down onto the sand, cold now that the sun had gone away, and as the stars pricked their lights above our heads we lay side by side and I mapped with my fingertips the constellation of tattoos across his body. He closed his eyes, pressing his face against the pulse at my neck, breathing hard with pleasure, and it was as though my happiness rebounded, redoubled upon itself, a force so sudden and sweeping that I wondered, dizzy, if we had created a new kind of magic, a synergy, something just ours that sprang from the tattoos on his skin and the wild force within me to envelop us both.

His fingers and hands pressed against me, down my bare arms, across my neck, my shoulders, my chest, while my ears filled with the sounds of my name and of his breaths like waves. There's an ocean inside us all, and I put my hand to his chest and felt the current there, closed my eyes and held my breath and let myself get lost at sea as he whispered to me, just once, words that all together were an invocation, a reminder, a dare, a prayer, a promise:

Never regret, Avery. Never regret.

Twenty

I CARRIED MYSELF SLOWLY BACK THROUGH
the gray streets of New Bishop, and although I knew I should
be exhausted, hungry, instead I felt electric, as though within
me something glowed and burned, warming my cheeks, my
stomach.

The sun rose, a lump of orange melting over the slate-blue
clouds, turning the streets warm and alive. The working men
of New Bishop, the sailors and shopkeepers, would already
be awake and out on the streets, but here, up lighthouse in
the high-class neighborhood, the homes stood silent, and so I
walked back to my mother's house alone and unwatched.

Or not entirely alone, for when I breathed in, I could smell
Tane on my skin and my clothes, and my lips felt raw with the
memory of him; and his voice, his quiet breathing filled my

ears, even though I had left him still sleeping down on the cold sand.

The farther away I got from the beach, the more I felt the night before strain at my muscles and pull at my eyelids. Although Tane had slept, I stayed awake. I didn't want to fall asleep and dream of my murder and jerk awake, crying. Not that night.

So during the long night hours I stared up at the skies and breathed in and out the cold night air. And I was delighted to discover that the angles of Tane's shoulders and ribs and hips fit just exactly against my body. He rested his head on my chest, his face tilted up at me so that when I looked down, I could examine his fine fringe of eyelashes, his straight, dark eyebrows, the perfect contours of his face. Sometimes he would move, turn, a frown crossing his lips before he reached out for me again, pulling me closer even in his sleep while I held my breath and my heart drummed out a beat of pure happiness.

I hoped he would understand why I left, and I hoped he knew I would return to him. But I needed to eat and sleep and wash the sand from my hair. I wasn't free from my mother yet. I would have to make an appearance or risk her seeking me out.

When I opened the front door, I almost expected her to leap out, eyes wild, but the front hall was empty. So too was the little parlor just off to the left, and I picked my way carefully down the hall toward the back staircase that led to the kitchens. A noise from the dining room startled me, and although it was too early for breakfast, there my mother sat, skin as fresh as a white rose, her long hands wrapped around a fragile, pale teacup.

She said nothing, staring at me with her black eyebrows arched delicately above her eyes, and tapped a finger gently on the table. She wanted me to sit down, but instead I stood just inside the doorframe, my muscles tense and my eyes narrowed.

"Where did you go last night?" she asked, her voice slightly scratchy, and I noticed that she wore the same dress as the day before. Had she really sat there since dinner?

"Out," I said, and a muscle in her face twitched.

"That's not safe, Avery. I didn't give you permission to leave this house just so you could wander around alone at night."

Apologize. The little voice whispered in my head. *Say you're sorry and then you can leave her.* But I didn't want to lie about Tane. I didn't want to think of him as something bad, something to be ashamed of and kept secret. My mother might be scared to get close to anyone, but I was going to die soon, and I needed her to understand this: I had found someone caring and wonderful who loved me, all of me.

I lifted my chin. "I wasn't alone."

In the silence, I realized she had stopped breathing, her face very white. "What?" she asked softly.

"I wasn't alone. I was with someone." I swallowed and took another breath. "A boy."

A crash resounded through the room as my mother's teacup smashed to the floor. She had jumped to her feet, fingertips tense against the tabletop, poised like an animal about to spring.

"I'm not going to hide him," I said, fighting the quaver in my voice. "I don't care what you think about him. I love him and—"

My mother leaped for me, and before I could move she had her hand wrapped around my arm.

"Love him! How? When? Avery, *what did you do*?" With every word, she shook me hard enough to rattle my teeth.

"I didn't do anything wrong!" I cried, but she ignored me, yanking me so that I let out a yelp.

"We were so close! We were going to leave, I had it all settled, I thought—" Fear and confusion clouded her face, a shudder ran over her body, and for a moment I thought my cold, blank mother would actually break down in tears. But just as quickly, an iron rod seemed to slip down her spine, pulling her up, in. Her mouth set into a straight line, and she dragged me by the arm out of the dining room.

"We have to leave. We have to leave now, right away; we can't stay here anymore; it's not *safe*."

"That's—that's what I'm trying—" I struggled against her grip, but she ignored me. "I know you're scared, but he's not going to hurt me! He's kind and warm, and he's not afraid of what I am!" I wrenched free and my mother stared at me, eyes narrowed.

"It doesn't matter. It doesn't matter who he is or what he cares about," she said, breathing hard.

"You don't know him!" I shook my head. "You don't know anything about it!"

"*I* don't know?" Her hands curled into fists. "Avery, how could you be so foolish? I *told* you: We're cursed; magic destroys the thing you love!"

A shiver tingled across my skin, and she grabbed my shoulders, holding me tight.

"You never listen to me," she whispered. "Why did you never listen to me? I never wanted this to happen to you."

She stared into my eyes, her mouth twitching as though she had something to tell me but didn't know how to say it.

"I never wanted you to know this," she said softly. "I never wanted you to know how we become witches."

My stomach flipped within me.

"How?" I asked, the word slipping from my lips like a wisp of breath.

"*Pain*," my mother said softly. "That's what makes us witches."

The air in the room went still. My skin began to tingle.

"It takes a lifetime of pain to make our magic," she continued, so quietly that had she not been a handbreadth away, I would not have heard her. "Not the kind of pain that comes from cutting your skin or breaking a bone—no. It's the pain of ache, heartbreak, and disappointment. The pain of falling in love for the first time...and losing it. Loving someone and having that person hurt you in ways you've never imagined. It has happened to every single one of us, Avery, every Roe woman. We're *cursed*, we fall in love and are hurt, and that pain, that sacrifice, is what makes our magic."

The words slid out from her, cool and quiet, and when she stopped speaking, I realized I'd stopped breathing. I took a breath then, and then another, and then it was as though my heart whirred inside of me and I could not breathe fast enough to keep up, and all the while my mother stared at me, waiting for my response, her head cocked in something that, in another light, could be called triumph.

"I don't believe you," I said, speaking quickly. "What you say doesn't make any sense. I've felt pain before. I've hurt, but I've never made spells before; I'm not—" My words broke off as a memory floated back to me: leaving my grandmother's house, falling into the sea, reaching the water and breathing it in as though it were air, and Tane, pulling me out, saying something that I hadn't heard, hadn't understood at first. "I thought you had died," that's what he said, and all I could do was stare at him.

I breathed underwater. Only magic could have made it happen, but before I realized what I was doing, the magic vanished. It vanished as soon as I realized that I still had something good and worthwhile in my life: the instant Tane touched me.

"It's a curse. We're all cursed," my mother whispered. "Every Roe...it's happened to all of us. Don't you understand? Every Roe woman fell in love and every one had that love taken away from her—brutally. Our magic *feeds* on pain, and every time a witch makes a spell, it *hurts*, it hurts just like it did the first time! Whenever I make a spell, I feel...I feel..." Her voice faded, disappearing like smoke, and I stared at her, surprised to see her icy eyes filled with tears, her fingers creeping up to touch the scar on her face.

"Maybe this boy cares for you now," she said, "but I promise you, he will hurt you. He will do it in some way you can't even imagine, but it will happen."

"He would never," I whispered, and she shook her head. "He's the kindest, gentlest person I've ever met and he *loves* me. Nothing could make him hurt me, not even magic."

"What he would or would not do doesn't matter. It's a curse, Avery, and no Roe woman has ever escaped it. No matter the person, no matter what he thinks about you now, even if he really cares about you, it doesn't matter. You might think you've found a good man, but trust me," she said, and she grimaced, stretching the skin along her scar, "whatever power makes our magic can and will change him."

Change him?

"I never wanted that for you, don't you see? A lifetime of pain? What good is magic if all day, every day you feel...? I never wanted that for you."

In the quiet I heard my heartbeat, loud in my ears.

"Listen." There was steel in her voice again; she had become once more the woman who always knew the right thing to say and do. "It's not too late. He hasn't hurt you. Maybe the curse hasn't touched him yet. We can leave the island, right now, and you will never have to see him again."

I seemed to hear her speak as though underwater, her words indistinct and muffled, and I felt her hands grip my arms.

"We have to go and you have to forget about him and maybe, maybe you'll be safe." She shook me a little, a scale of panic in her voice. "Do you understand? You won't be the witch, but you'll be safe away from him. Avery? I'm going to take you away."

She expected me to say something, but I felt too dazed, too confused to respond. "I...I can't leave," I mumbled, and her hands tightened.

"You have to. If you stay, if you get pregnant—"

"Pregnant?" Ice slipped into my stomach, and my mother's face soured.

"It's...it's the other part of the curse."

"Curse," I repeated, the word dull in my mouth.

"We were born that way...a-all of us," she said, stumbling a little over the words, and she released her grip on me, sending tingles of feeling back into my arms. "Our mothers fell in love, they lost their men, they became witches, and all they had left was their...daughters. That's what it means to be a Roe. We're all just consequences of our mothers' bad decisions."

One of her hands lifted to my cheek and I knew she was trying to comfort me, to be a mother to me, but I was just a consequence of her bad decisions, and I turned my face away.

"I tried to stop it for you," she said, her hand still in the air, reaching, trembling. "I tried....I found you a good boy to marry, a boy who would never fall in love with you. I gave the captain of the *Eagle Wing* three hundred dollars to hire Tommy Thompson. I brought you to parties, concerts, the very best kind of life a young girl could possibly enjoy. No love, no magic, but you could have had a wonderful life. Maybe you still can. You made a mistake," she whispered, and I flinched to hear Tane called a mistake. "But we can stop this now. Before you get pregnant and the curse claims another girl. The line has to stop. Now."

Every muscle in my body seized with a sudden coldness.

"That's what you want, isn't it?" I asked, jaw clenched to keep my teeth from chattering. "You want me to leave this island forever. You want an end to the Roes."

"You should want it, too. I know you love this boy now, but Avery—all that will come of it is pain and heartbreak, I promise you, for you and—and for him."

Him? Fear shuddered through me, and my mother saw it and snatched at it.

"You want to protect him, don't you?" she asked, her voice low and harsh. "You say that he's good and sweet, that he's gentle, but I promise you, he will hurt you. What if our curse changes him and *makes* him hurt you? Don't you see? Everything about him that you love will be destroyed, and he will be changed forever. Do you really want that for him?"

A tremor worked through my body and I felt my eyes go glassy with tears. Magic could change people, I knew. How many times had I seen my grandmother tear through a man's anger, turn him blank as a doll? And I had stood with my mother two years ago in a clapboard church as a soppy-faced Pastor Sever leaned in like a drunk to kiss his bride. Magic could change people.

"I...I don't..."

"Avery, you can save him!" My mother grabbed my hands, whispering furiously. "Just come with me! Leave with me, forget all about him, and you and he will be safe!"

I could feel the word on my lips: *yes*. I never wanted to leave the island, but Tane's face swam before me and my resolve slipped through my fingers. Dazed, I opened my mouth to tell her I would go, when I recognized the gleam in my mother's eyes: desperation, almost madness. And I remembered, she would do anything to stop the Roes.

"No." I shook my head and wrenched my hands away. "No, you're trying to scare me." I backed away from her, moving down the hallway toward the front door. "You're trying to trick me into leaving the island. I don't believe we're cursed, I don't; Granma never said anything about a curse, and you, you! Am I supposed to believe that you were in love with the man who gave you that scar?"

She shuddered and a spasm crossed her face—the look of someone caught in a lie. "Please, just listen to me. All I've done is to protect you from our family's curse!"

"How? By putting me in pretty clothes? By marrying a rich man? How is that protecting *me*?"

"Money gives us opportunities! Was I supposed to keep you in that old apartment to starve to death? I'm trying to give you a good, honest, secure life! Avery, don't you understand? I always wanted you to be the kind of woman people admire, an upstanding woman, someone with choices. Magic tries to control us, but if you can control your own life, Avery, *that* is real power!"

"No, no!" I backed away from her, my blood sizzling through my veins. "You only care about my reputation; you only care about what people would think if they saw me alone with Tane; you only care that they would think I'm ruined!"

"Are you?" My mother almost leaped at me with her question. "Avery, did you—"

"That's all you care about! You know that no man will ever look at me twice if my *virtue* could be called into question, and you're worried that all your plans will fall apart." I shook my head, still backing away from her. "That's what this is really about, isn't it? Not curses! It's always been about you! *Your* life was ruined, *you* grew up poor, *you* picked the wrong man, and he destroyed the only thing that really made you special, and now—what? You think you can make up for your terrible life by turning me into a proper, pretty lady with a wealthy husband!"

She said nothing, tears pooling at the corners of her long eyelashes, and I knew I'd hit the mark.

"I almost believed you," I whispered, and now I'd nearly backed up to the front door, my mother still following, almost groveling, in my wake. "But Tane—I *know* he would never, he could never..."

"It doesn't matter! The curse, the magic, it will do things to him, I know, I—Avery, we have to leave, *now*."

Heat blossomed at my hip, and I knew she was casting a spell on me right then, right at that moment, but my tattoo shook it off, broke it, and shattered it while I kept moving backward, away from her.

"Stop it!" I shouted. "Stop lying to me! I don't believe you!"

She moved so fast it must have been magic, springing toward me, one hand reaching out, but the moment she touched me I screamed, "No! Get away!" and I felt something inside of me rear up, throw her back while she hissed like a cat, like a monster.

"You don't know what you're doing! I'm taking you away from him! He's only going to hurt you!" she said, her hair all in a mess at her shoulders, her white skin blooming roses on her cheeks. She looked like a real witch now, tense and crouched, hands curled into claws, and fingers of her magic scraped across my skin. But as the realization hit me that my mother had always lied to me, had always hated the Roes and would do anything to end our line forever—bind me to her side, send away Tommy, *manipulate* me—lightning suddenly burst through my veins. I felt pain and I felt magic and I knew that despite the endless lies, my mother had at least told the truth about the source of our power.

The fire within me arced toward my mother, and she let out a strangled scream and crumpled to the ground.

"Avery," she whimpered, blinking back tears, and she looked so pathetic now, cowed by my magic, reaching for me.

"Stop it," I said, my voice quavering. The door was just behind me and I reached for it, opened it, and smelled the fresh, cool air. "You aren't going to trick me. You can't control me anymore!"

Before she could speak, before she could move, I darted from the house, feeling with every step the magic inside of me build, build, build before—*CRACK!*

I spun just in time to see the roof of the big white house cave in, cut perfectly in two, wrenched apart in a cloud of splinters and dust. As shouts of panic exploded behind me, I turned and ran.

Twenty-One

PAIN MADE MAGIC. ISN'T THAT WHAT MY grandmother always said? "It's supposed to hurt. That's just how it should be."

I ran from New Bishop, feeling, for the first time in years, the thrum of magic through my veins, only this time I wasn't a conduit for my grandmother—*I* could control this. My mother had hurt me, just like my grandmother had hurt me, and for a few amazing minutes my blood sizzled with power.

But seconds later, I remembered what else my mother had told me about love, about Tane, and as his face rose up before my eyes, the hurt fell away and with it, my magic, until I was just Avery again, just the dream-teller.

That much was true, then—that heartache fed my magic, and maybe enough heartache would change me forever into a powerful witch. The magic didn't last, but I did more today than I'd ever accomplished with all my experiments. I'd nearly ripped apart my mother's house, cracking the roof in two like a ceramic figure. *Was anyone hurt?* Part of me worried, even though that seemed unlikely—no one would have been in that part of the house so early in the morning. Certainly my mother, in the front hall, was fine, as I'd kept her from following me outside with my magic. *My magic.* Real Roe witch magic, not just telling dreams. Hope rose up within me as I remembered my dream, my future. *You can't kill a Roe witch.*

There was a way, a way to stop my dream, but then... According to my mother, I'd only become a true witch after Tane broke my heart, after the thing I loved more than anything else in the world hurt me.

Impossible.

Unless...

Unbidden, a very small voice whispered inside my head: *Your mother says the curse will change him. She says he'll change into the kind of person who will hurt you. She says you cursed him, just by loving him. She says you can't stop it.*

I told the little voice to shut up, but the doubts stayed. What if I *had* cursed Tane? What if it was still my destiny to become a witch, but first Tane had to become a monster? Or worse, what if the magic changed him, took away everything good and sweet and turned him into something cruel and terrible, and I *still* died?

My grandmother would know. Of course she would. For

years she'd told me that she'd explain it all someday. At night in my trundle bed, I was a tiny thing, watching her work, and I'd ask why I couldn't make charms like her if I was a Roe. Six years old, tying the winds on her lap, why couldn't I do it myself? Seven, eight, nine years old, she'd sit me at the table in the cottage and give me Almira's book of languages and Frances's book of plants and tell me to study and I'd say I didn't want to study, I just wanted to know how to make magic. Ten years old, I told a dream for the first time, felt my magic stir for the first time, but I wasn't a real witch, I couldn't make magic, and *why*, Granma, why? *Why won't you tell me?*

And she'd take my face between her hands and say, "Not yet, dear. I'll tell you later. I'll tell you when you're older. I'll explain it all someday, I promise you."

Well. I was older. And I didn't care anymore that she'd turned me away, that she'd thrown me away, that I'd failed her and she'd rejected me. Tane might be in trouble, and I deserved to know the truth. It was time to remind my grandmother of her promise.

I arrived by midday, sweat dripping down my neck, my feet tired and my throat parched. I walked up to the door and didn't bother to knock. This cottage still belonged to me, no matter what my grandmother said. I pushed inside, expecting to find her at the table or in bed, but the cottage was empty and cold.

Sunlight filtered in through windows that I'd never seen so dirty, illuminating the stained and threadbare sheets of her bed, the shards of broken plates piled into the corner—signs of decrepitude that had been hidden in shadows when I visited four days ago. I crossed quickly to the fireplace in the far corner, my nose wrinkling as I neared what appeared to be a string of rotting fish. Heat, faint but there, warmed my fingers as I held my hand over the ashes, and I let out a tight breath. She had been here recently. She wasn't dead or hadn't disappeared or whatever happens to our women when they go.

But she also wasn't in the cottage. I pushed back a water-stained curtain and peered through the layer of dust and grit that coated the window. Movement on the rocks caught my eye, and I rubbed my palm against the glass and looked again. My heart flew into my throat—there she was, my grandmother, walking barefoot down the sand to the water, covered in something billowing and black.

I turned and ran down the path that led to the beach.

"Granma!" I shouted, and although she was close enough to hear me, she didn't turn around. Her gray hair floated in the wind, the black sheet lifting like a hot-air balloon, and I saw with a wrench in my stomach that underneath, she wore no clothes.

Sand and small rocks sprayed under my feet as I slowed to a stop, but she still didn't seem to hear me, walking slowly and carefully up to the water.

"Granma," I said again, and this time I circled around her,

walking almost into the waves to stop her, and when I saw her face I had to choke back a gasp.

Four days. I last saw her four days ago, but to look at her now it could have been four decades. Her eyes sat far back in their sockets, dull under half-closed eyelids, and her mouth hung open, a fine stream of spittle suspended from her parched lips. Dust seemed to cling to her skin, grimy and gray, and her wrinkles had deepened, elongated so that her face appeared nothing more than a collection of slashes and pockmarks.

She held her hands loosely at her sides, wrapped up in the black cloak, and bile rose into my throat to see the sores across her emaciated body, all bones and sagging skin save for a round paunch at her stomach.

"Granma," I said again, my voice wavering, and this time her eyelids fluttered in my direction, her vacant expression showing the barest sliver of recognition.

"Wh...what..." she said slowly, almost whispering, and for just a moment she seemed to change, shift closer to the woman who was my grandmother. But the change didn't last; the empty skeleton reappeared, and she turned back out to the water.

"Granma!" I said, and I grabbed for her shoulders. Her hands rose up quickly, defensively, and I just managed to pull away as she slashed at me with a knife hidden in her left fist. Her face darkened with anger, but soon the expression drained from her like water from an overturned bottle, leaving her blank and cold.

"Granma, it's Avery."

Again she slowly stared at me, her eyes unblinking and unfocused.

"I thought you were dead," she finally said, her voice low and creaky. "Are you dead? Am I dead?"

I shivered.

"Let's go inside," I said.

Carefully, I reached a hand out to her, and when she didn't strike at me, I tried to pull her back from the water. After a moment, she let herself be led away, but only a few feet from the waves she stopped and stared back over the ocean.

"Listen," she said, lifting a hand—the hand holding the knife—toward the horizon. "It's singing."

"Come on, Granma," I said, wrapping an arm around her thin shoulders. "You should sit down."

"Yes," she said, and I thought she might let me bring her back up to the cottage, but instead she sank down to her knees and settled into the wet, rocky sand. She was tiny, frail like a kitten, and if Tane were with me, he could have easily scooped her into his arms and carried her back to the cottage, but I didn't trust my exhausted limbs to work properly, so I just swallowed the lump in my throat and sat beside her.

Her shoulders rocked, unsteady and fast, causing her head to bob like a dandelion in the breeze, but she didn't appear to notice the tremor, her attention still caught by the sea.

"Are you all right?" I asked, although clearly she wasn't. At my voice, her head swiveled in my direction and a corner of her mouth puckered into a half-smile.

"You fell in love," she said. "Was it the boy with the lantern?"

A chill danced down my spine, but of course, she was gifted with picking up other people's emotions, and even in her ruined state, it seemed, she could sense the threads of feeling stitched through me.

"My mother said that's how we fuel our magic," I whispered. "She said when a Roe falls in love, that man breaks her heart, and that pain transforms her into the witch. She said I can't do anything to stop it. Is that true?"

"You're younger than most," she said, the smile growing slack. "I was twenty-four when I met my man. But then, you always showed such skill." Her face twisted as if she'd just smelled something rotten. "Pity you won't become the witch."

"You say I won't," I said, heart beating faster. "What does that mean? My mother says the curse will change him into a monster, just because I love him, but if I'm not going to be the witch, is he safe? Will it happen to him?"

Her shoulders lifted into a slow shrug. "How can I know? How can anyone? You are not the witch because you are going to be murdered, and no one can murder a Roe witch."

"But the curse—"

"The curse..." She breathed out, long and shaky. "Roe women, unlucky in love... always picking the wrong men..."

"Tane's not wrong," I said quickly. "He would never hurt me."

"You sound just like your mother. Thought she was clever,

thought she found a safe man, but she still ended up broken. The magic...changed him...." Her face took on a faraway expression. "Listen to that *music*."

Frustration rose inside of me and I wanted to grab my grandmother's bony shoulders and shake her, shake her until the skeleton was gone and I had my grandmother back, sharp-tongued and sharp-witted and full of advice. I drew in a breath.

"I love him. And I know I'm going to die; I know I'm going to be murdered," I said, clenching my jaw. "I'm supposed to die, Granma, and if I won't be the witch, that means he won't ever hurt me, will he? Is he still cursed? Will he change? What will the curse do to him?"

"Do to him?" she repeated, staring at me.

"Yes! He's kind and calm and caring," I said, speaking fast. "Will the curse take all that away from him? The kind of person he is now—Granma, he would never hurt me."

She closed her eyes tight. "He would never hurt me," she said, slowly drawing her fists up to her chest. "Oh, oh, Caleb..." Sunlight glinted off the knife clutched in one hand and my stomach flipped.

"Who?" I shook my head. "Caleb?" I frowned. "Caleb... Caleb Sweeny from the Caleb's gifts? That captain who insulted you?"

Her body folded around itself and she leaned forward, her chin almost resting on her knees. "So many secrets," she whispered. "So many secrets."

A spasm of pain crossed her face and she whimpered like a

kitten. I felt something grow around her then: magic, for what I couldn't tell, but I recognized her expression of pain. It was how she always used to look after making a spell. It was how she looked when she taught me to tie the winds and pressed her hands to my chest and told me that magic was supposed to hurt.

"Granma, I don't understand. Why are you talking about Caleb Sweeny? Did you... did you love him?"

"Hmm?" My grandmother lifted her face, open and expectant like someone had called her, but she didn't seem to be paying attention to me. Instead, she gazed out at the water.

"Did you fall in love with Caleb?" I asked. "Did he change? Did the curse change him? Is that why he slighted you?"

"Hmm?" She had forgotten about me, staring off at the water, and I dropped my face into my hands. This was useless.

"I killed him," she said, her voice flat, and it was as though a huge fist reached into my chest and squeezed my heart.

"What?"

"He loved me. I loved him... the only man I ever loved... the first man I ever loved. Come away with me, Jennie Roe, come away with me and be mine.... I'll surprise him, I'll meet him early, what a lovely surprise!" The dreaminess on her face dissolved into a mad hiss. "What's that? Who's that with him? Nelly Mower! Come away with me, Nelly Mower! All the same! Take my heart and break my heart and when I asked him for answers he laughed at me and called me a silly girl." She shook her head, her gray hair flapping around her eyes.

"Let him go. Let him leave. He's not worth it, Jennie Roe, he's a captain and twenty-eight and beautiful as sunshine; and two days out of port, I sent that ship to the bottom of the sea."

I couldn't breathe. I felt very cold, listening to her, the wet sand creeping its chill through my dress and into my skin. It's one of the most famous stories about my grandmother, the captain who was rude to her and lost his ship and his life out on the ocean, inspiring a generation of captains to give her beautiful presents. But I never knew it was a story about my grandfather, too.

"So much pain... Revenge... I thought it would help," she said, and she seemed to be gasping, wheezing for breath. "I thought it would stop the pain, but it didn't, it didn't!" She lifted her hands in the air, the cloak hanging loose from her shoulders, the knife upright and shining. "Caleb! Caleb! Forgive me!"

Runny tears clung to her wrinkled cheeks, and I had to look away, more embarrassed to see my grandmother's tears than her naked body.

"It never ends," she whispered. "The pain never goes away. I had to stop. I *have* to stop. I want... I want to die. I should have gone years ago but I hoped... I hoped..."

The words slipped out of her as soft as breaths, and guilt stabbed through me. She had stayed for me. Her last few years had tormented her, turned her mad, but she had hung on for me.

No. For nothing.

"I'm sorry," I said softly, and she raised her wide eyes to my face.

"Sorry?" she croaked. "Sorry? Death is a comfort, Avery." A smile split open her chapped lips and I looked away again. "All I feel now is pain. Pain and power and Caleb...calling for me."

One of her cold, bony hands grasped my wrist, stronger than I could have anticipated. I glanced at her and for once, she looked deep into my eyes, the way she used to.

"I hope you don't experience it. I hope you die before it happens to you."

What could I possibly say to that? I felt sick to my stomach, thirsty, and exhausted, and still I did not know what would happen to Tane. Gently, I pushed myself to my feet and was surprised when my grandmother followed.

"I'm sorry," she said. "I thought you were already dead. I thought it was all over."

"What...what do you mean?"

"When I go, my magic will go with me," she whispered. "There's always been another witch to keep the spells going, but it will all go when I die."

My skin crawled as I realized what she meant—all her magic gone, all her charms useless, everything this island had come to rely upon for centuries vanished.

"It will be hard on you," she said, and she reached out a hand, not the one with the knife, to me. "I am sorry. But"— she choked suddenly—"I cannot stay!" She turned and faced the sea, her skin bloodless, almost translucent. "I've stayed too long, and Caleb...Caleb..."

At her words a low moaning wind wrapped around us,

whipping her hair and cloak across her body, and the waves churned and boiled while a huge, angry swell of magic crashed at our feet. I brought up a hand to shield my face from the stinging sand and didn't realize until too late that my grand-mother had begun to walk into the waves, the knife still gripped in her fist, her face dreamy and lit up.

"Wait!" I shouted, but the wind wrapped around my voice and whisked it away. I lurched forward, for this all felt terribly wrong, like my grandmother wasn't walking into heaven but hell, but before I could reach her, she lifted her arms into the air and, with a final screech, brought the knife quick and hard into her own stomach.

Too shocked to cry out, I stood, frozen, as she dropped the knife and staggered deeper into the waters. A wave knocked her off balance and she stumbled, splashing, and when she tried to get her footing another wave came for her, crashing water over her head and dragging her from shore. I screamed for her then, fear and confusion maddening me, and while the hungry waves tumbled her about in the sea, her face turned, just for a moment, and I could see she was no longer a skeleton, no longer even my grandmother, but a young woman, Jennie Roe at twenty-four and full of life, and as she slipped into the water, one hand lifted into a wave, and I swear she saw me, I swear she smiled, smiled to leave this world forever.

Twenty-Two

MY HEAD THROBBED. I'D GONE BACK TO the cottage to drink from an earthenware pitcher in the corner and to eat the stores of my grandmother's pantry and to sleep, but now it was the day after my grandmother's terrible death, and I felt sick, my skin itchy and greasy, my face puffy with exhaustion.

My grandmother, the last real witch, was dead, and I'd finally learned what happened to Roe women at the end of their lives. Was that what it meant to be a witch? Heartbreak, then a life consumed by pain until it became too much to bear?

Perhaps an early murder wasn't as bad as I thought. Perhaps even my mother's world of fancy dresses and pretty parties made sense. A safe home, an indifferent husband, warm clothing, and good food and music. No love, but no heartbreak, either. How did she put it? "The best kind of life a Roe could ever expect."

And maybe it was; maybe my mother had a point in trading magic for a pain-free life, but I remembered then what else my grandmother had told me.

No more Roes. Everything we'd built, all our magic, gone forever. Centuries of work undone in an instant, and that was my mother's fault, no matter how you looked at it. Even if she didn't want my grandmother's life, she chose her own comfort over the legacy the Roes created.

What would happen to us and our reputations when the islanders discovered that the charms to keep the whale men awake at night, to keep the tryworks from catching fire, to keep their masts steady and their limbs free from whale jaws and their sons safe from drowning had all failed?

I sat on the edge of my grandmother's bed—my bed—no one's bed—and rubbed my aching temples as I thought about what I had learned.

The first person a Roe woman fell in love with ended up breaking her heart.

This broken heart transformed the Roe woman into a witch.

I loved Tane. My mother said that he would hurt me, would maybe even turn into a cruel, hateful person to do it, and that my broken heart would make me a witch. My grandmother said that I was going to die and would *never* become a witch.

Questions, questions swirled through my head: Was my

mother lying? Was Tane cursed? If in the end I was going to be dead no matter what, if I would never unlock my magic, never get my heart broken, would Tane still change into a monster?

I had to believe that it wouldn't happen like that. I loved Tane and I was going to die and he wouldn't change; he would have his happy life, his ships and babies and love. But still, doubt gnawed at me.

I knew at least that I couldn't stay here in the cottage for the rest of my short life. For one, I would soon starve. My grandmother, as a sea witch, knew how to turn salt water into fresh and how to call fish to her nets, but I did not. The temporary burst of magic I'd felt leaving my mother's house had left me, and now I felt cold and lonely.

I wanted Tane. I wanted to tell him what had happened. I wanted to hear him say that it would be all right, that no curse would ever change him, that loving him was a good thing. And so I pushed myself from the bed, fetched my grandmother's ancient boots, and began the long walk back to New Bishop.

I was still half a mile outside town when I noticed the first signs of change. Wind whipped around my skirts, tugging at my hair, churning the normally calm waters at New Bishop's shore. It was then that I remembered the spell my grandmother would perform annually, every spring, renewing the magic of Lenora Roe from all those decades ago. She'd pour a little water collected from the harbor into an upturned seashell, a promise for sound waters and a safe port (and in return, the town supplied a repairman to reset her windows or clean her chimney or patch up her roof).

Even as the southern factories of New Bishop came into view, I kept to the beach, to the churning, swirling waters, boiling and white-foamed like I'd never seen before. I stood silent and awed, facing the ocean, with the town behind me, and watched the waves crash furiously against the shore.

My stomach rumbled. It had been a long while since I had eaten. With the wind at my back, I turned and walked up the beach toward town, making my way to Main Street and the food stalls and grocers.

Puffin Canned Goods and Grocer still had its lanterns lit, and although I didn't have any money on me, the shop owner, a man named Pendleton, had been kind enough a few days ago to extend some credit when I came asking for food for Tane. But this time, I scarcely had the door open when he threw an arm out to wave me away, his face dark and red.

"Not you!" he said, coming out from behind the counter to shoo me. "I won't serve another Roe ever again!" He pointed to a back corner of the store and a damp pile of splintered wood that smelled conspicuously like vinegar. "I paid thirteen dollars for a charm that the witch *said* would keep my barrels from leaks! My boy goes to move one of the barrels for delivery today, and it bursts! Every one of them bursts! That's more than two hundred dollars of lost profits!

Not to mention the barrels that need replacing and the orders that I missed!"

My stomach dropped, and I opened my mouth, I suppose to apologize, although I didn't know what to say.

"You get out of here!" he said, and I noticed a tall shadow in the corner: his broad-shouldered son, watching me. Without another word I ducked out the door and into the streets, my cheeks red as I realized that already, already the Roe name had changed into something terrible.

I went to the fish stall next, but when I asked for a plate of the daily catch, Mary Barker, the curly-haired fishwife, crossed her arms.

"Think you see any kind of catch here, Avery *Roe*?" she asked, her mouth puckered into a sour frown. "We sold out half an hour after we opened this morning, and it weren't because e'ryone got a hankering for some fish." She pointed a fat hand into my face. "You tell your grandmother those spells she promised for better catches een't worth a bucket o' slop! You tell her that from me!"

"I'm sorry," I said, my words tense and clenched, and I turned around back the way I'd come.

I walked quickly down the street, but I knew there wasn't a shop on Main Street that didn't have my grandmother's magic woven through it in some shape or form. And was it my imagination? Or already, already did the people of my island watch me pass with narrowed and angry eyes?

My feet brought me farther from the center of town and I

had just crossed a corner when I felt the warm pulse of familiar magic. *Tane*. I turned to follow the feeling beckoning me down an alley between the blacksmith's shop and the barber.

I saw his shape at the end of the alley, darkened by shadows, and I was halfway to him when he struck a match to light a cigarette. I paused, confused, because he never smelled like tobacco, and just then he raised the match nearer to his face and I stumbled to see it wasn't Tane at all but a fair-haired sailor with a sunburned, unfamiliar face.

Frozen, I meant to turn, but he spotted me and pulled the cigarette from his lips.

"Somethin' you need?" he asked, and though his voice was low and gruff, I knew he couldn't be out of his teens. He leaned a shoulder against the wall, and as he turned, his arm was suddenly illuminated by a shaft of light from the streetlamp. He wore a tattoo, one of Tane's kind.

"Where did you get that?" I asked, pointing at the man's arm, and when he lifted his cigarette with a frown, I shook my head. "The tattoo, I mean."

"Like it, do you?" He leaned forward and rolled his sleeve higher so I could see, and I was sure now that it was the same magic as Tane's tattoos—a fisherman's charm for good catches. "Got it in the South Pacific a few months back. Little island."

"Hovell Island."

The man's eyebrows lifted and he smiled.

"Yeah," he said. "Yeah, that's right. How'd you know?"

"They don't tattoo outsiders," I said, and he shrugged.

"Maybe they didn't used to, but they did when I was there. Traded this one for a peek inside the ship's medicine chest. Hey." He licked his lips, studying me. "Why d'you know so much about them?"

"I'm looking for the men who murdered them."

At this, he lifted his hands defensively, shaking his head. "I don' know nothing about murders," he said. "I wasn' even *there* when it happened!"

"You *know*?" I took a step closer to him.

"Sure I know," he said. "But I didn' have anything to do with it."

I felt my hands curl into fists. "Why should I believe you?"

He lifted his lip in a sneer. "I'm alive, ain't I?"

"What does that have to do with it?"

"Listen," he said, glancing at the open mouth of the alley. "I'm a cooper on the *Sachem* and we were at Hovell Island right before it happened. 'Bout eight months ago we spent a few days there and when we left, another boat, the *Robin*, landed. They got into some sorta tussle with the natives—you know how it is."

I frowned. Attacks by natives were common enough, so common that sailors often came to my grandmother asking for charms. But while she could promise safety at sea or love charms for island girls, she knew no magic against arrowheads or knifepoints. Round-eyed boys who survived attacks told breathless stories of sudden and inexplicable swarms of angry natives, although I generally doubted the sailors' total innocence, especially when captains bragged of buying supplies from natives by "paying with the fore-topsail"—that is, promising payment but sailing away.

"So this...tussle," I said, tensing my jaw. "What happened?"

"No one knows for sure what started it. Something about a native girl, and then two of the savages killed the first mate. The men of the *Robin* just wanted vengeance."

"Some vengeance. They killed children. Women. Slaughtered them."

The man shrugged again. "They were drunk," he said, as though that excused it all. "Hadn't a whale kill in months, so they said. And those natives were in bad shape before the *Robin* ever made port—sick, you know. Said they had the typhoid, the grippe. Weren't more'n a hundred when we landed, and a pretty shabby bunch at that. They wouldn't've been able to put up much of a fight against the *Robin*. I heard the crew just meant to go after the men, but they burned the village and the fire got out of control and the natives too weak to stop 'em..." He trailed off. "Anyway, the *Robin*'s crew got what was comin' to them."

I studied him. "What do you mean?"

"Those devils musta had a curse put on the *Robin*, because it wasn't long after that she went down, foundered off the coast of Australia on the clearest day a man could ask for. Two other ships saw her go. Said it was like the sea jumped up and swallowed 'er whole."

A curse. That was powerful magic, magic that existed after the caster had died, and I rubbed my temples, wishing I understood.

"There's more, too," the man said, leaning in slightly. "One of the men of the *Robin* switched ships after they left Hovell Island. Same day the ship sinks? He gets a knife in his belly in a bar fight."

"Then they're all dead," I said, dazed, and the man nodded.

"And it was a curse that done it, I'm sure."

I had no more questions the man could answer, and I turned suddenly and ran from the alley, followed by his surprised shouts.

Dead. The men responsible for the murders of Tane's people were all dead. No wonder I could see nothing in his dreams; Tane couldn't very well hunt down men already rotting at the bottom of the ocean.

The man's words echoed through my skull as I made my way back to the lighthouse. What would I tell Tane?

I paused for a moment, one hand resting against the wall of a building. What if I didn't tell him? He'd promised to give up hunting those men, but what if, when I was gone, he needed them? What if he needed something to live for? Vengeance had sustained him for so long. It had carried him through the worst moments of his life. What would he do now that it was gone?

When I reached the lighthouse, butterflies rose up through my stomach, and memories of my night with Tane flashed through my head, turning my cheeks pink. So much had happened since I'd seen him last: my mother's terrible truth, my grandmother's terrible death, the story of the tattooed man. And yet all I could think of as I crossed the sand was his hands on my skin, his mouth on mine, his whispers filling my ears— and how to keep him safe.

I touched the door of the lighthouse, cold twisting in my stomach. Would my family's curse change him? Had it *already* changed him? I'd been gone from him for almost two days. What if I came back to find him a different person?

Sighing, I pushed the lighthouse door open and walked inside. Everything was quiet, so quiet I wondered if he was even here, but as the stairs curled up into the lamp room, there he was, leaning against the window, his fingers tracing patterns along the glass. My footsteps had been loud climbing the stairs, but he didn't move, head bowed and silent, and a shiver ran through me.

"Tane?" I whispered, hesitating at the entrance to the lamp room. His shoulders stiffened.

"Where have you been?" he asked, his voice smooth and even, and—and *cold*, colder than I'd ever heard before.

"I...so much has happened."

He turned, and although it was dark in the lamp room, the only light coming from a solitary, flickering candle set into the floor, I could see something strange, almost angry, burning in his eyes.

"I didn't know where you went," he said, shaking his head, and that blank, detached voice made all the hairs on the back of my neck stand up. "I woke up on the beach and you were gone."

"I'm...sorry," I said. "I meant to come back and..." I reached for him but he didn't move, staring at me like a stranger, and I pulled my hand away and held it tight to my chest, fighting back a cry of anguish. He'd never spoken to me like this; he was so different, and was this the curse? Had it happened already and was he going to hurt me now? Break my heart?

"How could you leave like that?" he asked, and I felt my insides crumple.

"I...Tane, I'm sorry," I said, my voice whisper-weak. "I always meant to come back, I...I had to see my grandmother. Tane, she's...she's dead."

His eyebrows lifted for a moment before settling back into his neutral stare.

"There's no Roe witch anymore. All my family's magic is...gone."

Tane glanced out the window, dark except for a few scattered lights in New Bishop. "All day men have complained that their charms didn't work properly, and someone guessed that it was because the witch was dead." He turned to me, his face hard, and then the expression broke, melted into a look of misery and anguish. "Avery, I thought *you* were dead."

He was so upset—he cared about me so much—and relief soared through me as I realized that I was wrong—he *loved* me still, and nothing had changed him! I wanted to laugh at myself now for doubting him, for thinking that magic was strong enough to make him stop loving me, and, dizzy with happiness, I ran to him and wrapped my arms around his waist.

"You left me," he said again, talking into my hair. "You said you would stay and I woke up and you were gone." He pushed me away and held my shoulders tightly in his hands, looking into my eyes, and I could see his were bright with pain. "Don't do that again."

"I'm all right," I said, but he shook his head.

"Avery, you're in danger," he whispered. "What will happen when the people on this island learn that all the magic is done with? They'll want you to make them spells and you know you can't, and then they'll get angry. They'll blame you!" His hands tightened around mine. "Can you help them? Is there any magic you can do? Is there anything your mother can do?"

I let out a bitter laugh. "If she was going to return to magic and help the people of this island, she would have done it long ago. This is what she's always wanted: an end to the Roe witch. No doubt she'd be glad to hear that all the charms have gone awry."

"But if they blame you, won't she try to help?"

I took a breath. "I don't think she wants anything to do with me anymore. We... argued. I never want to see her again."

"But then, she won't take you off the island?"

I blinked in surprise. "I... I suppose not."

Tane squeezed my hands. "She won't take you, and it's not safe for you to stay. You must come with me."

I shook my head. "Tane, it's not safe for me anywhere, remember? I'm going to be killed."

He smiled, one hand reaching across my cheek to tuck a strand of hair behind my ear. "Maybe not," he said softly. "I had another dream."

"A dream?"

He nodded. "It means something important; I'm sure of it. I've never felt this way about my dreams, not since the one about my family. But this one—it will give me answers, I know it, and I have a feeling...I think it's about you."

Dazed, I pulled away from him. "Tell me."

He took a breath. "I am back on my island, and it is night-time. Two birds fly to my shoulders and I recognize them—they are my youngest sister's pets."

I felt the little curls and tugs of magic, tingling at my fingertips, turning my stomach, and I fought to keep my face blank and calm.

"I walk along the beach with the birds on my shoulders and I see a shadow has crossed my path. The shadow grows and becomes a man with a knife. He lunges for me and I turn and the knife hits one of the birds on my shoulders. It cries out and floats to the ground. The man runs then and I chase him, one bird singing in my ear, and this time, when he turns and lunges for me, I stand still and let the knife hit me instead of the bird. The bird flies out and attacks the man's face, and he disappears into shadows again. The last thing I see is the bird flying into the sky, and then I wake."

My teeth clenched, I pressed my fingernails into my palms and tried to hide my shock, my confusion. What his dream showed me was impossible, something I'd never seen before.

"Well?" he asked.

"Say it once more," I said, and when he had repeated the dream, nearly word for word, a frown pulled at my lips. The same strange impossibility.

My breath ran ragged in my chest and I thought back to the day we met, when I held his coin in my fist and told him, "It's not good. If you don't want to hear, you can have your money back."

"Avery?"

He couldn't know, he couldn't even know it was bad.

"Avery, what does it mean?"

I took a breath, looked into the face of the boy I loved, and lied.

"Nothing. It means nothing."

Confusion crossed his face. "Nothing?" He shook his head. "I... I don't believe you. I know it means something. Is it about you?"

I clenched my jaw and kept silent.

"Is it... my family? Is it about the men who killed them?"

"Your family? You promised you'd given up avenging them."

"Is that it, then?" he asked, speaking quickly. "The dream has something to do with them. With whoever killed them!"

"No," I said, shaking my head. "I *told* you, it doesn't mean anything." Anxiety turned into frustration turned into anger and I scowled at him. "You promised me you would forget about revenge! You swore you wouldn't spend your life hunting down killers!"

"And you promised to be honest," he said, a corner of his mouth twisted with distaste. "But I know you lie to me now."

"What if the dream did have to do with those men?" I asked, my voice lifting with my temper, for my grandmother's emaciated, pain-riddled body suddenly filled my thoughts. I'd seen, truly seen, what revenge did to a person and knew now how ineffective a balm it was. "What do you think you would do?" I demanded. "Would it make you feel better, to kill them? Would it erase all your pain? Or would you find yourself only more damaged by taking their lives?"

"Who are they?" he asked, grabbing quickly for my shoulders, his face alive with anger in a way I'd never seen before, never even imagined. "Tell me, Avery!"

"They're dead!" I shouted. "They were sailors, and they slaughtered your people in a drunken rage, and soon after they left your island, their ship faltered and they died!" I pulled away from him, my arms tingling from his grip. "If you were to chase them, you'd be chasing flotsam and jetsam and corpses in the ocean, nothing more."

Shock turned his dark skin ashen and he blinked at me, shaking his head so fast that it was almost a tremor. "I don't believe you," he said. "You don't want me to find them, and this is why you lie to me."

"It's not a lie. I met a man in town, wearing one of your people's tattoos. He was at your island. He knew the men who did it."

But Tane's face darkened with distrust. "My people don't give tattoos to sailors. You know that."

"He said they were sick, desperate. He traded a tattoo for medicine. And he told me your people put a curse on the sailors. He told me they avenged their own deaths."

"I don't know anything about curses like that. Why are you lying to me?"

"You left as a child!" Color rose to my cheeks. "You can't know how your island changed or what measures they took to protect themselves!"

"Enough!" He turned from me, shaking his head, and when he glanced back at me, I had to swallow my gasp to see him so angry, so cold, so unlike my Tane. I could almost feel the sparks of anger flying off him, his muscles tense, and he drew himself up, a dark stone statue of judgment and betrayal.

"This is something I need to do," he said, his words careful. "Even if you don't want to tell me, even if you think I might get hurt, I deserve at least to know who really killed my people. You promised me once that you would tell me everything my dreams meant, every little thing, and trust me to make my own decisions. I know there is something waiting for me in my future. I want to know. Even if it's bad. No matter what, I want to know. Avery"—he took a breath—"what does my dream mean?"

Goose bumps tickled my arms at the unnatural timbre of his voice. But I would never tell him.

"Nothing," I said. "It means nothing."

The silence was awful, like all the air in the room had turned to glass or ice and we were stuck, frozen, staring at each other, neither daring nor able to move.

I wanted to tell him, *Trust me, forget all this, believe in me,* but he gazed at me with his dark eyes and I told him nothing.

First, his hands curled into fists, and then he slowly, slowly drew the fists to his chest, but still I didn't move, didn't even flinch, and I wondered if this was how my mother felt, watching her man slip the belt from his waist.

I heard my mother in my ears: "Magic can and will change him"; my grandmother: "Be careful of that boy." Roe women, unlucky in love, find the man who can hurt them the most and give them pain enough to make their magic, but I wouldn't look away from him. I wouldn't run. I trusted him; I trusted that he wouldn't ever hurt me and that he was strong enough to withstand a curse, that *we* were strong enough to withstand a curse.

Whatever happened next, I'd take it with my chin held high and my heart pounding.

He seemed to tremble, a shudder working through his muscles, and when he moved toward me, his body light and quick as a cat's, I jerked away.

But he didn't hit me. He didn't even touch me. He spun around me, head bowed, and made for the lighthouse stairs.

"Wait!" I said, turning to follow him, but when he stared up at me, his eyes were blank as a stranger's and the breath froze in my lungs.

"I'm going," he said. "I can't stay, I can't..." He shook his head, lips pressed tightly together, and without another word ran down the stairs, his footsteps rattling, reverberating through the whole lighthouse.

The door slammed behind him and I felt the floor shake, or perhaps it wasn't the lighthouse at all but me, my own trembling, uncertain body. I slid to the floor, and all the nerve and desperate strength that had filled me seemed suddenly to drain out as I thought, again, of what I'd seen in Tane's dream.

This was what I did not tell Tane: His dream showed not one future but two. I saw something no dream had ever shown me before.

I saw a choice.

Tane's dream showed me that I would die. I would be murdered by a man angry about something terrible that the unraveling of my grandmother's magic had wrought.

But it showed me something else as well. It showed me that Tane would sacrifice his life for mine, that he would stop this man, and that in the struggle he would die but I would live. It was an impossibility, both these futures coming true, because Tane could not save my life if I was to be murdered, and he could not die saving my life if I was killed first.

Two futures, and only one would come true.

And I could choose which one. I could choose to hold up

my head and face my own murder, or I could choose to let Tane die for me.

That's what the dream showed me: two futures, a choice, and one more thing—that the events of the dream would take place within the next twenty-four hours.

Come the following dawn, one of us would be dead.

Part Three

The Island at the End

Twenty-Three

I DIDN'T DECIDE RIGHT AWAY. I ADMIT THAT.

Alone, I crept down the lighthouse stairs and into the night. The sun had gone down and it was very cold, or at least I felt cold, my hands stiff and shaking. I didn't want to stay in New Bishop. I didn't want to return to my mother's house, smashed and broken. In less than a day, Tane or I would be dead, and I had to decide.

I had to decide.

I could feel the island underneath me, the steady rock below my feet, and slowly, without even realizing at first, I began to walk. I walked along the beach, not south and toward the town, the docks, but north, keeping so close to the water that my feet sank into wet sand with every step. With the ocean always on my right, I passed at a distance the well-to-do neighborhood, the grand houses lit up for dinner, for social calls. I walked north, and when I couldn't walk north anymore, I followed the curve of the island, circling, counterclockwise, my comma-shaped home.

I listened to the wind whistle through the grasslands to my left and kept walking. I made it out to the Great Gray Slough, which sang with nighttime sounds of birds, insects, the rare slap of a fish against water. I didn't stop to listen but continued south down Prince Island's western shore, and by the time I reached the fishing village, Weld Haven, the sky had just barely, just a bit, begun to lighten.

On the beach, fishermen gathered to check over their little boats, their supplies, while their wives' silhouettes patterned the windows of their tiny huts and cottages. I kept far enough above shore that at first I didn't think they saw me, but it takes more than quiet footsteps to fool a fisherman. One and then another and then all of them turned their sun-leathered cheeks and crinkly eyes up the dunes to watch me.

They, like the sailors, must have known that my grandmother's spells had failed. Maybe they even knew, with their preternatural feeling for the ocean, that she had died. More than the sailors or the people of New Bishop, they depended on Roe magic day by day to keep food in their children's mouths, and as they watched me, their quick fingers quiet on their lines, I tensed.

But then, as though by some unspoken agreement, they turned back to their work, and a few lifted their hands parallel to the sand and water, wavering their palms like fishes slapping across the deck: the fisherman's greeting and farewell. Hello and good-bye, witch girl. Hello and good-bye, magic. They pushed off into the ocean and didn't look back.

My grandmother's house was only an hour away and, as I had done the day before, I stopped to sleep and to finish off her meager stores. She had a big tin tub in the corner, and with the last of her precious water, I gave myself a bath, first heating the water over her fire before pouring it luxuriously into the tub.

I scrubbed the sand and sweat from between my toes and under my fingernails and washed my face until my skin seemed to sing. Carefully, I untangled each black hair on my head and sat, for a long time, facing away from the fire, feeling my hair dry and curl and fluff against the muscles of my back. My grandmother did not have many fine clothes, but I found stuffed in a cabinet a white dress with a blue ribbon at the waist that did nothing as far as matching my grandmother's old boots but did, at least, make me feel pretty.

Fed, washed, and dressed, I studied the silent cottage and slowly walked to the foot of the bed. There it was. The big black chest, just as I remembered.

My fingers tingled as I lifted the huge lid, and inside... I saw my grandmother's supplies, neat and organized. I saw Almira Roe's book of languages and Frances Roe's book of plants and their uses, illustrated by H.K., a man she loved. I reached in and touched the onionskin papers jotted with notes and drawings from Roes going back decades, generations. There were other trinkets in there, things that had nothing to do with magic: a flower pressed between glass, a necklace of scrimshaw, a ring. Little bits of themselves to love and remember and keep safe, to remind their daughters and granddaughters and great-granddaughters that they were more than just powerful witches but women, too.

I stared at the things for a long time, and then I picked up my discarded dress from the floor and reached into the pocket. Tane's drawing, the drawing of me, was still there, a little wrinkled and worn from having been carried around so long.

The girl in the drawing looked at me, and I reached out and touched her eyes, the lines of her mouth. This was the way Tane saw me: scared but strong, daunted but determined. Decided.

I understood.

I would never be the witch. But perhaps I could still keep Tane safe.

And carefully, I placed the drawing into the chest with all the other Roe memories and shut the lid.

I was done. There was nothing to do but get started back to New Bishop. It was late afternoon, and if I made good time, I could reach the town just by nightfall.

Time to go.

Get up, time to go.

Avery? Come on now, don't be difficult.

And so I pushed myself from the floor and stood in the center of the room. Before I walked out of the cottage, though, I needed to do one more thing (and maybe I was procrastinating, but could anyone blame me?). Lifting the still-hot coals from the fireplace, I carefully scattered them around my grandmother's cottage, coughing as thick black smoke reared up at me. By the time I made it out the door, the little gray cottage was burning in earnest, a miniature sun up on the cliff, a beacon, a lighthouse that, no doubt, the fishermen could see even now.

With the smell of smoke in the air, I turned my back and set off for town.

I don't know what the people of my island will make of my story, the story of the end of the Roes. Will they blame me when their ships splinter? Will they remember that I fought for years against my mother, that I tried to go home and set it all right? Will any of them know that I gave up all of it—magic, my own life, and their livelihood—for a tattooed harpoon boy?

But even if they will never know this whole story, it's helped me to remember why I've made this choice, to remind myself that although I will die tonight, in only a few hours, it will be to save the life of the boy I love. It has helped me know what to do and it has brought me to this moment, standing at the outskirts of New Bishop, watching the lamps come on in the houses while the sky turns crimson-orange in a sunset that seems to know it will be the last I'll ever see and is showing off accordingly.

I stand, my feet in my grandmother's boots, her dress swaying in the breeze, and I wonder where to go first (find Tane? Or, no, stay away from him?) when I hear the bells.

Every whaling town has its own way to spread news of an islander's death at sea, and in New Bishop, we use bells. A six-note tune, to be specific, followed by one tone for every Prince Island man confirmed dead.

As the tune begins, chills run down my spine, and I, along with every other person in town, count the number of bell tolls. We have never, in the entire history of my island, had more than six men die at one time, and when the bells reach six and keep ringing, keep ringing, I feel my head swim, hazy with shock.

Ten. Fifteen. Twenty. The bells continue until it seems they will never stop, but when they finally, finally fall silent, the absence of noise rings as loud as the bells themselves.

Thirty-two.

Thirty-two dead.

A whole ship.

It is my grandmother's magic, quickly unraveling, turning seemingly seaworthy ships into wreckage, and amid my fear and confusion, I ask myself the question that half the island now wonders: Which ship was it?

People will gather at the wharf, where William Bliss, the dockmaster, will announce the details—such as they know, for even with the telegraph bridging faraway worlds, the sinkings of ships are often murky, misunderstood events.

Still on the darkened outskirts of town, the echo of the bells rolling through me, I duck my head and walk quickly in the direction of Main Street and the wharf, stopping only at the Abels' backyard, where Mrs. Abel has hung a gray traveling cloak with the rest of the laundry. I grab the cloak and throw it, still damp, around my shoulders, taking care to pull its hood to the edges of my face.

Already the streets are full of chattering islanders, their faces grim with worry. I hear women whisper to each other and watch as one older woman bends over a crying girl, touching a necklace made of shell—one of so many protection charms my grandmother wrought.

"There, there, Judith," the woman says. "Benji's all right! You've still got your necklace, haven't you?"

So the news of my grandmother's death hasn't spread entirely, not yet, and I shiver and keep walking.

At the wharf, I have to skim the edges of the crowd in order to see anything; it looks as though the whole of Prince Island has packed itself into the water-lined courtyard, illuminated by the sickly light of the streetlamps and by a few pragmatic souls' lanterns.

I see William Bliss pacing at the end of the wharf, the docks and his clasped hands behind him. A knot of sailors stands off to the side, their eyes never leaving his face. Pressed up against a building, I crane to look over the heads of the crowd, but I don't see Tane with them. I don't see him anywhere.

The sharp whispering of the crowd falls silent as William Bliss climbs atop a stack of wooden crates and stares out at us all.

"Tell us what's happened!" a woman shrieks, and another girl cries out, "Is it the *Valhalla*?"

A chorus of shushes rises from the crowd, and William Bliss raises his hands.

"This afternoon, we received a telegram from the captain of the *Martha Porter* in the Azores," he says, his voice shaky but loud. "He told us that he'd received reports that the *Eagle Wing*—"

Dozens of shouts and sharp cries drown out the rest of William Bliss's words, and I clutch at the cloak around my neck, my legs rubbery and unsteady. The *Eagle Wing*...no, no...*Tommy*...

Over the cries of the crowd, William Bliss lifts his voice, shouting the details that I can barely hear, that the *Martha Porter* found the wreckage, found the bodies, buried them at sea, but it doesn't matter, it doesn't matter because we already know that every man on that ship is dead and because I know that Tommy Thompson, my sweet friend, is with them. I hear names, men's names, rise up from the churning, grieving people of my island, and when no one calls Tommy's name, I tilt my face down to the ground and whisper for him.

"*Tommy*," I say, my whole body shaking, vibrating as tears sting my eyes and fall to the cobblestones at my feet. Why?

How did this happen? He was seventeen and didn't deserve to die. He had spells to keep him safe—he should have been safe—and just like that my grief turns to anger. I'm not alone.

"That ship wasn't supposed to sink!" a man shouts.

"What happened to all those charms! Unsinkable!"

"The witch promised the *Eagle Wing* would never falter! How did this happen?"

Amid the grief of crying women—wives, sweethearts, mothers—I hear, feel another howl, a howl of betrayal and desperation. Other towns lost ships. Other towns built memorials to the dead lost at sea. But not Prince Island, not the island where sailors leave port weighed down with trinkets and wishes and promises.

"Find the witch!" The voice jumps from the crowd like a bolt of lightning. "Find the witch and make her pay!"

The people of my island roar their approval and I blink, stunned to see what my grandmother tried to impress upon me so many times: how delicate our balance with the islanders truly was and how easily it could topple. And now I press myself against the building at my back and pull my stolen hood down over my eyes and watch the people I thought loved the Roes scream for our blood.

I have to fight the urge to slip away unseen and leave behind the mob before they find me. It has to be like this. Someone in this crowd, someone angry at what has happened, will kill me tonight. Shaking, I move to lower my hood, to step into the crowd, when a single voice rises above the shouting.

"Wait! Wait!" So much authority in that voice that

everyone quiets, confused, and looks for the speaker. I see him leap atop the crates next to William Bliss, his calm face now tense and stern, his skin shining in the lamplight. Tane.

"The witch is dead!" he says, and when the crowd mutters their confusion, he continues. "She is dead, and her magic with her!"

Frowning, I bite my lip. What is he doing up there? Why is he involving himself?

Others seem to wonder the same thing, shouting up at him to stay out of it, that this is island business and no place for foreigners, but William Bliss steadies the crowd.

"I've seen him around the Roe girl," he shouts. "Let him speak!"

"No, Tane," I whisper, my heart in my throat as he studies the crowd.

"Avery Roe told me yesterday that her grandmother is dead," he says. "She also told me that all the witch's magic and charms are now useless and ineffective."

"What'll that mean for our ships?" a man shouts, twisting to be heard over the cries of panic and confusion. "The *Valhalla*'s got just as many spells as the *Eagle Wing* did! It can't fail!"

"You can no longer rely on the witch," Tane says, and am I wrong? Or do I hear anger in his voice?

"Where's the girl?" a man asks. "Where's the Roe girl? The little witch? Make her fix it!"

"And the mother," a pinch-faced woman shrieks. "Let's not forget about *her*!"

"Come on," says a burly man with a lantern, and I recognize him as one of the dock stevedores. "We know where Pastor Sever's house is! We'll drag the witch out!"

Shoving breaks out as the men struggle to align themselves but then a high-pitched voice calls out, "Stop!" and I recognize Lucy, my mother's twelve-year-old kitchen maid. She's pale and thin under the lamps and the attention of half the island, but she stands bravely and says with tears in her eyes, "They're gone, all of them! The house near caved in two days ago, hit by a spell, they 'spect, and last night the pastor lit up and left with all the drawers in the house still full! Took a chartered boat to the mainland with his family!"

"The witch woman, too?"

Lucy nods. There's a scuffle and I see Mrs. Plummer, the cook who would tell me stories about Almira Roe, standing at Lucy's elbow. Her face is drawn, serious, as she places her hand on Lucy's shoulder, and she hisses something to her, something about the Roes, the island, a debt. But Lucy shakes her off, her voice tense and high-pitched as she says, "Leave off! It's the Roes' fault they're all dead!" She turns to the crowd, eyes shining with tears. "The woman left, but not the girl! I haven't seen her in three days, and I'd bet anything she's still on the island!"

Mrs. Plummer shouts something else—I only just hear the word "calm!" ring out—and then another woman yells at her to keep quiet, that I'm a menace to the island, and more voices join her, screaming for me, *me*, Avery Roe, who failed the Roes and failed them all and didn't do what she was supposed to.

"She tried! She tried!" It's Billy Macy, the rope-maker who wished me well on my escape, but louder voices shout him down, beat him back, and when I catch his face between the flailing limbs of the crowd, I see a thin line of blood stream from his nose.

I wish I could melt into the building at my back, my skin sweaty and cold, but I don't dare even to leave the crowd for fear of drawing attention to myself. I hear them shout to each other about where I might be, when one young man, an island-born sailor, leaps onto the stack of crates at the edge of the dock and seizes the front of Tane's shirt.

"You know where she's at, don' you?" he asks, voice crisp with malice. "You can tell us!"

He pushes Tane as he speaks, and when they stumble for balance and fall from the crates, my blood turns icy in my veins, immobilizing me completely, and I don't know if it's fear or instinct or love or just plain desperation that forces me to action, but I throw back my hood and press into the crowd and scream at the top of my lungs, "I'm here! I'm here!"

There's a moment of surprise and in that moment I see them all, frozen, every face in town turned to me and every face a mix of anger, of betrayal, of grief and revenge and hurt. And then the dam breaks and they surge toward me, hands and teeth and fingernails bared and wicked and so furious that fear crests through me and I wonder if this is how I'll die: literally torn to pieces by the islanders.

William Bliss leaps off the crates and into the crowd and

presses his arms around me, scant protection as he pulls me back to the edge of the wharf, and he can't prevent a few islanders from taking swipes at me, raking their fingernails across the exposed skin of my cheeks and arms. I feel my cloak choke at my neck before it's lost to the mass of outreached hands, while another hand—belonging to a woman, to judge by the satisfied screech—pulls out a stinging chunk of my long hair.

William Bliss sets me atop the crates, facing the islanders, so that I'm alone on this makeshift stage, so that every islander can see me now, can roil and boil and shake their fists at me as I stand before them trembling like a rabbit before wolves.

I want to tell them they know me: I'm Avery, I'm the Avery they said "good morning" to and the Avery who told their dreams. I'm the Avery who's seen their faces my whole life, who grew up with them and played with them and laughed with them, who knows that Betty Shelley lost a baby last spring and Henry Snider likes clams for breakfast and Emily Wells can't speak to a boy she likes without a stutter. I'm the Avery who learned by heart the curve of Main Street and the rickety places on the docks and the smell of the refineries like sweet, rotting fish. I'm Avery Roe with the prickly temper and fights with my mother, the girl who loves this island and wanted, *wanted* to be their witch.

But just like the islanders forgot my grandmother was once a regular girl, Jennie Roe with the laugh and the bright eyes, and saw her only as the witch, my people look up at me now and see me only as a failure.

I can't look at them anymore, and I search instead for a kinder face, one that loves me, but when I finally find Tane, he stares up at me with an expression of blank confusion. He blinks, dazed for a moment, and then he seems to hear the roar of the crowd, seems to notice at last the hatred thrown at me, and just as I expect him to offer me something—hope, a smile, protection—his whole face darkens, his warm brown eyes turn black and cold, and slowly, slowly his lips stretch into a grimace that sends a shiver of shock through me.

"Avery Roe!" William Bliss climbs up onto the crates with me, but he faces the crowd. "What do you have to say about the news that your grandmother is dead?"

Tearing my gaze from Tane's face, I turn to the crowd and want to clear my throat, but instead I end up mangling my words: "I-it's true."

"And does this mean that all your grandmother's spells are useless?"

"Yes." I swallow. "Yes, they're useless now."

William Bliss glances at me sharply. "And will you ensure the survival of the Roe witch's magic?"

My body trembles. "I...cannot."

"Why is that?" William Bliss asks over shouts of anger. "Why is that when we've all heard from you, many times, how you will take your grandmother's place?"

I take a breath but it's not enough, I'm gulping down air, wide eyes tripping from face to face. "I do not know how to do her magic. I am not a witch."

Protests of "Liar!" leap out at me, and William Bliss says, "We know that is not true! You tell dreams and you have for years!"

All I can do is shake my head. "Dream-telling is different. I can't do her magic."

"She split the roof on the pastor's house!" Lucy pipes from the crowd. "Tore the whole thing in half, practically!"

"I can't—I couldn't—" I wheeze for air, my head swimming. "That was only one time!"

William Bliss's strong hands grip my shoulders, forcing my gaze onto his cold face. "Your family's spells are responsible for the deaths of thirty-two of our men," he says, and although he's quiet, almost whispering, I know the whole crowd can hear what he speaks. "Most likely that number will only grow when more spells fail. Your grandmother is dead. Your mother has fled the island. You are the only Roe woman left on the island and the only person able to save the lives of our men on the sea. If you refuse to help, their deaths and the deaths of the crew of the *Eagle Wing* will be on your head. We will hold you responsible. You, Avery Roe, for failing to live up to what your family has promised us. Will you fix your grandmother's wrong and ensure this island's survival?"

I close my eyes, just for a second, and in that second I think of all the times I have wished for a moment like this, when the people of my island would turn to me as their savior.

But it's not meant to be.

I open my eyes and look out onto the crowd and say, with as clear and strong a voice as I can muster, "I cannot."

The people surge forward but William Bliss stands in front of me, and in the roar of so many furious, betrayed people I can hear him call for the sheriff. A lantern illuminates the chief of Prince Island's paltry police force: a red-faced and round-stomached man, pushing forward in the crowd, his heavy iron handcuffs dangling high over his head. He reaches for me, moving to strike the cuffs across my wrists, when a voice calls out to stop.

And it's Tane, my beautiful Tane, striding forward now, the crowd parting for him like stalks of wheat, all eyes on him.

"Don't get involved," I whisper to him, although he's too far away to hear. "Please, please go!"

But I know also that he wants to save me, I know he will try something desperate like this, I know it for certain up until the moment when he turns and faces me and I see with all the force of a slap that this is not the boy I love anymore, that I'm too late to save him—I'm too late, the curse has changed him, stripped away all that's good and left him a monster with flashing, furious eyes and a cruel mouth, and he stands in front of the crowd and says with a strength and authority that no one could possibly challenge:

"She is a sea witch. Let us throw her into the sea."

Twenty-Four

"NO! TANE, NO!" I SCREAM, AND LUNGE forward, but I'm caught around my waist by strong hands, angry hands that trap me on the crates. I'm shouting, shouting for him, shouting because I'm scared and angry and *too late*— the Tane I know would never do something like this to me and I'm too late to stop my family's curse and now the magic has changed him, turned him from the boy I love into a monster.

Everything falls into confusion around me, men shouting, women screaming, footsteps on the docks, and Tane's voice rises above the commotion, clear and angry as he barks instructions at the men.

"She says she's not a witch!" Tane turns and points a long finger at me, and I can hardly recognize him, I can hardly *breathe.* "Throw her into the ocean! If she's truly a witch, she'll save herself!"

"But if she's innocent, she'll drown!" It's woman's voice, and I recognize Ethel, one of my mother's housemaids, face contorted in worry, but soon a chorus of voices silences her.

"She's a witch—she'll save herself!"

"A test! She needs a test!"

"We can't let more of our sailors die!"

Tane leads the way down the stairs to the docks behind me, and when he glances back at me, there's no love, only a cold, black anger that I don't recognize, and I can't believe it: I can't believe how much he's changed and so quickly, and my mother was right! The magic transformed him, made him hurt me, and he's doing it now, he's doing it and I don't know how to stop him and I don't know how to get him—the real Tane—*back*!

"No, no!" I cry, and it has nothing to do with the rope someone loops around my wrists or the rough tugs at my grandmother's finest dress. Strong-handed men wrestle me down from the crates, dragging me to the docks, and I pull against them, screaming Tane's name.

When my boots trip up, one man hoists me to his shoulder, and, craning my neck, I see he's taking me down to the very last boat at the end of the pier, golden-prowed and white-sailed and ready to take off from harbor at a moment's notice: the *Modena*.

They mean to sail out to sea and drop me in the water, and this is it: I'm going to die, now, right now, and Tane is still locked in my family's curse—*forever?* How do I help him? What do I do? There's no more time!

"Tane!" I shriek, but he's disappeared into the crowd of men who swarm the *Modena*, busy loosening the ropes that keep her sails furled. Two more men work the chain that tethers the anchor, while others slip ropes off the cleats on the dock.

The person carrying me climbs up the gangplank and sets me roughly on my feet, and I stare, dazed, at the thrum of activity surrounding me, the sailors working quickly to set the *Modena* out to sea, when it hits me that they're taking me off the island. I will be away from my home when I die—I'm leaving the island forever, and I want to cry or scream or for someone to just kill me, now, now while I can still see my island, or no, I want there to be a problem with the ship, a loose rigging, a torn sail, no wind and no current and the ship never leaving the waters of the harbor, but I don't even get that. It takes the space of two hundred fast, shallow breaths for the men to ready the ship, and then they stand, tensed and silent, on the main deck, watching William Bliss for directions.

"She'll only need six men," he says, and I'm not sure if he means me or the *Modena*. "Come on, lads, most of you will need to come off."

The sailors stare at him silently and I look into their faces, wondering if they will be relieved or disappointed to have to leave the boat. Why won't one of them say something to me? Why won't one of them just look at me? But their expressions show no guilt or hesitation. Instead: anger. Betrayal. I let them down. I made them think they were safe, and now their friends and brothers and cousins are dead. *I'm angry, too*, I want to tell them. *I lost someone, too, and it's not what I wanted.*

One by one, they slip to the gangplank and back to the docks until only a few remain at their ropes. Other than a tall man who I think is the *Modena*'s captain, I know them all. There's Horace Green, who once bought five love charms in a single summer. And old Jake Kilrain, who used to bring me sweets whenever he visited my grandmother. I spot round-faced Neely Campbell at the foremast, and manning the mainmast, the dock jokester, Frank Leroy. I peer into the darkness, looking for the sixth sailor, and when I find him, hysteria creeps up inside of me and I scream out a protest.

"Not you! Anyone but you!"

But Tane ignores me and stands beside Neely Campbell, the end of a thick rope in his hands. I cry and try to run to him, to stop him, because even though my family's magic has changed him, I still want him to be safe. As long as I live, his life is in danger, but when I shriek at him to get off the boat, the *Modena*'s tall captain catches me and pushes me roughly to the deck.

The men on board and the men on the dock say nothing as the captain readies himself behind the wheel, and then they begin their song: calling out to one another to man positions, ready sails. Music of the docks, the rhythm of shouts and grunts and squeaking ropes, and it raises shivers on my skin.

Sometimes a ship launch can be tricky, the wind and water uncooperative, and captains must call for towlines and tugboats, but they are lucky tonight. A fine wind blows into the sails, pushing the *Modena* out from the docks with a sudden wrench, and I am jolted to realize that, for all the days and months and years I've spent at the docks, with my thoughts wrapped up in sails and seas, this is the first (and only) time I have ever set foot on a moving whaler.

The ropes squeak and whine and the sails flap dully in the breeze and the men call out, "Heave! Heave! Heave!" as though this is just another whaling expedition, a different sort of hunt. I hear the strain of the sails mingle with the sailors' grunts, and the white wings stretch above me, fluttering and full. They snap and balloon with air, and we're already moving fast enough, the whaler stretching to the harbor, waves slapping at her hull.

I twist my head around to look over the edge of the ship and a force like a knife blade sweeps up into me. This is it; this is when I leave my island! I want to leap to my feet and throw my body over the bulwarks and swim for *home*.

But I can't. Either Tane or I will die tonight and I've already made my choice.

"Good-bye," I whisper, and I close my eyes and let the *Modena* carry me to sea.

For all the *Modena*'s size, all she needs is a hand on the wheel and sails full of wind to keep her moving, and one by one, the sailors drift down to the main deck where I sit. Horace Green and Frank Leroy lean against the tryworks while Neely Campbell climbs the rigging to peer down at me, blinking round eyes in the lamplight.

Footsteps from the upper deck make me turn, and I see Tane walk slowly to join the others, his eyes on the black ocean.

"Tane," I whisper, staring at him. "I know you're still in there. You've been cursed, Tane, and that's why you're doing this."

"Quiet," Horace Green says, not harshly.

"Please," I whisper, and Tane's face grows drawn and tense. "Please, this isn't you! I know it! Tane, Tane, I love you."

The men don't move, heads bowed. Whale men to the end, keeping their noses out of a fellow's business, but I can feel their attention on my skin as surely as the wind. I stare into Tane's face, searching for any spark of life or love, but the voice that slides from him is black and icy.

"I do not love you."

His words float on the air, and I can feel my body crumpling, my ribs crushing around my heart, the ache in my stomach expanding. I failed. I lost him. I will die but it doesn't matter, and Tane won't have any kind of life, no happiness or love or babies because the curse has changed him, destroyed him, turned him into a monster; and what my mother said was true: "He will hurt you in ways you cannot imagine."

I try not to cry, pressing my lips and eyelids so tightly closed that I feel veins standing out on my temples and neck. A pit seems to open up within me, tearing at my stomach and chest with so much force that I actually place my bound hands to my body, feeling for the edges of a hole.

And then: a spark.

It blazes before me in the darkness, although I still have my eyes shut, and then the pain inside of me bursts into flames, seizing my stomach and my skin, forcing my eyes open, my lungs to gasp for breath. Magic—horrible, raw, burning magic lunges through my veins, setting me aflame, and just like at my mother's house, when her terrible words fed the pain that fed my magic, I feel Tane's betrayal sink into my skin, pierce me full of a million holes, and bubbling up through the holes is *power*.

The witch inside of me roars with delight as all around, I feel the network of life, of magic. I feel the heartbeats of the men, still unaware of what's happening to me, and I feel the pull of the tides, the breath of the wind, and I know that I can control it, all of it, all of them.

The ropes at my wrist fall apart with a sizzle and a snap, and, instinct taking over, I pull a length of the rope tight between my two hands as the memory comes back to me: six years old, my grandmother's lap, her breath stirring my hair.

It is easier this time, so much easier and so much faster, the magic surging through me, the wind whipping up my hair and clutching at the sailors, who shout with confusion and run for their ropes. Through the pain of my spell I feel pleasure, too, the pleasure of knowing that I am, at last, doing what I have always been meant to do, and I laugh, a laugh that sounds nothing like me, and as the wind curves into a screech, my hands fly unnaturally fast, just as they did once before, one-two-three times, making knots in the rope that tethered and bound the power of the wind.

I stand up, the knotted rope in my fist, and one of the sailors notices me, shouts, "She's doin' a spell! Stop her!"

But they're too far away, and I yank open the first knot.

A gentle breeze, that's all it is, and out here, a mile at least from the shore, the island tiny and distant, I can barely tell the difference between it and the ocean wind. I don't give it a moment's thought, because in another instant I tug free the second knot: the fine trade wind, strong enough to press against our faces with cold steel hands.

Only a moment has passed since the sailor's shout, and as I reach for the third knot, their voices rise with fear and they lunge for me, to stop me, only I cannot be stopped, not now, maybe not ever, and even though I feel, dimly, that what I am about to do will likely kill them, will likely kill—*oh no*, will likely kill Tane!—whatever concerns the Avery of ten minutes or ten seconds ago might have had are now obliterated and overwhelmed by the wild thing living inside of me, which grabs for the last knot—the hurricane knot—and screams in a voice entirely unlike my own, "*You cannot kill a Roe witch!*"

My hands slip on the knot, tug, pull it free, and for a moment the men can only stare at me, *Tane* can only stare at me, his eyes wide and blank with shock, and I feel a sudden rush of regret, of worry, but then it's too late, it's too late because my magical wind has swept down over us and grabbed us in its claws.

A roar like an animal's howl crashes over the decks, bringing with it sheets of rain and bright, sudden flashes of lightning. The *Modena* lurches hard to the starboard side as a huge wave topples over the decks, ruining my grandmother's best dress and chilling me to the bone. Shouting, screaming men run across the decks, already so waterlogged that I can't tell them apart, but their wide eyes flash white with fear and I know they understand that this is no ordinary storm.

The wind picks up around us, tossing and spinning the *Modena* like a toy, tearing the sails loose from their rigging. My hair and then my dress and then my body lift into the air, and I clutch for a rope and snake it around my wrist.

Screams whip past as bodies fly up around me, and something hard—a piece of the whaler, a lantern, a barrel—smashes into my shoulder. Something like a giant, unsteady hand topples me, tears the rope from my wrist with a crack and twists me head over toes into the swirling black mass in the sky and I know I should be afraid, should be screaming like the men, but the witch within me loves this, loves the rough tossing of the sky and water, the flashes of lightning, the power of the world unleashed.

I spin and float, my arms and legs and hair pulled in a thousand directions at once before I slam into the water, a force so sudden and surprising that it's as though I jumped from the top of a mast straight onto the deck, and I can only gasp and choke and swallow a mouthful of sea.

The waters are no less wild than the air, and I feel swirling, sucking powers reaching for me, but I fight them, I can fight them, and I bob to the surface and burst up, the screaming wind blistering in my ears.

I tread water, blinking furiously at the stinging salt, and as the cold leaches through my skin, shocking sense into me, I am overwhelmed at last by what I have done. A wave lifts me, raising me into the air five, ten, twenty feet before it crashes back into the ocean below, and I spin like a cork, my teeth and bones rattling.

I have to stop this—I have to or I'll drown—but it's not so easy now, the fearless witch silenced and cowed by the fury of the ocean, and besides, my grandmother never taught me what to do when spells get out of my control.

Another wave spins me, and this time I'm barely steadied before more water crashes onto my head and pours itself down my throat. The fire inside of me quenched, I feel panic clutch my chest, and I scream into the air.

"Avery!"

His voice almost gets swallowed into the wind, but I hear it and, impossibly, my heartbeat quickens. He's alive! Tane's alive! Power surges through me along with happiness, and I feel the threads of the sky and sea quiet.

"Tane! Tane!" With each vibration of my voice the roar of the storm dies, just a little bit, until the waves turn smooth as glass and the storm clouds pull back as suddenly as if someone has opened curtains in the sky. I feel a terror creep through me to see the world go so terribly still at my bidding, not even the break of waves to disturb the silence.

Silence. *Silence.*

Fear shoots through me, and I call for him again, spinning frantically in the black ocean, too dark and too quiet.

But then my name rings out into the air, white-foamed

splashes light up in the darkness, and I swim forward, my dress dragging me under but my heart a buoy to keep me upright, and in the terrifying emptiness of the ocean, I find him again.

He's laughing and crying and kicking furiously underwater, reaching out to me with one hand. We twine our fingers together and he pulls me closer, and as I bob against him, he kisses me, over and over and over until I weep with relief because he's back, truly, the Tane I know and love.

. I push away from him, trying to make out his features in the darkness. "I thought I had lost you!" I whisper, tears pricking my eyes.

He laughs, a tight, exhausted laugh. "I'm here," he says, but I shake my head.

"No, no, my mother said—she said that my family has a curse, that whoever we love is destined to hurt us. I thought... I thought you—"

"I wouldn't hurt you," he says. "Not even if I were cursed."

"But at the wharf," I say, tears striking my cheeks, "you said—"

"Out on the water, I could grab you and swim. I could get you away from five men. But I can't steal you away with the entire island watching. I can't break handcuffs and I can't break jails."

"But"—and I know I should stop, just be grateful, but I shake my head—"you said you didn't... you didn't love me."

"What else was I going to say in a boat full of men ready to let you drown?" Under the water, he grabs for my hand, cold and small in his, and stares at me, fierce and blazing. "Avery, I love you. I will always love you, always. I am not cursed and I never will be. I love you, I love you!"

He's crying and I'm crying and it feels so good to hear him say that, to feel him on my skin. We lean forward and kiss as best as we can, laughing, floating in the ocean, treading water and breathing hard, and finally Tane breaks away to scan the ocean for the *Modena*.

She lists heavily to the port side, and her foremast and mainmast—two of her three backbones—stick out at strange angles, shattered and useless. Sails hang in tatters like bunches of cobwebs, her ropes and riggings an impossible tangle. The surrounding waves must once have been full of jetsam, but everything now is swept clean, and with no wind and no waves, the *Modena* bobs in the water like a buoy. She won't sail, maybe ever again, but several of her whaleboats—thirty feet long, with oars and lanterns—remain lashed to her sides.

We splash toward the ship, my hurt shoulder burning from the effort. Tane finds a piece of rigging stretched into the ocean and helps me up. My hands slide and slip on the wet rope, my shoes scrambling for purchase on the smooth hull, but I manage to haul myself over the bulwarks and onto the deck, where I sprawl out in my soaked dress, gasping for air.

Tane lands heavily beside me, breathing hard, and for a moment all we can do is lie side by side, staring up at the blazing constellations of stars shining through the last wispy traces of my magical storm.

"You're really the witch," he says softly, and I reach down and grip his hand tight in mine.

"What happens now?" I whisper.

He rolls to his side and kisses me again before we stand up and look out at the ocean. Nothing. No men, no murderer, just black, swirling waves. Darkness except for a handful of faraway lights: Prince Island, my home.

"We can't go back there," Tane says, his voice steady.

And I know what he says is true. I know there's no life for me on the island, not anymore. But still, I feel it call to me, sing to my blood and heartbeat.

"We can get in a whaleboat and row," Tane whispers, close at the side of my face. "We're only a few miles from the mainland. We can make it there by morning. I have money. We can do it."

I turn to him but, like a spell, the moment he stops speaking I pull away, my eyes on the lights of my island.

"Avery?" His wet fingers twist around mine. There's a plea in his voice, plaintive and nervous, as though he knows that despite everything that has happened, I will still leave him.

"What about your reputation?" I ask. "Your contract?"

He spreads an arm over the ruined deck. "I was contracted to sail the *Modena*, and she'll never sail again."

"But..." Tears fill my eyes. "I wasn't supposed to be the witch. You were supposed to be cursed. I was supposed to die tonight. Your dream...it wasn't about your family, Tane, it was about me. My death."

"No one will hurt you," he says, fierce, shaking his head. "Maybe our fates are too complicated to tell in dreams." He pauses. "I thought I was supposed to avenge my family."

I stare at him. "You know, then, that I wasn't lying. Those men really are dead."

"Dead or not..." He takes a deep, shuddering breath. "You were right. I can't...My sisters, my parents...they wouldn't have wanted me to spend my life seeking revenge."

"You wanted to kill them. I wanted to be Prince Island's witch," I say, and despite the warmth of his hand, I feel a cold dread settle into my stomach. "What do we do when everything we've wanted falls out of reach?"

A frown crosses his face and he lifts his hands to cup my cheeks. "That's not true," he whispers. "I want you, and you are right here." He presses his forehead against mine, eyes squeezed tight. "I want to show you the world. I want to marry you. I want you to come with me in a whaleboat and sail away." He opens his eyes and looks into my face. "What do you want?"

What do I want?

And I am ashamed to say what I want, what I truly, deeply, desperately want: to pull away and plunge into the water and swim for my home, for the only place in the world that makes sense to me.

Maybe Tane knows what I mean to say, because before I can open my mouth he kisses me, and it's as if a drop of heat slides down my throat, hits my chest and spreads, spreads out through my arms, my legs, my fingers, my toes, and all the fear hidden inside of me disappears because he's here, because he'll be with me to remind me that I'm strong enough to leave behind the world I've always known and trust that what's waiting on the outside is even better.

My magic blazes up around us, hot and strong, and I know he knows my answer; he can feel it in my pulse, in the beat of my saltwater heart, and he pulls away from me and sees my smile and throws his head back and laughs. He is such a boy, laughing and cheering, running around the deck grinning, and I laugh back at him and feel within me a happiness so astonishing that it is all I can do to breathe. Breathe and be grateful.

He returns to me and kisses me once, his face lit up with a smile. "Ready?"

"Yes," I say, and I mean it this time. "Yes."

He turns and makes his way to the edge of the ship, where the long, narrow whaleboats hang suspended from pulleys. I watch at first as he loosens the ropes, my heartbeat drumming so fast that I feel as if I might float in the air.

"I'll need a hand," he says, leaning over the edge of the boat. He turns to glance back at me. "Do you think you could—"

A moment's silence and then Tane lunges for me, his eyes wide, his arms outstretched, and a cry of fear crosses my lips before his heavy body smashes into me, forcing me down onto the deck. The world spins and I just manage to roll out of the way of a heavy black boot aimed in my direction, and my eyes travel up the boot to a leg, a body, a face so twisted with rage that I almost don't recognize him: Frank Leroy, a Prince Island sailor, wet as a seal and holding a knife and screaming something, something terrible, that it's my fault, that I killed his son, that the murderous witch has to die.

Twenty-Five

I'M ROLLING, SPINNING, SEARCHING FOR my footing on the slick deck while around me I hear the thuds, the groans and moans and cracks of Tane and Frank Leroy, dim shapes locked together and thrashing. When I finally scramble to my feet, I can just make out the two of them: Tane, bigger, younger, faster, and Frank, the slash of his bright knife more than making up for his lack of strength.

"Don't hurt him!" I shout, and I stretch out, frantic and terrified, for the threads of feeling that can stop him, but I find myself empty and powerless, no longer in pain and no longer a witch, and maybe no longer free from my fate, my dream: Maybe Tane or I will still die tonight.

But a choice! I have a choice! If I die, he lives, and that means I can save him now with my own death! With my eyes squeezed tight and my breath choking in my lungs, I spring on top of the rolling, stumbling, shouting bodies, hoping that Frank's long knife finds its place in my gut.

A shoulder hits me square in the chest, knocking the air from me as my head falls against the deck, and I hear Tane's gasp of surprise and feel the tangle of limbs—arms, legs—wrap around me. In the confusion I don't know which is Tane and which is Frank, but I buck my body as much as possible, screaming, "It's me you want!"

Warm hands wrench me away: Tane, Tane pulling me to my feet and tossing me, dizzy, to the deck, and when I blink the bursting stars from my vision, I see Frank running up the stairs to the upper deck, Tane on his heels.

"Get away from him!" I shout, and I don't know if I'm shouting to Tane or to Frank, but neither listens to me, and I scramble to my feet, my legs shaking. The main deck is slick with salt water, tangled with messy coils of rope, and I stumble a bit as I run to the upper deck, following the noise of their fight.

The long, narrow bow stretches out in front of me, and at the end, Frank Leroy raises his knife against Tane, his face so contorted to be almost unrecognizable.

"No!" I shout, but Tane lifts up a thick piece of wood to parry the blow, and when Frank stumbles, off balance, Tane slams the wood into Frank's side. I hear a crunch and Frank crumples in pain, but his knife still slashes out, bright as sparks, and, wary, Tane backs up.

I run to them and force myself between Tane and Frank, throwing my arms in front of Tane's body.

"Dead, dead," Frank mutters, one hand steadying himself, the other whistling the knife through the air. In the faint moonlight I see tear tracks etch his sweaty, feverish skin, see the anguish written deep on his face, and although it does not matter now, not really anymore, I remember that Frank Leroy's twelve-year-old son, John, was the *Eagle Wing*'s cabin boy.

"Tane, get back," I hiss, edging away from Frank slowly, and Tane just manages to say, "Avery—"

"No!" With a howl, Frank springs forward, barreling into me and Tane, and I feel my body wrench in one direction while my foot catches between two broken planks. Tears of pain rise to my eyes as my ankle twists under me, and when I look back at Frank and Tane, I see that Frank has overshot himself, rolling to a stop several feet away. He picks himself up and moves to lunge back at me, but Tane is in his way, arms stretched out to stop him, and for a moment I think that Tane has him, but then Frank turns and leaps into the air, grabbing one of the ropes hanging from the tangled mess of the rigging. His knife still grasped in one fist, he climbs, and Tane jumps after him, the ropes squeaking in protest.

"Tane, stop!" I shout, and I rise to my feet, but waves of crippling pain radiate from my ankle, and besides, even well and whole, I lack the skill to climb ropes like these two whale men.

Frank climbs, climbs without any purpose that I can figure, and Tane follows him, the two of them now twenty feet in the air and far out of my reach. Tane catches up to him, an arm outstretched to snatch his ankle, but Frank lifts his foot and kicks back, connecting with Tane's face with a sickening crunch.

Blood, bright and thick, flows from a split in his cheek, and I'm filled with anguish so terrible and unbearable that the hungry beast inside of me eats it up, snarling and mad. Power, magic flows back through me, and this time I manage to hold my head long enough to try to use it without hurting Tane.

The boards under my feet tremble as waves foam against the sides of the *Modena*, striking and churning against her hull. I stumble for balance, ignoring the stinging pain in my ankle while, above, Frank Leroy lets out a cry. The boat begins to move forward, slowly at first and then faster, and then she turns sharply to the left, throwing both Tane and Frank off balance. I limp quickly to the port side of the boat and look over the edge into the swirling water.

A tight knot of magic billows up from beneath the surface, coiling and pulling and sucking at the *Modena*: a whirlpool. I glance up at Tane and Frank, still clinging to the rigging, their eyes round and white with fear. The *Modena* lurches, her port side dipping low into the water, and I hear a cry of surprise as Frank slips in the ropes and swings out over the edge of the boat, only a dozen feet above the waves.

We spin faster, faster, the *Modena* creaking and cracking, the spray licking Frank Leroy's boots, but still he clings to his rope, his knife in his hand, his face dark with anger and fear.

"Almost there," I whisper, urging the water to reach for Frank, "almost there!"

Frank tries swinging, throwing his weight back and forth against the spinning of the boat, and I see what he's doing, trying to launch himself to the deck, to me, and I stumble to my feet, hobbling to the rigging where Tane still clings.

"Get down!" I scream to him, but it's impossible to hear over the roar of the whirlpool. I wave my arms, frantic.

A crack like a cannon shot fills the air, and I'm thrown forward against the mast as the *Modena* splits across her middle. Tane's hands slip from the rope, and for one terrifying moment I imagine him slamming into the deck below, but he's a spider up in the rigging; he knows those ropes, and he catches himself, jerking his fall to a stop. I let out a quick breath of relief and reach for him just as Frank Leroy's heavy body swings forward, slamming into Tane and knocking them both from the ropes and into the boiling sea.

All the breath vanishes from my lungs and I run, run, run and leap over the edge of the ship and into the icy vortex. It's madness, complete madness, my body pulled deep into the sucking forces of the water, and I'm blinded by waves and darkness and pain and fear, but I still reach out with my water witch's senses for Tane, for the boy I love who cannot die tonight, not tonight, not for me.

When my hand fits around an ankle, I can't be certain whether it is Tane's or Frank's, and it doesn't matter anyway, so quickly am I wrenched away. But it's enough to know I'm not alone, that I can find them, and I grab hold of the forces swirling and drowning around me and *pull*.

The water shudders as it slows and stills, knocking me against debris and bits of wood and bodies—bodies! I reach out and clutch the nearest one and am rewarded with a shock of pure, hot, familiar magic, and it's Tane, it's Tane, still alive.

"Avery!" he gasps, his dark hair plastered to his forehead, falling into his eyes, his split-open cheek dribbling blood across his face, and I'm too exhausted to laugh, too exhausted even to be happy, my every nerve alight with thoughts of our survival. I twist my fingers around his shirt and turn and pull him from the faint, swirling remnants of the whirlpool, scanning the surface for any sign of Frank.

"Avery, what—"

When his words break off so suddenly, I know it can mean only one thing, and I spin in the water, just managing to see Frank Leroy rise from beneath the waves like a shark with a single bright tooth that glides, slow and even and calm, right into the space where Tane's perfect heart sits.

I scream and Frank jerks below the surface as though some giant fist had pulled him under the waves, and for a moment everything is forgotten—the water, the burn in my muscles, even Tane beside me—and I give myself over to the black-eyed creature burning through my veins, letting the waves twist and tear and wrench at Frank Leroy's body until what finally bobs to the surface moments later seems more a dark tangle of wet rope and jetsam than a man.

"Avery."

The witch flees as Tane's gasp fills my ears, and I swim to him, my heart rising into my throat. He's breathing hard, fast, his eyes darting blindly across the surface of the water; and when I finally reach him and touch my hands to his skin, he is so cold that a second wave of terror fills me.

"No," I say. "No, no, no!" I reach under the water and press a hand to his chest. The knife handle sticks out between my fingers, lodged into him so sure and steady that it seems as if it belongs there, as if it is now a part of his body.

He lets out a strange sound, part breath, part moan, his eyes widening with something—fear, I think, it's fear—he's afraid, he thinks he's going to die—but that's impossible, he can't, he was fine just a moment ago, he was perfect seconds ago—and then he looks at me, turns right to my face with shallow breaths and wide eyes like he expects me to save him.

"It'll be all right," I say, and the words are so fast and high out of my mouth that I can barely understand them, and I have to repeat myself, over and over: "You'll be all right, you'll be all right, you'll be all right."

Shaking, I slip one arm under his shoulder and reach with my hand under the water, feeling for the knife in his chest. My fingers slip against his skin, so much warmer than the ocean, and to keep from screaming I take a breath, force myself to focus. I have to do something to save him. I have to do it, and do it *now*.

His blood is just water.

His skin is just clouds.

I can control water and clouds, spin them to where they are supposed to be.

But magic and blood slip around my fingers and when I touch his skin the pulse of him fades, fades, and I let out a cry of frustration, because I am no healer witch, and what good is my magic? What good does it do to control the skies and winds and waves if I cannot mend a knife wound to the chest while bobbing in the middle of the Atlantic Ocean, not even to save the life of the boy I love?

Anger rises within me. I need to get him into a boat, for every second he treads sends more of his blood churning into the water, but only wreckage floats around me, the *Modena* hopelessly crippled and split into two pieces at least a hundred feet from where we bob. I dip my hands into the water, wondering, vaguely, if I can call one of the little whaleboats, but as the waves boil around us Tane lets out a cry of such pain that I jerk my hand back into the air, terror cresting through me.

"I'm sorry!" I say to him. "I'm sorry! I'm sorry! I won't do it again."

His breathing slows, his eyes flutter open, his teeth are gritted; and I reach out and grab a three-foot-long piece of wood and lodge it under his arms, just above the black handle of the knife.

"Hold on to this," I whisper to him, stretching his arms over the piece of wood. "Don't leave me!"

He nods, jerking his chin so that it splashes a bit, his

unsteady and unfocused eyes pointed in the direction of my voice. I tread water beside him, helping him support himself with the wood, and we are so close that his rattling breath strikes my cheeks. I lean forward and kiss him, not to save him but because it's the only thing I know to do now; I kiss his mouth, his eyes, his slashed-open cheek, and feel with my lips the faint tangle of magic within him.

"You're going to be all right," I whisper, kicking hard under the water. "We will be all right. Do you hear me? You promised me that we will make it to the mainland. You promised to marry me, and you look like a boy who keeps his promises."

A smile limps to his lips and he nods, his eyelids slumping low over his eyes, and I am glad at least that I can make him smile, right now, at this moment when we both know that my magic can't save him and we are alone on the ocean and every breath he takes shaves another few seconds from his life and there is nothing to do, no one to scream at, no one to hate— not even Frank Leroy, his twisted remains swaying in the currents, his knife shining below the surface of the water.

"You can't stop," I tell him. "You have to keep swimming."

And he nods again, but the small voice inside of me asks, *Why? Why keep swimming? Who will save you now?*

"Listen to me!" I splash the water and a little lands on his cheeks, the bones of his face reflecting back the light of the moon, and he is so beautiful, he cannot die; he cannot. "I want a blue house. All right? A blue house with yellow shutters. I want a porch and somewhere to sit after dinner with a cup of tea."

His eyelids struggle to stay open, but his smile grows.

"And when we have our children," I whisper, "I want a boy. I want a little boy. My family is done with little girls."

And he keeps on nodding, his eyes closed now, his face tight with pain and shiny with sweat, and when he stops nodding, I shake him.

"You can't die!" I say, furious. "Tane! You can't go!" Another nod that fades away as quickly as it came, and I choke out a sob and crush his hand in mine. "If you die, I'll never forgive you! Listen to me! If you die—I'll... I'll follow you!"

He gasps then, his eyes snapping open, fixing on my face, his mouth moving softly, silently, and I lean in closer, crying, trying to hear what it is he means to say to me, and at first I think it might be my name but then I hear it: "Saved you... safe... safe..."

I am so close to him that I see the edges of his lips curl into a smile. His breath slides from his lungs, warming my cheek before disappearing into the cold air and when I feel no more warmth from his lips I know that all his breaths are gone and with them goes my Tane, my love.

I am angry.

Furious.

I reach a hand from the water and slap his cheeks, scream curses at him, but his beautiful body is nothing but a heavy shell, still leaking blood into the water.

"This wasn't supposed to happen!" I scream, tipping my

face up to the sky. "I had a choice! I chose him! I chose to die! This wasn't supposed to happen! I wasn't supposed to live!"

I don't know who I scream to—life, fate, magic, and nothing answers me—but in the silence I hear that small voice, not much more than a whisper inside my head: *Who said it was a choice? Who said you'll survive the night?*

And I know it doesn't matter whether or not I am the witch; it doesn't matter what I can control. Right now I am just a girl in the water, clutching at the body of a dead boy, alone and cold and scared.

His body begins to sink then, his face slipping below the water, and hysteria takes over me, because I won't let the waves have him. I wrench him up from below, holding on to him until my muscles cramp, while desperation like a gaping hole opens up inside of me.

I start to give myself little challenges: First I have to keep his face above water, and then when the water reaches for him and pulls him under, I tell myself I just have to hold on to him, some part of him, and when that becomes impossible, too, I tell myself I can rest, just for a moment, but in that moment he slips away from me so suddenly that I gasp with fear and snatch him back and tread water again, even though my body burns so much it's as though a heavy, hot weight sits on me, pushing me ever deeper.

I don't swim. I don't let go. I hold on to Tane's ever-colder wrist and cry saltwater tears and wonder if I'll make good on my promise to follow him into death. Right now, the idea of death feels delicious, warm and soft, like sinking into pillows, like falling into Tane's arms.

I could let go and swim and make it back to my island.

I could hold tight and stop kicking and let Tane's weight pull me down.

I bob in the water and close my eyes and try to be nothing, no longer Avery Roe or the witch or even a girl in the ocean but nothing, nothing and no one. I close my eyes and call for death to take me and wait to be answered.

It doesn't take long.

Something bumps against my leg and I think of Frank Leroy and jerk wildly in the water, sending drops of sparkles into the sky. Another smooth, insistent nudge, and this time when I twist I see its form: huge, long, longer even than a whaleboat, a powerful black muscle with a bulbous black head.

It is a whale.

It circles me, its flukes rising in the water like great leathery wings, and then it disappears, swimming down, down, down into the deep.

A tug from Tane's body and I scream and grab for him. I feel the whale's massive head at my feet, lumbering around Tane's legs, its jaws open and reaching for him, and I scream again, batting at it frantically with my magic, but the whale only retreats a bit before returning, more insistent now.

"Get away!" I say, gasping. "Don't touch him!"

A massive wave rolls over me as the wake from the whale's tail rises through the water and I sputter and cough, still holding tight to Tane's body. The whale swims faster now, circling and darting, so much bigger, so much more powerful than I am, and my eyes widen to try to follow its movements underwater, to try to put myself between its jaws and Tane's body, when it suddenly slams into me, knocks loose my hold on Tane's arm, and snatches him away, down deep under the waves.

I swallow a breath and dive, but this is the whale's world, not mine, and they are gone, gone with nothing but the motion of the water in their wake.

Kicking for the surface, I cry and choke, anger and aching filling me and with it, the hot power of my magic. I could kill the whale now for stealing Tane, for leaving me alone, and I spin, scanning the waves for any sign of it.

Vibrations, vibrations in the water along with a strange series of noises: *click-click, click-click*. It is the sperm whale's song, not the deep, mournful call of the great humpback whales but the quick, precise ticks of a hunter.

The vibrations tickle my skin, sending goose bumps along my arms and legs, but I clench my fists, ready for the whale. It swims closer, closer, and the closer it gets, the more powerful the vibrations of its song, until I can feel every bone rattle within me, my blood sizzling in my veins, the weight of my heart shivering in my chest.

It swims for me and I wait, listening to the whale's wild,

manic song, my magic coiled around me, when it lifts from the water with the force of a cannon, waves and foam and spray rising in a collar around its massive body, and I just have time to lift my arms, to scream a final witch's scream of fury as it opens its gaping jaws and the whole world crashes around me.

Twenty-Six

IT HURTS TO DIE.

It feels nothing like I thought, nothing at all like falling into warm pillows or into the arms of someone I love. Actually? It feels like getting my skin sliced off, piece by piece. It feels a little like someone has reached inside of my chest and pulled out my heart and my lungs and my stomach and forced me to walk around like that, with nothing but emptiness inside.

And I must always remind myself that I am dead. That is the worst part about it.

Sometimes I will forget and think that I am still a girl with air in my lungs and things to be happy about and then I must tell myself that I have utterly failed at everything: protecting someone very dear, keeping promises, magic, life.

It is hardest when the fogginess fades a little from my eyes and shadows loom around me, talking at me like I am a real living girl, saying horribly stupid things about bones and fevers and pulses, and me too weak to tell them, *Please stop talking about me like that. Please let me stay dead.*

Please let me stay dead.

"Death is a comfort, Avery." But where is that comfort my grandmother spoke of? She smiled when she slipped under the waves.

Twenty-Seven

I DON'T LIKE THAT THE SHADOWS GROW clearer and smaller. I don't like the light. Even when the darkness behind my eyelids turns red, I keep my eyes tightly shut. Voices drift into my ears, but I ignore them. Only after someone presses something to my lips, something spongy and wet, do I make my protests known, snapping open my eyes.

The indistinct person in front of me lets out a cry of surprise and I scream at him, "Go away!"

He mumbles something, hand outreached, and I slide under the blankets and squeeze my eyes shut and scream again and again, *"Go away go away go away go away go away!"*

There's a sharp, bright light and then a crash—lightning, thunder—and the man stumbles and runs away. I wait until he's gone before I open my eyes.

It's all wrong. I'm dead.

The room swims hazily, my head spinning and dizzy, but I can make out just in front of me a little stool, and on the stool sits a lump of bread and a bowl of something white and steaming and a knife.

A knife.

A knife right in his chest like it belonged there.

My hands reach out and gather up the knife, and I watch, detached and uninterested, as one of my hands decides to take the edge of the knife and press it against the inside of my arm.

The door explodes open and I hiss as strong hands I do not see or understand press down on me. All I feel is numb and all I hear is soft rushing and then it's black again.

Even though I'm dead, I still dream. I don't have any dreams about whales or harpoons or angry men who want to kill me. I don't have any dreams that mean anything as far as my own future. Instead, I dream about a blue house with yellow shutters and a porch and cups of warm tea.

They aren't nightmares or terrible dreams—they are lovely, happy. I close my eyes and feel his hands on my skin and hear him laughing and I forget that I'm dreaming, that I'm dead.

When the dreams fade and I open my eyes, I feel sick and groggy. My whole body aches and my stomach turns and my skin itches and burns. All I want is to close my eyes again and go back to the place where I don't hurt and don't think and where he still lives.

And because there's nothing to be done when I wake up, nowhere to go, no one to see, and because this world is gray and empty with sharp corners and bright lamps and harsh sounds, I close my eyes and go back to sleep. I'm good at sleeping.

The next time brightness pierces my eyelids, I try to move, but my hands are locked in cuffs and tied with a rope to the side of the bed in which I lie. I breathe slowly, staring at my hands until they blur, thinking no thoughts.

Go blank, Avery. Dead girls don't have thoughts. Dead girls don't feel guilty.

The door opens, but I don't move or look up. The shadow of a figure creeps closer, stopping at my feet.

"Go away," I say, and my words feel limp and gray in my mouth.

"I am the captain of this ship," a man's voice says. "You don't give me orders."

"Go away," I say again. I still don't look at him.

"I saved your life," he says. "Maybe you should be a little more grateful."

I feel the urge to laugh explode inside of me, but I don't move a muscle. Instead, I let my eyes slide over to the man's face. He holds a cigarette between his lips, smoke curling past his face. I know him. He is the man from the Codfish. The smuggler.

"Why am I here?" I ask.

"You tell me," he says. "I was sailing for Boston when my ship was attacked by a mad whale. I called my men to kill it, but when they looked over the side of the boat, the whale had disappeared, and instead they found you floating in the water."

I breathe very slowly, listening to what he says, studying his face.

"That is impossible," I say softly. "I'm dead."

His eyes widen, just a little, just barely, but he does not react except to say, "I suppose on that point we have a difference of opinion." He pauses and takes another puff of his cigarette. "What were you doing out alone in the ocean?"

I look away.

"Did it have anything to do with the news that your witch grandmother is dead?" he asks. "And her magic with her? Did it have anything to do with the sinkings of the *Eagle Wing* and the *Modena*?"

He's making fun now.

"You seem to know the whole story," I say. "Why do you ask what happened?"

"Because it's all anyone can talk about," he says. "One week ago, six strong men sailed out to sea with a girl who claimed she was not a witch, and since then none of them, save you, have been seen again."

None of them, none of them. His words bounce painfully around my skull.

"Did you kill them?" He doesn't sound scared, although he appears to already know the answer.

"Let me go," I whisper, and he shakes his head.

"I won't have you hurting yourself. It's bad luck for a woman to die on a boat."

"I'm already dead," I say, and he stares at me for a long time.

"You know...you're not dead," he says. I laugh, a high-pitched, nervous sound.

"I was murdered. I had a dream about it. It was my fate." The corners of my lips stretch into a grim smile, a corpse's smile. "I thought it meant someone would cut my throat or stop my heart. I thought it would be all right, because I knew it was coming and I was ready for it. But I didn't know there are different ways to die. I didn't know someone could murder you without even touching you."

Sacrifice, Avery. Don't you realize what you must sacrifice?

Take my heart and break my heart and when I asked him for answers he laughed at me and called me a silly girl.

They died, but I died, too, and it was my punishment that although I was dead there was still breath in my lungs and I still could walk and talk and think.

And feel, Tane, and feel. That's the worst part of all.

The voices in my head swim around me, but I keep my

eyes on the smuggler's face and stretch my smile bigger, bigger, because I know I'm right. I know my dream told the truth from the beginning and that Frank Leroy murdered me when he slid his knife between Tane's ribs. I know Tane's dream told the truth, too: not a choice between futures in which I would be murdered or Tane would sacrifice himself, but the same future. Neither one of us was going to survive.

The smuggler watches me grin as he smokes his cigarette. He breathes in, the embers at the tip of the cigarette burning bright and red, and before I know what's happened, he pulls the cigarette from his lips and sweeps it down and presses the hot end against the sole of my right foot.

My skin sizzles and I scream and jerk away, anger and confusion riding high in me, my breath coming faster and harder. With my hands tethered, all I can do is coil into a ball, and I tense, ready to strike out against him if necessary.

But he doesn't even move except to return the cigarette to his lips.

"What was that?" I hiss.

"You're not dead," he says. "Dead girls don't jump when they get burned."

I narrow my eyes at him, my breath still fast and shallow.

"I won't disrespect you and say you don't deserve your grief," he says, looking me in the eye. "But as long as you're on my ship, you won't hurt yourself. You'll eat and gain strength and get out of your dreamworld." He puts his cigarette to his lips again before dropping it to the floor and crushing it with the toe of his boot. He pulls open the door to my berth and pauses before he leaves, glancing back at me with a hard, appraising stare.

"Maybe you did die, girl," he says softly. "But you're alive now."

He leaves, and I turn my face to the wall and try to go back to sleep, but it takes a long time.

When I next wake, two kindnesses: My wrists are no longer chained, and a bowl of broth sits on the stool in front of me. I stare at it for a long time. Although I can't remember the last time I ate, it might as well have been a bowl of sand.

Feelings, memories crowd around me, piercing me like a million tiny needles, and I wince and shake my head and force myself to concentrate on the little room I'm in. There's a bed. There's a stool. Otherwise, the room is empty, a typical small ship's berth. A round window sits in the wall behind my head, the glass lashed with heavy rain, and when I twist around to look at it, thunder booms, loud and strong enough to raise the hairs on my arm.

A moment later, the door opens and the smuggler appears. His eyes take in the untouched bowl before settling on my face, his expression smooth.

"How did you know I was awake?" I ask, and his eyebrows lift to the ceiling.

"You always announce yourself," he says, and I frown at him for a moment before I realize what he's saying.

"I'm controlling the storm," I say, my words flat and dull. Indeed, I could feel it now, like a nagging thought in the back of my mind. It's powerful magic, controlling the weather. Not even my grandmother, the storm-raiser, could take over the skies for more than a few hours. But I'd done it for days, most of the time unconscious. I tensed and another flash of lightning lit up the berth.

"The storm's made it impossible to sail," the smuggler says. "We've been docked since we picked you up."

"Where?"

"A cove. Not far from Weld Haven."

I blink, unsure whether I am happy or sad to hear it. I am home, but this island can never be my home again, not after what the islanders did to me. "Why did you take me back here?"

"*You* took us back here." He crosses his arms over his chest. "I told you, we were on our way to Boston, but when we picked you up, we got caught in this squall that blew us off course. We stopped at the closest place we could find."

"And now what?" I ask. "Will you hand me over to the dockmaster? Or the sheriff?"

"If I was going to do that, wouldn't it already be done?"

I shrug. "If I were a sailor on Prince Island whose friends were killed by a witch and then I found out that witch was alive and well somewhere, I might pay a nice coin to get my hands on her."

The smuggler laughs. "Your storm destroyed half the docks and a quarter of the ships in New Bishop, and folks say it's punishment for putting you on trial. If *I* were a sailor on Prince Island and found you were alive, I'd get my apologies ready."

I look away. "They wouldn't take me back."

"Wouldn't they?" The smuggler pauses to study me. "Half their ships aren't seaworthy, not now they've been stripped of magic. The whole industry's in ruin, and they'd need a miracle to be profitable. Or a powerful witch."

"You said there aren't enough whales now to compete with your kerosene. You said the witch would have to know to call whales to the hunters."

"I did," he says lightly, "and I found you riding atop a whale as docile as a toothless dog. If the sailors knew you could perform that trick, they'd make you into a queen, no matter how many ships may have gotten lost."

I close my eyes. I could go back to the island. Rebuild the cottage. Live like my grandmother, my great-grandmother, her mother, and back and back and back. The Roe women would be reborn and with them, the island. It would be salvation and I would be their savior.

And I would live out in the cottage alone and every time I performed a spell I would feel the pain of Tane's death again and the more I felt the pain, the more I would want to make magic, like trying to quench a thirst with seawater, like an addiction I had to feed. I would live like that until finally the pain became too much to bear, and then I would walk out into the waves with tears on my face and look for rest in the waters of the sea.

I have nothing to live for, not even revenge. This could be something to live for.

Except... I hear Tane's voice in my ears, excited, full of life and hope and promise, telling me of a world outside the walls of my island—not the world of art and culture, my mother's world, but something else. There are things out there he wanted me to see, to experience. And that could be something to live for, too.

"I have nothing left," I whisper, more to myself than the smuggler. "My grandmother killed herself. My best friend went down with the *Eagle Wing*. The boy I love..." Waves of pain radiate out from the center of my chest, and I feel as though I am teetering on the edge of a great, black pit. I shake my head. Can't say it. Not yet. "Even my mother left me for her church in the mountains."

"Your mother hasn't left you."

I glance sharply at the smuggler. "What do you mean? She went with her husband to Pennsylvania. Her own kitchen girl saw her board a boat."

"Maybe she did board it," the smuggler says, lifting his shoulders into a shrug. "Her husband and his children certainly did. But she didn't go with them. She didn't leave the island. She's in New Bishop now. One of my crew heard some folks in town talking about her. They say they'll leave her alone, for now."

My heart thumps painfully, but I ignore it. "It doesn't matter," I say softly. "Everything that happened . . . it's all her fault. I don't want to see her. I don't even want her to know I'm alive."

The smuggler is quiet, and when I turn to look at him, I see he's studying me, his dark eyebrows knit in concentration. He walks over to the side of my bed and moves the bowl of broth to the floor before sitting down.

"I was mistaken before," he says.

"About what?"

"You do remind me of her. Stubborn and sure of yourself, even when you're wrong."

"How? How am I wrong?"

"Instead of putting aside your anger and speaking to your mother, you'd rather she mourn you," he says, and there's an edge to his voice. "She stayed here for you, you know."

I shake my head. "She stayed because we can't leave, none of us. The island . . . You wouldn't understand. It's like a magnet. We can't leave, and that's why she stayed. It's got nothing to do with me."

"She's always wanted to leave the island," he says softly. "Maybe before you cut her from your life, you should ask her why she never did."

"Why don't you tell me?" I ask, my voice sharp with acid. "Seeing as you seem to know so much."

But he just shakes his head, a smile pulling at his lips. "No," he says. "But I do want you to have something, before you make up your mind."

"Haven't you listened? I *have* made up my mind. I'm not going to see her," I say, but he shakes his head again and reaches into a pocket on the inside of his jacket and pulls out a crinkled piece of soft paper: a photograph. He looks at it for a moment, then holds it out to me.

It's my mother, before my father hit her, before her face became a battlefield. She is just as beautiful as I've been led to believe, her cheekbones high and full of light, her lips round and smooth. But it's not her beauty that holds my gaze. She stares straight ahead, her eyes focused, almost angry.

No.

Defiant. One hand hangs close to her body, drawn into a tight fist, while the other sits on top of a slope of fabric just below her rib cage. She looks like a wild animal, a witch, proud and powerful and protecting the little bump under her dress. Protecting me. I stare into her beautiful face for a long time.

"Why do you have this?" I ask, but the smuggler is quiet. I remember what my mother told me about my father, his soft hands, and I set down the photograph on the bed and reach for one of the smuggler's hands. It's warm, strong, and he lets me run my fingers across his callused, rough, sun-darkened skin.

"You're not him," I say, and I'm not sure how I feel, disappointed or relieved. I pull my fingers back and lace them quietly in my lap.

"He's dead." The smuggler glances up at me, uncertain. "Did you know that?"

No.

"Years ago," he said. "At the end of the war. You would have been about twelve. Why did you think she came for you when she did? She only left you with your grandmother for that long because she thought he'd try to hurt you, and your grandmother's specialty was handling angry men. She left you there to keep you safe from him."

We say nothing, both of us looking at the picture in my hands.

"When the storm hit the island, she broke her leg," the smuggler says quietly. "It's not mending well. Rumor says she might die."

I can hear the urgency in his voice, the worry. And the love. I study the creases in the photograph and the spots where fingertips have softened its edges. I flip the photograph over and see a single line of browned ink. *Essie*, it says. That's my mother's name. Essie Roe. I don't think I ever mentioned that. On one of the very rare occasions my grandmother spoke of my mother, she told me that she'd named my mother for the sounds of waves on the shoreline, whisper-quiet in the morning: *Ehhhss-eeee ehhhssss-eeee.*

"I wanted her to carry water with her everywhere she went," my grandmother said, and I remember that she pursed her lips in a frown. "For all the good it got her."

"You say you have nothing left," the smuggler says, and he pushes himself up to his feet, his eyes on the little photograph in my hands. "But it's not true."

"I don't want her," I say, and he lifts his shoulders into a shrug.

"I didn't say that you wanted her," he says, turning to the door, and he pauses at the frame and studies me. "I said that you have her."

Twenty-Eight

THE RAIN BEATS STEADILY OVER ME AS I leave the smuggler's boat with his cloak over my shoulders and his photo of my mother in my pocket. He tells me it's midday, but the sky overhead is dark with clouds that roll and boil and blot out the sun. *My* clouds. I pulled them up there, like a veil over the island, and they'll stay there until I send them away.

The smuggler wouldn't take anything from me in return, although it must have hurt his business to have docked for so long. I offered, too. I had enough pain, eating away inside of me, that I knew I could make him any charm he asked for, something that would turn his sails and bow invisible in the water or that would keep his hull free from breaks or bumps. But he said no, that he'd never needed a witch to keep him safe in the waters and he wasn't about to start now.

I leave without looking back, without even asking his name. His final words to me ring in my ears:

"If ever you want to sail away from here, you're welcome on my boat."

But now that I am back on my island, I can't imagine leaving again. The rain makes the landscape in front of me green and gray and soft, the colors blending and bleeding together. I breathe in the smell of wet earth, growing grass, lightning in the air, and lift my face to the sky. I am home.

With every step, my newfound power thrums in my veins, a sweet beckoning that reminds me that I am a witch now, as good a witch as my grandmother ever was. The whole world sings to me, and I drop to my knees and pull a blue flower from the grass, wet with rain and mud. My grandmother used these flowers in luck spells and, curious, I reach out to my magic, let it flow into the flower and fix itself there, perfect and preserved like an insect in amber.

I gasp.

It is as though a whirlpool opens up underneath my feet, like I've opened a dam, like I've unleashed a raving, starving monster. I feel Tane's blood slip between my fingers, hear his dying breaths in my ears, and, panicked, I pull away from the magic, thrust it deep inside of me, and fall, shaking, to the ground.

A howl of grief crawls up through my stomach, through my lungs and throat and out my mouth. The sound feels heavier than just noise, more solid than air, like I'm screaming out a black weight that thuds into the dirt. It's such a high pitch, this screech, so high that it hurts my ears and my throat, and finally I have to ball up the smuggler's cloak and stuff it into my mouth while my whole body shakes so hard I am not sure it will ever stop.

I want him. I want him back. I want him alive, and all I can do is huddle against the black mud with his name *Tane Tane Tane* echoing through my head. I know he is gone, but it's as though my spell has resurrected him only to let him die again, teasing and torturing me. And with that pain, more magic, more power, and I know that I could truly do anything I wanted now, a thought that terrifies as much as it intoxicates.

Every spell I make, I will feel Tane's death again.

Every time I feel him, I will get a bit stronger.

No wonder the Roe women live short lives. No wonder my grandmother went mad and ran to death.

The little flower seems to glow in my hand, its vivid blue cheerful and bright, changed from a flower to a perfect charm. I toss it away, trembling, and stumble to my feet to continue my walk to town.

When the first few buildings emerge from the mist, I notice signs of the terrible storm I brought upon the island. On every building, a film of mud four feet high marks the line where the waters rose. At the warehouse near the docks, it's a custom to preserve these marks with paint, along with the year the flooding occurred and a little note about the storm. I wonder what they'll say this time, if it will be something like "We tried to kill a water witch, and this is what she did to us."

Trash and splintered wood and twisted metal and glass litter the streets, but no people. A ruin. New Bishop looks a ruin. It seems impossible that no one but my mother was hurt in the storm, and I tuck my chin deeper into the smuggler's cloak and quicken my pace.

My walk takes me past the little graveyard beside the white clapboard church at the center of town, and I pause for a moment. Shadows in the fog line the edge of the graveyard's wrought-iron fence, and as I grow closer the shadows darken and solidify into a neat row of perfectly cut gravestones, their edges sharp and clear. I stare at these just-made stones, sitting atop a carpet of undug grass, before I realize that they belong to the men of the *Eagle Wing*.

My hand seems to push open the graveyard gate by its own accord; my feet carry me down the row of stones, thirty-two, clean and rain-washed. No. Not thirty-two, thirty-six. Tacked on the end in slightly darker stone, four more names: the four islanders who left the island with the *Modena* and never came back. Just the islanders, because this graveyard is not for outsiders like the *Modena*'s captain, who will have his own gravestone erected by his family, or Tane, who will have nothing.

I stare at them for a long time, trying very hard to feel nothing or else I will feel everything.

I wish my magic didn't go toward killing things.

I stand still just long enough to catch my breath, and then I continue down the line, taking in every name until I see the one echoing in my head.

Thomas Thompson.

I frown. He was never *Thomas.* I bend down and pull up two pieces of grass, the green bright and alive in this gray fog, and arrange them carefully in the shape of a *y*, just over the *a* and *s* so that the name now reads *Thomy Thompson.* It's the best I can do.

I press my fingertips against the stone. Under my feet the ground is empty of his bones and body because he's been buried at sea, buried beneath waves. It's how every sailor prefers to be laid to rest, but then I remember what he said to me when he said good-bye: "I wanted roots."

He should have been buried underground.

My head swims and bright points of light pepper my vision and I realize I've stopped breathing. When I open my mouth for air, a whimper escapes my throat, and for the second time today I'm standing at the edge of a black, bottomless pit, crumpled by grief and whispering to myself, "I want him back, I want him back. . . ."

What a mess. What a disaster this has all been.

Roe magic did this. The lack of it or the reliance on it— either way, it's a Roe's fault that Tommy is gone forever, his body a part of endless ocean instead of here where he belongs.

I push myself, shaking, hiccoughing, to my feet, and pause

again to lay my hand on Tommy's gravestone before closing my eyes and leaving the churchyard.

I wish I were a good enough witch to bring his body home. But when has my magic gotten me anything I wanted?

I don't bother heading up lighthouse; the pastor is gone and his house a ruin. Instead, I turn south, down to where the factories and refineries once chugged out black smoke and profits.

My mother has an old apartment there, and it was to this apartment that she took me first, when she dragged me from my grandmother's cottage. We spent two years there, choking on smoke from the refineries next door until she managed to marry the pastor, but since our move, she hasn't sold the little apartment. I knew I would find her there now.

The apartment sits in a back alley, the smell of wet garbage rising like steam to greet me. The first-floor window is dark, but when I tilt my face up to the rain, I see a glow coming from the second floor, her bedroom, and I open the unlocked door.

I walk carefully, silently, my heartbeat thrumming within me. Apprehension causes my fingertips to tingle, and yet underneath that, something hotter, fiercer. I do not know what to think except that everything that has happened—Tane's death, Tommy's death, the sinkings of the *Modena* and *Eagle Wing*—is her fault. Had she left me safe in my grandmother's cottage, I would have grown to be the witch. Had she taken the role meant for her, she would be the witch now and I her apprentice and none of this, none of this would have occurred.

The sound of her breathing travels down the hall as I climb up the rickety, dark staircase, loosening the cloak from my shoulders. She is alone. I roll the balls of my feet gently over the floorboards, taking care not to raise any telling squeaks, and when I reach her slightly ajar door, I am certain she hasn't heard my arrival.

Slowly, I push open the door, and the mournful wail of the hinges makes her turn her face in my direction, her labored breaths quick, her blue eyes wide with surprise.

"Avery!" she says, gasping. Her voice has lost its precise snap, her pale skin no longer clear and lovely but deadened, waxen, and covered in sweat as she watches me from her narrow bed.

I take a step into her room, and my head spins with the heavy smell of blood and sweet medicine. Tears fill her eyes but I ignore them, all our arguments running together in my mind, all the hatred I felt for her whirling through me. I take another step, another, and my hands automatically curl into fists. I want to make her pay. I want to make her understand what she has done to me, to this island, to Tane, and when I am inches from her bed I feel the hot breath of a vengeful witch on my neck. As she trembles in her sweat-soaked sheets, I open my mouth, too overwhelmed even to speak, too overwhelmed even—even to—to—!

My legs fall away from under me, my bones and body

crumpling, crumbling to the ground, and what comes from my lips is not a hateful declaration of judgment but the soft, timid mew of a kitten in pain. I clutch the side of her bed, my forehead pressed against her mattress, while sobs, coughing, choking, uncontrollable sobs explode through my body.

My mother says nothing, and the mattress shifts suddenly as though she's edging away from me, and I feel stupid, so stupid, reaching out for a woman like her, expecting—I don't know—kindness? Understanding? And I am ready to jerk to my feet and leave her forever when something light as a bird wing touches my hair: her fingers.

I press my face into her sheets and kneel at the side of my mother's bed and she strokes my hair, gentle, even, her long nails untangling the knots at my scalp, sending waves of tingles over my skull. My skin turns hot and cold, and I pour out the emptiness I feel into my mother's thin mattress.

I cry for Tommy, who never wanted to go to sea but did it because of me.

I cry for my grandmother, walking into the water like it was her last hope.

I cry for my beautiful Tane, slipping beneath the waves.

I even cry for my mother, for her ruined face and for the secrets she kept from me. And all the while, my mother's sloped nails scratch gently against my scalp, the pads of her fingers soft and warm.

"Mama," I whisper. It is the first time I have ever called her that, and we both feel the power of the word. Small magic, except what is happening now does not feel small but huge, and my mother nudges me, helping me onto the mattress. She wraps her arms around me and says nothing.

Without meaning to, I begin to speak, the words spilling from me unbidden (there's magic in talking aloud, like drawing out poison, like exposing a wound to air). My mother holds me in her arms while I whisper to her about Tane, about his tattoos and magic, his dark hair and calm eyes. I tell her about my grandmother, her mother, who went into the sea desperate and deranged. I tell her about my dream, what it always meant. I whisper to her all my fears, my guilt, and let the magic of talking exhaust me, let it for once silence the cacophony in my head.

My mother says nothing to me, the only acknowledgment of my words the occasional intake of breath, but when I finally, finally close my eyes to sleep, she whispers back to me strange, hazy, half-spun stories that bleed into my dreams. After I wake, she falls silent, her face very white, her lips pinched together, and I know that this peace between us is too fragile for her to say anything to my face. So I close my eyes and feign sleep and hold my breath until I hear the hot whisper of her words in my ear.

She tells me about her time as a girl, when she was Essie-Roe-the-prettiest-girl-in-New-England-and-maybe-the-world. Just like that, like that was her full name.

She tells me of her days in the cottage on the rocks, when my grandmother was young and still in her prime. She tells me that she would make the long walk up to New Bishop only to have the other little girls throw rocks at her while the little boys stared and laughed. She tells me of the only child on the island who would speak to her, a green-eyed orphan boy who slept out on the grasslands in the center of the island and promised her what she was too timid to accept: that one day she would become a powerful witch.

And she did. Only a few short years later, her magnificent face and her magnificent bloodlines emerged, and like the day I discovered I could tell dreams, one morning she woke and knew she had power over love, trust, passion, feeling. My mother's voice grows short and clipped to tell of what it did to her. I think about the fierce-faced woman in the photograph in my pocket and try to imagine her the way she imagines herself: haughty and cruel, with more power than a beautiful seventeen-year-old girl knows what to do with.

Boys died for her, going recklessly to sea to prove some-thing and coming back corpses. Men left their wives for a taste of her beauty, driven mad by it and by the wild force she was too proud to control. And she tells me something I already know, that the magic was like a drug, an addiction that kept her begging for more, like a shipwrecked man dying of thirst and drinking deep the salty waters of the ocean.

But for all that I know—the legendary beauty, the wild run of power, the heartsick men of Prince Island—there is more I learn about the woman who is my mother. She wanted to be the witch. It is a revelation so sudden and surprising that I almost can't keep feigning sleep.

She wanted to be the witch. She wanted the power and the

pain and knew how it would happen. She had always known, for her mother had told her on her thirteenth birthday: "You will fall in love only once and that person will hurt you terribly and out of that pain you will become a witch." But she thought she could outsmart the curse. She thought she could change her fate. *We are more alike than I imagined.*

This is what she believed: that the same man she fell in love with, the same man who would hurt her, would also be the father of her child. That was how it had always been, and even if a Roe invited someone else to warm her bed, she would not have another child. My mother could prepare herself for pain and heartbreak, but she could not bear depriving her child of a father. So she had a plan. She would find someone to break her heart and open her magic, someone she was assured could not have children. And then she would take her time looking for someone good, kind, caring: a father worthy of her daughter.

"He bragged about it," she whispered, the words fast and feverish against my cheek. "A string of women and never had to worry about leaving them with child. Other men might have been ashamed, but he bragged. Hated children. Such soft hands, like a little child's. Not a good man and not the right man, but such soft hands."

She's quiet for so long that I wonder if she's fallen asleep, and I am about to move when her arms tighten around me.

"I picked him, even though I knew I could never love him," she whispers. "I forgot the others who loved me. I forgot my only friend. I forgot him. He told me to be careful so many times. Hated him for it. Jealous, I called him. Wanted me all to himself. Thought it would be him at the end, loving me. I thought it would be him at the end. First love gets the curse. First love. Second love's safe. That was what I hoped."

She murmurs the words over and over, talking about her green-eyed friend, the orphan who loved her, the plans they had made together: First she would get her heart broken, and then she would go back to her friend. But she didn't count on magic doing the impossible, like giving her a baby from a man who swore he couldn't father children.

"My friend…he would have been a better father," she says softly. "I thought I was so clever, pushing him away, waiting, giving myself to a man who wasn't supposed to be able to have children. I shouldn't have done it. . . . I picked wrong. . . . I picked wrong. . . ." Her words fade into a spiraling whisper that makes her seem younger, more fragile than I have ever imagined her, and I wonder to myself, *Where is the tentacled lady with the cold, calculating heart?*

"My baby," she mumbles, and although I'm trying so hard to keep still, I can't help a flinch. She doesn't notice. "He thought she wasn't his. Everyone thought she wasn't his. Laughed at him, laughed at all his bragging. Can't father children, but Essie Roe's round as a drum. He didn't believe me when I told him it was the magic, changing him. Magic will change him. . . . He didn't believe. . . . They're all whispering, Essie. They say it's that orphan's. They say, they say…I could have stopped him. The belt. I could have stopped him. Just a spell. Could have made a spell and stopped him."

I open my eyes and stare into the dark center of my mother's room, my heartbeat loud in my ears, waiting, waiting.

"I thought he would have stopped on his own." Her head droops low over my shoulder, the heat from her skin dry and sticky. "He loved me without spells. Not a good man but... never had to use magic on him... He loved me. I thought he loved me. I didn't think he'd ever..."

I lie very still, not breathing. I imagine this is just a bedtime story, just a fairy tale and not a history lesson in my father's brutal treatment of my mother. I wish I could pull the covers tight up to my chin, wide-eyed and worried about the witch who will have a child, and I wish my mother could laugh and tell me that at the last moment, the green-eyed orphan boy burst through the door and rescued the witch and beat the mean man with the soft hands and they all ran away together, and the witch became a queen and the little girl a princess and the orphan boy a father and they lived together happy and safe until the end of their days.

But instead my mother says nothing, and I lie awake for a long time, listening to her ragged breathing.

"I'll come back for her," she whispers, and even though I'm supposed to be asleep, I turn and study my mother. But she doesn't even notice, her eyes closed, her lips partly open.

"I'll come back for her," she says again. "He was going to

kill my baby. I'll come back for her.... Don't know any spells to stop him, but Mother...go to the cottage; Mother can stop an angry man, can keep her safe, keep her safe.... I'll come back for her, he said. I can't stay there or he'll find us. I can't take her with me.... Leave her there and go away. Don't teach her magic, I said, just keep her safe.... I'll come back for her...."

My heartbeat sounds very loud in my ears, thumping through my entire body, and I study my mother's tangled face. Love and pain. My grandmother fell in love with Caleb, a captain, and found him in bed with another girl, mocking everything she thought they had. I fell in love with Tane, who hurt me in a way I could never imagine: dying in my arms. And my mother? She met my father, and he beat her, and that was her love and pain, wasn't it? Wasn't it?

My skin itches, my whole body burning as though it's on fire, and I sit up suddenly, breathing hard. The movement wakes my mother and she blinks, blinks in the candlelight.

"Wha-what?" she asks, and her voice is weak but closer to the cool, calm woman I know.

"Tell me something," I say. "Don't lie to me. Not anymore." I take a deep breath. "I feel him. When I make spells now, I feel him, dying in my arms again." I stare at her and she stares back. "What do you feel?"

Her eyelids flutter, as though still asleep, and she struggles to sit upright. "I feel..." Her voice quavers. "I feel pain."

"*I* feel pain," I say, spitting out the words. "When I make a spell, his blood is on my hands again and I am in that moment. What moment do you find yourself in?"

She shakes her head and I jump from the bed, pacing, breathing hard. "Tell me," I say. "Tell me or I'll never know. I'll never understand you! I don't believe that you fell in love with my father, so what is it? Is it your face? Is it your orphan boy? Tell me!"

She breathes in, a tight little gasp of surprise, her mouth falling open, her eyes bright with tears.

"Failure," she whispers. "I feel failure at keeping you safe." She closes her eyes and a tear falls down her cheek. "I feel the moment I picked the wrong man to be your father. I feel the fear of knowing he wanted you dead. I feel the mistake of leaving you with my mother instead of keeping you with me. I feel all the hatred you threw at me when I dragged you from the only home you knew." When she opens her eyes again they are blue, blue, the rain-washed blue of a summer sky. "That is what I feel. And that is why I could never be the Roe witch. I could never live a life like that."

"I thought our curse broke first love," I say, my voice trembling. "The first person you ever fall in love with hurts you in ways you never imagined."

"Yes," she whispers. "Yes."

And she reaches up.

She places a hand on my cheek.

She smiles.

"My little love."

A chill corkscrews through my stomach, up to my chest, out to my fingers and toes, and I jerk away from her. All I can do is stare at her, at her outstretched hand and soft smile and the look in her eyes, the *love*. My skin itches, my heart pounds, I feel dizzy and strange, and still she just watches me, watches me like she can't believe I couldn't have figured this all out. She fell in love with me. And I broke her heart.

I don't know what to say to her—and finally I just shake my head and ask, my voice soft with pain, "Why didn't you just *tell* me all this from the beginning?"

"I didn't want to burden you. I didn't want you to think that I blamed you, somehow, for what happened to me—"

"No. No, I mean, why weren't you honest with me about how we get our magic? You could have told me from the beginning what would happen if I fell in love with someone, but you didn't."

"Do you really think it would have stopped you?" My mother shakes her head. "Avery, if I had told you that the secret to our magic lay in making a man fall in love with you and then that man breaking your heart, would you have turned away all men? Or would you have run into the street, looking for the first likely fellow?"

I open my mouth to protest, but the sincerity of her question stops me. What *would* I have done, armed with that information? I never cared for marriage or love. I would have thought it a cheap price for what I've always wanted, for saving my own life. And like a pantomime play in my head, I see a vision of myself, made up in my new-bought finery, leaning close to Tommy and whispering to him, "You've always loved me, haven't you? *Haven't you?*"

"I'm sorry," she says softly. "I am so sorry for everything that has happened to you." There's a hitch in her voice as she speaks. "I am so sorry for this. I wanted better for you. I always thought...you'd have to live a life without love, no matter what happened to you. Why not spare yourself the heartbreak? If you could never fall in love and never experience magic, I wanted you to have the best life available. I thought if I could only make you see how wonderful your life could be, you would forget about magic."

I let out a short, bitter laugh.

"There isn't anything you could have said or done to make me forget," I say, and I know that it's true, that my mother could have laid out all her plans and her ideas and her worries and it would not have made a difference. "And I have nothing left now."

My mother's face contorts with emotion, and her hand falls down and touches, so lightly, the spot just below my abdomen.

"That's not true. You have her."

I don't breathe. I don't speak. I slide my hand under hers and try to imagine what she's feeling: life, a kick, a heartbeat, a piece of Tane. But after a moment I push her hand away.

"I'm not pregnant."

"What? But I thought..."

I look away, and I'm back on the beach, Tane's beautiful

body next to mine. He told me not to regret. He made me promise. When he slid his hands along my skin, every atom in my body lit up like a cloud of fireflies and I wanted him, I wanted all of him, I wanted him to have a part of me, something special, something only he could have, something he could always carry with him. No regrets. But even in that moment, I was bad at keeping promises. I pictured him, the weight of a dead girl on his shoulders for the rest of his life, and I pushed him away. I couldn't do it.

A sudden sob racks through my mother, breaking my thoughts, and I'm so surprised, scared even, wondering what it means, but then my mother's crying turns to laughter, and she grips my hands, breathing fast.

"Avery, do you see what this means?" She closes her eyes and a tear slides down her cheek, and when she looks at me again, she's smiling. "You haven't continued the curse. You're *free.*"

Although her hands are warm around mine, her eyes soft with happiness, I pull away, suddenly cold. An image fills my mind: a little ghost-girl, all my own, a little girl with dark hair and dark skin and a calm, even temper; and an aching wrenches inside of me, a sudden grief that I didn't anticipate. I have nothing of Tane, not even a lock of hair, but a little girl—she would have been something to hold on to. Something to love.

"She wouldn't have been a curse," I say. "I'm not just a curse, either."

My mother's face tightens. "I know that," she says. "That's not what I'm—" She cuts herself off, exasperated, and I feel the muscles in my jaw tense, the same old anger needling the fragile peace between my mother and me.

"I'm trying to tell you . . . a baby . . . she would have tied you here, to the island," my mother says. "But there's nothing here for you anymore."

"I know I'm alone," I say, shaking my head. Tears fill my eyes as a cold hole widens within me. "I know it."

"No, Avery, what I mean is—" She takes a breath, her eyes darting across my face like she's looking for the right words. "Every Roe woman was born because of the curse." Her hands flit up to smooth the hair at my temple. "Do you understand what I'm saying? We were all born because our mothers fell in love with men who hurt them. That's what the curse does, leads us to the wrong men."

"Tane wasn't wrong."

"No. He still hurt you, though." Her fingers tangle in my hair, twisting a lock that falls past my shoulder. "For every one of us, that man, the first man we ever gave ourselves to, left us a baby, the next Roe witch. But you . . . you fell in love and had your heart broken, same as the rest of us, but if you didn't . . ." She trails off and, when I just stare at her, continues. "You aren't pregnant. The curse hasn't made another witch."

"What does that mean?" I ask, my voice tight and quiet, and my mother pauses.

"I think . . . I think it means there won't be another Roe witch, after you," she says softly. "I think you are the last. I think you can leave the island."

Leave the island? The words stir up frightened feelings in my chest, and I shake my head. "But—none of us can!"

"No. No, that's not true. I couldn't leave while I was pregnant with you and when you were born…" She takes a breath. "She convinced me that I couldn't take you away. Your grandmother. She told me I would be taking away the only place in the world where you truly belonged and that you would hate me for it someday." My mother lets out a cold, dry laugh. "She always knew the right thing to say to make me do what she wanted.

"Later, I could have left. I had so many chances, Avery. A man…my friend…he came to me after you were born. He was scared that your father would hurt you and me, and he tried to get me to leave the island, but I told him no."

"Why not? Because of me?"

She squints her eyes as though wincing. "Yes, of course. I could never leave you, but even so…this island is my home, my daughter's home. I would have left for him, not for myself, and I would have hated him for it someday." She shakes her head. "Love doesn't last in such rocky soil."

I look away, my lips pressed tight together. I am not my mother. I am not, and her life is not my life. I tell myself that I would have gotten into a whaleboat with Tane and rowed for shore and built a blue house with yellow shutters and a lovely little porch. We would have been happy together, all our days. And I would have forgotten the pull of my island, the sea that flows in my veins. I would even have forgotten that it was Tane who made me leave the only thing I ever loved, other than him. This is what I tell myself as my mother's words bounce against my skull.

"Pastor Sever came the closest to getting me off the island," she says, a little laugh breaking her words. "He got me on a boat and swore to annul our marriage if I didn't leave with him, but I made him turn around and take me back to you. He was...very angry."

"Why didn't you just make a spell so that he loved you?" I ask, eyes narrowed. "You could have done that this whole time, and then maybe you could have had a happy marriage."

"No," she says softly. "I wouldn't have been happy, knowing it was all a trick....I decided a long time ago that I would never make someone love me."

She catches the sleeve of my dress, gives it a little tug. "Magic makes things too easy sometimes, Avery. So easy that we forget what we give up when we shape our worlds to our liking." She gives a rueful little smile. "In any case, I don't think I'll ever see Pastor Sever again."

I can't help it. "Pity," I say, speaking through my teeth, and my mother laughs softly.

"I chose to stay here for my daughter. But you, Avery"— her eyes shine with tears—"you can *go*. You can have—"

"Don't say it. I don't want to marry someone I don't love. I don't care about the opera or museums. Those things—they were always things you wanted, never me."

My mother blinks, and for the first time, acts as though she actually hears me. "All right," she says. "I know. I've always known. But, Avery"—she reaches for my hand and holds it between both of hers—"there's still a whole world out there to see. You miss so much on this little island. Aren't you even curious? Don't you want to know what it's like?"

No.

Yes.

I don't know.

I've heard those words before and they've felt like traps, tricks, distractions, but this time they sound different. They sound like encouragement. Or hope. And beneath the grief, beneath the power, I feel the tiniest spark of wonder.

But after a moment, I shake my head, because of course I still have responsibilities, a ruined island to fix.

"I won't let good men die," I say, and I know suddenly that this is how it started, all those years ago, when the first Roe woman came to the sea and knew she could control it and felt she could use her abilities to help ease the lives of others. Did she ever think of what she would have to give up in return?

A gift. That's what my grandmother calls our magic, and my mother says it's a curse. But it's not really either of those.

"No one is making you do that," my mother says. "And you would go mad to try. You would end up like your grandmother, like all the rest of them."

"You asked me once why I wanted to be the witch," I say. "I didn't have a good reason then, but I do now, even now that I know what it means. I can save lives. I can keep men safe. I can keep food in children's mouths and keep an entire island from turning into a ruin. And if I can do it, I should. For them."

"Avery..." My mother shakes her head. "They were ready to kill you."

"They were scared," I say, and I think of Mrs. Plummer, of Billy Macy, of the islanders who tried to defend me. "And besides, there are good people here, too. I can help them."

Silence, and I wonder if I've managed to convince her that both she and my grandmother are wrong about our magic. Neither a gift nor a curse but a responsibility. Our responsibility and our choice.

"I'll do it."

My mother's voice rings in my ears. I am so surprised I can only stare at her, taking in the firm set of her mouth, her confident, steady eyes. Witch's eyes.

"I'll do it," she says again, and now she sounds even more confident, the beautiful, powerful witch she always was. "I'm not dead yet, I'm not dying. And I can do it. No charms. No new spells. They'll have to learn how to get along without a witch to help them, but I'll keep them alive until they do. I'll do it so long as you promise to leave the island."

A promise. Not a demand. For her and me, that's progress. She holds out her hand to me, not like a mother but straight out like we're equals.

My grandmother chose to give in to the magic and it ate her away.

For years, my mother chose to run from it and now will take it up, a burden, a sacrifice, for me.

And what will I do?

I stare at my mother's white, outstretched hand. It shakes a little as she holds it out, but she's strong. I could take her hand now and promise to leave the island, like she never could. I could say no and walk away and become the witch and fulfill what I have always been told is my destiny. I could do it, but it wouldn't be fate. It would be my choice.

Twenty-Nine

WHALES HAVE LONG MEMORIES. THEY SPEAK
to one another, warn one another. Their massive hearts pump
hot blood through their veins, blood the same as ours. Their
infants drink milk, same as ours. They are the most human
thing in the ocean, but they live in a world we can't imagine.

These whales dive down, down, down where the sun
doesn't reach, the home of monsters, and when they emerge
their skin has been crisscrossed by scars, patterned with the
circular suckers of creatures even bigger and more powerful
and more mysterious than the whale.

Once, a sailor came to visit my grandmother, to sell, he
said, not to buy. This happened from time to time, when
she needed some artifact or object that couldn't be found on
the beach.

"Sit," she said, gesturing to the scrubbed-down table. He moved quickly to the chair and as he lowered himself, I could hear something rattle, a dry, smooth rustling noise. I was supposed to be doing something, some chore probably, and visits from sailors were frequent enough to lose their novelty, but this, I felt, I needed to see. I dropped whatever I was holding and stared over at the table, at the man.

My grandmother sat down across from him, her long-fingered hands held in front of her, palm-up on the table. The man reached to his belt and drew out a papery-thin bag tied tightly with string.

"We caught an old whale," he said, gently pulling the string. "I could tell he'd been swimming since my granddad was young, and I was curious, right? They say you can find funny things in whales' stomachs, especially the old ones."

The string off, he lifted the paper bag over the table and turned it upside down. My eyes widened as beautiful, bright objects fell through the air, scattering all across the surface. One fell to the ground, sliding to my feet, and I bent down to pick it up. It was small, no bigger than a coin, in the shape of a triangle and vibrant red. One point of the triangle curved, wickedly sharp, and as I ran my hands over it, the tip caught a fold of skin on my finger, pulling at me like a thorn.

I had no idea what it was, and I glanced up at my grandmother, waiting for her to speak. But she only gathered the little objects between her hands and stared at them. As her hands swept them together, they clinked against one another, delicate and fragile.

"What are they?" I asked. I held the thing in my hand up and watched the light shine through. "Shells?"

"No, dear," my grandmother said. She picked up another object, this one as big as my palm, but the same triangle shape, a shape that seemed so strange but still familiar.

"Beaks," the sailor said, and I frowned.

"Whales don't eat birds," I said, but as I turned the object in my hand, I could see it now, the top of a beak, curved and bright.

"Not birds," said the sailor. "Underwater creatures. Squid. Octopus. Great big tentacled things." He wiggled his fingers in the air, laughing, before turning to my grandmother. "How much will it be, then? You won't get another lot like this, not for a long while."

Squinting, I stared down at the curved beak, but there was no animal in my mind that lived in water and yet carried the beak of a bird. It seemed stupid and unreal, like the sailor wanted to play a trick on my grandmother. That happened sometimes, cocky boys thinking they could pull one over on an old woman, but of course, you can't fool a witch. Angry, I crossed to the table and threw the little beak down, glaring at the sailor.

"There are no animals like that," I said, and the sailor's eyebrows lifted. "You can't trick us."

"Hush, Avery," my grandmother said, but absently, and when I turned back to look at her, I could see her studying the beaks carefully, running her fingertips over their smooth surface, her eyes gone far away.

"Thirty dollars," she said, and I gasped. It was an absurd sum of money, more than six months' wages for a green-hand whale man, but even more absurdly, the sailor shook his head.

"Fifty," he said. "That's the fair price."

I felt my hands ball into fists, a burst of anger rising through my chest. I took a step closer to the sailor, but my grandmother placed a hand on my shoulder.

"Yes," she said, and she stood and crossed the cottage to a plain iron box sitting on a shelf above the bed. This was where she kept her money, as everyone on the island knew but didn't have the guts or stupidity to steal. I watched as she counted out the bills, ragged and oily from whale men's hands, and turned and handed the stack neatly to the sailor.

"Bring me another lot," she said, "and you'll get the same."

He nodded once, quickly, before tucking the bills into his pocket. As he walked to the door, he glanced back at me and his face broke into a smile.

"Listen to your grandmother, girl," he said. "She knows there's more out there than you can imagine on your little island." And with a wink, he opened the door and left.

I was so mad I wanted to kick over the table, and maybe my grandmother knew this, because she walked quickly to the beaks and swept them all back into their bag. And my pride was so wounded that I hoped she *had* been cheated. But of course she was right, as she always was, and she sold the beaks, woven into necklaces, for eight dollars each. It was a bargain for what it promised: force, power, invincibility, that the bearer would never be defeated in a battle of strength, whether with man or whale or underwater creature.

Beaks. Beaks from under the water. It is a strange and surprising world.

The rain beats down on my black hair as I stand on the beach before the smuggler's ship, looking out beyond the little cove to the ocean. All I must do is get in the rowboat and row to the ship and climb aboard. All I must do is quiet the clouds and settle the winds and then we will leave. It has all been decided. Boston, first. From there, I will work my way inland, exploring the country between two oceans. The smuggler tells me there are lakes and mountains and rivers and deserts (deserts! a world without water!), and I would like to see them. But first I must get into the rowboat.

You have to leave the island.

I hear my mother's voice in my ears and I see her: young, no longer beautiful, her belly round and tight as a drum. She stood at the edge of the dock, her toes curled around the wooden board, her hands pressed against her stomach, pressed against me, her baby. Tears fell on her cheeks and she brushed them away, not wanting anyone to see. A pregnant girl crying. People will make assumptions.

She stood at the edge of the dock, waiting for the ferry, wondering what would happen to her when she left her island behind. Would she die? Would she be free? Idly, she made a fist and held it against her chest. The magic was there inside of her, curled up and strong. It had blazed, ever since her man left her beaten and bloodied, since he'd vowed to return with a knife to cut out the bastard child he believed wasn't his. The magic burned like a cheerful flame in a pot of whale oil, bright and clear and smokeless, but what would happen when she left the island? Maybe the magic would die out, maybe she would leave these shores a free woman to live scarred and scared but unshackled, the terrible tension gone from her chest forever.

The baby, little baby me, gave a shake, rolling over, and the witch moved her fist from her chest back down to her stomach. What would happen to the baby? This little baby, this girl, made out of magic, out of heartbreak, made to remind her of her many mistakes and failings. The baby only existed because of magic. What would happen if she took the baby away from the island?

One low, long call: the ferry whistle. Already, the clouds seemed to thin, the long bow of the ferry piercing the waters of New Bishop. It would be here in minutes, and then she would have to decide: stay, or go? Stay, raise her daughter in the net of magic, remain a powerful woman, a witch. Or go, go and leave magic and heartbreak behind. Again, though, she thought: What would happen to the baby? There were no rules for this sort of thing.

The witch's mother urged caution—"How can a Roe witch be born off this island? What if leaving makes you lose the baby? Why would you take that risk?" But it was caution wrapped up in motives, to keep the baby here on the island, to raise her to be the next witch. And wasn't that just exactly what she wanted to avoid?

Another ferry whistle and this time a broad-shouldered man asked her politely to stand aside and join the other passengers. He held a rope in his hands, a rope as thick as the witch's arm, and she stared at the rope for a long time before moving.

The ferry's docking was smooth and almost silent, nothing but the slap of the waves to announce its arrival. The witch waited as the people riding the ferry disembarked. They were mostly men, mostly sailors, whale men, looking for work. Some might even have arrived just for charms and spells. Her mother would be busy today.

The ferryman called out in a deep voice for the departing passengers to come aboard, and the witch moved forward, slowly, walking as if in a dream. The magic inside of her whipped up into a fury, like a bird beating itself against the bars of its cage, all flapping feathers and fearful chirps, but she ignored it, ignored it until the sole of her shoe touched the ferry deck and the baby inside of her wrenched, hard, a pain so intense that the witch gasped and clutched at the gangplank railing.

Dimly, she heard strangers ask if she was all right, but she could only focus on the stabbing inside of her, her baby writhing as though it were burning alive. She turned and ran, ran down the gangplank and to the docks and back into town, ran and ran, gasping all the while, and she did not stop until she reached the cottage on the rocks and her mother's grim, satisfied expression.

She could not do it. She could not leave the island, not if it would harm the innocent thing inside of her. She would take her chances with the net of magic, with the heartbreak. She would do all she could to protect her daughter from her own fate, even knowing that simply being born a Roe woman on Prince Island meant the only thing waiting for her was pain.

She promised to stay with her child, but the sailor with the soft hands who had broken her heart and ruined her face promised her that he would find the child and kill her. To stay at the cottage was to invite him there and leave the baby in danger. So she left her girl, and when she made her mother promise never to teach her magic, she knew it was a promise that wouldn't be kept.

"Ready?"

I turn my head toward the smuggler's voice. No, not "the smuggler" anymore. I got my mother to tell me his name, and I smile to myself remembering what she said: "Mal. Malcolm really, but he was such a naughty thing that the pastor called him Mal. It was supposed to shame him, but Mal liked it."

I left his photograph back in New Bishop, in a drawer in

the shabby little apartment where my mother would be certain to find it and maybe, if she ever got strong enough, follow it to him.

"Avery? Are you ready?"

I have to answer him.

"Yes," I say, because saying the word is so easy, and I let him help me into the little rowboat. The boat sways and bobs as he rows to his ship, waiting for me in deeper water, and I clutch the sides of the rowboat, remembering.

We can get in a whaleboat and row. We're only a few miles from the mainland. We can make it there by morning.

I turn my face into the wind.

We reach the ship and Mal asks me to hand him my bag. It's small, just big enough for a spare dress, a nightgown, and the money my mother squirreled away from her husband over the years. And one more thing: a slim book. I went back to the lighthouse, and even though the broken windows had let in rain and dampened the pages, it is still possible to make out the drawings. Tane's drawings. He'd taken his dream journal and his boarding-house had thrown away the rest, but this one, his last one, the one filled with images of his island, his family, remained. And I feel, just a little, that even though he is gone, some part of him survives.

Strong hands and warm faces pull me onto the ship, and Mal tells me it's time. It's time. There is only one more spell to do—undo, really—and then I will be done with magic. I reach up to the knots in the sky, the storm I made almost a week ago, and hold my breath and pull. I tense, expecting to see him again, slipping below the waves, but unmaking must be different from making. The spell unravels as gently as pulling a ribbon from a bow.

Without my magic, the rain pauses, the clouds roll away, and the waves cease churning and fall, shapeless, back into their normal tides. I hear the crew call to one another their heaving songs, and the sails unfurl like wet butterfly wings, flapping in the breeze. We move, just barely, but it is enough to begin a keening inside of me, a wail of pain and loneliness and sorrow.

My home. My island.

I run back to the stern, dodging ropes, masts, crew, until I reach the very end of the boat, and I grab the edge and lean, lean, lean over, my knuckles white with tension, my toes arched as though I am about to take flight.

You have to leave the island.

And I am amazed that all it takes is not moving, letting my body get carried away. Stillness, stillness outside and stillness inside, and I turn my back on my island, on the islanders who relied on us and hated us and loved us and feared us and now must learn to forget us. I turn my back on the waters that hold Tane's body, my grandmother's spirit, Tommy's memory. I turn my back on my mother, lifting her tired and broken body to do the work that she once hoped to leave forever. I turn my back on the land of my ancestors, the land of the Roe women, the water witches.

I leave them, but they still live inside me, like ghosts.

I am Jennie Roe, discovering the man she loves in bed with another girl.

I am Essie Roe, who felt she failed as a mother from the moment she became a mother.

I am my great-grandmother Almira, the one gifted with languages, laughing as a handsome sailor leans in close to her and says, "You will never have to kiss a foreign tongue." And I am Frances, who also loved an artist, and her mother, Martha, too, who read minds and must have known her man didn't love her and still gave him her heart. I am far-seeing Ida, never able to let go, and Lenora, who could erase memories but never erased her own pain, and Abigail, reaching through a curtain to speak with someone she lost. I am all of them, all the way back to Madelyn, the first one, the one whose blood sang for salt water and who made the first charm for the first sailor and who fell in love with the wrong man.

I am their magic and their pain. I am their heir, no matter what my grandmother said about my suitability. I hear their voices, whispering to me in my dreams, giving me the advice they could never follow. And I listen. They are smart women after all, brave and passionate and strong. But in the end, it is my decision. I am the one who has to live, who has to wake up every morning with Tane's name on my lips.

If I could, I would take a running leap from the deck and scream like a boy and hit the water with a tremendous splash and dive, dive, dive and swim, as far as my arms and my legs could carry me until I collapse, exhausted, into the cold water.

If I could, I would turn my body into a whale's body and turn my memory into a whale's memory and learn about the currents of the ocean and teach my babies to fear big ships. If I could, I would kiss Tane, one last time.

The Roe women murmur to me their worries, their plans, their hopes. My ears fill with advice and wishes and histories, and my muscles burn as they cling to me, climb onto my shoulders to see with my eyes and hear with my ears the world they've only imagined. And whispers—always, always I hear their whispers.

Love will lead to ruin. Death is a comfort. You can't kill a Roe witch.

But the words that carry me into the fog toward my uncertain future, the words that set me free, belong only to Tane:

Never regret, Avery. Never regret.

AUTHOR'S NOTE

What I knew about whaling before writing this book is probably what most people know: oil and harpoons and *Moby-Dick*. But as I began my research, I was amazed to learn more about the whaling industry, from the vast impact it had on the development of America and the Industrial Revolution to the sincere, strange, and thrilling stories of whale men at sea. Writing *Salt & Storm*, I knew I would have to take some liberties with the facts, but in the end, the vast majority of Avery's world—even the magic—came out of real-life events, people, and folklore.

I began to imagine the Roes themselves after finding descriptions of real people who sold charms or curses to sailors. In Iceland, captains could visit "wind wizards," and Scottish "witches" in the seventeenth century were accused of raising storms in retaliation for personal slights. Avery's experience "tying the winds" in three knots is based on the witch's ladder, a real historical practice in Finland. And New England folklore is full of stories of "witch women" who lived alone near water, sometimes on islands, seeking payment for safe passage of ships or for crafting good-luck charms. With the tradition of sailing and superstition going back centuries and continuing to this day, I didn't have to look too far to build a plausible history for the Roes.

The American whaling industry was a more egalitarian profession than most, with emphasis placed on skill rather than race or class, and it attracted sailors from a wide range of backgrounds. With that in mind, I created the character of Tane, a boy from a fictional island in Polynesia, a roughly triangle-shaped collection of more than a thousand islands that includes Hawaii, New Zealand, and Easter Island. I imagined Hovell Island, Tane's home, to be closest to New Zealand, and Tane's cultural background to be similar, although not identical, to the indigenous people of New Zealand, the Maori. Some common words Tane uses—*toka* (rock), *tuahine* (sister), *matua* (father), and *whaea* (mother)—are, in fact, from the Māori language, which serves as a root language for many Polynesian communities.

Tane's tattoos also represent an important aspect of Polynesian culture. The word *tattoo* is believed to come from the Samoan *tatau*, and tattoos themselves were largely introduced into American culture by sailors visiting the Pacific Islands. Tane's tattoos were inspired by Southeast Asian *sak yant* tattoos, which are said to grant special properties like strength and skill, and by the maritime tradition of tattooing good-luck symbols, such as the nautical star, which is supposed to help the wearer find his or her way home. For the majority of Polynesian cultures, however, tattooing was and is a deeply personal process done to connect the wearer to his or her own community and its history. The magical aspects of Tane's tattoos are fiction, a product of *Salt & Storm*'s world, where magic is common and integrated into society.

When thinking about what could have happened to Tane's community on Hovell Island, I looked to the Moriori people of the Chatham Islands, near New Zealand. Like the Hovell Island I imagined, the Chatham Islands are small, isolated, and subantarctic, and they support a limited number of people. To conserve their resources, the Moriori kept their population low and renounced war, and they were especially ill equipped when foreigners arrived, bringing disease, competition for food, and conflict. Only a few decades after the first outsiders landed on the Chatham Islands, more than 90 percent of the indigenous population had died. I imagined Tane's people having a similar fate: Their numbers severely diminished by years of hunger and disease, and lacking any knowledge of warfare, the entire community could be wiped out by a smaller, stronger, and better-armed enemy.

On the Chatham Islands, the Moriori primarily suffered at the hands of sealers and neighboring invaders. Attacks from whalers, like the kind described in *Salt & Storm*, were less common, although conflict between whalers and natives did occur. Whale men typically fought with indigenous people over precious resources, access to native women, and violations of cultural taboos, and there was deep mistrust on both sides. Some whaling captains really did pay for supplies "with the fore-topsail" (reneging on payment by sailing away); when other whaling ships subsequently visited the island, the sailors were often surprised and bewildered by the deep suspicion and anger shown by the natives, leading to unjust accusations that the Pacific Islands were full of "bloodthirsty savages."

As for the whaling itself, I followed the history of the industry. The whaling business began to slip in the late 1860s, when Avery's story begins, for the reasons described in the book: the aftermath of the Civil War, overhunting, dangerous conditions in the Arctic, and the development of kerosene. Prince Island is meant to reflect the biggest whaling centers in nineteenth-century America, with Martha's Vineyard and Nantucket serving as geographical inspirations, and the elegant but industrial fictional town of New Bishop is based on New Bedford, Massachusetts.

There were a few conscious breaches of fact that I hope you will forgive. In real life, Avery would probably not have been named *Avery*—it was a man's name in the nineteenth century. Similarly, *Tane* is not a historically accurate name, as Pacific Islanders contracted to whalers usually adopted Anglo names like John, Joseph, or even George Washington. *Tane* is a common word in many Polynesian languages, usually translating to "man," and I chose it for Tane as a way to suggest that he left behind the identity he carried in his old community.

There were so many details I discovered in researching *Salt & Storm* that I never, in my wildest imaginings, could have come up with on my own. (Who knew, for example, that whaling blacklists could be so catty? One poor sailor earned the descriptor "an excellent DO-NOTHING," which is my new favorite insult.) Fact is so often stranger than fiction—wilder and weirder and funnier and fiercer—that figuring out where one ends and the other begins can be very hard indeed. But that, of course, is the fun.

ACKNOWLEDGMENTS

I like reading the acknowledgments. They're usually the first thing I turn to when I pick up a book. I like being reminded that, for all writing is supposed to be a solitary profession, it takes a team to make a book. Here are a few of the people who helped get *Salt & Storm* out of my head and into your hands.

This book would not be what it is without my insightful and sensitive editor, Bethany Strout. How Bethany is able to see the story I'm trying to tell and how she can bring that story out with just a few smart comments remains a mystery to me, but a mystery I'm forever grateful for.

Thank you to Sara Crowe, my agent and tireless advocate. Whenever the stresses and nerves of being a first-time author threatened to overwhelm me, I felt criminally lucky to say these magic words and watch all my troubles fly away: "Sara's got my back."

A whale-sized thank-you to Beth Fama for, quite literally, everything. Chicago would have been a lot lonelier and my road to publishing a lot rockier if not for your warm friendship and thoughtful advice. (And thank you also to Matt Noto, for introducing us after correctly thinking that the YA-writing wives of economists would probably hit it off.)

My crit partner, Natasha Sinel Cohen, read the very first novel I ever tried to write and is the go-to recipient of all my most despondent e-mails (subject line: "UGH"), a fact that will forever keep me in her debt. I am so grateful for her humor, optimism, and talent, which inspires me every day.

To the wonderful team at Little, Brown Books for Young Readers: Thank you for all the hard work you've done to bring *Salt & Storm* to life. Never would I have dreamed of finding a more perfect home for my book than Little, Brown, and I am so humbled and grateful for all your support and enthusiasm.

Michael Dyer and the dedicated staff at the New Bedford Whaling Museum graciously answered my many (and increasingly weird) questions about whaling and the lives of sailors. Thank you for your assistance and for all the amazing work you do keeping this fascinating history alive.

Thank you also to the crews of the tall ship *Windy* in Chicago and the *Adirondack III* in Boston for allowing me to pepper you with questions about traditional sailing (and letting me pull the rope to make the sail go up the thing! Those are the technical terms, right?).

Merci beaucoup to Juliette Caminade for help with the French translation and for explaining the complex and fascinating dynamics of French conversion. *Gracias* to Carlos Correa and Karen Moskow for help with the Spanish.

Many people read and commented on this manuscript in

its earlier forms, and thank you especially to Annie Berndtson, Nate Bernhard, Danielle Corea, Eileen Michael, Karen Moskow, Rebecca Senville, and Steve Toniatti.

Thank you to my wonderful friends, who were always ready with the champagne to celebrate my every accomplishment (no matter how small!) and who said the greatest thing imaginable when they heard the book was going to be published: "Well, duh!"

Music carried me through so much of this book. Thank you to the Decemberists, for setting the tone of the book and giving Avery her name, and to Sea Wolf, for bringing this story home.

I am so thankful for the wonderful support I've received from the friends I've met online. Thank you to the fabulous community of writers and bloggers who have championed *Salt & Storm* from the very beginning.

To the Kennys, Michaels, and O'Rourkes: I could not wish for a better family. Thank you for your love and encouragement and for always believing I could make this dream a reality.

Thank you to the Toniattis, my second family, for the mountains of support I've received over the years and, especially, for your friendship and love. A special thank-you goes to Mark and Anne, for always treating me like another daughter and for applauding my successes like the proud parents they are.

My parents, Denise and Keith, and brother, Sloan, were my earliest supporters and the ones who never failed to encourage my writing and never batted an eye when I told them I was going to use my college degree to write books for teenagers. I love you guys.

My puppy, Abby, gets a mention, if only because her constant encouragement to nap more, go for more runs, and set aside some time every day to appreciate a squeaky toy keeps me sane and grounded.

And finally, it is not an overstatement to say that none of this would exist without my husband, Dave. There is no way I can thank him for all his support and love, for putting himself on the line for me, for encouraging me and taking care of me and reminding me that pursuing a dream is a wonderful thing, even when it's tough (maybe especially when it's tough). I love you. This is for you.